PRAISE FOR GR

BLACK RAIN

"Action-packed . . . The fast pace . . . will keep readers forging ahead."

—*Publishers Weekly*

"A unique and compelling thriller that will keep your interest start to finish. *Black Rain* is fast-paced, dangerous adventure at its very best. A sequel is in the works, and I can't wait to read it."

—FreshFiction.com

"Exotic location, innocents in danger, overwhelming odds against the good guys and the inability to know who they can trust—this enjoyable read is very frightening. . . . A lively read."

—*Romantic Times*

"*Black Rain* is an adventure that's not only a terrific read, but is smart, intelligent, and poised to shake up the whole thriller community. Every copy should come with a bucket of popcorn and a John Williams soundtrack to play in the background. I loved it."

—Linwood Barclay, #1 internationally bestselling author of *Fear the Worst*

"*Black Rain* sizzles with tension and twists that both entertain and magnetize. The plot envelops the reader into a brilliantly conceived world, full of strange and amazing things. Graham Brown is an exciting new talent, a writer we're going to be hearing a lot from in the years ahead. I can't wait."

—Steve Berry, *New York Times* bestselling author

ALSO BY GRAHAM BROWN

BLACK RAIN

BLACK SUN

a thriller

GRAHAM BROWN

BANTAM BOOKS
NEW YORK

For those who believe

A Bantam Books Mass Market Original

Published in the United States by Bantam Books, an imprint of The Random House Publishing Group, a division of Random House, Inc., New York.

BANTAM BOOKS and the rooster colophon are registered trademarks of Random House, Inc.

ISBN 978-0-553-59242-9
eBook ISBN 978-0-553-90791-9

Cover art and design: Carlos Beltran

Printed in the United States of America

www.bantamdell.com

2 4 6 8 9 7 5 3 1

ACKNOWLEDGMENTS

To my agent, Barbara Poelle, thanks for the trust and support, and the laughs. I don't know how someone so brilliant can also be so funny. To Marisa Vigilante, my editor, whose ability to see through the mist sharpened the leading edges of this novel more than I can say. To Alison Masciovecchio and Dana Kaye, my in-house and outside publicists, who do the hard work of turning unknown writers into the known. To Evan Camfield and the copy editors at Random House, who put up with my penchant for inventing new words and strange new uses of punctuation. To the sales and promotion staff at Random House—without you guys pushing hard every day, all the writing in the world would get us nowhere.

And finally to the readers, who put up their hard-earned cash, trusting that we will entertain them and sweep them away for the four hundred or so pages of each book. Thanks for the faith. I will do all I can to never let you down.

PROLOGUE

Bering Sea, November 2012

The fifty-foot trawler *Orlovsky Star* pushed on through frigid Arctic waters and a lingering fog that seemed to have no end. The sea was unusually calm and the wind nonexistent, but with the outside temperature dipping to fifteen degrees Fahrenheit and the water holding just above the freezing point, the conditions were anything but benign.

Alexander Petrov stood at the wheel inside the darkened pilothouse, a grim air surrounding him. His weathered face, shaved head, and clenched jaw all suggested a burden his broad shoulders were struggling to carry. He stared into the darkness ahead of the boat, listening to the thrum of the engine and the occasional muted thump of ice banging against the hull.

So far the ice had been thin: small, free-floating chunks that his boat could slide through at half speed. But the pack ice formed quickly at this time of year, spreading south like a plague, and just an hour before there had been no ice at all.

Guiding the boat on feel as much as sight, Petrov considered the danger: If the ship didn't reach warmer waters soon, they'd be trapped and the thin hull ground into metal filings long before any rescuer could reach them.

Then again, perhaps they deserved such a fate for what they were attempting to do.

As another impact reverberated through the cabin, a voice spoke from behind him. "It's getting thicker. We need to make better speed."

Petrov glanced into the recesses of the darkened pilothouse. A heavyset man gazed back at him. This was Vasili, a Russian of mixed European and Asian descent and the broker of their unholy deal, the keeper of their unusual human cargo.

Despite the cold, Petrov could see a thin sheen of perspiration on Vasili's upper lip. If Petrov was right, Vasili's mind was reeling in a battle between greed and fear, between the possibilities of life-altering wealth just days away and a horrible death in the crushing embrace of the ice.

"What are you really worried about, Vasili?"

"That we're lost," he said bluntly, glancing at an exposed circuit board and what had been their navigation system.

The GPS receiver had shorted out eight hours before, the screen flashing and the casing catching fire in a shower of sparks. Petrov had examined it briefly but saw that it was clearly beyond repair. For an hour he'd used the stars to guide them, but the fog had thickened and he'd been forced to rely on the vessel's compass.

"I was a fisherman before I joined the navy. I learned to navigate at the hands of my father," Petrov assured him. "I know what I'm doing,"

Vasili stepped closer to him. "The crew is worried," he whispered. "They say our journey is cursed."

"Cursed?"

"Orcas followed us down the channel," Vasili explained. "And we've seen sharks every morning. Far too many for such northern waters."

That had seemed odd, Petrov thought, as if the predators of the sea were shadowing them, waiting for a meal to be delivered into their hungry bellies. But he hoped it was mere coincidence.

"It's almost dawn," Petrov said, changing the subject. "We'll have a few hours of light, nothing more, but it should be enough. The fog will lift and we'll make better time."

Petrov's statement was designed to ease Vasili's fears, but even as he spoke, they found another mass of ice and a grinding resonance traveled down the starboard side. From the sound alone, they could tell it was thicker and heavier than those they had hit before.

Petrov reduced the speed to five knots. This was the trap he'd been hoping to avoid, one he'd warned Vasili about: Thicker ice meant slower speed and thus more time for the ice to form in the waters ahead of them.

He switched on the overhead lights, but the fog swallowed the beams and reflected the energy back, blinding him. He shut them off.

"We need a spotter," he said.

Before he could call the crew, the boat slammed something head-on. The nose of the boat pitched upward and their momentum died, as if they'd run aground.

Petrov cut the throttle.

In utter silence he waited. Finally the boat began to move, sliding backward a foot at a time and then settling once again. He breathed a sigh of relief. But he dared not touch the throttles.

"We cannot stop here," Vasili said.

A crewman popped his head into the control room from the lower deck. "We're leaking, Captain," the man said. "Starboard, forward."

"How bad?" Petrov asked him.

"I think I can seal it," the crewman said. "But we don't want any more of that."

"Wake the others," Petrov said. "Get them into their survival suits. Then do what you can."

It was a precaution only, and also a bluff meant to calm the fears of the men. But even in their suits, they would not last long in the water.

He turned to Vasili. "Give me your key."

"I don't think so," the broker replied.

"So you will take him, then?" Petrov asked. "If we have to leave the ship?"

Vasili hesitated, then reached under his sweater and pulled out a key that dangled around his neck.

Petrov snatched it and then pushed his way outside.

The fog hung in the air, cutting at his face like shards of suspended glass. Not a breath of wind could be felt, and with the engines shut down the silence was complete.

He looked around. A thick layer of frost covered the deck while daggers of ice hung from the bridge and the ladder and the rail. Every surface, every line, every inch of the vessel had become encrusted in ice.

The ship looked dead already.

Vasili came out a moment later, bundled from head to toe, but still too stupid to put his survival suit on. "Why did you stop?"

"So we don't rip the boat apart."

"But we can't stay here," Vasili replied.

Of course they couldn't, but they could no longer risk moving in the dark. The fog made it impossible to see the danger, and impatience would destroy them. But to some extent they seemed to be in luck. The fog was beginning to lift. In addition, the thin light of the approaching dawn had begun to illuminate things. This far north, the sun would never get off the horizon, but the light would grow quickly. Petrov hoped it would show them a way out.

And yet, even then something seemed wrong. The sky was darkest ahead of him. It should have been just the opposite; the brighter light should have been out in front of them. It had to be some illusion of the fog, but it seemed as if the sun were coming up in the wrong place.

Before he could come to terms with this, something heavy bumped the boat and pushed it to the side.

"What was that?" Vasili asked.

The slight impact could have been an iceberg moving on the current. But as he looked over the side, Petrov saw that the waters remained dead calm; the ice wasn't moving.

"Alexander," Vasili said.

Petrov ignored him and moved toward the bow. The fog had thinned considerably. Replacing it was a sight Petrov could hardly fathom: a field of solid white.

Unbroken ice that stretched to the horizon in every direction.

"My God," he whispered.

The ice was clearly impenetrable, but the truth was more damning than that. The sun had finally begun to peek its face over the horizon, not ahead of them and to the left as it should have been, but behind them and to the right.

Even Vasili realized the mistake.

"You've taken us the wrong way," he shouted. "We've been sailing to the north all night!"

Petrov reeled from the error. Relying on a magnetic compass was tricky around the poles, but he was no amateur. And yet somehow they'd spent hours tracking toward the danger, into the thickening ice pack instead of away from it.

"How could this . . . ," he began.

"You goddamned fool," Vasili cursed him. "You've driven us to hell."

Petrov's legs almost buckled from the realization, but urgency pushed him on. He glanced toward the stern. The ice there had not yet formed into a solid block. If they moved quickly they might just survive.

He brushed past Vasili, driving for the pilothouse. Before he could open the door, something slammed into the boat again, but this time the blow was sharp, a solid impact, rolling the boat ten degrees or more.

He shouted to his crew. "Reverse, reverse! Get us the hell out of here."

The engines rumbled beneath the deck and *Star* began to back up, but another impact shoved the bow to the right, crashing it into the ice floe.

Yanking the door open, Petrov went for the wheel and pushed a crewman aside. His hand found the throttles and moved the engines from a quarter astern to half.

"Something hit us!" the crewman shouted.

"Ice, moving on the currents," Petrov said, strangely certain that he was wrong.

The impact had been powerful, deliberate, more like an intentional ramming. He began to think about the orcas and the sharks.

Vasili stumbled back inside the bridge. "It could have been a submarine," he said. "Remember the FSB."

Petrov thought of their cargo and the importance it was deemed to hold. Agents of the FSB, the Russian successor to the old KGB, had hunted them for weeks, trailing them across much of Siberian Russia. No doubt they were still looking, but a submarine, a ramming? Perhaps it made sense; certainly they would not risk destroying the vessel with a torpedo.

He spun the wheel, bringing the nose of the vessel around. After swinging through ninety degrees, he shoved the throttles forward. The boat began accelerating, bulling its way through the ice, pushing toward gaps of black sea, spots of open water where he could make better time.

If they could just . . .

Another impact caught the boat, jarring it to the right, lifting the bow and then dropping it. The hull couldn't take much more.

Petrov gunned the throttles, grinding the metal hull and risking the props.

"Captain, you have to slow down," the crewman said.

"One mile!" he shouted back. "Then we'll slow."

But even before he finished the words, a crushing impact hit on the port side. An alarm began ringing as water flooded in.

"Get everyone topside!" Petrov yelled.

The crewman shouted something back to him, but the alarm drowned it out.

"Maybe we should make a distress call," Vasili said.

Petrov glanced at him. "Too late now."

A voice shouted from the deck. *"Akula!"*

It was the Russian word for shark. Petrov glanced out the window and saw a dark shape slicing through the black water toward them. It hit them below the waterline and Petrov was thrown to the floor by the impact.

Another blow followed, stronger and heavier, multiple thuds, likes fists pounding on a door. The sharks were slamming themselves into the hull, ramming it like living torpedoes, hitting the boat with such force that they had to be injuring themselves.

"What the hell is happening?" Vasili yelled.

Petrov could not fathom it. He had never heard of such a thing. It was as if some sort of madness had infected them.

He glanced to starboard. They were about to hit the ice.

"Hold on!"

The ship slammed into the ice shelf, then recoiled from the impact. It rocked wickedly in one direction and then back in the other. For a brief instant it rolled to a level beam before beginning to list.

"Abandon ship!" Petrov shouted. "Abandon ship!"

The order was unnecessary. The men were already

near the stern, readying the lifeboat. He counted five men there. Only Vasili and the crewman beside him were missing. And their passenger.

"Go!" he shouted. "Go now!"

As they pushed through the hatch, Petrov charged below deck.

Dropping into the swirling water, his feet went instantly numb. He waded to a closed cabin door and pulled the key he'd taken from Vasili. He unlocked the door and forced it open.

Inside, sitting cross-legged on a bunk, was a twelve-year-old-boy with a round face and dark hair. His features were indistinct. He could have been European, or Russian, or Asian.

"Yuri!" Petrov shouted. "Come to me!"

The boy ignored him, chanting and rocking back and forth.

Petrov charged forward, lunging and grabbing the child off the bunk. He slung him over his shoulder in a fireman's carry and then turned toward the door, just as another impact rocked the boat.

The *Star* groaned as it took on water. Petrov braced himself against the wall that now leaned at a twenty-degree angle. Regaining his balance, he fought his way out into the hall.

With Yuri clinging to his neck, Petrov fought against the rushing water and made it to the stairs. He clambered onto them, dragging himself and the child upward, pushing through the hatch as the boat passed thirty degrees. She would roll over at any second.

He looked to the rear deck. The survival boat was gone, floating thirty yards from the foundering stern.

But something was wrong. The men were in a panic, looking around, pointing to something.

A shape erupted underneath them, a huge gray body with a triangular dorsal fin. The life raft flipped, sending the men flying into the sea. Dark tails slashed between the sheets of ice, cutting the surface like knives. Petrov heard the horrible sound of his men screaming.

Akula, murdering his crew. He had never heard of such a thing.

The *Star* tilted farther and items came pouring out of open cabinets. He pulled himself through the doorway and stood on what had been the bridge's side wall. It began dropping away beneath his feet. The ship was rolling. A rush of air came up through the water.

He jumped.

Landing hard on the pack ice, he tumbled. Yuri was flung free of his grasp, sliding and sprawling on the ice.

A thunderous crash erupted behind him and Petrov turned to see his boat plunging toward the depths of the sea. Pockets of air exploded as the vessel went down; concussions echoed through the frigid air and waves of debris came rushing to the surface.

And then it was quiet.

Roiling black water, floating wreckage, and small chunks of ice swirled where the ship had been, but the noise of the struggle had ceased.

He looked to the south. The survival boat was gone and the only sign of the crew was a pair of empty life-jackets. In places he saw the sharks crossing back and forth, searching for anything they might have missed. Only he and Yuri remained.

Somehow they had landed on the edge of the ice

pack. Three feet thick and as hard as concrete, it might as well have been solid ground.

He turned to look at the boy.

Their cargo, paid for at a cost of ten million dollars, with the lives of his crew taken for interest. Did he even know what he was? What he could do? Did it even matter anymore?

Already shivering, Petrov stood. He raised his eyes to what lay beyond them: a shelf of brilliant white, the barren wasteland of the ice pack, floating on the salt water of the sea. It was a continent in all but name, with only two citizens to inhabit it. And in all likelihood, they would be dead before the sun rose again.

CHAPTER 1

Southern Mexico, December 2012

Danielle Laidlaw scrambled up the side of Mount Pulimundo, sliding on the loose shale and grabbing for purchase with her hands as much as her feet. The frenetic pace of the ascent combined with the thin mountain air had her legs aching and her lungs burning. But she could not afford to slow down.

Thirty-four years old, attractive, and athletic, Danielle was a member of the National Research Institute, a strange hybrid of an organization, often considered a science-based version of the CIA. That they were currently searching for the truth behind an ancient Mayan legend seemed odd, but they had their reasons. The fact that another armed group was trying to stop them told Danielle that those reasons had leaked.

She glanced back to one of the men climbing with her. Thirty feet downslope, Professor Michael McCarter struggled. "Come on, Professor," she urged. "They're getting closer."

Breathing heavily, he looked up at her. Imminent exhaustion seemed to prevent a reply, but he pushed forward with renewed determination.

She turned to their guide, a twenty-year-old Chiapas Indian named Oco. "How much farther?"

"We must get over the top," he told her, in heavily accented English. "It is on the other side."

A few minutes later they crested the summit. McCarter fell to his hands and knees, and Danielle pulled a pair of binoculars from her pack.

They stood on the rim of a volcanic crater. A thousand feet below lay a mountain lake with a small, cone-shaped island bursting upward at its center. The island's steep sides were thickly wooded but unable to disguise its volcanic nature. Yellowish fog clung to it, drifting downwind from vents and cracks.

"Is this it?"

Oco nodded. "*Isla Cubierta,*" he said. Island of the Shroud.

Danielle studied it through the binoculars. If Oco was right, this place would be the key to finding what they were searching for: a Mayan site that legends referred to as the Mirror, a reference to Tohil, the Mayan god of fire, who wore an obsidian mirror on his forehead. It was a symbol of power and might, and if Danielle, McCarter, and the NRI were correct, a symbol of far more than that. But so far the Mirror had remained hidden. To find it they needed help, help that supposedly existed on the Island of the Shroud.

"Are you sure?" she asked.

"The statue is there," he insisted. "I saw it once. When I came with the shaman. He told me that the time was coming, the time when all things would change."

Danielle scanned the terrain. To reach the lake required a hazardous descent, down a steep embankment of loose and crumbling shale on the caldera's inner cone. It would be rough, but much easier physically than the climb they'd just completed.

She tied her hair into a ponytail to let the breeze cool her neck, then settled her eyes on McCarter. He'd managed a sitting position now, though his chest still heaved and fell. His loose linen shirt was open; the T-shirt he wore underneath was drenched in perspiration. Sweat poured down his face, leaving brackish, salty trails on his dark skin.

McCarter was in good shape for a sixty-year-old university professor. And they'd brought only small packs and limited supplies, having discarded all else in the name of speed. But three days of constant hiking and climbing had taken its toll.

"Ready?" she asked.

He looked up, clearly in a state of unreadiness.

"It's all downhill from here," she promised.

"I've been hearing that load of tripe since I turned forty," he said, between breaths. "And so far nothing has gotten any easier." He waved her on. "Go. I'll try to catch up."

McCarter and Danielle were an unlikely team, but they'd formed a bond two years earlier, when Danielle had recruited him for an expedition to the Amazon. Things had started well enough, but in the depths of the jungle everything had gone horribly wrong. By the thinnest of margins, the two of them and a very few others had survived.

In the aftermath of that mission, Danielle had quit the NRI and McCarter had gone back to New York to teach. At the time, he had seemed far more likely to sue the organization than to ever work for it again, but in answering to his own curiosity he'd agreed to do just that. Despite her own reasons not to, Danielle had rejoined as well, in hopes of protecting him. The way she figured it, she owed him that much. He would never have heard of the NRI if she hadn't recruited him. After eight months in the field and several close calls, including a car bomb and two shootings, she wasn't about to leave him now.

Besides, her only chance of returning to Washington, D.C., and the semblance of a normal life she'd been building was to finish this job and deposit McCarter safely back in New York.

"We stick together," she said. "Besides, you're the expert here. You're the one who needs to see this. All we have to do is get down there before them, learn what we need to know, and follow the lake out."

"And what happens when they catch us?"

"They want the statue. They're not going to chase us."

She extended a hand, which McCarter eyed suspiciously before reaching out and grasping.

She helped him to his feet and the three of them went over the side, skidding and sliding and running where they could. As they reached the bottom, she could hear shouting far up above. Their pursuers had come to the crest.

"Hurry," she said, racing across the last ten yards of solid ground and diving into the cold mountain lake.

When they were halfway across, gunfire began cracking from the ridge. Shots clipped the water around them and she dove under the surface and kept kicking until she could no longer hold her breath.

She came up shrouded in the sulfurous mist. McCarter and Oco surfaced beside her.

The gunfire had ceased but another sound caught her attention: a distant rhythmic thumping reaching out across the mountains. It was the staccato clatter of helicopter blades, somewhere to the east. Apparently their enemies had a new trick in store.

"Where is it?" she asked Oco.

He pointed toward the summit. "At the top," he said. "Hidden in the trees."

They climbed the steep angle of the island's slope, using the trees as handholds. They found the statue at the dead center. A great block of stone with the outline of a man carved into it, a Mayan king in full regalia. In his right hand he carried what looked like a net holding four stones. In his left was an orb of some kind. Hieroglyphic writing was scrawled across the bottom and a great snake twisted across the top, with its large open mouth stretching down as if to devour the king with a single bite.

"Ahau Balam," McCarter said, reading the title glyphs. "The Jaguar King. Spirit guide of the Brotherhood."

Oco, who was of Mayan descent, fell silent in awe. McCarter did likewise.

Danielle was more concerned with the danger closing in on them. From the sound she guessed that the helicopter was no more than three minutes away and that the men behind them had to be scrambling down the cliff by now.

"We need to get this information and disappear," she said. "What do you see?"

McCarter studied the writing, eyes darting here and there. He touched one glyph and then another. He seemed confused.

"Professor?"

"I'm not sure," he said.

The sound of the helicopter lumbered closer, growing into a baritone roar.

"We have two minutes," she said. "Maybe less."

He shook his head in disbelief. "There's no story here. No explanation. It's mostly just numbers."

"Dates?"

"No. Just random numbers."

Her mind reeled. She couldn't believe what he was saying.

"Maybe if I—"

She cut him off. "No time."

She pulled out her camera, snapped off a shot, and then checked the screen. The stone was so weathered that the glyphs didn't come out clearly. She took another from a different angle, with a similar result. There just wasn't enough definition.

The helicopter was closing in. She could hear the men on foot shouting as they came down the caldera's embankment.

"It's not clear enough," she said.

McCarter stared at her for a second and then tore off his shirt, dropped to the base of the statue, and pressed it up against the raised hieroglyphs. Holding it there with one hand, he began rubbing fistfuls of the volcanic soil against the surface of the shirt. Oco helped him.

The helicopter thundered by overhead. Slowing and turning. *Looking for a place to land.* She thanked the heavens that there wasn't one to be found.

She dropped down beside him to help. The shapes of the carving began to emerge, the edges and the details. It looked like a blurry charcoal drawing, but it was working.

As they worked, pine needles, leaves, and chaff began to swirl around them. The helicopter was moving in above, its downwash blasting everything about.

"That's it," she said. "No more time."

McCarter rolled up the shirt and tucked it into his backpack while Danielle grabbed a large stone and began smashing the surface of the statue. The glyphs of the priceless work crumbled under the blows, shards flying like sparks from a grinding wheel.

Suddenly, weighted ropes dropped through the trees, unfurling like snakes.

"Run!" she shouted.

McCarter and Oco took off. Men clad in midnight blue slid down the ropes, crashing through the trees.

Danielle wheeled around, pulling out a Glock 9mm pistol. Before she could fire, two metal prongs hit her in the back, penetrating her shirt. A shock racked her body. She fell forward unable to move or even shout, crashing hard like a sack of flour and convulsing from the Taser.

Lying on her side, she saw Oco go over the edge and McCarter running after him, wires from the Taser darts trailing after him. He managed to dodge them, then lurched suddenly at the hammering of a submachine gun. A spatter of blood flew and he went tumbling over the steep embankment.

The next moments were a blur. She tried to move, only to have another jolt from the Taser rack her body. As she was rolling on the ground, men surrounded her and zip-tied her wrists behind her back. All around the trees bent and whipped beneath the thunderous symphony of the helicopter's downwash.

She glanced up. A dark shape filled a gap in the trees. It was a Sikorsky Skycrane, a huge beast, shaped like a hovering claw, with an empty space for a belly where it could secure incredible payloads. Tractor trailers and small tanks could be suspended beneath it. The thing would have no trouble with the stone monument.

Heavy chains dropped from the monster and were secured. The whirling blades roared, the chains snapped taught, and the statue was pulled free.

The man beside her grabbed a radio from his hip. "We have one of them," he said.

He looked toward the rim over which McCarter and Oco had flown.

"The local boy got away. But the other one's dead."

Danielle's heart fell; the words left her sick.

"Take her out past the mist," she heard the guard say. "They're going to drop a basket for her."

Danielle was forced to stand and then dragged off. As she was pulled past the spot where McCarter had fallen, her legs nearly gave out. McCarter lay unmoving on his side, thirty feet down the steep slope, wrapped awkwardly around a tree. His back was bent at an impossible angle and his eyes remained open, staring lifelessly into the distance. His T-shirt was soaked with blood.

She hesitated, her legs feeling as if they might give out. A shove in the back sent her moving again.

Five minutes later she was in the cabin of the giant helicopter, the carved relic secured in the bay, with McCarter, Oco, and the Island of the Shroud disappearing far behind her.

CHAPTER 2

Professor McCarter lay unmoving on the black volcanic slope. His eyes were open and fixed, staring forward at the oddly tilted landscape. He'd tumbled down the slope of the wooded island, slamming the base of his spine against the tree. The backpack had flown out of his hand, disappearing farther down into the mist. McCarter himself had come to rest looking up the hill, watching as both Danielle and the statue were hauled away.

He lay motionless but not by choice. His body was numb and cold. He couldn't feel his feet or legs or anything below his waist. He could barely feel the tips of his fingers. He could barely breathe. He couldn't have called out for help, even if he'd wanted to.

Alone now, fear had begun to grip him. McCarter guessed that he was paralyzed, and to the men up the steep slope from him it must have looked as if he were dead.

He'd been hit in the leg. And though the flow had slowed quite a bit, McCarter had never seen so much blood.

And now he could feel nothing, even as blood followed the course of gravity and seeped from his elevated leg up his torso and soaked his shirt. It was a strange thing to him: The mind worked, the mind attempted to make the limbs work, and when nothing happened the mind made its conclusions and rendered its report.

For several minutes he lay like that, wondering if his fate or Danielle's was worse. But instead of his breathing growing weaker and coming to an end, he began to feel a dull sensation in his legs. It wasn't pain, but an uncomfortable buzzing, like pins and needles.

It grew in shapeless waves and he soon found that he needed to attempt moving, just to fight against it. He rolled to his left and a tactile sense began returning to his hands.

With great effort he managed to untangle himself from the tree. The fact that he was not paralyzed was a great relief; the fact that he was in considerable and growing pain was the opposite. Stiff and weak, he crawled a few feet and then collapsed. He lay there for another minute, face pressed into the soil of the sloping ground, before finally raising his head.

Looking up the hill, he thought he saw a shape standing above him, the outline of a person, a woman.

He blinked to try and focus and the shadow was gone.

He tried to put the image down to his injured state, but it seemed real to him. Real enough that he attempted to scale the hill.

Crawling, he struggled upward, making progress for a few yards. But the slope was too steep for his weakened body, the footing too loose. It crumbled under his hands and he began to slide, first to his original position and then farther down into the mist. A tumbling, unstoppable descent brought him down to the flatland at the water's edge, right beside the backpack he'd lost half an hour before.

He looked at the pack tentatively and then pulled it to him, zipping the compartments shut and trying to thread an arm through its straps. Before he could succeed, the sound of movement in the water reached him.

It was Oco wading toward him.

"They took the statue," Oco said. "In the helicopter. I saw them."

"I know," McCarter said. "We need to get help."

With Oco's assistance, he wrapped and dressed his wound and then pulled a satellite phone from its watertight container in his pack. He powered it up, giving thanks for the green light that told him the signal was getting through.

In his clouded mind, McCarter tried to remember what he was supposed to say, the acronyms Danielle had briefed him with over and over again. Terms and contingencies he didn't want to think about, the worst of which had now come true.

He pressed the initiate button and waited for the satellite to link up. An answering voice came on the line, a staff member in a secured communications room in Washington, D.C.

McCarter needed someone of higher authority.

"This is Professor Michael McCarter," he said. "Attached to Project Icarus. My code is seven, seven, four, tango, foxtrot. We've been attacked. Our status is Mercury. Now get me Arnold Moore."

CHAPTER 3

Twenty-four hours and five thousand miles from where Professor McCarter had called, Arnold Moore, director of the NRI, waited. For the second time this day, he had bad news to deliver.

The first time had been to a former operative of his named Marcus Watson, who had left the NRI years prior. He now taught at Georgetown and was rumored to be engaged to Ms. Danielle Laidlaw.

Despite all the tact and promises Moore could offer, the meeting had ended in rage. "You had no right to ask her back," Watson had insisted. "I told you that a year ago. God damn you, Arnold. You find her."

Marcus had been dead set against Danielle going back to the NRI, and Moore had pushed every button he could think of to convince her to do so. The NRI was where she belonged, but that was not to be explained at a time such as this.

"You know I'll do everything I can to find her," he'd promised.

"And what if it's not enough?" Marcus had said.

Moore had no answer for that. It was a contingency he did not want to consider. His old friend had stormed off, slamming the door on his way out with such force that it shook the building.

Now, hours later, sitting in the Oval Office, smoothing his unruly gray hair, Moore waited on another old friend: the president of the United States.

Sitting behind the impressively large desk, the president ignored Moore for the moment, signing a series of papers one after the other.

Slightly older than Moore, with dark hair that the newspapers were desperate to prove was dyed, President Franklin Henderson had been Moore's superior once before, twenty years earlier, when both of them worked at the State Department. They'd remained friends, if distant ones, ever since. Moore kept Henderson's trust and respect, partially because he made it a rule never to ask his friend for anything—at least, that was, until now.

The president stacked the papers neatly for an aide to retrieve and then looked Moore in the eye.

"Can't say I'm happy to see you," the president began. "Every time you come up here you tell us things we don't want to know. Why don't you just stay over in Virginia, or better yet retire?"

"Mr. President, this is my retirement," Moore said. "This is the reward, or perhaps the punishment, for thirty years of government service."

"Well, from what I remember you're not much of a golfer anyway." The smile appeared as he finished, the same easy, confident smile that had touched so many voters during the election. The one that said, *It's going to be all right.*

Unfortunately, Moore knew better. "Mr. President,

the NRI has a problem. Two, actually—maybe more. By my count they seem to be multiplying."

The president looked around. "There's a reason we're the only ones here, Arnold. I was told you couldn't give me any kind of prebriefing. I figured it was serious. What are we talking about?"

Moore pulled two sheets of paper from his briefcase. He placed them on the president's desk. The first was a satellite photo depicting a fleet of Russian ships, steaming headlong through the Pacific toward Alaska. The second had multiple photos inset with text, showing similar movements from the Chinese navy and even a few merchant ships.

"I've seen these already," the president said. "Talked them over with John Gillis this morning." Gillis was the navy's chief of staff. "It's not like the Russians are going to invade Alaska with a couple of cruisers, a dozen destroyers, and a few reconnaissance aircraft. Nor are the Chinese."

"I realize that," Moore said. "It's obviously not an invasion force. If you look carefully you'll see that both groups are made up of fast ships only, and both began to fan out as they approached this point, here." He touched the map indicating a spot in the Bering Sea, near the International Date Line.

"Gillis thinks they're search parties," the president said.

"I agree," Moore said. "Which begs the question: What the hell are they searching for? Does the navy have any idea?"

The president glanced at the satellite photo but remained silent.

Moore pressed him; he needed the information. "Mr. President, I can find no evidence that anything went down in that part of the Bering Sea. No distress calls were recorded on the channels we monitor. There are no oil slicks or debris fields visible in the recon photos. Nor any heat spikes on the continuous infrared scans that would indicate an explosion. There is literally nothing to suggest that either side lost an aircraft or vessel of any kind. And yet both sides launched massive search parties within hours of each other."

The president was direct. "What are you asking me, Arnold?"

"Do we have any submarines in the area? Do we have any sonar information suggesting either the Russians or the Chinese had a submarine in the area at the time?"

"Unfortunately, we don't," the president said. "But why would that matter, unless you think that's what they're looking for."

"I'm not sure what they're looking for," Moore said.

"But you have a hunch. Otherwise you wouldn't be here."

When intelligence agencies had an idea they went to the president, and when things were amiss they hid in their offices desperately searching for answers before the president or his staff came looking for them.

Moore explained what he knew. "Several hours before the Russian fleet launched, we recorded a gamma ray event in this exact location. Not a big burst by any stretch of the imagination but an unusual type of energy, for certain."

"Gamma rays?" the President asked. "I went to law school, Arnold. Mostly because I didn't like science. So why don't you tell me what this means in layman's terms?"

"Gamma rays are high-energy electromagnetic waves," Moore said. "They're used for many different things, including a type of nuclear surgery, or as hyper-powerful X-rays that can see through walls and steel containers. There's even research being done on ways to use them as weapons, either to bring down missiles or to use against troops."

The president seemed impressed. "Why didn't Gillis tell me this?"

"He wouldn't know," Moore said. "His satellites don't scan for this type of thing. The data I'm showing you comes from an NRI bird launched earlier this year."

As the president absorbed the information, Moore continued.

"At almost that same instant, four of our GPS satellites, all in geosynchronous orbits over the Arctic Circle, went momentarily dark, forcing automatic resets to bring them back on line. The service interruption lasted less than a minute, but the event was recorded."

He handed another printout to the president. "As you know, the GPS works by sending signals coded to the atomic clocks on board each satellite, which allows for very accurate time and distance measurement. According to the logs, the satellites went down all but simultaneously, to the billionth of a second. It's impossible for any ground-based system to be timed that accurately into four different locations."

"Which means?"

"They were taken out by a common event."

The president looked at the paper and then up at

Moore. "You think this was a weapon of some kind, based on a submarine. Maybe something went wrong, an overload of some kind. An event like that would likely destroy the platform itself, with the search parties scrambling for the wreckage."

"That's one possibility," Moore said, though there was another that he didn't want to get into. "Both Russia and China are working on energy weapons, just like we are. Either of them could have had a test bed out there."

The president slid the papers back over to Moore. "All right, Arnold. What do you need to follow this up?"

"I need time and access. I want the keys to the NSA's data vault, and control of the listening posts and the Pacific sonar line. And I need it done with a block on data sharing and without having to field stupid questions from NSA, CIA, or anyone else for that matter."

The president reacted as if he'd been punched. "Damn, Arnold, why don't you just ask for their firstborn while you're at it?"

Moore didn't respond. At times in the past, he and the president had spoken about the NRI's unique role in the intelligence system. And whether it was because of their friendship or the value that the NRI provided, the president had always supported Moore when it was needed.

"I can give you everything but the sonar line," President Henderson replied. "With the Russian fleet prowling around, Gillis will go apeshit if we block him, but I'll have the navy forward the information to you. You have forty-eight hours. And don't be surprised if I shorten the leash or if events supersede your request."

Moore nodded. It would be enough to start with.

"And now for the second problem," he said, folding his notes and putting them away. "I have a favor to ask."

"Personal?"

"In a manner of speaking," Moore replied. "One of my people has been kidnapped. I have reliable data implicating a group working for Chen Li Kang, the Chinese billionaire. I want to go after her."

The president's face turned grim. "Right now? With all this going on?"

"Yes, Mr. President."

"Why?"

Moore was surprised by the question; he thought the answer was obvious. "What do you mean 'why'?"

"Does she have information that they could use against us?" the president asked.

"No," Moore said. "Nothing that's not compartmentalized. But she deserves better than being left to Kang. In his hands, she's as good as dead . . . or worse."

The dark look on the president's face spoke volumes. "You and I have both taken that risk in our lives," he reminded Moore. "It's one of the hazards of being an operative."

"She's not just an operative," Moore said, reluctantly. "She's someone I dragged back into the business personally."

The president paused. "What are you telling me?"

"It's Danielle Laidlaw," Moore said.

The president winced. Moore knew Henderson would

recognize the name, that he would understand what Danielle meant to him: the daughter he never had, a protégée he now lived vicariously through in some ways. He hoped that would sway the president's decision, but if it moved the needle at all, it wasn't far enough.

"Arnold, you knew the answer to that question before you came in here," he said. "Things with China have been spiraling for years. New kid on the block flexing his muscles, waiting for a chance to show the old boss that his days are numbered. This isn't the time to stir that up."

"Kang's not a member of the government," Moore pointed out. "He's a private individual, a Chinese citizen who's kidnapped an American citizen."

"There are no private individuals when you get to his status," the president said curtly.

"We can do it quietly," Moore said insistently.

"This discussion is over," the president said.

Moore took a deep breath. He knew better than to press an argument he could not win.

As he relented, the president threw him a bone. "We'll work through back channels. We'll talk to a few people."

Moore nodded, but he knew it wouldn't be enough. He stood. "I'll update you regarding this gamma ray burst as soon as I have anything."

Moore turned to leave and the president looked back to his stack of documents, grabbing one that he'd yet to review. Without looking up, he spoke.

"You don't think there's a connection between these two things?" he asked.

Moore had been in the intelligence game long enough

that withholding information came naturally to him. One volunteered nothing, not even to the president of the United States.

Now the president looked at him. "Chinese fleet racing through the Bering Sea. Chinese billionaire kidnapping one of your people from Mexico. Is there a link in there somewhere?"

"Let's hope to God not," Moore said.

"Why?" the president asked. "What were your people working on down there anyway?"

When Moore spoke, his tone was both glib and deadly serious. "In a manner of speaking, Mr. President, the end of the world."

CHAPTER 4

Western Congo, December 2012

The battered jeep rambled down an uneven dirt road, a ribbon of red clay that twisted through the dark green foliage of the lower jungle.

The jeep had no doors or roof, but it carried some minor armored plating around the engine and a .50-caliber machine gun mounted atop the roll bar. It also carried three men: an African driver and his fellow gunner, wearing dark camouflage, and a white man in the passenger seat, whose own fatigues were stained with blood, sweat, and smoke and whose tanned face was coated with soot and grime.

Looking as if he'd just come from fighting a fire, he slouched in the seat, turned outward at an angle with one foot resting on the jeep's running board and a long-barreled SIG 551 assault rifle resting in his hands.

His manner brought to mind that of a weary soldier daydreaming, but behind the dark sunglasses, his eyes were moving constantly, flicking from one section of the trees to the next, scanning up and down the dusty, reddish road.

He didn't see anything to alarm him, hadn't seen anything on the entire drive. And that bothered him. He'd expected at least one more wave of resistance.

He turned to the driver and asked in an American accent, "How far to the village?"

The African driver kept his eyes forward, a tense determination never leaving his body. "A mile or two," he said. "We will be there soon enough, my friend. I promise you, the Hawk does not need to fight anymore today."

The man, whom the others called Hawker, turned away from the driver and stared down the curving road. They'd been through hell to get this far and some instinct deep inside told him the work might not be done.

He glanced backward over his shoulder at the small convoy following them. Two hundred yards behind, a group of trucks filled with medical supplies, grains for planting, and sacks of rice traveled in single file. Accompanying the trucks were a pair of vans filled with doctors.

They were brave men and women who'd come here, beyond the reach of their governments, beyond the reach of the UN, in a valiant effort to treat the maimed and the wounded of Congo's endless civil war.

He admired them. They abhorred fighting enough to risk their lives trying to stem its carnage in some small way. And yet they were conflicted now, having seen it up close for the past few days, not as observers or angels of mercy, but as prisoners and victims and combatants.

Hawker could feel the change in them. They looked at him differently now, avoiding eye contact or any real conversation. Perhaps he and his men were part of the problem instead of part of the solution.

To be honest, he didn't care what they thought. In a few minutes, a village that had been under siege for years would be seeing food and medicine and a break from the constant predation of the strong against the weak.

The jeep rounded a long, sweeping curve and the village came into view directly ahead of them. It was nothing more than a ramshackle collection of corrugated tin and, in places, mud-walled adobe buildings.

At the center of the village, the dirt road turned a circle. A simple wooden church stood off to one side, its steeple and walls bearing the scars of bullet holes below a white painted cross. In front of it stood the town's most prized possession, a solar-powered pump that drew clean water from a thousand feet below.

He'd expected people to be gathered around it, but the fields and the village appeared empty, and all was quiet as Hawker and his compatriots rolled in.

Hawker's jeep rounded the circle at the center of town and slowed to a stop.

With the engine idling and the vehicle's nose pointed toward the safety of the dirt road, Hawker and the two men with him watched for any sign of movement. He brought a walkie-talkie to his mouth.

"Hold the convoy," he said quietly.

A double click told him the message had been received. He placed the radio down.

The smell of a cooking fire lingered in the air, but there was no noise or movement. Hawker turned to the driver. "I thought you said someone would be here to meet us."

The man looked around nervously. "My brother is here," he said. "Somewhere."

Across the plaza, the door to the church cracked open.

"Cut the engine," Hawker said.

As the rumbling of the exhaust died away, the door opened farther. A moment later two men stepped out: one dressed in the garb of an Anglican priest, the other in a loose gray shirt and black pants.

"Devera," the driver shouted as he jumped from the jeep.

The man in the gray shirt smiled broadly. "Brother," he said. They reached out and clasped in a strong hug.

"Did you bring the doctors?" Devera said. "Some of the people have been wounded in the fighting."

"We brought them," the driver told his brother excitedly.

Hawker clicked the radio. "It's clear," he said. "Come on in."

Moments later, the trucks entered the town accompanied by additional armed jeeps and the two vans with red crosses painted on them.

Devera and the priest watched the vehicles pulling in.

"We were told that Jumbuto had stopped you," Devera said. "Most of the people fled, fearing a reprisal."

Jumbuto was the local warlord. And he *had* stopped them, ambushing the convoy after promising free passage. His men had killed two of the drivers and one of the guards and had then kidnapped the doctors, hoping to ransom them to their relatively wealthy families back in Europe and America.

Hawker and his people had gone after them, something Jumbuto had never expected. Forty-eight hours later, the warlord was dead, his garish compound burning in the hills. The few of his men who had survived were running for their lives.

It had been a bloody, horrible battle. Thirty men had been killed, four of them Hawker's people. Three others were badly wounded, but the siege had been broken.

"He did cross us," the driver said, "like the snake he's always been. But he won't do it again. I tell you we killed him," he said excitedly. "I saw it with my own eyes."

Devera looked thrilled, the priest less so. "You see, Father, I told you about this one." He pointed to Hawker. "I told you he would get through."

Laughing heartily, Devera grabbed Hawker in a huge bear hug, shaking him.

Hawker accepted the man's gratitude, but he didn't smile. He knew there were no simple solutions to the problems of such a village. There would be new oppressors to deal with before too long.

The priest seemed to know this as well. And though a sense of relief had appeared on his face, he did not smile, either. "We can only hope the next devil will not be worse than the last."

"Oh, you're too glum, Father," Devera said, still reveling in his joy. "God has sent us deliverance."

"God's deliverance does not come with bullets and blood," the priest replied.

Hawker gazed at the priest. Burn marks covered his

hands and a scar from some terrible blade cut across his forehead and disappeared up into his hairline, but the man's eyes seemed devoid of malice. Even after all he must have seen, his face offered kindness and peace.

For a moment Hawker felt he should say something, explain himself perhaps, or at least his actions, but he couldn't find any words and instead nodded silently and then began to walk away.

Behind him the unloading got under way, and as Devera had expected, the proper rejoicing began.

CHAPTER 5

Three days after Hawker's arrival, the African village was filled with life, like a garden after a long-awaited rain. With seed now available, the overgrown fields were being plowed and planted. Children were playing among the doctors as they administered vaccines, treated infections, and removed bullets or shrapnel from a surprising number of men and women.

To Hawker, the liveliness of the village was both a blessing and a curse. If another warlord set his sights on this place, the people who now laughed and danced would find a new subjugation more painful than having never being freed in the first place.

Weary with this knowledge, he found himself alone in the church, sitting in a simple wooden pew, one row from the front. He wasn't praying or reading or meditating. He was just sitting there, bathed in the darkness and the silence.

A former pilot, Hawker had once been a member of the CIA, but after disobeying a direct order, he'd spent the past decade on the run, living as a pariah. He was a mercenary now, running weapons, fighting, flying.

And while the days were often filled with war, it was

the nights that held the darkest alleys for him, dreams that twisted and bent back on themselves—mistakes, failings, friends who trusted him suffering and dying.

Neither awake nor asleep could Hawker escape death.

A sliver of light cut across the floor as someone opened the front door. The light widened and then shrank and he heard the footsteps on the crude wooden planks. A match flared and was touched to a candle.

"Are you troubled?" the priest asked him.

"Aren't we all?" Hawker replied, only half joking.

The priest sat down opposite him. "Of course we are. It is the nature of our existence. But perhaps I can help you."

Hawker considered the offer. He felt somewhere beyond help. "What happened to you?" he asked, touching his hair in a spot corresponding to the scar on the priest's head.

"In the early days of Jumbuto, a man who worked for him attacked me with a machete."

Hawker's jaw clenched for a moment as he imagined the crime. "Well, perhaps he's gone now."

"Oh, no," the priest said. "He's quite well, thank God."

Confused, Hawker narrowed his gaze.

"The man who attacked me was Devera," the priest explained. "He was young and wanted the kind of life he saw the warlords having. But it was not in him, or, if it was, God took it from him. One day, months afterward, Devera came to me for forgiveness. His eyes were red with tears, his face stricken, his arms covered in blood where he'd gashed them over and over in some form of self-inflicted penance."

The priest shook his head sadly. "Even after I forgave him, it was a long time before he chose to forgive himself. But he worked day and night to help this village and the people here. Eventually he was one of us again. Part of something more. Part of us, part of life instead of death. And then finally the darkness left him."

Hawker stared at the priest.

"If he had not attacked me," the priest said, "he would have killed others, perhaps many. He might not have found his way back to the narrow gate."

"You could have died," Hawker noted.

"God works in mysterious ways," the priest replied. "Change is often arrived at only through enough pain."

For the second time since meeting this man, Hawker was struck silent. He looked down at the floor and then away.

"I did not mean to disturb you," the priest said, "but there is someone here to see you."

"To see me?"

"A white man. He says he flew into Dwananga and then drove up."

"When did he get here?"

"An hour ago," the priest said. "He insisted that he needed to see you right away, but I made him wait outside. This place is a sanctuary. Here one should not be disturbed."

An hour. Had he really been in the church for that long?

"Did he give you his name?"

"He did not," the priest replied. "He said that you would not speak with him if you knew who he was."

It seemed like a strange admission from someone who'd come to see him.

Hawker stood. "Thank you, Father."

He walked to the door and pushed through, leaving the darkened quiet of the church for the brightness of the outside world. Squinting across the courtyard, he saw a gray-haired white man wearing slacks and a dress shirt with rolled-up sleeves. The man stood with his back to Hawker, talking with Devera beside the water pump.

As Hawker walked up, Devera looked his way.

The white man turned with him. "By the pricking in my thumbs . . . ," he said, loud enough for Hawker to hear.

The man was Arnold Moore, director of the NRI.

CHAPTER 6

The words came screaming from the darkness. "What are you looking for?"

Danielle strained to see their source. She felt her body shaking, extreme cold and hot all at the same time, as if poison were coursing through her veins.

A blinding flash of light scalded her eyes.

"What are you looking for?" the voice demanded again.

It felt like a nightmare, like a disjointed dream of terror. Her head was swimming, as if she had vertigo and was falling. She reached for something to hold on to, feeling behind her, but there was no back to the chair, nothing to lean against, only edges like on a countertop or table.

The blinding light vanished and a more subdued light came on. A face moved close. It was Asian in complexion and features, slight and fine-boned. He came so close that all she could see was his eyes. His hands grabbed her. They were cold and shaking. He gazed into her eyes, as if he were searching her soul.

"Don't worry," he said, smiling. "We know what you're looking for. More artifacts, like the one you found in Brazil." He pulled away, laughing a sickly laugh.

He began to laugh harder and it terrified her. She forced herself to move, scurrying backward and then falling. The jarring impact with the floor sharpened her senses for a minute. She looked back toward her oppressor. He sat in a motorized wheelchair, his body twisted and withered, shaking slightly from some internal tremor.

As strange as it seemed, a feeling of pity came over Danielle. And when the man seemed to recognize it, his face contorted in fury.

"Take her," he shouted.

Two large men grabbed her, picked her up, and slammed her back onto the examination table. A third man approached with a dripping hypodermic needle.

"No!" she screamed, struggling to break free.

The men held her down. The blinding light flashed again and then the needle pierced her flesh and everything vanished.

She woke, curled up in the fetal position, her heart pounding in her chest. It was more than a dream, but how much more she couldn't know. As the images faded, she struggled to parse them into coherence, to separate reality from what must only be nightmarish imagination. Try as she did, she could not be sure where the boundary lay.

She sat up slowly. White walls and beige furniture surrounded her, including an art-deco-like desk and several chairs that occupied the far side of the room. There were no windows in the room. No clocks, radios, or televisions; no computer sat on the desk. It was as if she'd fallen asleep in some downtown office building and woken up in the *Twilight Zone* version of it.

If only that were the case.

She was a prisoner. One who had been treated roughly for some period of time, a few days or even weeks perhaps. She had no concept of how long it had been, of where she was, or what she might have told them.

Her last clear thought was of Professor McCarter lying dead on the side of the hill, wrapped around a tree, like a car that had gone off a cliff.

A wave of depression swept over her.

She felt great responsibility for McCarter. To begin with, he'd only been exposed to the NRI after she'd talked him into joining the Brazilian expedition two years before. He was a civilian and at the time not even cleared to know the truth behind the mission. Yet together they discovered a precursor of the Mayan religion, one that predated the rest of the culture by at least a thousand years.

And then they'd been attacked, first by a group of mercenaries, later by a tribe of xenophobic natives, and finally by a relentless pack of mutated animals that seemed to spring from the Mayan underworld itself.

They'd never found what they were looking for—elements that NRI scientists believed could lead to a working cold-fusion device—but just prior to departing, they'd recovered something else: a large, glasslike stone, which seemed to radiate energy in a manner that no one could yet explain.

The NRI hid the stone in a vault beneath its Virginia

headquarters and began to study it. McCarter went back to New York to begin teaching again and Danielle watched the machinery of government move on, unconcerned with those who had suffered for what they'd found.

It was enough to change her long-held beliefs of what mattered in the world. She quit the NRI and become a lobbyist for causes she believed in: education, health care, the war against cancer. For the first time since college, her life had taken on a sense of normalcy. There was peace and contentment and traffic; there were office parties, shopping malls, and bills.

And there was Marcus.

She sat back, trying to fight the waves of nausea. Deep, slow breaths helped calm her, but tears welled up in her eyes as she thought of the man she'd spent her year of civilian life with.

Leaving the NRI had been harder than it appeared. There was a definite disconnect with the regular world, a feeling of being a stranger in a strange land. But Marcus Watson had been at the NRI when she started there. They knew each other, even had a past together. He'd already made the transition to the real world and he helped show her the way.

It had been a great year, an easy year after so many hard ones. Their joint experience with the institute gave them common ground to work from, and in many ways it had been nice to let someone else hold the reins for once. But even as Danielle took to this new, normalized version of life, a strange reversal of circumstances had begun.

At his university in New York, Professor McCarter

had grown increasingly interested in the artifacts they'd found. He soon began pestering her for information and then, realizing she no longer had access, he went directly to Arnold Moore.

As it turned out, McCarter wasn't the only one with the artifacts on his mind. The NRI scientists were becoming concerned with a growing wave of energy emanating from what they now called the Brazil stone. When McCarter explained a theory he'd developed, that the stone was one from a group of four, Moore decided it was imperative that the NRI find the remaining stones before anyone else did.

McCarter volunteered to begin the search, but shortly afterward, he was attacked in Guatemala. It became clear that he needed protection, but McCarter didn't trust the NRI. It was an uneasy alliance to pursue something he wanted to find. He wouldn't have some gun-toting bodyguard at his side like a chaperone.

Fearing for McCarter's life, and for the success of the mission, Moore came to Danielle and begged her to return.

The timing could not have been worse. Marcus had just asked her to marry him, and she had hesitated. Moore's arrival was gasoline on a fire and it triggered endless fighting. It was a special kind of hell, having someone she loved ask her to leave a friend to the wolves.

She spent three days trying to make him understand and then, after an argument for the ages, she'd gone to the airport, bought a ticket, and left for Mexico. She'd boarded the plane fairly certain that she'd destroyed everything. And after all that, she'd failed to help McCarter anyway.

"What have I done?" she wondered aloud. "What have I done?"

As a new wave of sickness broke over her, she felt a great urge to lie back down. How much easier it would have been to just give up and die. But the thought disgusted her. As guilt-ridden as she felt, she knew that any hope of making up for what had occurred, any hope of seeing the people she cared for again, began with getting out of that room.

Relying on sheer willpower, she stood and crossed the floor. The carpet felt soft and well padded under her bare feet.

She reached the door, checking it just to be certain. Of course it was locked. There was an electronic keypad on her side, probably a card reader on the other. She moved to the desk and opened every drawer, one after another.

Empty, all of them.

She slammed the last one shut and sat down, her head throbbing ever harder. Either the lights were absurdly bright or something was wrong with her eyes. It almost felt as if her pupils were dilated, which suggested that strong drugs had been used against her. The terror of her dream and the disjointed, fragmented pattern of her memories and sense of time since her capture only made it more likely.

She looked at her right arm. There were at least four needle marks, maybe more. Bruising around the injection sites made it hard to tell.

Sodium pentothal, she guessed. Or scopolamine.

Both drugs were barbiturates that could be used as truth serum. They didn't exactly work that way, but people had a tendency to talk and give up secrets they might otherwise have withheld, especially under higher doses; doses that were dangerous and often resulted in amnesia.

She thought that might explain the dryness in her mouth and the flaring of the lights.

Before she could consider the thought further, the door clicked open and two Asian men came in. Both were muscular and fit, wearing suits, pressed shirts, and silk ties.

The leader stepped toward her.

"Put these on," he said, placing her boots on the desk. She noticed a small bruise under his eye, a scabbed cut. She hoped it was her doing.

She took the boots. "Why?"

"Because you're going to want them where we're taking you."

Not liking the sound of that, Danielle pulled the right boot on. As she tied it, she thought of using the left as a weapon, but even if she were to overpower these men, where would she go from there?

Out into the hall? Which led where, exactly? To what? For all she knew there would be another locked door twenty feet away. She would only get one chance, if that. She could not waste it.

She pulled the other boot on and the men walked her out the door to an elevator. Entering, they used a key to access a panel beneath the other buttons. It popped open and the man who'd given her the boots pressed the lowest of the buttons. The indicator illuminated, the doors shut, and the car began to descend.

Danielle did a quick count of the buttons, three rows of twenty, but the way the elevator was moving—and her ears popping—she guessed it was the express. That meant the building would be closer to a hundred floors than sixty. She tried to think of the buildings in China that were over a hundred stories. There were a number of them, but one in particular came to mind: the Tower Pinnacle, owned by Kang and sitting on prime real estate at the edge of Victoria Harbour.

She was in Hong Kong.

"I want to talk with the American consulate," she said.

"No," the man with the cut said. "You've done enough talking. At least to us."

The elevator slowed and then stopped. The doors opened, not to a spacious lobby, as Danielle might have hoped, but to a metal threshold beyond which lay darkness and what looked like aged and blackened stone. The place had a dank smell, like garbage or urine.

"What the hell is this?"

The man with the scab got off the elevator.

"Please step out," he said, holding a Taser and energizing it. The electricity snapped across the prongs.

Reluctantly Danielle moved forward into a hallway of some kind. It looked to be made of natural rock and mortar, like the interior of some medieval castle, only dark and wet with condensation. A heavy wooden door to her right was rotting off its rusted hinges. A single bulb attached to a bare cable cast little light.

Danielle came to a gate made of iron bars.

Before she could react the men shoved her forward. She tripped over a slight ledge and sprawled to the ground, skinning her hands on the stone.

She sprang back up and rushed the gate, but they slammed and locked it in her face.

"Why are you doing this?" she shouted. "What do you want from me?"

"Nothing," the scabbed man said.

She glanced into the darkness around her. She heard movement: shuffling, groaning, and breathing, as if her arrival had disturbed some resting beast. The stench of the surroundings grew suddenly worse.

"What is this place?" she shouted.

The men were in the elevator now, the doors closing, cutting off the light. One of them replied as the doors slammed shut.

"This is your new home."

CHAPTER 7

In the heart of the African village, Hawker stared coldly at Arnold Moore. He knew Moore from a mission he'd taken with the NRI two years earlier, the same expedition to the Amazon that had involved Danielle Laidlaw and Professor McCarter. Hawker had been promised a certain type of absolution for his efforts, but in the aftermath that followed, the deal had fallen through.

"What the hell are you doing here?" he asked.

"Looking for you," Moore said.

"You're not exactly dressed for the bush."

"No," Moore said in agreement. "Our intel had you in Kinshasa, drinking and spending money like you'd printed it yourself. But after three days of looking it became clear that you weren't there. I almost went home. But then I heard about a firefight going on up here, where the bad guys were getting the worst of it for once."

"Sometimes bad things happen to the right people," Hawker said.

"And sometimes to the wrong ones," Moore replied cryptically. "I need your help."

Hawker studied Moore, acutely aware of their differences. Moore was an important piece for one side of the world. Not the white king, perhaps, but a bishop at the least. A mover of pawns and a shrewd one at that. Hawker had once been a part of that side, but no longer. In fact, he wasn't part of any side at this point in his life. In some strange, surreal way he'd become a type of third player, a red knight on a board of black and white. He had no alliances, no one to answer to, and thus no real limits. Reaching out to him could mean only one thing. Moore had a job no white piece could do.

"The last time I worked for the NRI it didn't turn out so well," Hawker said. "In case you forgot, you guys never came through on your end. Though you seem to have set yourself up pretty good."

"The CIA got involved," Moore said. "They think you still owe them a few chits."

"They must. They sent a couple of thugs out to try and collect."

Moore nodded, grinning. "Yes, well . . . once you put those men in the hospital, I lost any say in the matter."

"You also lost the right to ask me—"

"It's Danielle," Moore said, stopping Hawker mid-sentence and speaking bluntly, like a man running out of time. "She's been abducted. I know who took her and where she is, but she's out of my reach."

Hawker stared at Moore as if he'd been punched. He and Danielle had initially clashed in Brazil. But as things had gone from bad to worse, he'd watched her change from a win-at-all-costs alpha female to a person who cared more about her team than she did about herself. At the darkest moment of their journey, she'd even been willing to sacrifice herself to give the others a chance at survival.

Going through that had created a bond he could still feel when he thought of her. Enough that not getting a chance to see her again had been the worst part of how things ended.

"I heard she'd quit," Hawker said angrily.

"She did. But she came back to help a friend."

"You?"

"No," Moore told him. "McCarter."

"McCarter?" Hawker's mind reeled. Danielle returning to the NRI was one thing, but Professor McCarter? His gaze sharpened, focusing on Moore like a laser. He understood.

"You're looking for more of what we found in Brazil."

Moore nodded. "And who else could I possibly send?"

Of course, Hawker thought. Moore needed to keep his secrets. A theory called containment symmetry held that it was best to send agents who already knew those secrets, perhaps especially with what they'd found down there.

"McCarter is still missing," Moore added. "He's injured but he escaped and has gone into hiding. I have teams looking for him and we'll find him, but Danielle is beyond my grasp. And she will die where she is, but not quickly."

Hawker clenched his jaw. "Who took her?"

"A Chinese billionaire named Kang," Moore said.

"And he's untouchable?"

"So goes the order," Moore said. "That's why I'm here. That's why I had to come in person. This is not an institute mission, it's a private one, a deal between you and me, to help someone we both care for."

Hawker studied Moore. If there was a redeeming quality to the man, it was that he cared for those who worked under him, especially Danielle. Coming to Africa to solicit help for her was a desperate act, one that could not only end his career but see him off to Leavenworth for the rest of his life. A pariah in the making. Hawker suddenly found new respect for the man.

"You should know, a big part of why she quit the NRI was our inability or unwillingness to help you," Moore told him.

"You don't have to sell me," Hawker said.

"I'm not," Moore insisted. "I just want you to know it was my decision not to press that fight, and she took issue, strongly."

It was good to hear. Hawker couldn't deny that.

"I've set up an account," Moore said. "I've transferred all the money I could lay my hands on into it. Use it, go to Hong Kong, and get her back."

"It won't be that easy," Hawker replied.

"It never is," Moore said quickly. "You didn't do this because it was easy. You did it because it needed to be done. Because no one else would do it. And somewhere deep inside, that pisses you off more than anything else. Danielle's situation is the same. If you don't help her, no one will."

Voices could be heard in the distance, singing and joking. The villagers were coming back from the fields they'd spent the day planting. Hawker had already made up his mind, but he didn't want to leave the village undefended. He hadn't thought about it much beforehand, but now it seemed vital. One flower in the barren garden.

"You protect these people. I don't care how you do it. You get word to the right men that they're not to be touched."

Moore nodded. "I can do that. Just find Danielle and get her away from Kang."

Hawker would do what he could, but he wondered if it would be enough. "And if I'm too late?"

Moore did not blink. "Then you find that son of a bitch, Kang, and you kill him. Even if you have to burn down the whole damn island to do it."

CHAPTER 8

Professor McCarter lay flat on his back staring at a ceiling made of thatch and sticks. He was a guest in Oco's Chiapas Indian village, thirty miles from the base of Mount Pulimundo.

With Oco's help he had made it back to the village but it had taken several days and his condition had grown worse each day. The bullet wound in his leg had become infected and neither the prayers of the local shaman nor his potions had helped.

Fearing such treatment might hasten his demise, McCarter had asked Oco to get him a proper doctor or at least a treatment of antibiotics. The young man had run off for the next town, but the village was so remote that it would take him two or three days to make the round-trip. McCarter wondered if he would last that long. And when his hosts moved him to the shaman's hut, he hoped it was not for last rites of some kind.

A wood fire crackled somewhere to the left of him, but he couldn't turn toward it. Since the shooting and his collision with the tree, his body had grown stiff, as if a metal rod had been run up through his spine. Any attempts to twist or bend caused ripping pains and he found it best to lay still.

He stretched his left hand down to his thigh, where a swollen wound marked the entry point of the bullet that had hit him. But he was fortunate: The jacketed bullet had gone right through.

He'd doused the wound with antiseptic and bandaged it on the shore of the island, but the infection had taken hold anyway. Beneath the bandage, the swelling had grown and become heated. McCarter drew his hand back and remained still, blinking the sweat from his eyes.

How had it come to this? The thought ran through his head as if he didn't know the answer, as if it were all the result of some unforeseen event. But he knew exactly how it had come to this. It was a situation of his own making.

A year and a half ago, long before he'd been reunited with Danielle and the NRI, before he had even begun to consider such a course, he'd crawled out of bed on one of many sleepless nights and gone to his study. His notes from the Brazilian expedition were sitting untouched on a shelf. He'd pulled them down and begun leafing through them.

There were so many unanswered questions related to what they'd found down there. Given the chance he would have stayed in the Amazon, but in the wake of so much violence, death, and destruction, there hadn't been the opportunity.

Initially they had been looking for a site the Mayan people called Tulan Zuyua, a place associated with their creation myth, similar to the Garden of Eden. Whether that was what they'd found he couldn't say. Nor had he much thought to ask in the final days of that madness. Survival had become all that mattered.

But sitting in a robe, sipping tea in his study, McCarter began to wonder. He was able to study his notes and consider them with more insight. And that had led him to something unexpected.

There were glyphs in the Brazilian temple that spoke of sacrifice. Nothing unusual about that—it was everywhere in the Mayan culture—but this particular set of glyphs described it differently, not as an act or a ritual but as if the sacrifice were a thing. Sacrifice of the Heart was one description.

And then he remembered the item they had finally recovered down there, the stone that seemed to generate power. The natives had called it the Heart of Zipacna, named for a mythical Mayan beast.

If the stone they'd found in Brazil was Sacrifice of the Heart, then what was he to make of other glyphs referencing the Sacrifice of the Mind, of the Soul, and of the Body? Were there three others like it?

Intrigued, McCarter had begun going over the rest of his notes, thinking and working through the night. Knowing what he did about the origin of the Brazil stone, McCarter found himself ascribing great purpose to it and any of its brethren that might exist. This was how it had begun.

Reviewing other notes and even photographs that had been taken, McCarter came to believe that these four stones had been separated by long journeys, one remaining in Brazil, two traveling over land, and the last out over the sea.

The record ended there. It seemed something had befallen the rulers of this Brazilian temple, an uprising or some type of disaster, but the subjects and the artisans and the builders had vanished. McCarter suspected that most had traveled west and then north into Central America. And he tried to pick up the trail there.

Searching the record for anything similar, McCarter settled on the stories of the earliest Mayan people carrying their gods with them in special stones. A carving at an ancient temple south of Tikal told of two stones traveling by land and one sent over the sea. The remnants of a mural there showed a stylized view of the world, nothing that could be called a map or globe, but because he believed that was exactly what he was looking at, his deduction yielded a stunning possibility. Two stones had been taken farther north to the Yucatan and one had been placed on a continent across the sea, in what could only be northern China or southern Siberia.

The fact that this dispersion had taken place here, hundreds of years later than the description in the Brazilian temple, told him it had been planned. There was a purpose to it, a reason. It was more than a simple inheritance or a division of spoils. The act had to have a meaning to it, a greater intention in the grand scheme of things.

At that very moment, McCarter had felt the urge—no, it had been a need—to look for these stones. He had gone to those who could help him: Arnold Moore and the NRI.

It all seemed so foolish now. Not the theory but his pursuit of the proof. Who did he think he was? Some spy, some agent of change for the world? It had ended so badly, he wished it had never begun. And yet even in such despair, some part of him knew that if he managed to get healthy he would continue on.

At the sound of someone entering the room McCarter tried to look up.

"Oco?" he asked.

A different voice answered. "Oco has not returned from Xihua."

McCarter saw a younger man who spoke English and who had acted as an interpreter between McCarter and his primary caregiver. Right behind him stood the shaman himself, in full regalia.

"When will Oco return?" McCarter asked.

"Tomorrow, maybe," the interpreter said. "But we cannot wait. The poison of the blood is spreading."

McCarter looked around, desperate to see what preparations might be under way. "What are you going to do?"

"The shaman say, he now understands why you are sick," the interpreter said.

"I'm sick because someone shot me," McCarter managed to say. "I have an infection."

Apparently the shaman disagreed.

"He say, you are looking for something," the interpreter said. "But you not admit to yourself what it is you want to find. He say, you fear it will be taken from you. And your spirit fights against that truth."

Great, McCarter thought. Now he was getting his horoscope and medical treatment all from the same person. Not his idea of comprehensive medical.

He laid his head back, the strain on his neck too much to bear. He found the shaman's statements utterly confusing, but he lacked the energy to ask anything more. At another time he would have enjoyed speaking with them, exchanging words and concepts and trying to gain an insight into their unique view of the world. But at the moment, he couldn't have cared less.

The shaman spoke some words over him. "The poison blood has brought bad spirits to you," the interpreter said. "They control you in your sleep, bringing the dark dreams. The healer is going to force the spirits to leave and then the medicine will be able to work properly."

At that, McCarter heard the fire being stirred, felt another wave of heat, and heard the shaman begin to chant. The interpreter was grinding some type of medicine in a cup, mixing it with goat's milk. Seconds later McCarter was drinking it.

The taste was bitter enough to make him close his eyes. When he opened them a moment later, he felt dizzy once again and quickly the room began to blur.

Around him, the chanting continued as the shaman fanned the flames of the fire. The room began to spin and McCarter felt his head growing heavy. It felt as if the sounds had become distorted. He heard voices: the shaman chanting, the interpreter as well. And then, he thought, another voice.

"Oco?" he said hopefully.

The voice reached him again. A woman's voice, though he couldn't make out the words. They were just whispers. Hidden.

The shaman passed through his field of vision, casting ash into the air. The fine dust floated down, catching the light of the fire. In it McCarter saw a face.

He tried to focus but the shaman waved a hand through it and the dust scattered on the current.

"What have you given me?" he asked weakly.

The young man answered. "The potion is to calm the dark ones, to make them unaware."

McCarter could not follow anymore or even pay attention. He felt less pain, that was for sure, but he was more certain than ever that he was on the way to the great beyond.

He thought of his wife, who had died from cancer several years earlier. There were people in this life that made it seem worth all the trouble, made it feel like things would always get better no matter how bad they were. McCarter's wife had been one of those people.

As college students in the mid-1960s, they had endured racial slurs and threats together. And of the two of them, it had been she who'd insisted that minds would change. When their first child had been deathly sick with pneumonia, she'd promised him that their son would be fine, and he grew up to be a strong young man. And even when she'd lain dying herself and McCarter had stood at her bedside, she had been the one to comfort him.

"If this is my time," he whispered, "then let me find you."

The shaman moved past, chanting and whirling like a dervish, shaking some feathery wand. It was all a blur.

McCarter ignored him now. "Let me see you again," he said aloud to his wife. "If it's time, bring me to you."

The shaman was over him now, gazing through the smoke and the haze into McCarter's eyes. There was something in his hand.

McCarter looked past him. "Bring me to you," he said again, and then he heard the woman's voice. It was his wife. She whispered back to him.

"No," she said. *"Bring me . . . to you."*

And then the shaman raised a cast-iron rod from the glowing embers of the fire and plunged it downward. The molten tip burrowed into McCarter's open wound; his head tilted back and he screamed.

CHAPTER 9

Lantau Island, three miles east of Hong Kong, December 2012

Hawker arrived at Chep Lap Kok Airport shortly after midnight. He stepped off a cargo flight from Nairobi dressed as a member of the crew and helped to supervise the unloading.

Then, instead of reboarding the aircraft or entering the brightly lit passenger terminal, he traveled with the freight to the huge warehouse at the edge of the ramp.

The whole thing had been prearranged, the night foreman and a customs officer dutifully taking their bribes and hiding him. A new set of clothing was handed over, along with travel papers and a stamped passport. Thirty minutes later Hawker was streetside with the rest of the second-shift crew, stepping onto a bus that would take him to Hong Kong's central district.

At two o'clock in the morning, the city was ablaze with lights, skyscrapers outlined in white and yellow, others up-lit by colored floods, while the ever-present glow of the orange halogen bulbs reflected on the layer of clouds that hung over the city. Though not quite deserted, the streets were quiet, at least by Hong Kong standards.

Hawker wandered around the district for twenty minutes or so, getting his bearings, stopping for an English language newspaper and a bite to eat: Cantonese chicken and a cup of green tea.

In many ways Hong Kong was the same as Hawker remembered, the same neon face for the world to see, the same subconscious buzzing of energy, even at night. It even smelled the same; food cooking and salt air mixed with the exhaust of idling traffic.

To many that would have seemed impossible a decade and a half earlier, as the British prepared to hand the territory back to the Chinese and the threat of communist rule loomed. Many had expected a muting of Hong Kong's vibrancy, with the imposition of communist taxation, regulation, and bureaucracy. A duller, grayer place was the likely outcome. Certainly money had been fleeing the island for years before the switch.

But it hadn't happened that way. Aside from growing bigger and brighter, Hong Kong remained the same densely packed bundle of energy it had always been. The place was New York or London on speed, a more youthful and less restrained Tokyo. Its spirit, rather than being dulled, had infected the mainland, right up to the highest levels of the Communist Party, with mini versions of the great city sprouting in Shenzhen, Tianjin, and Chongqing. As it turned out, China hadn't taken over Hong Kong after all; Hong Kong had taken over China.

As if further proof were needed, Hawker's last foray into China had been with the state as an adversary. That monolithic source of power no longer existed in the same way. In all likelihood, Kang could be as much an enemy of his own country as he was currently an enemy of Hawker and the NRI. And that fact was important, because though any action against Kang would be dealt with harshly in the aftermath, especially if linked to the United States, the machinery of the state had better things to worry about in the meantime. If he was right, the only real security he would have to deal with would be Kang's.

Hawker made his way to the Peninsula Hotel and checked in under the assumed name on the passport: Mr. Thomas Francis.

"Are there any messages for me?" he asked.

"There is one message," the clerk replied in English. She handed Hawker an envelope.

Hawker opened it. A single sheet of hotel stationery. No name, only three words. It read: *Enjoy the view.* He put it in his pocket and went to his room.

Sitting down, he flipped open a laptop computer that Moore had given him and signed on to the Internet. Using an encryption program, he secured the connection and checked for any messages. There were none. Next he tapped the account that Moore had set up.

Once the security protocol went through, Hawker saw the balance for the first time: $1.4 million. A life's savings, pledged to save a life. But then Danielle wouldn't have been in danger had Moore not convinced her to work for him once again.

Hawker stared at the screen. The truth was, he would have come for Danielle without any payment at all. But the money in front of him wasn't without meaning. It was enough to change Hawker's life, enough that he could escape the world he'd lived in for the past twelve years. And the thought had a magnetic attraction that he could not fully deny.

He transferred half the money to an account of his own. The rest would wait; that was the deal. Then he logged out of the site, closed the browser, and shut the laptop.

Glancing at the note he'd been given at the front desk, he stood and walked to the picture window of his seventeenth-floor room. Moving his face up against the glass, he exhaled, creating a slight fog on the windowpane.

A small arrow appeared in the condensation, drawn with fingers and the subtle oils that resided on them. From Hawker's point of view, it led directly to a moped rental kiosk on the opposite side of the street far below.

He reached out with his hand and wiped the window clean. He would meet his contact there in the morning.

CHAPTER 10

Danielle stood in the darkness, the filth in the air surrounding her. Hearing more movement, she stepped back in a defensive posture, waiting for something or someone to attack her.

"Show yourself," she demanded.

A voice called out to her. "You disturbed our rest. So why don't you show yourself."

An oil lantern was lit, lending a fraction of light to the room. As her eyes adjusted Danielle saw a figure moving forward: an older Asian man, with a scraggly beard and mustache. Four or five bodies lay on the floor around him, covered with filthy blankets. She guessed they were sleeping. Beyond them were more stone walls and the remnants of cast-iron bars rusted and flaking.

"What is this place?"

"This is the brig," the older man said. "You cross Kang, there is no court of law. Just this place or worse."

"Stop talking, old man," a stronger voice demanded.

Danielle looked and saw another prisoner, younger and larger. He studied her in return and she felt certain that his intentions were anything but pure.

"Who are you?" she asked bluntly. "And why the hell should he do anything you say?"

The younger man seemed insulted by the directness of her questions, but that was the point, to establish dominance or at least a position of strength.

He stood up, throwing off his blanket. He was at least a foot taller than she was, and probably seventy pounds heavier. In comparison to the others, he looked well fed. She guessed that he stole their food. That made him the head rat in the cage.

"You call me *Mister* Zhou," he demanded. "You're going to be here with us a long time. Better you learn right now, how things are."

He stepped toward her and Danielle prepared for the fight.

"Stop," the old man said. "No fight, not now." He pointed toward the far wall. Through thin slits that might have once been gunports, the blackness beyond had turned a shade of blue. The day would be breaking soon.

"They feed us now," he said. "No food, if we fight."

Danielle stole a quick glance at the old man. He was skin and bones. She turned back to Zhou, and with her eyes locked on his, she stepped backward toward one of the stone bunks.

Zhou sat back down, waking another man and pointing Danielle out to him.

A few minutes later, as thin slivers of light crept across the stone wall, the rest of the prisoners began to wake. It seemed she had six cell mates: the old man, Zhou and his friend, an Indian woman who did not speak or make eye contact with anyone, and two others, who appeared to be Caucasian: a male child who looked about ten to twelve years of age and a man in his early sixties. He was short but stocky with broad shoulders.

He did not rise or look particularly well. In fact, he seemed to be dying.

CHAPTER 11

Hawker stood in line at the rental kiosk as the morning sun filtered through the skyscrapers. The streets were already clogged with a mad rush of cars, trucks, and people. Bicycles and pedestrians cut between the vehicles, seemingly unconcerned with the thought of a collision. Double-decker buses swerved around other traffic, changing lanes as if guided by Formula One drivers in training. Horns were almost omnipresent and brakes squealed at every intersection.

Renting a moped to enter that madness seemed about as smart as charging into a stampede with an umbrella for protection. But based on the line of people at the desk, both Chinese and foreign, it must have been a preferred means of transportation.

The clerk looked down the line and waved Hawker up. "Come, come," he said. "Your bike is ready."

Hawker stepped around a line of jealous customers and followed the clerk through the shop. He hadn't ordered a bike of any kind, and assumed the man had recognized him.

"This way, this way."

Hawker followed him out through the back, where a

line of forty mopeds waited. As he stepped through the doorway he spotted a group of four Chinese men with weapons on display. The clerk threw up his hands as if to say he knew nothing about it and hurried back into the shop.

This was not the start he had intended.

One of the men waved Hawker toward a workbench. He was forced to sit and was then searched.

Nothing unusual was found. He sat quietly. Perhaps he'd been wrong to think Kang's people were all he had to worry about. Looking at these men he guessed they were either the secret police or members of the Ministry for State Security, the Chinese equivalent of the FBI. Still, he was surprised to be targeted so soon, since he'd yet to do anything wrong.

Hawker's passport was pulled and thrown over his head to someone behind him. He heard the smack of it being caught and then the pages rustling and finally a voice. "What are you doing in Hong Kong, Mr. . . . Francis?"

"I'm here on business," Hawker said. "I thought I'd do some sightseeing first."

"You must have a taste for danger," the voice said. "Businessmen don't rent these contraptions; they hire cars."

The passport was dropped on the workbench beside him and a boot stepped onto the frame. He heard the slide of a gun racking behind his head.

"So what kind of danger are you looking for?" the man asked.

Hawker didn't answer, not because he wasn't ready to, but because he'd suddenly noticed something about the man's accent. The English words were heavily accented, but the pronunciation wasn't Cantonese or Mandarin, or any other Asian form, for that matter.

The man standing behind him, the man pointing the gun at him, was Russian.

CHAPTER 12

In the depths of the stone brig, Danielle watched as the food was brought to them by armed guards. It was an almost Dickensian scene, with dirty bowls of some rancid, salty broth and some hard, stale bread. Seven servings for seven prisoners, but no one moved toward the food until the guards had locked the iron gate and reentered the elevator.

Zhou stepped forward first, taking the largest bowl of soup and gathering all the bread for himself. As he did the boy jumped down and snatched a heel.

Zhou grabbed for him, but the child was too quick. He raced back to his shelf.

"I cut your hand off for that," Zhou said.

The boy didn't respond. He was trying to feed the bread to the dying Caucasian man.

Zhou stormed toward the child. "Give me the bread!"

Danielle stepped in front of him. "Just let him have it," she said.

Zhou pushed past her and snatched the bread from the child's hand, then slapped the child across the side of the head. The young boy screamed and began to cry.

As the others cowered, Danielle stared Zhou in the face, an act he correctly viewed as a challenge. He did not back down.

"You must be something nice, I think." He let his eyes fall across her hair and down the length of her body. "Otherwise Kang would have killed you."

She stared back at him, now fully engaged in the test of wills.

Zhou seemed to enjoy it. "Concubine or whore," he said, curling his lip. "I'm going to find out just what it is that you do."

Zhou had leaned in toward Danielle, staring down at her in an obvious attempt to intimidate her, but the move had left him vulnerable, his legs straight, his body off balance.

Danielle sat down on the shelf of a bed, sliding back and creating some space between them, as if she'd been cowed by his threat. From her sitting position, she watched him smile disgustingly. She smiled back and in the blink of an eye pivoted and thrust her right leg out, slamming her heel into Zhou's knee. The joint snapped with an ugly sound, like a firecracker going off. Zhou crumbled backward, howling in pain.

As he fell, he swung at her, but she dodged his fist and stood. With Zhou on the ground, she slammed a second kick into his face and his nose exploded in a spray of blood.

Zhou's friend leaped from his bunk, charging toward her. He tried to tackle Danielle, grabbing for her throat, but she blocked his hands and using his own momentum against him, flung him into the wall.

Even as he crashed into the stone she held his arm, twisting it around backward and dropping a hammer blow onto his elbow. The man's arm folded in the wrong direction and he screamed in agony. She slung him onto the floor next to Zhou, his face a bloody mask of shock.

She glared down at him. "That's what I do, you son of a bitch."

Zhou slid himself backward along the floor. His friend crawled alongside, and they dragged themselves to a deeper, darker part of the brig.

Around the room, the others looked on, approvingly it seemed. The old man was laughing, giggling at the entertainment. He moved forward, taking back the bread and proceeding to eat.

"Take it all," he said to the others. "Don't save any for them." He was giddy. "With no teeth, they will not be needing food today."

The young boy jumped down and took the largest bowl of soup, bringing it back to the dying man and trying to feed him.

"You eat it, Yuri," the man said. "You need it."

His voice was Eastern European, maybe Russian. She wondered what he and the child had done to Kang to warrant such treatment. Certainly he did not look like much of a threat. With great effort, he got to a sitting position.

"They will try to kill you now," he told her. "They will want revenge."

She thought back to the words of one instructor. *If you move, make sure you do enough to prevent any countermove.* She felt quite certain she'd done that.

"With those injuries, they'll be immobile for weeks, maybe months without proper care."

"Be careful when you sleep," the Caucasian said. "They will come for you." He pointed to the boy he'd called Yuri. "He can watch for you at night. He never sleeps," the man said.

Danielle looked at the boy, perched on the shelf like a little bird.

"Is he your son?" Danielle asked.

"No," the man said. "I kidnapped him, to sell him to Kang."

Danielle found this revelation hard to fathom. The man seemed to have great affection for the child. "Kidnapped him?"

"I took him from the people he knew, though they were not his family. I took him from the only place he has ever known, though it was not a home."

"He's Russian, like you," she guessed.

The man nodded. "He was under the care of the Science Directorate. They did experiments on him."

The hair went up on the back of her neck. "Experiments?"

The man began to answer but went into a minor coughing fit first. "I wish I could say we were trying to save him, but that is not the whole truth. Kang wanted him. He promised us his safety and his fair treatment. But we did it for money."

"What happened? How did you end up down here?"

The man coughed harshly once again, fighting to control it. "Things went wrong on our voyage. The navigation system, the radios, everything failed us, and my vessel lost its way in the Arctic. My crew thought we had been cursed. And maybe they were right."

"I don't understand," Danielle said.

"We were tracking south through the night, following the compass. But when dawn came we realized we had been going the wrong way. *Akula,* orca, they followed us as if they knew we would soon fall into the sea. They pushed us onto the ice, slamming into our boat over and over again. Three and four at a time. The crew made it to the escape raft, but they were attacked and killed. And as the boat went down, I escaped to the ice floe with Yuri."

Danielle looked him over. He smelled of decay. He had a stump wrapped in rags where his foot should have been and his hands, nose, and other parts of his face were black with gangrene. The child didn't appear to have suffered the same way.

"How come he's not frostbitten?"

"I used my knife, I dug us a small cave, and I surrounded him as best I could," Petrov answered. "We were there for three days. Days almost without sun. I was certain we would be dead on the fourth, but a helicopter came. Kang's people found us."

"Why did he put you down here?"

"We were so far off course, he believed we meant to betray him."

Danielle looked at Yuri. "All this for a child?" she said. "Why? Who is he?"

"He's no one. He has no family that I know of, but he is unusual," the dying man said. "He was born with a degenerative neurological disorder. His parents could not care for him and he was given to the Science Directorate. They use him in experiments, and somehow they stopped the progression of his disease. But there was a strange result, a side effect. They say he senses things, sees them."

The man spoke in a wavering voice and she wasn't sure the information was any more firm than the voice. Certainly it sounded odd.

"What do you mean?" she asked. "Like a psychic?"

The man shook his head. "No. Physical things. Magnetic anomalies, electromagnetic disturbances. They say he can see beyond the normal human spectrum."

"Can he really do this?" she asked.

"I don't know," the man said, coughing badly. "Kang thought he could."

"Then why is he down here?" Danielle said, realizing he'd used the past tense. "Does he not think so now?"

The man shook his head. "Yuri would do nothing he asked," he said. "No matter the beating or incentive. No matter the threat. He only talks to himself or sings. And he would not leave my side. So Kang sent us down here. His men told Yuri that he would see me die and then he would have only his new master to cling to."

Danielle looked at the young boy, slurping up the soup broth. "Does he even understand what Kang is asking?"

"I think so," Petrov said. "He just doesn't respond."

Suddenly the boy looked up. His eyes darted toward the elevator door. Nothing happened, no sound could be heard, but seconds later the car slid into place at the bottom of the shaft and the doors opened.

The guards stepped out with their Tasers in hand.

"What's your name?" she asked.

"Petrov," he said. "Alexander Petrov."

He went into another coughing fit, his body racked with spasms for twenty long seconds, and this time when he pulled the rag from his face, it was covered in blood.

CHAPTER 13

When Hawker didn't respond to the man who questioned him, one of the thugs raised a gun and aimed it at his eye.

"You really won't get much out of me if I'm dead," he told them.

The thug was unmoved but the man behind him laughed. "Bring him with us," he said.

Hawker was blindfolded and dragged into a waiting van. From there it was a short trip to the waterfront and a forced walk onto a waiting vessel, a diesel-powered junk.

As they rumbled out into the harbor, Hawker tried to guess their direction or speed.

"Where are you taking me?" he asked after a minute or two.

"I'll gladly answer that, once you tell me what you're doing here," the Russian voice said back to him.

Hawker gave no answer. He was still trying to figure out the dynamics of the situation. Why should he, an American, have to explain to a Russian what he was doing in Hong Kong?

The motor beneath the deck cut back to idle and then

died away. Soon the boat's momentum ceased and the vessel began to rock back and forth in the chop of the waves.

"Stand up," the man said.

Hawker stood, holding the rail, as one of the man's guards pulled the blindfold away. He began to turn.

"Eyes forward!"

A rifle jabbed him in the back.

Hawker did as he was ordered. They were a mile out into Victoria Harbour, looking back at the skyscrapers of Hong Kong.

"You are a man without a home, or so I hear. A man with debts to pay, who is wanted even by his own country."

Hawker did not respond.

"You go by the name Hawker," the Russian said. "An interesting metaphor this word. Where I come from, it means a seller in the marketplace, a shill, offering goods or services."

The name had come to him as a code, one he'd kept for his own reasons. He didn't try to explain.

"At any rate, you are here plying your trades, both gross and fine, only in this case, it is at the behest of your own nation's security apparatus. Care to tell us why?"

Hawker held the rail. He guessed that the man already knew the answer, or some version of it. He remained quiet.

"Come now," the Russian said. "You're among friends here. To prove it, I'll answer for you. You're here to do something that might infuriate the Chinese. Something the people who hired you don't want to be known for. Murder?"

"I'm not a killer," Hawker said.

"You are a killer," the man replied, emphatically. "But not a murderer, perhaps. What then?"

Hawker thought of leaping over the rail, but guessed he'd be riddled with bullets before he hit the water.

"It's not so complicated," the man said. "In fact, the answer is right in front of you."

Hawker looked across the water, staring straight ahead. The boat had been lined up with Kang's Tower Pinnacle, its white marble façade gleaming in the morning sun.

"They have something your people want back," the man added.

Hawker's eyes followed the contours of the tower down to the bedrock at its base. Whatever cover he'd once thought he had was nonexistent at this point.

He turned around slowly, and this time no one stopped him.

Ten feet away, hidden in the shade of the boat's pilothouse, stood a short, gaunt figure of a man. He wore a black peacoat and leather gloves. No more than five foot six, his round face was marked by sunken cheeks and whitish stubble the same length as the buzzed gray hair on his head.

Hawker guessed the man's age was close to seventy. His face was pale, his eyes almost gray. Apparently his host was a confident man. His henchmen had vanished and no gun or weapon could be seen.

"Who are you?" Hawker asked.

"My name is Ivan Saravich," the man said.

"Are you my contact?"

"No," Saravich said.

"What happened to him?"

Saravich waved a hand in a manner of swatting away an insect. "Don't worry about him. He chose a bribe over a job. I treasure men like that."

"What do you want from me?" Hawker asked.

Saravich explained. "I want to help you get at Kang, to help you recover your missing person."

"And in return?"

Saravich stepped into the light, shielding his eyes from the sun. He walked to the rail, looking toward the Tower Pinnacle in the distance.

"Kang is not a very discriminating man," he said. "In addition to your missing friend, he has taken one of our citizens, a child, whose mother is a prominent member of our Science Directorate."

That sounded like a legitimate possibility from what Hawker had been told, but there had to be a reason. "Why would he do that?"

"She's an expert in high-energy physics," Saravich said. "What Kang cannot buy he steals; what he cannot steal, he extorts. He wants information from her."

Information on high-energy physics. Hawker wondered if it were related to what Danielle and McCarter had been working on.

"For weapons?" Hawker asked.

Saravich shrugged. "No one knows," he said. "Kang is rumored to be very strange, obsessed with exotic areas of science and compulsive in regard to other things like medical oddities and genetic deformation. It is said he has a zoo of humans born defective."

"Charming," Hawker said. "Why do you need me to deal with him? Why not take him out yourself?"

Saravich exhaled. "I would prefer it," he said. "But certain niceties must be observed. You, on the other hand . . . well, a man with no home does what he does. There can be no proof of whom he works for or why." He shrugged. "There can be suspicions, yes. Whispers and rumors. Of course. These things will always fly, but in the end it will never be clear, and that is what we prefer. Just as your people do."

"Of course," Hawker said. "Everyone's afraid of the dragon these days."

"Don't want to wake it," Saravich said.

"You want me to get the kid back?"

Saravich nodded. "You can get them both at the same time."

Hawker might have asked what the alternative was, but it was fairly clear to him that there was none. He was now working for Moore and the Russians. He smiled at the irony, wondering what Moore would think, footing the bill personally with his cold war enemies riding along for free.

Perhaps it was for the better not to try this act alone. He turned back toward Kang's fortress of a tower. "You think they're inside?"

Ivan nodded. "We have surveillance video showing them entering the building and no indication of their departure."

It had been eight days since Danielle's capture in Mexico. "That's not exactly conclusive."

"We know Kang." Saravich was insistent. "We know his ways. If your friend is alive, then she's there. And he wouldn't have brought her here if he planned to kill her quickly."

He studied the building. "Well, that narrows it down to a hundred floors or so."

"Actually," the Russian said, "we have only one floor to worry about." He handed Hawker a spotting scope. "Look at the foundation."

Hawker trained the scope on the black bedrock from which the tower seemed to sprout. He saw the remnants of fortifications and old stone walls, even a broken set of stairs leading down to the water.

"Kang built his tower on the ruins of Fort Victoria," Saravich explained. "A fort those hardworking Brits carved out of solid rock in 1845, before building Fort Stanley a few years later. Kang uses the old brig as his private gulag. Down there he keeps those who owe him what they cannot pay or those who cross him and survive. A very rare few have even been ransomed out."

Hawker studied the jagged black stone, wet from the spray of the waves.

"He has both of our people," Saravich said. "I promise you, he has them there."

CHAPTER 14

Byron Stecker, current director of operations for the CIA, had a phone to his ear. On the desk in front of him lay an internal report, one that was highly critical of a fellow organization. An organization that had been a thorn in Stecker's side for years: the NRI.

Since the NRI's creation, there had been those at Langley who disapproved of what they considered a competing agency. Few were more vocal than Stecker, and for the past two years he'd fought to bring the NRI under the Agency's control. So far it had been a losing battle.

In hindsight, Stecker assigned the bulk of that failure to a situation beyond his control: the president's friendship with Arnold Moore. But after two years of running into that particular wall, Stecker had come up with a new plan, one that would turn that personal connection between the two men from a roadblock into an advantage.

The president may have been Moore's friend but he was a politician first. And like all politicians he feared the appearance of impropriety. In fact, if he was like most of them, he feared the appearance of impropriety more than the actual act of impropriety itself.

With this in mind, Stecker realized what he needed: a scandal at the NRI. If such an event could be managed correctly it would shine a harsh light on Arnold Moore. And the president, ever mindful of how their friendship looked, would be forced to act more harshly than another man. Even if just to prove that he played no favorites.

Stecker would get everything he wanted and this time he wouldn't even have to ask.

A click on the phone line told Stecker he'd been transferred into the Oval Office. The president came on the line.

"Afternoon, Byron," he said politely. "What have you got for me?"

Stecker looked down at the report; there were several disturbing rumors to choose from, including one that suggested the NRI was conducting some type of dangerous nuclear experiment at its headquarters in the suburbs of Virginia. He doubted that could be true, but the other information his people had dug up would be damning enough.

"Mr. President," Stecker said, speaking with a melodious southern drawl and at this moment an exaggerated sense of concern in his voice. "I have a warning flag to run up the pole for you. Have you checked on your good friend over there at the NRI lately? Because he seems to be turning up the heat on a few people whom you might want him to leave alone."

"What are you talking about, Stecker?" the president asked.

"I'm afraid Moore's gone off half-cocked," Stecker

said. "Hired some mercenary ex-agent of ours to start himself a private little war over there in China."

"What gives you that idea?" the president said wearily.

"I have confirmed sources reporting from Kinshasa and Hong Kong," Stecker said. "I'm afraid the NRI has overstepped its bounds yet again."

Stecker knew he was laying it on a little thick, but what the hell, he had Moore dead to rights this time. Might as well enjoy it.

The president didn't reply, but the ringing silence had an edge to it and if Stecker knew anything, he knew this dart had hit the bull's-eye.

"You bring me those sources," the president said eventually. It sounded to Stecker as if he were talking through a clenched jaw. "And you bury this story. Understand? If it comes out before we can deal with it, I'll know who to burn."

Though leaking the information would have been personally satisfying, Stecker would not let it happen. Better to show the president who had control of their organization and who didn't.

"Of course, Mr. President," he said. "Honestly, if Moore has gone off the rails, I would consider it my duty to keep it quiet if at all possible."

"Cut the crap, Stecker," the president said. "You're not the one running for office here. Be at the West Wing foyer tomorrow morning, seven a.m., sharp. Drive your own car and don't bring any assistants."

The president hung up, the snap of the phone ringing Stecker's ear. He felt he'd made his point, but there was more to it than that. The president was angry, but he didn't actually sound surprised. No, it was more like disgusted, like a man hearing of an accident he thought he'd already avoided.

A grin formed on Stecker's face as he put the phone down and closed the report. Perhaps this would be more interesting than he'd guessed.

CHAPTER 15

The view from the 101st floor of the Tower Pinnacle was nothing short of spectacular. A curving, tinted wall of glass created a panoramic view. It began on the far right with the skyscrapers of central Hong Kong. In the center was Victoria Harbour, Kowloon, and the busy shipping channels between them, while off to the left lay the open waters of Sulphur Channel, Discovery Bay, and Lantau Island, where the new airport had been built.

There was a time when Kang considered the view a treasure, but now such beauty vexed him.

"Close the shutters," he ordered.

A male secretary hustled to his desk and punched four buttons in rapid succession. Steel shutters descended from slots in the ceiling, blocking off the priceless view. In ten seconds they were down and locked and the room was illuminated by the soft recessed lighting.

Kang turned his head slightly and the sound of electric motors became audible as the powered wheelchair that supported him began to move. He crossed the floor, acutely aware of the eyes upon him: his secretary, several technicians, and his head of security and unofficial chief of staff, a burly man named Choi.

Though they tried to disguise their gawking, Kang could feel their pity and disdain. He had once been an imposing figure, nearly six feet tall, one hundred and eighty pounds, but several years earlier a rare neurological disorder had attacked him, first draining his energy and coordination and then progressing to steal the strength from his body. Kang could walk, and he did at times, during treatment and therapy. But his condition was deteriorating, and for expediency he now spent most of his time in the chair, his body twitching and shaking from both the disease and the electrical stimulators that had been attached to him to keep his muscles from atrophying further.

That the others stared was perhaps not surprising. But he despised them for it. Even more because he was forced to rely on them and Choi in particular.

"The girl is in the brig?" Kang asked.

"She has been placed as you requested," Choi said. "But I think—"

Kang cut him off. "I do not ask your thoughts, nor will I suffer them today."

"But sir, she is no use to us now," Choi said. "She knows nothing that we don't already know. We should kill her now or sell her. We know many who would pay well for such a woman. As long as she remains here there is a chance the Americans will move against us."

A chance, Kang thought. *There was far more than a chance.*

He offered Choi a dose of pity. "You are limited in what you know. Your view of things does not extend to what I can see."

He turned the chair a fraction, until he faced Choi more squarely. "The woman is of no use to us at this moment, this is true. But a time will come when she has utility for my purpose. If I were to indulge your bitterness and kill her or deliver her to the brothels, what would I receive in return? Two things I do not need: vengeance and a trinket of wealth. Should I really trade a cup of spite for what I desire?"

Kang watched Choi trying to work it out. He and Choi had come up from the streets together. Though Kang's modern empire included manufacturing, shipping, and construction, he'd begun as a criminal, a racketeer who dealt in extortion, prostitution, and smuggling. Be it human cargo, drugs, or endangered species, if there was a price for it, Kang and Choi had sold it. And they had not been alone.

Originally their cadre included three others. But Kang had been forced to kill them, one by one, as their thoughts turned from following to leading. Still in the prime of his health, he had ripped one man's throat out with his bare hands. He remembered the feeling of such strength, such visceral power, the man's life and warm blood pouring out over his fingers. He longed to experience such a feeling again, such proof of his own potency. And he would not let Choi get in the way of his quest.

"But, sir," Choi said.

"I will not be questioned!" Kang shouted. His voice reverberated around the room, startling all who heard it.

Choi's mouth clamped shut but Kang could see the continued disagreement and defiance in his chief servant.

Choi had long been loyal, but Kang could see it beginning to fray. It was inevitable.

He turned his chair and guided it forward toward the door of the conference room. It opened at his approach to reveal two objects and several men who seemed to be technicians of a sort.

The first object was the stone statue taken from Mexico. Two of his men were examining it, using electronic equipment to penetrate its depth.

"What have you found?" Kang asked.

"There is nothing within the statue," one of the men said. "The granite is solid. No cavities or electromagnetic discharges. No sign of anything that the NRI was looking for."

"Of course there isn't," Kang said. "The boy would have sensed it, when we brought him up here. What about the inscription?"

A second man sitting at a computer terminal answered. "We're using the computer program to match the woman's photographs with the remaining portion of the damaged stone. The resolution is poor but we have enhanced it and are now comparing it with all known hieroglyphic codes."

"How long?"

The man shrugged. "The damage is extensive."

"We'll keep trying," one of the other techs said.

"Time is running out," Kang said. "We must do more than try."

He saw their reactions, and from the corner of his eye, he saw Choi exhale in exasperation. He sensed all of them mocking him, as Choi did behind his back. And at that moment he wanted to kill them, to have them slaughtered for their contempt. But he restrained himself from ordering such an action. He would be healed soon, and once he was healthy again he would kill the insolent with his own hands.

CHAPTER 16

Hawker stood on the bow of a harbor tug, beneath a spitting rain and an overcast sky. He wore a heavy wool coat, boots, and a black cap pulled down over his ears. He looked like a longshoreman or a sailor, just one of the crew watching as the tug pushed its cargo southward.

The barges ahead of them were heavy with coal, destined for an outlying power plant. With this legitimate cargo in play, the tug would make a slow pass right in front of the Tower Pinnacle. As it did Hawker would go over the side and swim underwater to the base of the tower and the remnants of the old British fort.

He and Ivan had discussed several options for rescuing their respective citizens. Ivan's preference was to get them while being moved. He believed with certainty that Kang would not keep them in the old brig forever. There would be a chance to take them when they were in transit somewhere, a weak link in the chain.

That plan presented several problems. To begin with, it required intelligence as to when and where the prisoners were being transported, but more important, it was standard attack doctrine; prisoners were always considered more likely to escape during a transit and were often guarded more heavily as a result. Beyond that, the plan required waiting, something Hawker was not well adapted to, and something that would only increase whatever suffering was going on behind the heavy stone walls.

After looking at the schematics of the two structures, they'd determined that the old fort used an ingenious sanitation system built by its original inhabitants. Latrines led to a waste holding area, which had separate tunnels connected to the river. When the tide rose, the British soldiers would open wooden doors and the river's current would divert water through the tunnels, flushing out the system and washing the waste downstream.

"Enter through the sewers?" Ivan had asked. "Like some kind of rat?"

It seemed like a perfect solution, until a surveillance run had shown that the old wooden doors had been replaced by plugs of concrete. That left only one real option and now was the time to make it happen.

Hawker looked up into the sky. Evening was coming and the rain and the darkness would help hide him. He walked back into the pilothouse of the tug, shook Ivan's hand, and grabbed his gear.

"Have the helicopter ready," he said. "We'll only get one chance at this."

In a minute, Hawker was slipping into the water on the far side of the tug, wearing a black wet suit and carrying a rebreather. It was almost dark.

Descending under the surface, Hawker waited for the tug to pass and began swimming toward the rocks. He moved slowly, kicking in a rhythmic motion fifteen feet beneath the surface.

His air came from a device known as a CCR, a closed-circuit rebreather. This type of diving gear had several advantages over scuba tanks. First, it was lighter and easier to maneuver than standard scuba gear, and second, it reprocessed the exhaled gases, filtering them out and reclaiming the oxygen, which could be recirculated back to the diver.

"Rebreathing" the air meant there would be no trail of bubbles to appear on the surface and mark the diver's location.

Hawker honestly doubted that anyone would be looking for such a threat, but Kang was known to be a paranoid man. If he did have people watching, Hawker wasn't giving them anything to see.

After several minutes of swimming, Hawker had made his way across the channel and bumped into the rising ground near the edge of the harbor. The murky water was so dark that he didn't see anything until it was inches from his face. He followed the sloped embankment up. After several feet, the muddy silt gave way to rugged black rock.

Two feet from the surface, he stopped his ascent and rolled over onto his back, gazing upward. There was still some illumination coming in through the water, but it wasn't from the fading December sun. It came from the city lights now, especially the white floodlights of the Tower Pinnacle.

Hawker guessed it wouldn't get any darker, but as he checked his watch he found himself ahead of schedule, so he waited, resting on the rocks and watching the water's surface above him.

The ripples from the rain formed a hypnotic pattern. A cascade of minor rings hit and spread into one another in unpredictable order. He watched the pattern grow stronger, the light drizzle giving way to a steady rain. Hawker smiled at his luck.

He had many reasons to love the rain. In this case, the precipitation would degrade the visibility, making surveillance feeds blurry while keeping foot patrols short and sweet.

It probably didn't matter much anyway. If Hawker was right, he'd be in before anyone knew what had happened. And on his way out he'd go in the one direction they'd never expect.

Cautiously, he surfaced.

The rocks ahead of him rose up in a jagged, sloped pattern. Higher up, set back an additional eighty feet from the water's edge, was the base of the monstrous tower. A hundred and eleven stories clad in Italian granite. Garish white lights shone upward onto the sides of the tower to blinding effect, making it almost impossible for anyone to see a man in black crawling across the dark rocks beneath it.

Hawker sank back down, pulled off his flippers, and released the CCR. He reemerged, pulled off his mask, and climbed onto the dark stone, moving up and across it like a crab.

He found the gap in the rocks that he was looking for and ducked into it. Ten feet in, he scaled a minor chasm and pressed himself against what had once been the wall of the fort. Foot-thick stone had been cut and laid precisely, but over the years the mortar had eroded and the structure was now held together as much by its sheer weight as by anything else. Three stories above, what had once been the roof of the fort now held a manicured yard, a flower bed, and a walkway that led back to the doors of Kang's tower.

Hawker hugged the wall until he came to an indentation through which a thin vertical slit had been cut. A foot high and no more than six inches wide, this slit had been a gunport for the old fortress, not for cannon but for musket shot. The indentation design was necessary to allow the British soldiers to aim their muskets across a wide field of fire, but it created a thin spot in the wall, a weakness that Hawker would use the explosives to breach. Designed to repel invaders, the gunport would be Hawker's way in. But first he had to make sure he was in the right place.

He pulled off his backpack and set it down. From inside the pack he pulled what appeared to be a small box made of clear plastic. Visible through the plastic, like the innards of some transparent fish, were a small battery pack, a transformer, a microphone, a camera, and an antenna.

The NRI-built device was called a spider. Moore had sent it to Hawker along with several other pieces of high-tech equipment. At the press of a button, eight mechanical legs with articulated joints extended from the machine. The thin legs gave the spider the ability to move over incredibly varied terrain. It could even hop up a full flight of stairs, though if the plans Saravich had shown him were accurate, this particular spider would only have to go down.

Hawker retracted the legs, took a quick look in through the gunport, and dropped the device inside. He heard it bounce once and then stop.

Crouching down, he pressed his back into the recessed section of the wall. Sheltered for the most part from the falling rain, he pulled the control unit from his pack and slipped a headset over his ear. It included a speaker, so he could hear what the microphone picked up. A tiny LCD screen covered his right eye, to let him see what the camera saw.

He powered the device up and focused on the eyepiece. Ahead he saw the interior of a sixteenth-century brig, filthy and cramped, with a low ceiling and rusting metal here and there.

It looked medieval except for the support pylon in the far corner, a ten-foot-thick column of steel-reinforced concrete that plunged through the brig itself and into the bedrock below. It was a foundation piece of Kang's tower; next to it was an elevator shaft.

Hawker pressed the button that extended the spider's legs again and the camera view shook from side to side. A moment later the spider was off and hunting.

CHAPTER 17

The occupants of Kang's prison lay sprawled out on the raised sections in the various stone recesses of the prison—anything to keep them off the cold, wet floor. The men Danielle had fought had taken shelter in another cell, but Petrov, Yuri, the old Chinese man, and the Indian woman remained in the cell with Danielle.

Of that group, only Danielle and Yuri were awake. It was still early in the evening but the others had been in the prison a long time and were not well in any case. Sleep was a necessity for them, and perhaps a respite from their predicament.

Danielle hadn't reached that point yet and promised herself she never would. She would keep her mind sharp, her spirit strong, and her body as healthy as possible. And when the chance came, she would act, decisively.

She glanced over at Yuri.

Without moving his head, Yuri turned his eyes to her, as if he knew she was watching. If Petrov was right the boy never really slept.

She smiled.

He smiled back.

She blinked and he did the same. She wondered if he was unconsciously mimicking her or perhaps even playing.

Suddenly his head jerked a bit, like he'd heard something. His eyes turned and focused on the corridor.

She listened for any sound, but could hear nothing but the patter of rain. Not even the whining of the elevator that Yuri had detected before.

Yuri sat up, looking down the corridor. He pushed aside his thin blanket and stood cautiously.

Danielle waved him over. "Come here," she said.

He hesitated and then moved her way and climbed up to sit beside her.

She thought of the few Russian words she knew, but could come up with nothing that might form a coherent question to the child. She brushed the hair out of his eyes and he relaxed for a moment before stiffening again.

He pointed to the ground. "Down," he said, speaking Russian and pointing at the floor. "Down."

The word he used meant "down" or "floor," but she didn't know what that *meant* in the bigger picture.

She thought of waking Petrov, but before she could move, she heard a noise, a rapid little ticking almost like a drumming of fingernails on a hard surface.

It started and then stopped and then started again. And then through the darkness she saw something scamper around the edge of the cell door.

For a second she thought it was a rat. It would certainly not be the first they'd seen down here, but even in the gloom of the dank prison she could see that its movements were too precise and its stillness too complete once it stopped.

Yuri pointed at it insistently. Despite the fact that it was ten feet away from them on the floor, he repeatedly pushed an outstretched palm toward the object, as if he was trying to shun it or force it back.

"Machine," he said. "Machine."

"It's okay," Danielle told him.

Gently she eased his hand back to his side and then stepped off the shelf and moved toward the object.

It was indeed a machine, one that she recognized.

Her heart began to pound. The spider was NRI equipment. It meant help had arrived from somewhere.

Knowing it carried a microphone, she began relaying details of the situation to whoever was controlling it.

"There are seven prisoners down here," she whispered. "No guards on this level, no cameras, either, but I've gone through every inch of this place and there are no exits except the elevator. Do you copy?"

The little spider pivoted up and down on its front legs, in a sort of nodding gesture.

Danielle looked around and then back at the device. "Are you on a surveillance run?"

The spider moved side to side.

"So this is a rescue attempt?'

The spider nodded yes. And then, after a pause, it continued nodding yes, bowing and rising repeatedly.

After three or four identical moves it stopped and Danielle looked at the thing dumbfounded. What the hell was the operator trying to tell her?

"I don't know what you want from me," she said, almost laughing at the absurdity of the situation.

The little spider nodded three more times and then stopped. She shrugged, and almost simultaneously, a thunderous explosion rang out.

The shock wave knocked her off her feet. A cloud of dust surged throughout the old brig.

Coughing, she looked up. Yuri had grabbed her arm and was pulling her. The others in the cell were awake and stunned and hacking on the dust just as she was.

"What happened?" the old man asked.

She heard the muted wail of some alarm high above. An earthquake or fire alarm, she guessed.

She got back to her feet just as a figure came in through the swirling dust.

"Are you all right?" the new arrival said.

The voice was strangely familiar, but in a distant way. And then as the person crouched beside her she recognized him.

"Hawker? My God, what are you doing here?"

"Getting you out of trouble," he said. "It's what I do best."

It was the dry sense of humor she remembered. After the way things had ended in Brazil, and especially after her own departure from the institute, she'd sadly guessed that she would never see him again. Certainly not in a situation like this.

He dropped down and began digging into his backpack.

"I was telling you to get down, before the explosion," he said.

"Suddenly it makes sense."

A new set of alarms began ringing and she guessed that the incursion had been detected.

"We need to get moving," she said.

The old man and the woman were standing around her; Yuri was tugging on her sleeve.

"Where do we get out?" the old man said.

"At the front of the room," Hawker said. "By the gunports. Go across the rocks and swim to the south; you'll have the current and the tide with you. But go now if you want to make it."

The two prisoners moved quickly and disappeared.

Hawker looked around. "I thought you said there were seven."

She pointed to the cell across the corridor. Zhou and the other man she'd beaten cowered there.

"What happened to them?"

"We had a little disagreement," she said. "They're kind of my bitches now."

"Someone's got to be king of the yard," he said. "I should have figured it would be you."

"Yeah," she said, glad to be talking with him, but thinking they could catch up later. "Can we get the hell out of here?"

"Not just yet." He looked at Yuri. "Grab the kid."

"You know about him?"

"He's part of the deal," Hawker said. "Sort of."

There was something in his voice that concerned her, but before she could say anything, Hawker moved to the gate that separated them from the elevator. He stuck a shaped charge of C-4 to the lock and stepped back.

Yuri began to yell. It was unintelligible wailing, but he covered one ear with a hand and pointed toward the elevator.

"Look out!" she shouted.

The elevator doors flew open and a wave of darts came streaking through the air, trailing wires back to some riflelike Taser device. Danielle ducked behind the wall but saw one hit Hawker and his body stiffen, and her immediate thought was, *This can't be happening again.*

CHAPTER 18

Hawker felt the sting of the dart hitting his body but he was already moving for cover and even as his muscles wrenched tight he fell behind the stone wall, his chest scraping against it and thus ripping the prong of the Taser out.

Spared the full burst of electricity, he still writhed in pain from the half second of shock.

He rolled over, angry at himself. He'd been waiting for security to come down in the elevator; in fact, he'd been counting on it. But the occupants of the car had doused any light inside it and the screaming Russian kid had distracted him.

He shook his head to clear it and looked around. Danielle was pulling the child into safety behind her with one hand and grabbing the carbine rifle he'd dropped. As she fired down the hall, a man screamed in agony at the far end.

"One down," Danielle shouted.

A second wave of darts came flying in, which Hawker deflected with his backpack.

He pressed the detonator switch and the C-4 on the

gate exploded, flinging it open and taking out the second guard.

Before they could rejoice, a third guard opened fire.

Bullets ricocheted around the brig and Hawker pulled a grenade from inside his pack. While Danielle fired back, he tossed the grenade.

The concussion knocked the remaining attacker down and Hawker ran to the man's position, ripping the Taser-like weapon from his belt and using it on him. The five-second ride left the man writhing on the floor and Hawker guessed he would no longer be a problem.

He looked toward the elevator. A racket of the competing alarms poured down through the elevator shaft and in through the hole he'd blown in the wall. Out on the rocks, beams of light were playing through the smoke. Shouting could be heard.

It would take a minute or so for any guards to scale down from above, but exiting that way now would be suicide.

He shouted to Danielle. "Come on!"

Through the smoke he saw Danielle and the child trying to help another prisoner stand.

"Leave him," Hawker shouted.

"I can't," Danielle said.

"We don't have room. If this guy wants out he has to run for it . . ."

Hawker's voice trailed off as realized the man had only bloodstained rags where his feet should have been.

"I'm not leaving him," Danielle said. But the man pushed her away and then fell back onto his stone ledge of a bunk.

"Go," he said in Russian. "Take him with you." He pointed to Yuri.

Hawker looked at Danielle. "We only have room for three."

Angry, she grabbed Yuri and tore him away from Petrov. The child began to scream.

"Give me a weapon," the man said.

Hawker handed him a fragmentation grenade, in case he didn't want to be a prisoner any longer. And then he turned and led Danielle and the child toward the open elevator doors.

"We're taking the elevator?" she asked.

"Right now they're cutting off the exits, surrounding the perimeter to try to keep us from escaping," he said. "We're going to head deeper inside."

They piled inside.

Danielle pointed to the guard's key still in the slot. "I'm guessing if we turn that, we go up."

"Gimme a second," Hawker said. He dropped down and pried open the control panel.

"What are you doing?"

"Overriding their computer," he said, pulling out an electronic interface that looked like a comb connected to a calculator.

He pulled the elevator's own mess of wires from the unit interface and jammed the comb side of his contraption into the same spot. He typed in 102 on the keypad and hit LOCK. The doors closed and the elevator began its express ride.

As it rose up, Yuri continued to cry. Danielle attempted to comfort him, holding him with one arm while gripping the assault rifle with the other. A modern woman.

Hawker checked his readout. They'd passed the twentieth floor and were accelerating. The device he'd plugged in had come direct from the manufacturer, via the NRI lab and Arnold Moore. Not only did it override the security protocols of the elevator's main computer but with NRI's reworking, it sent a signal to the tracking system, fooling it into thinking that the elevator was still in the subbasement of the brig.

While Kang's security forces were surrounding the fort, scaling down the walls outside, and frantically pressing the elevator call button in the lobby, Hawker, Danielle, and the kid were passing right by them, headed for the roof.

He only hoped that Saravich and his helicopter would be there.

He pulled out three harnesses, each connected to thin steel wires with carabiners on the end. One for him, one for Danielle, and one that would go to Yuri.

"Put these on," he said, stepping into his own.

Danielle slipped hers on, legs first and then arms. She helped Yuri into his. The crying had ceased, but his eyes remained red and swollen.

"How did you know I was here?" she asked.

"Moore sent me."

"How did he know?"

"McCarter called in, after you were taken."

"McCarter?" Her voice was suddenly filled with surprise and hope. "I thought he was . . . ," she stammered. "I thought I'd gotten him killed."

Hawker smiled at her. He liked being the bearer of

good news for once. "Apparently he's tougher than you thought."

For the first time since he'd known her, she seemed to be overcome with emotion. He looked up at the rapidly increasing number on the elevator readout. "Ninety. We'll be at the top in fifteen seconds."

"And then?" Danielle asked.

"There should be a helicopter waiting."

"Why the harnesses?"

"There's nowhere for it to land."

The doors opened to a black night and an empty, wet roof.

"Where's the helicopter?" Danielle asked.

Hawker stepped out. It wasn't there.

The rain was still coming down at the same steady pace. Heavy gray clouds loomed close above them, lit by the city lights just as they had been on the night Hawker arrived. Perhaps it was the quarter-mile ascent to the roof, but the clouds seemed much lower to Hawker than they had when he'd stood on the tug in the harbor.

Ordinarily no one in their right mind would risk flying around skyscrapers under such conditions, but if Hawker was right, Ivan's pilot would do whatever Ivan ordered him to do. And if Ivan wanted this kid back as badly as Hawker thought he did, the helicopter pilot would make the attempt even if the visibility dropped to zero.

He walked to the edge.

God, it was a long way down, and with not even a fence or a wall on this roof, just a sharp, flat edge, like some infinity pool. He pulled back feeling dizzy from the false sense of movement created by the uplighting and the sheets of falling rain.

"Where is our ride?" Danielle asked impatiently.

Hawker listened through the rain. He heard nothing, until the muted sound of a distant explosion echoed through the night. A slight vibration was felt even on the roof.

She looked at him and then turned away. They both knew what that meant. Petrov had used the grenade, either on himself or the guards or both.

"At some point they're going to realize our elevator is not stuck at the bottom floor," she said.

"You think they're smart enough to pop open a door and look up?" Hawker asked.

"Sooner or later."

As if to affirm her thought they heard the sound of heavy machinery whirring, slow at first, then louder and faster. The second elevator car was moving.

"Looks like they chose sooner," he said.

"I hope you have a backup plan."

He looked at her blankly.

"Great."

Hawker pulled a pistol from the satchel, took cover behind a huge air-conditioning unit, and waited. Danielle crouched down beside him, pulling Yuri close and pressing the carbine into her shoulder.

The elevator pinged.

He could see the light beneath the doors. He raised the pistol, aiming. The doors opened . . . to nothing. The car was empty.

"Put down your guns!" a booming voice shouted from behind them.

Hawker cringed. The stairs.

He dropped his weapon and heard Danielle's rifle clatter to the rooftop.

"Turn around."

Hawker turned slowly to see three guards flanking a heavyset Chinese man. He didn't know him by sight, but Kang's head thug was a man named Choi. Hawker guessed that's who he was looking at.

"Get on the ground!" Choi shouted.

As Hawker put his hands on the rooftop, he caught the sound of a reverberation. As he lay flat, the sound grew rapidly until a sleek, European-built helicopter came roaring up over the side of the building.

He looked up just as shots began to rain down from the open door of the helicopter.

Two of the guards went down. Choi and the other scrambled for cover.

The helicopter swept past and turned around.

Hawker grabbed his weapon and began firing, pinning down Kang's people in the stairwell.

The helicopter had turned and was coming back. It trailed a steel cable. As Danielle took over the firing, Hawker dove for the wire and grabbed it.

"Come on!" he shouted.

Danielle raced toward him, dragging Yuri.

The helicopter hovered, but shots rang out and sparks could be seen where shells hit the fuselage.

"Hurry!"

Hawker clicked in and then locked Danielle and the kid in as well.

The helicopter peeled off as Choi and the guard came out of the stairwell firing.

Hawker fired back, just as the slack was used up. With a jolt they were yanked off their feet, flung over the edge of the tower and falling.

The three swung through the air like jumpers on some absurd thrill ride, arcing toward the water, accelerating forward like a giant pendulum. It was an insane rush, racing at a hundred miles an hour through the dark and the rain with nothing around them, and the waters of Victoria Harbour a thousand feet below.

They swung forward and up, weightless for a second before dropping back. After two or three smaller arcs they were stable, trailing beneath and behind the helicopter as it moved across Victoria Harbour.

The rain stung their faces like pellets from a gun. Hawker gripped Danielle and Yuri tightly to reduce the friction and the swaying. The helicopter's winch could not raise the weight of three people at once, so the plan was to get over to the Kowloon side, land, and then disperse.

Danielle held on tight. "Who's flying this thing?"

"No one you know," he said.

She shouted above the wind. "What aren't you telling me?"

He tried to explain his allies. "These guys are Russian."

"I thought Moore sent you."

"He did," Hawker said. "But I needed help, and they sort of made me an offer I couldn't refuse."

Hawker squinted at her, the wind stinging his eyes. He could see Danielle shivering in the cold and rain, but they were descending and slowing. In a few minutes they'd be down on the ground.

"They want this kid back," he told her. "Kang was using him to blackmail one of their scientists, the kid's mother."

Danielle cocked her head as if she'd heard him wrong. "They lied to you," she said. "Yuri's an orphan. They've been doing experiments on him."

Hawker cringed. He figured Ivan had told him only half the truth, but this was not what he'd expected.

"Are you sure?"

"As sure as I can be," she said.

He looked at the kid and then back at Danielle.

"I'm not giving him back," she insisted.

He didn't know what to say, how to explain just what kind of a man Saravich was. How there would be no compromise.

"I gave someone my word," she said. "And I'm not going back on it."

Her eyes were unyielding. Despite the wind and the spray and the rain, she glared at him.

He watched her glance toward the shore. Fifty feet high now, five hundred yards from land, they were doing only thirty knots.

"You don't understand!" he shouted. "I made a deal with them."

She pulled free from his grasp and stretched upward, reaching for the steel line.

"Well, I'm breaking it."

Before he could stop her, she pulled the release bar and the three of them dropped like stones.

It's amazing what the mind can do in the blink of an eye. It took all of a second and a half for the distance to be used up, but as he tumbled through the darkness, two complete and distinct thoughts ran through Hawker's head.

First: that if they somehow survived the fall, he was going to kill Danielle for causing it. And second, if they did survive the fall and he relented on his first thought, where the hell could they possibly go, that Ivan wouldn't find them and kill them both.

And then he slammed into the water like a man running full force into a solid brick wall.

CHAPTER 19

Building Five, Virginia Industrial Complex

Arnold Moore had been expecting the worst, with the president and the head of the CIA coming to see him together. The two men had chosen Monday morning for a short drive out into the countryside to NRI headquarters at the Virginia Industrial Complex, affectionately known as the VIC. Moore hadn't been given a reason, but he assumed it had something to do with Danielle's rescue, and he was right. Partially.

After several minutes of haranguing by the CIA's chief, Moore glanced at the president. So far the commander in chief had remained oddly silent at a bawling-out session he'd specifically called for. It almost seemed as if he'd turned the whole thing over to Stecker, a thought that worried Moore considerably. And yet Stecker seemed just as puzzled at the president's silence.

"The point is," Stecker said, launching forward once again, "when we hear about someone hiring a fugitive, a mercenary who used to work for us, we don't expect it to be the head of a fellow agency."

Moore could see the outlines of the trap now. If he

denied the meeting to the president, Stecker would produce proof. And if he admitted what he'd done, he'd be seen as a reckless fool.

With nowhere else to turn, Moore threw up his only defense, weak as it was.

"I wasn't acting in my official capacity," he said.

"What the hell does that mean?" Stecker asked.

Moore clarified. "No NRI funds were used in the operation."

"Then where did the money come from?" Stecker asked.

"My own personal account," Moore said, before adding with some glee, "My CIA retirement was a big part of it. I'd like to thank you for that."

Now Stecker glanced at the president as if waiting for him to lower the boom. When President Henderson remained silent, Stecker scowled. He turned back to Moore.

"You must be out of your mind, Arnold," he said. "You know you can't act as a private citizen. Not in your office. You endanger the very fabric of—"

"If Ross Perot can go rescue his own people from a hostile nation—and be a hero for it, I might add—then I can rescue mine. When a private citizen of a foreign country acts against the law, I don't have to be bound by it in protecting one of ours."

Stecker exploded. "God damn you, Moore, you're out of control! If you worked for me I'd fire your ass or have you arrested."

Moore sat back. At least Stecker had exposed his true purpose. "Ah yes. So that's what this is really about. The

CIA's never-ending campaign to take over the NRI and all its assets."

"It's called Central Intelligence for a reason," Stecker replied.

Moore raised his eyebrows. "I'll give you the Central part," he said. "But Intelligence . . . really, that's been kind of hit-or-miss."

Moore watched Stecker's face go red. He looked like a tourist who forgot to use sunblock on a Florida beach.

Before his head could explode, the president raised a hand.

"I'm going to ring the bell here, gentlemen." He looked at Stecker. "Byron, I have you ahead on points, but Arnold has a knockout punch waiting for you, one you'll never see coming."

This was news to Moore.

"Arnold only took action after getting a verbal executive order from me."

Stecker was clearly stunned. "A verbal executive order?" His brow wrinkled in confusion. "With all due respect, Mr. President, what the hell does that mean?"

"It means," the president said, "that I didn't want this thing blowing up in my face. But I also don't like the idea of foreign nationals kidnapping our citizens and hiding behind a wall of legitimacy. If this had happened on the high seas we'd have called it piracy and had the navy take the SOBs out."

The president glanced at Moore before continuing. "Truth be told, Kang is lucky he lives in a country we care about. And given that fact, the only way I was agreeing to this was if someone else's ass was on the line in case it went down in flames."

The president smiled. "Trust me, Byron, if the operation had blown up you wouldn't be hearing about it from me."

Stecker seemed flabbergasted. Moore was just as confused. The president had issued no such order. The fact that he was pretending to have done so put Moore heavily in his debt.

"And with that settled," the president added, "let me bring everyone onto the same page and back to the real reason we're here."

Apparently the first payment was about to come due.

"Less than twenty-four hours ago, Byron came to me with some disturbing information," he said. "It seems the CIA has heard rumors about your organization that go beyond the travel plans of its director. One rumor that caught my attention was that the NRI has built some type of experimental fusion reactor beneath this building, one that might be endangering the good citizens of the capital."

Moore remained quiet. The details of the rumors were false, but there was a kernel of truth in the story. The president knew this, of course. He'd been briefed from day one, and he could have easily given the details to Stecker or whomever else he chose to inform. There was no need for the trip to Virginia to get that done.

So there had to be another reason for the drive out, one that Moore guessed at easily: It was time to come clean.

Moore had long dreaded this day's arrival, doing all he could to postpone it. But it appeared the president wanted the CIA informed and perhaps involved with what the NRI had hidden beneath Building Five. And to really understand what that meant, the truth had to be seen.

"So we're here for show-and-tell," he said.

The president nodded and Moore rose from his seat. "With your permission."

CHAPTER 20

Moore led the president and the confused head of the CIA down the hall. The president's security detail followed them until the three men stepped onto a secured elevator, where the president held out a hand.

"Smoke 'em if you got 'em, boys," he said. "This is going to take awhile."

Moore punched in a code and the doors closed, leaving security behind. He thought of making a last-ditch plea to the president, but one look at Henderson's stern face told him the time for discussion was over. The president wanted the CIA informed and involved.

Moments later the three men stepped out into a darkened laboratory. The hum of an air filtration system was the only real sound. The light around them was soft and off-color, coming from special blue and white LEDs embedded in the wall.

In the quiet darkness, two NRI technicians monitored computer readouts. They stood awkwardly when they realized who their guests were.

"As you were," the president said.

Moore walked to a pane of glass in front of them. Inclined forward at forty-five degrees to allow easy viewing of an object below, the "glass" was actually a two-inch-thick plate of clear Kevlar, strong enough to stop a high-powered rifle bullet.

Five feet below them, lit by a circle of LEDs and raised up on prongs like the setting of an engagement ring, lay a triangular stone with softly beveled edges.

The stone was the size and thickness of a large dictionary and as clear as any glass ever made. Where the blue light caught its edges, they shone like thin strands of neon, while the white light seemed to penetrate and reflect from deeper within.

"Any change?" Moore asked.

"No, sir," the lead technician replied. "Nothing since the twenty-first."

Stecker stared at the object. Moore could not help but do the same, despite having seen it many times. He'd even held it once, one of the few in the NRI to have done so.

The president had only seen it on two occasions, but he seemed to regard it with a new unease this time. Moore understood that, too: Events and time had changed things and the stone had gone from an object of curiosity to a subject of concern.

"What am I looking at here?" Stecker asked.

"We call it the Brazil stone," Moore said. "A group of our operatives recovered it from the Amazon, two years ago." He nodded toward Henderson. "The president was informed along with ranking members of Congress."

Moore walked to a different position, one where he could see both the president and Stecker. He needed to be able to read their faces to know where he stood.

"What does it do?"

"It creates energy," Moore said. "How, why, or for what, we're not exactly sure."

"Why is it down here?" Stecker asked. "Is it radioactive or something?"

"No," Moore said. "But this vault is designed to contain it and to protect the population above." He pointed to the walls around them. "We're fifty feet below ground level. The vault around us is constructed of a titanium box, lined with sixteen inches of lead, a four-inch layer of ceramic silicon, and a solid foot of steel-reinforced concrete. In addition we've set up monitors and a powerful electromagnetic dampening field."

"What the hell are you protecting us from, Arnold?"

"Electromagnetic discharges, including gamma and X-ray spikes: high-energy surges that not only fry electronic equipment, but can damage human tissue."

Stecker looked around. "All your equipment here seems to be working fine," he said.

"The bursts come at precise, regular time intervals, seventeen hours and thirty-seven minutes apart. We lock down the system and shield all equipment prior to the pulse. We power back up again once it passes. Easy as pie for the most part. At least it was until November twenty-first."

"November twenty-first," Stecker repeated. "The date rings a bell."

"That's right," Moore said. "The same day the Russians and Chinese launched their search parties. The same day we recorded a gamma-ray burst from a spot near the Arctic Circle that damaged a group of our GPS satellites."

Stecker seemed agitated, swimming in the deep water

now, not knowing which facts to connect. If Moore was right, he didn't know what to make of the situation; anger, curiosity, confusion, all three emotions were probably racing through his mind at the moment.

The president took over. "On the same day Arnold and I spoke about the incursion into Hong Kong, we had another conversation, centered on the Russian and Chinese actions. Like you and the chiefs of staff, he saw their fleet movements as a search party, only the NRI had one piece of information no one else had: a recording of this energy burst. Initially we guessed that one of those two countries had created some type of directed energy weapon and might have lost it up there. But we could find no evidence of that, and then one of his techs here was able to match the signature of that power burst to a minor fluctuation in the output of this object."

"You're telling me this thing had something to do with that?" Stecker said bluntly.

"No," Moore replied, "but something connected with it might have."

Stecker's eyes went from the glowing object to Moore to the president, as if to make sure everything around him was real and on the level.

"Is this some kind of an experiment?"

"No," Moore said. "We didn't develop this stone; we found it. We're studying it, and we're not yet certain about the implications of what we're learning."

"Which are?"

"I told you. This stone seems to *create* power. Manufacturing energy in a way we don't yet understand. One that violates the first law of physics."

"I'm not one of your scientists, Arnold. But I'm not an idiot. Talk to me in terms I'll understand."

This was the reason Moore dreaded bringing the CIA in the mix. The NRI was primarily a scientific organization, even if one wing of it was dedicated to stealing science from other nations. The CIA was about power, gathering knowledge on a more tactical scale. *If we do this, then they will do that.* Neither Stecker nor anyone else at the CIA would easily grasp what Moore and his people now believed.

"The First Law of Physics," Moore said. "Energy can neither be created or destroyed. To power your car you burn gasoline, the combustion creates heat, the heat creates pressure to expand the gases, and the rapid expansion drives the pistons. The energy is derived from the breaking of chemical bonds in the petroleum distillates. Chemical bonds that were slowly built up over thousands of years as the poor, dead dinosaurs turned themselves into crude oil."

He paused to make sure Stecker was with him.

"When you run your car you're releasing stored energy, not creating it. A nuclear plant does the same thing in a different way. It splits atoms, and the breaking of that bond does exactly what the breaking of the chemical bond in the petroleum does: It releases *stored* energy, but on a much greater scale. In both cases, however, the energy was always present, and its potential could be determined before it was used."

He pointed toward the stone. "But this thing is different. It's emitting energy through no process we are able to understand—at times, massive amounts of it. Our best explanation is that it is somehow creating energy or perhaps drawing it from a quantum background."

Stecker looked dizzy. He responded less arrogantly than Moore would have expected, perhaps because he was off balance.

"Okay," he said. "So that's what it does. You have a stone here that makes energy. Great, let's hook it up to the grid and stop the global warming everyone's so worried about. But that doesn't explain why it's so important, why so few people were told about it in the first place, or why you're telling me about it now."

Moore looked to the president. He nodded; it was time for the whole truth.

"Because," Moore said, "the stone is not some naturally occurring entity. It's not a rock, or some exotic new element found in the depths of the earth. It's a piece of machinery constructed by the hands of men and women. One that was found along with a horribly mutated human skeleton and a prophecy of doom, predicting the downfall of civilization. Billions killed in war, waves of disease and famine, punishment for the sins of human pride. All of it stemming from an event on December twenty-first, 2012."

Stecker scoffed at what he was hearing. "The Mayan prophecy," he said. "The one I can't turn on the damn TV without hearing about. Is that what we're talking about here?"

Moore nodded. "The glyphs McCarter found refer to it as the day of Black Sun."

"Black Sun? Like an eclipse? Like from a solar flare?"

"We don't know," Moore said.

"You don't know?"

"No, Byron," Moore said, exasperated. "We don't know. In case you didn't realize it, hieroglyphics don't come with footnotes and a commentary. So we're figuring it out as we go along."

Stecker didn't look convinced. "Come on, Arnold," he said finally. "The world is full of lunatics telling us the end is near; you can find them on any street corner if you want. Why the hell should we care about this one?"

"Because," Moore said, "in our case, the lunatic wasn't a prophet but a historian."

"Excuse me?"

The president stepped in and lowered the hammer of truth as bluntly as possible.

"Byron, we care about this doomsday prophecy because of its origin, because the NRI believes that it, and this stone, were created not thousands of years ago, but eleven centuries from now, by our descendants, three hundred generations removed."

Stecker's eyes went wide at what the president was saying.

Moore tried to explain. "The body I spoke of bore the remnants of advanced prosthetics that had been implanted into it or had been grown over by the living bone. From the description and its surroundings, our conclusions were that this person had suffered massive mutation or even purposeful genetic modification designed to help it survive life in a sulfurous acidic environment."

"I can't believe you're—"

"This is no joke," Moore insisted.

Stecker looked at the president, who shook his head solemnly.

Stecker exhaled sharply. Whether he believed what he was being told or not, Moore couldn't decide, but at least he'd stopped arguing the point. "So this thing's a problem?"

"Yes," Moore replied. "And it's not the only one. One of my people, a scholar named McCarter, studied the hieroglyphic data we brought back from Brazil. He concluded that this stone is one of four."

"There are three others out there?"

"We think so," Moore said. "Two in Central America, one somewhere in the Eurasian plain, probably central Russia."

"Have we told them about this?" Stecker asked the president.

Henderson shook his head.

"Well, that's something," Stecker said. "You got anyone looking for that one?" he asked Moore.

"Can you think of a way to do it, without alerting them?"

"No," Stecker said. "Good move." He appeared cordial for the first time. It didn't last long. "Okay," he continued. "So let's say I believe all this. What's the point?"

"We're not sure," Moore said. "But we come to one possible conclusion: A thousand years from now the world is not like the one we live in today. Our best guess: radioactive background, skies of acid rain filled with carbon and sulfur."

"And this . . . stone . . . is supposed to do something about that?"

"It seems logical," Moore said.

"Then why are you telling me about it?"

Moore looked at the president.

"Because," President Henderson said, "I want both of you working on it, both agencies, along with the best minds you can find."

"Why now?"

This time Moore answered. "Because the stone is building up a wave of energy, priming itself for something massive and sending out a signal that diminishes slightly in length with each new iteration. A signal that will reach zero, eleven days from now on December 21, 2012."

CHAPTER 21

Standing on the weather-beaten deck of a rusted, aging freighter, Danielle watched over the port rail as Hong Kong disappeared behind them. They'd bribed their way onto the vessel and sailed with it in the early hours of the morning. The ship, laden to the brim with small-engine parts and other manufactured goods, was headed on a southeasterly course toward its home port in Manila. Danielle's own home lay much farther away and if she was right it would be a long time before she saw it again.

While Hawker minded Yuri, she attempted to contact Arnold Moore on the satellite phone.

"Thank God you're alive," Moore exclaimed. "I honestly feared the worst. The explosion at Kang's tower was all over the news. Back channels are reporting Kang's security killing a number of people who they're calling terrorists."

She thought about Petrov. "I think some people were killed, but they weren't terrorists. And we're okay. But I'm worried about McCarter—Hawker said you'd heard from him."

"He reached us shortly after you were taken," Moore

said to her. "But no contact since. He said he was injured, but insisted it was manageable, so I have no explanations for his silence. I have several teams looking for him. But Mexico's a big country."

"He'd run even if he saw them," she said, thinking about how little McCarter trusted the NRI. "You don't think Kang has gotten to him?"

"Doubtful," Moore said. "Our data shows his people swarming all over the Yucatan. But nothing to suggest he's found McCarter. So wherever the good professor is hiding, let's hope he maintains the sense to stay there. Perhaps he'll listen to you, if we can reestablish contact."

After a moment of contemplation Danielle decided that was unlikely. Once upon a time she had dragged McCarter into things, but in this case he was a fellow zealot, all but possessed by the need to push on. The fact that he would not fly back to the States after what had happened was only the latest proof.

"Is Hawker with you?" Moore asked.

She looked ahead on the deck to where Hawker was watching Yuri, showing the boy how to use his hand like a wing and let it ride on the wind. Yuri didn't speak often but as he copied Hawker's actions his face beamed with joy.

She'd felt a similar wave of happiness at seeing Hawker again, mostly because he was rescuing her, but also because he was a friend. That was a precious commodity she'd pretty much run out of.

"He is," she said.

"And what's your situation?"

"I think our departure went unnoticed, but we're not without problems."

"Kang." Moore guessed.

"To begin with," she replied. "But it goes beyond that now. Do you know a Russian named Saravich?"

"Ivan Saravich?" Moore said, clearly recognizing the name. "I know of him. What the hell's he got to do with this?"

"Tell me who he is first," she said.

"Saravich is an old KGB hound. Back a few years he was listed as an enforcer, a problem solver for them. I'd have guessed he'd been put out to pasture by now."

"Not unless his pasture is the south coast of China," she said. "Apparently he bribed or removed your contact there and took a meeting with Hawker in his place."

"To what end?"

"It seems Kang stole something from mother Russia as well: a twelve-year-old boy named Yuri."

"Why?" Moore said, surprised.

"Saravich fed Hawker some line about the kid being used to extort information out of a Russian scientist. But I think the real reason has to do with his being a subject of experiments at the Russian Science Directorate."

She glanced at Yuri. "He seems a little restrained, almost autistic or something. He also seems to have a sixth sense regarding energy fields, electricity, and magnetism."

"Odd," Moore said. "You think it's connected with the search for the stones."

"Kang is after them," she said. "God knows why or

even how he heard about them but a person who could sense varying degrees of electromagnetism might be very helpful in such an event."

"I guess it makes sense," Moore said. "The Russians have been known to experiment with psychics, clairvoyance, and things like that for years. It doesn't surprise me that they had this kid in some type of program. But as far as I know it's always been a big joke to them, their version of the four hundred dollar hammers and the bridge to nowhere. Certainly nothing has ever come of it that I'm aware of. But if Saravich is involved, they must feel differently about this boy."

"The thing is," she said, "Hawker made a deal with Saravich regarding the kid. A deal I broke."

Moore was silent for a moment, a fact that concerned her.

"I'm guessing that's a problem," she said.

"Saravich will come after you," Moore explained. "And Hawker especially. He's a prideful son of a bitch. Even if he *could* let it go, he wouldn't."

"That's what I was afraid of," she said. "See if you can leak some misdirection, buy us some time. Otherwise I think Hawker is going to go after him, try to take him head-on."

It was something she didn't want to see happen, not just because she feared for Hawker but because she didn't want any more blood on her hands.

"I'll see what I can do," Moore said. "Where are you, now?"

"You know the proverbial slow boat to China?" she asked. "We're on the return trip. We'll be in Manila in a few days. How are things going on your end?"

"Not well," Moore said. "The CIA is involved now. A sense of fear has begun to develop about the stone. Even in the president's mind."

"That's not good news," she noted.

"No," he said, "it's not. The president wants two separate teams studying it. So we're getting joint custody, it seems. And he wants the stone moved out of Washington. We're taking it to Nevada. A lab is being set up inside Yucca Mountain, at the unfinished nuclear waste depository."

She realized there could be only one reason for that. "The energy pulse is still growing."

"Our containment building was in danger of a breach, but the bigger fear is detonation. We've pinpointed the parameters of the countdown and the zero state will be reached on December twenty-first, at 5:32 in the evening, Pacific time."

Danielle listened to the date. McCarter had recounted the story to her several times. At the end of this epoch, which had begun 5,114 years before, the Mayan Long Count Calendar rolled over, resetting its digits to zero. The prophecy spoke of the world ending in a flood of darkness. Dark sky, dark waters pouring from the heavens, dark earth. By itself the legend was just mythology, but when connected with the stone they'd found and its pending countdown and McCarter's theory that there were at least three others like it, the myth had taken on a disconcerting reality.

"When are you moving it?" she asked.

"End of the week. And if we can't figure out what this thing is supposed to do, or find the other stones in Mexico that might be doing the same thing, they're going to destroy this one, bury what's left, and hope for the best."

Since the day he'd seen it, Moore had treated the stone almost like a divine gift of some kind. He saw purpose in it. Danielle felt the same way, but sometimes she wondered if she could trust those feelings.

They'd sought to keep it hidden from the CIA and military because the first question from those organizations would undoubtedly be how to use it as a weapon. And now two years later, with the stone generating more and more energy and counting down to something, it seemed as if that might be exactly what it was.

"Do you want me to bring you home?" Moore asked. "You're entitled. And I'm sure Marcus would be thrilled to have you back."

She smiled at the mention of the name and felt a sudden wave of anxiety, all at the same time.

"You sure about that?" she asked. "I think the neighbors called D.C. Metro after our last fight."

"Pride does strange things to people. He's angry, but you know he wants you back."

She wondered. It had been a painful departure. "Does he know I'm okay?"

"Of course," Moore said. "I contacted him as soon as I got word. And I'll confirm it to him once we're done here. Unless you want to tell him yourself."

The offer caught her by surprise. She was an operative on a mission. It was a position that didn't allow call-ins to home. Still, she liked the idea. She wanted to hear his voice, to tell him she was okay. But something held her back.

"You'd be bending the rules for me," she said.

"Marcus was one of us once," he said. "I can bend them for both of you, or I can bring you home."

That offer sounded like a godsend. A huge part of her wanted to be done with the madness. She was drained emotionally and physically from everything that had happened. How nice it would feel to go home, sleep in her own bed, and wake up to Marcus making coffee for her. And even if their relationship was ruined, even if he'd moved on, or was still too angry to forgive her, she wanted to get home, to see him, even if just to explain more calmly why she'd made her particular choice. Yet as the thought crossed her mind she wondered why she should have to explain herself.

It seemed like the same old fight was already brewing. And McCarter was still out there, missing. She'd taken up the baton to protect him and she wasn't ready to relinquish it until he was safe.

Feeling a sick sense of déjà vu she decided. "If you're right, something catastrophic is about to happen," she said. "What good is coming back home, if I arrive on the wings of disaster? Unless you have someone better in mind, the best thing I can do for everyone is to press on."

She told herself it was cold logic, but she knew there was more to it. She knew herself well enough to sense the avoidance in her decision. She was ducking something: not the fight that would likely flare up once again, that came all too easily, but something else, something deeper. It was as if some truth waited there for her and she wasn't ready to see it yet.

Moore remained silent, but Danielle sensed that he

approved and perhaps had even expected this. "You sure?" he asked finally.

"I finish what I start," she said. "Please ask Marcus to forgive me."

"I will," Moore said. "Do you think you can find McCarter?"

Danielle thought about what had taken place in Mexico. The work she and McCarter had done. The discussions they'd had. It had been only eight days earlier, but she found it was like trying to recall what one had done a year or two ago. Still, something came to her.

"I have an idea where to start," she said.

"Good," Moore said, sounding proud of her. "What about Hawker? It might be helpful if he came with you. It'll keep him from going after Saravich."

"I'll ask," she said. "What do you want me to do with Yuri? I'm not sure bringing him along is a good idea."

Moore hesitated. "If you send him here, I can't promise you he won't end up with State or the CIA. Either way he could be sent right back in Russia. If you keep him close he might be able to help."

She didn't like that idea, didn't like the concept of using the young boy to aid in the search, but the thought of him being returned to Russia was unacceptable. "You'd better arrange travel for three."

"Where to?"

"Just get us to Campeche," she said. "I'll take it from there."

CHAPTER 22

Professor McCarter stepped out of a cramped, aging apartment building and limped into the heart of a tiny fishing village called Puerto Azul. He'd chosen this particular place to stay because it was not a hotel or motel, and because unlike most guesthouses in the area it had only an inside entrance that led to a set of steep, creaky stairs and a hallway with five doors, facts that he hoped would enhance his security.

But mostly he'd chosen it because it reminded him of the apartment he and his wife had stayed in on their honeymoon, which they'd spent in this very town, while McCarter had worked on a dig an hour inland.

He couldn't be sure if it was the familiar confines or the strange vision he'd had in the sweat lodge in the Chiapas village, but he had a sense now that his wife was with him. She was helping him. Watching over him.

He'd had several vivid dreams of her, some pleasant and others closer to nightmares. And at times both in public and in the privacy of his room, he found himself speaking out loud to her without thinking, as if she were right beside him.

He'd been in Puerto Azul for three days, after a week

in the mountain village recuperating. Oco's return with a bottle of antibiotics had saved him, both from the bacterial plague spreading through his body and the care of the shaman. And though the infection was not quite gone, he'd left the village as soon as he was strong enough to walk.

At the time McCarter hadn't known where to go. He guessed that the men who'd attacked him thought he was dead; otherwise they wouldn't have left him. But he considered the possibility that his reporting in to Moore would be leaked, or that Moore's subsequent actions on Danielle's behalf would lead their enemy to believe he might be alive.

So he'd hid and let his beard grow and returned, not to the town and hotel where he and Danielle had been based (and had left many belongings), but to Puerto Azul, eighty miles from Cancun on the northern coast of the Yucatan.

The town drew only a smattering of tourists, though enough that his presence would not be conspicuous. And though it was a long way from the interior and even the coastal Mayan sites, it remained within reach of the area where he and Danielle expected to find the next of the power-generating stones.

He stepped out onto the dusty street and began his daily walk, passing the street kids who'd taken to calling him *Moses Negro:* Black Moses. With the overlarge walking stick he used to support himself, a notebook in the crook of his arm, and the emergent bushiness of his graying beard, he must have looked the part. In some ways he felt the part, trying to lead the NRI to a promised land of sorts. He hoped it would not be forty years of wrong turns before they got there.

To find the Island of the Shroud, he'd combined what he'd learned from the cave in Brazil with Mayan writings found in Mexico and Belize. He'd used satellite imagery, infrared aerial photography, and the whispers of villagers who still lived in the old ways. It had brought them to the crater lake on Mount Pulimundo, to the monument of Ahau Balam, the Jaguar King. McCarter had expected to find the key to his search there. But the information they'd discovered was a blur, incomprehensible at the time, and only slightly more sensible after he'd transcribed the barely readable smudges from his linen shirt.

What he'd found prior to the Island of the Shroud told him this: *The path begins with spirit guide Ahau Balam. The tip of the spear reaches out from the great city to the temple of the warrior. There will be found the Sacrifice of the Soul. From there to the shining path, the footsteps of the gods and the Sacrifice of the Body. With these shall rise the Shield of the Jaguar.*

What it meant he, couldn't say. The king depicted on the stolen monolith had held no shield, and no spear. The only glyphs they'd found on it were numbers. Even if he was the king or Ahau that the legend spoke of, McCarter could not see how that would lead them anywhere else. It was like finding directions that said: "Take the road to the other road and then turn on the third road." Frustrated at his inability to come up with a meaning to this, he'd ventured out of his sanctuary. He needed more information.

He limped down the street, leaning heavily on the

staff. Halfway between the apartment and the beach he found an Internet café. After paying his money and settling into a rickety chair, McCarter logged on.

He wanted to tap into his university's system, where he would have access to data stored on its mainframe, data that included satellite surveys of the Yucatan. He rested, waiting for the connection to go through. He had no way of knowing if his account was being monitored by anyone but Danielle had warned him against any such actions on an insecure network. The people they were dealing with were extremely sophisticated and if they were monitoring the university somehow, tapping into his account would be like broadcasting to the world that he was alive and well in Mexico.

The thought of taking a bus to another town, to another Internet café somewhere, had crossed his mind. But he was too damned tired. He remained in recovery, weakened by the injury. The heat of the day sapped his energy and night sweats and chills kept him from sleeping.

Nervously he typed in his password.

As his finger hovered over the ENTER key, another thought went through his head. *Let someone else do this.* Simple enough, except others had more to lose than he did and he'd begun to think he might have something to gain.

He tapped the key. The hourglass flipped a few times and then he had access.

Zooming in close he could see some of the major ruins of the area and even some of the smaller ones. But he doubted anything they found in a tourist-ready environment would be helpful. McCarter was after older ruins, structures swallowed up by the jungle long before the great cities of Chichen Itza and Palenque were even built.

Modern theory said that Mayan civilization stretched back two thousand years or so. What McCarter and Danielle had found in the Brazilian rain forest suggested it had a precursor that existed long before that, and that the people who'd lived there had abandoned the site and moved north, journeying through the Andes and up through the isthmus of Central America, eventually settling in the highlands and the jungles of the Yucatan, Guatemala, and Belize.

The descendants of those travelers eventually became the Maya. And if McCarter and the NRI were right, the story of their exodus became part of Mayan prehistory, the departure from their place of origin, a place they called Tulan Zuyua, carrying with them the absolute essence of power: the spirit forms of their gods contained in special glowing stones, items eerily similar to the one that the NRI now possessed.

McCarter guessed that any similar stones would be found among the oldest ruins of the culture. And to find such ancient ruins he needed photos that showed more than the naked eye could see.

While the first set of visual images printed, he opened a second directory, this one filled with infrared images. The IR images peeled away the green of the foliage and showed heat. And the heat of different types of vegetation told him what he needed to know. The lowland Maya used limestone to build their structures and even when the forests had consumed those structures the heat they emitted was different than that of the regular ground.

As the image resolved on the screen McCarter felt hope growing quickly, followed by fear and a certain sense of hopelessness. There were hundreds of unexplored ruins in the Yucatan, two dozen or more within a twenty-mile radius. How the hell would he decide where to start?

A phone rang behind him, a cellphone in the pocket of another customer. It was a familiar ring, the same ringtone as his own, and it sent him into a moment of reflection. He recalled a conversation with Arnold Moore several months before.

"Hope I'm not bothering you," Moore had said. The tone in his voice was that of a salesman who knew he was in fact bothering someone and didn't really care.

"Do we have to do another hearing?" McCarter had asked, referencing the series of congressional inquiries that had focused on his few moments with the NRI.

"No," Moore had said, "nothing like that." A brief pause and then, "I understand you've been asking for access to the stone. I think I can arrange it."

That had surprised McCarter. "Terrific," he said.

"First I have some questions," Moore replied. "What do you know about December twenty-first, 2012?"

Two thousand twelve: the supposed end date of the Mayan calendar. For the next ten minutes McCarter tried to explain that the date did not mean the end of times to the Maya, which so many people perceived it to mean. At least not universally.

"How's that?" Moore asked.

"First off," McCarter said, "there are monuments

with inscriptions predicting events, often very mundane events that are supposed to happen well after that date. Second, the number of Mayan references to that particular date are relatively few given the overall hieroglyphic record. And third, because the Mayan Long Count was written like an odometer of sorts, some of the current theory suggested that even those apocalyptic descriptions were really references to things that happened on the previous rollover, 5,114 years ago."

He tried to use an analogy that Moore would be familiar with. "It's similar to the Revelation of John. Many biblical scholars would tell you that Revelation was not a prophecy of the *end* of times but a hidden description of contemporaneous events in Rome and the persecution of Christians in the first century."

"Yes, yes, of course," Moore said, or something like that. It sounded as if he wasn't really listening. Then, serious again, he asked, "Do you know of anything that would suggest otherwise, something reliable?"

McCarter racked his brain. "There is a monument, called Tortugero Monument Six. It's heavily damaged, but the glyphs that remain reference an event at the end of the calendar, the folding of the Thirteenth Baktun, the end of the thirteenth period of 144,000 days, which occurs on December twenty-first of 2012. They tell us that the god of change, Bolon Yokte, will descend from the Black something and carry out . . . something."

Stunned silence followed. "Something," Moore said. "What do you mean, something?"

McCarter shrugged. "No one knows. The glyphs that describe what those somethings are have been destroyed. Much like some of the glyphs we found in

Brazil. Almost as if they had been smashed deliberately."

"So not the ever-present concern for the Maya that we've been led to believe," Moore noted dejectedly.

"No," McCarter said. "More like one strand of thought. Perhaps an outcast strand. Like most apocalyptic beliefs it was not really considered valid or worthwhile to the greater culture itself."

"And yet it persisted throughout, unbowed," Moore said. "What does that tell you?"

McCarter considered Moore's words. What was Moore looking for? A strand of truth that could not be proved? All that could be proved by such persistence is that some group would not let the story die. A group within a group. A group with knowledge. The priests, perhaps. Or even a subset of them, making sure the date and the prophecy lived on despite its actual dismissal and unpopularity among the greater culture and its leaders.

"Keepers of the flame," McCarter said. "But still just a fanatical devotion."

"What if I told you I had something that might explain their fanaticism, something to indicate that an event of great importance will in fact occur on that day?"

McCarter knew what Moore was suggesting: the very subject of their call, the Brazil stone. "Then I'd tell you there may be others," McCarter said.

Silence followed once again, long enough that it almost seemed the call had been dropped. This time McCarter sensed calculation behind the quiet. Deliberation, even concern. Finally Moore spoke again, asking, "Have you been sleeping well, Professor?"

It was an odd question, and odder still because McCarter had been suffering terrible insomnia for months. "No, I haven't," he said.

"Neither have any of us," Moore replied. "You'd better come to Washington."

"Book me a ticket," McCarter said, "then we can talk."

A loud bang startled McCarter back to the present. He whipped around defensively. Another patron had stood up and accidentally knocked over a chair.

McCarter found his heart pounding and his hands shaking. The young man and his female friend were laughing. She was urging him to be more careful.

They were Americans. Several buttons adorned her jacket. One read, 2012, PARTY LIKE THERE'S NO TOMORROW. The second was a reference to Dick Clark's long-term stint as official Times Square New Year's host. It read, 2012, KUKULCAN'S NEW YEAR'S ROCKIN' EVE.

They just had no idea.

The pending date had brought thousands of extra tourists to Mexico for this moment. Most were from America, but large numbers had come from Europe and Asia, too. A few were there with legitimate interest, but the vast majority had come to enjoy the weather and another excuse to party.

Certainly McCarter couldn't blame them, and their presence had made it easier to hide among the crowds while he and Danielle conducted their research. But now he worried who else might be hiding among those crowds.

The American couple looked his way; the man stared at him. Suddenly McCarter needed to get out of there.

He gathered his papers, logged off the computer, and handed ten dollars to the clerk. Hobbling out into the street he glanced back at the shop. The clerk and the other patron were watching him and for a moment a wave of paranoia swept uncontrollably over him.

Getting into a rhythm with his walking staff, McCarter moved quickly, albeit awkwardly, down the edge of the street. So what if they were watching him. They were nobodies, university-age tourists. They're not with the enemy, he told himself. *They're not with the enemy.*

He could hear the thoughts reverberating through his mind, thoughts that seemed to grow stronger the harder he fought against them.

"Help me," he whispered to the air around him, in search of the spirit of his deceased wife. "Olivia, if you can, please help me."

Hearing no reply, he rushed forward, seeking the only place he felt marginally safe: his small room at the guesthouse. He needed to get there and sit down and study the printouts and the data. There he could make notes undisturbed and try once again to make sense of the inscription he'd seen on the Island of the Shroud.

But as he hobbled along a new thought occurred to him. His notes would be extremely valuable to their competitor. A treasure that could be found or stolen. Of course the very act of making notes and conclusions in the first place would endanger him, perhaps even make him superfluous if he were caught.

If they had my notes, my very thoughts, what would they need me for?

He tried to calm down. Needing his mind to stop whirling, he considered finding a bar and drinking himself into oblivion. But instead he slowed his pace and deliberately slowed his breathing. Somewhat calmer, he changed direction, heading down a random alley.

What he really needed was a way to make notes and then destroy them instantly: a shredder or a fire, or something he could scribble on and erase over and over again without leaving any evidence of his conclusions.

He needed a chalkboard. It was so simple but it was perfect. That would protect both himself and the mission. But unless he broke into a school somewhere, he wasn't likely to find a chalkboard in the sleepy fishing village of Puerto Azul.

The thought loomed like a giant roadblock. And then he looked up and found himself at the end of the alley, one narrow street from the edge of the sandy beach. With the tide going out, the sand was still smooth and flat and packed hard enough to draw in with ease.

McCarter had found his chalkboard.

CHAPTER 23

Hawker could feel things beginning to move. Not just in the physical sense, as the freighter began to push toward open ocean, but in a more personal sense as well.

Danielle had finally disconnected from Moore and slid the phone back into her bag. She was moving toward him with that purposeful look in her eye; on a mission once again.

"You guys okay?" she asked.

"We're fine," Hawker said. "I'm teaching the kid to fly."

He held his arm out like a wing once again and Yuri copied him.

"I—" she began.

"You don't even have to say it," he told her.

"I have to go back," she said. "McCarter's still out there and he won't come in."

Hawker could not believe what he was hearing. "Are you sure we're talking about the same guy?"

"Everybody changes," she said.

Hawker could not imagine McCarter changing that much, but obviously the professor felt strongly about what they were after.

"You're both OCD on this deal. You realize that, right?"

"I guess," she said. "Care to hop on the crazy train with us?"

"You want me to come along?"

She looked out to sea for a moment, hesitating as if she didn't know what she wanted.

"I don't want to lie to you," she said. "This mission is as odd as the last one. Maybe stranger. I don't know where it's going, but I know McCarter's in deep."

"And you feel responsible," Hawker said.

She nodded. "I owe you a lot, too, though. So no arm-twisting."

Hawker exhaled. For the first time in a decade he had within his grasp a free pass to a new life: Moore's money sitting in the numbered Swiss account. He could disappear, become someone else, and leave the darkness of his own world behind. He pictured a beach in St. Tropez, with a cool drink, warm sand, and beautiful women gallivanting about. In the ultimate fantasy, Danielle would join him. The two of them could travel the world on Moore's tab. Even if they were wasteful, the money would last for years.

But the fantasy would become a guilt-ridden nightmare if McCarter were to stay out and get himself killed or if Danielle were to go after the professor and both of them were to be harmed.

Knowing himself, Hawker could foresee spending the rest of his life and all of Moore's money seeking to punish Kang or Saravich for what they'd done. Not the kind of outcome he was looking for.

"I think you and the doc are both insane," he said to

her. "This doomsday thing, end-of-the-world prophecy, it's too far out for me to grasp. I promise you, if mankind's going down for all the things we've done, quick and clean is too light a sentence."

"I understand," she said, looking as if she were expecting him to say no.

"But I can't let you go alone," he added. "When you found me in Brazil, I promised I'd see you through, right to the end. I thought getting back to Manaus safely was the end, but obviously we were all wrong about that."

She smiled. And he loved that smile. He loved the fact that she wouldn't leave McCarter out there on his own, even though she'd almost been killed once trying to protect him.

"I'll go with you," he said. "I'll do what I can to help you find McCarter and to keep you safe. That's my quest. As far as these stones and everything else, that's your problem. The way I see it they're either some huge cosmic joke or some kind of Pandora's box we should never have messed with in the first place. But since you two are crazy enough to keep pursuing them, then I'll do what I can to keep you out of trouble."

"So *you're* going to be the voice of reason?" she asked, barely holding back a laugh.

Hawker put a hand on Yuri's shoulder. "Me and the kid here," he said. "We'll keep you guys on the straight and narrow."

Yuri looked up. He didn't say anything but his eyes were bright. He seemed to like the attention.

She looked incredulous but pleased. "Sounds like asking the fox to watch the henhouse. But . . . thank you."

He saw the gleam in her eye. "Just remember. When this is over, assuming the world hasn't blown up, I wash my hands of you two. You guys decide to go on another crusade somewhere, then go. I'll have a beach waiting for me somewhere."

A crooked smile crossed her face. "You retiring or something?"

"Actually I am," he said. "I've recently discovered the benefits of a 401(k). Not my own exactly, but those of others."

She looked at him with suspicion but he decided not to explain.

"Hmm . . . ," she said, playfully. "I guess that makes two of us."

"What are you talking about?"

"When this is over," she said, "assuming the world hasn't blown up, I'll be done with the NRI and all of this myself."

Her voice was higher than usual, as if she were playing. And yet in a way it seemed like a contest: who could quit first or best. And if there was one thing he knew about her, it was that she loved to win.

"Believe it or not," she said, "I had a normal life for a while. And I liked it."

He could barely contain the laughter. "Really?" he said, more surprised than ever.

"What? You don't think I could have a normal life?"

"Baking cookies and running errands?"

"Try lobbying for millions of dollars and thinking about running for Congress someday," she said sharply.

Her indignation amused him. "First off," he said, "that's not a normal life. And second, it's not that I don't believe you could have one. I just can't see you liking it for too long."

She laughed and shook her head as if she was greatly disappointed in him but her smile faded just a bit more than it should have, and he wondered if what he'd said had rung too close to the truth.

CHAPTER 24

Walking down to the sand, McCarter thought about the way he'd stumbled upon the beach. He and his wife had often traveled by car, and among the joys of those travels were the countless times he'd gotten them lost and she'd eventually gotten them back on track.

He wasn't sure he could chalk this up to some kind of spiritual intervention, but if there was anyone who knew he wouldn't stop and ask for directions, it was his wife.

"If that was you," he said, "thanks."

The sand near the top of the beach was soft and loose. McCarter stumbled a little as he walked in it. But he made his way past it, down closer to the surf. He stopped just beyond the reach of the waves, where they peaked and exhausted themselves before falling back toward the Gulf of Mexico once again.

The sand there was firm and he was soon drawing lines in it with his staff.

He started with what he knew from the statue that had been stolen out from under them. Its sculptors had been among the earliest Mayan artisans of the area and

McCarter had connected them with the tribe that had emigrated here from Brazil. The glyphs on the statue had been confusing to him when he'd viewed them. The vast majority were numbers, a long series of them that made no sense to him at the time.

Of course, the Maya had been obsessed with numbers; their calendars were only the most visible result of that. They had also been among the first cultures to discover and understand the importance of zero. They'd used mathematics in laying out their cities and building their pyramids. And some calculations, inscribed on stone at various cities, appeared to have been done for the sole purpose of proving they could do it. It was an ancient equivalent of trying to find the largest known prime numbers or calculate *pi* to more decimal points than anyone had done before.

A mathematician friend of his had once suggested that perhaps the Maya were numerologists and that the elite among them truly worshipped numbers in and of themselves. McCarter could not go that far, but he knew that a calculation of some kind held the answer to his current question.

He liked to work on the problem at night. So far he'd tested various theories and discarded them. The numbers did not seem to represent any specific place, or stand in for a name. Nor were they indicating time in years or months or some other permutation of the various Mayan calendars. They were just numbers, a long series of them without commas, he noted.

Then, in one of his sleepless nights, McCarter had stumbled to the bathroom, where he kept an antiseptic lotion he used to fight the lingering infection in his leg.

The antiseptic was concentrated and designed to be mixed with fresh water to form a solution. With the infection lingering, McCarter had decided to make the concentration stronger. He looked at the bottle for instructions.

What he'd found was a series of numbers designating specific mixing strengths: one for ophthalmic use in the eyes, another for topical use on the skin, and a third for treating broken skin or other open wounds.

The numbers had been in a series, in a ratio of water to medicine. It was 50:1 for use in the eyes, 30:1 for use on the skin, 10:1 for use on wounds.

McCarter had then mixed it at about 2:1, poured it into the festering bullet wound, and grimaced in agony as it burned. But as he flushed out the foaming mixture and the pain subsided, the truth had suddenly hit him.

The numbers on the statue were written in the same manner. They were ratios, with the second number always being the same: 90. And as he thought about them he suddenly realized what they were trying to tell him.

The first of the number sets stood for the east-west demarcation line. The other two were angles off it, angles that could be drawn from certain ruins and places the Maya considered holy. If he was translating things correctly, the lines would converge in an arrowlike shape. The Tip of the Spear—which would lead them to the Temple of the Warrior.

On the beach with his printouts and the numbers burned into his mind, McCarter had only to figure out which ruins, of the dozens in the area, the lines were to be drawn from.

Looking at his papers, McCarter continued to make his marks in the sand. He drew an east-west line as straight and accurately as he could and then began to fill in the surroundings. He used small piles of pebbles and shells for the bigger ruins that could be seen with the naked eye, and then scooped out divots of sand with his hand for the ruins that could only be seen on the IR scan and were still buried beneath the jungle.

He worked like this for an hour. Back and forth he went, hobbling around his diagram, crawling here and there to make changes. A couple walked by casting a disparaging look at McCarter and his masterpiece, but he didn't care; he wasn't building sand castles.

He drew in a river, and then adjusted the positions of certain landmarks until he was certain he had everything in the right place and in the right scale.

Stepping back, McCarter looked down on the layout and had to smile. To an onlooker it might be the scribbling of a madman, but to him it was the same as the satellite photo, and better yet, one that he could draw on and then erase.

Looking around to make sure he was still alone, McCarter began to work on the next stage of his project: deciding which ruins to draw the lines from.

The first line was to begin at the Great City by the Mouth of the Well. McCarter knew this to be the Yucatec Mayan name for Chichen Itza.

He found that particular spot on his beach map and tried to estimate the angle. For a moment he wished he had some type of protractor, but after erasing the line twice he came up with what he thought was a close approximation. He drew his line to the north, out toward the gulf and the foam of the lapping waves.

The origination point for the second line was harder to figure. His own translation told him it was the Temple of the Sunrise, but there might have been fifty sites in the Yucatan that had a connection with the rising sun. So that didn't exactly narrow it down.

A second line of description had called this temple the Place of the Wasp Star, Xux Ek, which to some Maya was another term for Venus. As McCarter considered the connection, the first temple that came to mind was the coastal ruins of Tulum.

He couldn't be sure, but what did he have to lose? He found the small pile of shells that represented Tulum and then measured his angle. Grabbing his staff, he began to trace the line to the northwest, cutting back across the Yucatan peninsula. The new line was angling toward his first line, as he'd hoped. And then finally they crossed.

He found only one problem: There was nothing on his makeshift diagram anywhere near the crossing of the lines. No stones or divots of scooped-out sand.

Disappointed, McCarter sat and checked his math and then his angles and then he studied the photographic printouts. Not only were there no ruins in the area of his crossed lines, but there was nothing on the Landsat photo, either. No hidden limestone signature, not even a smudge to hint that something might have been built in that vicinity. Nothing but miles of jungle-covered coastline.

McCarter exhaled in frustration. He rubbed his forearm across his brow to wipe the sweat away and only succeeded in covering his forehead with sand.

Aggravated and dejected, he looked out over the sloping beach. It was a little past noon and the warm sun bathed his back, while the sound of the small waves rumbling in toward the beach soothed his mind.

As McCarter sat there wondering what the hell he was trying to prove by staying on in Mexico, a speedboat zoomed out from the dock a half mile down. It accelerated noisily, running parallel to the beach a hundred feet out.

As McCarter watched it move off into the distance, its bow wave came ashore, merging with the smaller, natural wave on its way in.

Together they flowed up over the sand, surging higher onto the beach and cascading over the point where his two lines crossed. The water swirled for a moment, foam and silt frothing a few inches deep. And then it slid back, retreating to the gulf, leaving only a smooth canvas of sand where McCarter's lines had crossed to form the tip of the spear.

"Erasing my blackboard," McCarter mumbled. "Does this mean I have to start over?"

He stood wearily, guessing that it did. And then he noticed that nothing else on his diagram had been touched by the waves. A thought occurred to him. McCarter looked at his printouts once again.

He checked the photo and then the lines he'd drawn in the sand. He realized that he hadn't drawn anything to represent the coastline. But with the scale he'd chosen, the high point of the larger, boat-assisted wave was a fairly accurate equivalent of where that coastline should have been drawn.

He gazed out over the shimmering waters of the gulf. The Tip of the Spear pointed in that direction. The Temple of the Warrior was out there hidden somewhere beneath the waves.

CHAPTER 25

Choi stood in the communications suite of Kang's private Airbus A340. Stacks of electronic equipment, radios, and satellite transceivers lined the walls. The cramped space reminded Choi of the cockpit, without the benefit of windows, though at this particular moment they didn't need them. It was night and they were crossing the Pacific at thirty-seven thousand feet. There really wasn't much to see.

The radio officer handed Choi a printout, having decrypted it from the original satellite transmission. Choi looked it over. Pleased, he moved back into the aisle, walking forward to Kang's private section of the aircraft.

Normally Choi would have waited for morning to inform Kang, but Choi knew that Kang was awake and undergoing a treatment session from one of his many doctors.

Choi knocked on the cabin door and a nurse opened it. Inside he saw Kang wired up to a newer, more powerful electrical stimulator. Instead of electrodes that simply attached to the surface of the skin, he was now having wires surgically implanted into his body. The doctors were attaching them to specific nerves that they believed could be regenerated and possibly even used to control prosthetics.

It was a dangerous step forward in his course of treatment, but Kang was desperate to get out of his prison. So far he'd tried every treatment medical science was offering: stem cells, neurological transplants, untested drugs, and holistic remedies.

But he'd continued to deteriorate.

Of all the treatments, only the electrical stimulation had slowed the progress of the disease, and Kang had become more and more dependent on it. But keeping his muscles from atrophying was not the endgame he sought. At his urging the doctors had gone forward with a new theory: that the right electrical stimulation would force the nerves to repair themselves.

Choi watched. Each time the electrical stimulators fired, one of Kang's extremities would twitch, first his arm and then a leg. His fingers straightened and stiffened, shaking uncontrollably, and then the current was cut and they curled up into a lifeless ball once again.

Kang had been sick for so long that these movements startled Choi. He hadn't seen Kang straighten his left hand in years, hadn't seen Kang's legs move in over a decade. He found something disturbing about watching it now. When combined with the strange facial distortions that accompanied the shocks, it gave Choi an almost overwhelming desire to leave.

The latest series of jolts ended and Kang's body returned to stillness. He looked at the doctor who was watching the data displayed on a softly glowing LCD monitor.

"You wait too long to speak," Kang said. "Is the news that bad?"

"I'm sorry," the doctor said. "Your neurological response is still weakening."

"Then increase the stimulus," Kang said.

"It will cause a great deal of pain," the doctor said. "It will feel as if your skin is burning, as if a flame is cutting into you and you cannot pull away from it."

"Yes," Kang said. "And in my position you would welcome such sensations."

The doctor nodded politely. "I'll need a minute to adjust the settings."

As the doctor scurried to a new position, Choi stepped forward. Apparently Kang noticed the look on his face.

"You disapprove," he said.

"It is not my place to approve or disapprove," Choi replied.

"That is correct," Kang noted. "What do you have for me?"

"New information on the Americans. The one we thought had been killed in the mountains, the professor. It seems he might be alive."

"So one of your failures is erased," Kang noted.

Despite the anger he felt at Kang's derision, Choi maintained his composure. Dying men had a habit of lashing out and Kang continued to do so.

"Let us hope," Choi said. "What we know for certain is that either he, or someone using his password, accessed the mainframe at his old university. Information was downloaded, including satellite photos of the Yucatan."

"Do you know where he is?"

"Not precisely, but the terminal he used was in a small town, a large distance from where he and the woman were originally operating. And if she were to try and find him . . ." Choi let his voice trail off.

"Of course she will," Kang said. "Where are your people?"

"In Tulum and Puerto Morelos. And in Mexico City, at the Museum of Anthropology, where they did some of their research."

"This is good," Kang said. "Keep them out of sight. You moved too early last time."

Choi nodded and the doctor poked his head up from the equipment he was calibrating. "We're ready," he said.

Kang motioned for Choi to leave.

Choi bowed slightly and then stepped out through the cabin door, closing it behind him.

As he walked back to the communications suite, he heard a low buzz emanating from the room he'd just left. He also heard Kang grunting and wincing in unison with the electronic pulses. By the time Choi reached the communications room, Kang's voice could be heard down the aisle, screaming in agony and pleasure.

CHAPTER 26

Hawker sat in the front passenger seat of a dilapidated, rust-covered jeep as Danielle drove. Yuri sat in the back. The three of them had been motoring along in the Mexican sunshine for hours, a welcome change to the cold drizzle of Hong Kong and the South China Sea.

As they traveled up the coastal road toward Puerto Azul, Hawker watched the sunlight shimmering off the water. In the most bizarre way, it almost felt as if they were on vacation. He and Danielle traveling like some couple, their adopted child, Yuri, seat-belted in the back, wearing a touristy sombrero and oversized plastic sunglasses.

He was quiet, even when spoken to in Russian. Yuri did not often engage. But for the most part he'd been a model child, concerned with little things right in front of him far more than the bigger picture of his surroundings.

Even now he seemed more interested in the clicking sound made by the arms of the plastic sunglasses than actually wearing them. He repeatedly took them off, opening and closing the arms seven or eight times in proximity to his right ear, before Hawker would put them back on his face.

After the tenth round of watching this, Hawker turned to Danielle. "What do you think is wrong with him?"

Danielle glanced in the rearview mirror. "I don't know," she said. "He seems to be in his own world. In some ways it reminds me of autism but I'm not sure. He didn't exactly have a great start to life."

The look on Danielle's face was sadness, disappointment. They'd rescued Yuri from one prison but the future likely held another. Hawker understood it.

The rules were often blind to the facts and though he and Danielle could keep Yuri with them for the time being, and certainly would never return him to Kang, the diplomatic situation with Russia would be more difficult. Yuri was a Russian citizen, a ward of the state. And when the time came and the Russians demanded him back, legally there would be no way to stop them.

"Maybe we can keep him," Hawker said, joking.

"He's not a stray puppy," she replied. "But we can't send him back there."

Hawker watched as Danielle returned to scanning the roadside and the signs. The drive had been a long one. Nine hours cross-country with only a canvas targa top to block the sun. Sweat, sand, and grime coated their bodies and the urge to stop, shower, and sleep had been hard to resist. But time was short and so they'd driven almost nonstop.

And yet Danielle looked great to him, as stunning as he remembered, in some ways even better. In Brazil, pressured by superiors to get an impossible job done under a daunting timeline, she'd been very official and intense. But here, driving the old jeep, wearing jeans, a

T-shirt, and a crumpled cowboy hat, with her skin tanning in the sun, she seemed more natural, more at peace.

"You know," he said, "we could've found a car with air-conditioning."

She laughed, an easy laugh. "We have the two-sixty air conditioner."

"The two-sixty?"

"Yeah, two windows down, sixty miles an hour," she said.

"Great," Hawker said, wiping more sweat from his face. "I bet James Bond never had the two-sixty air conditioner. Maybe next time we could get an Aston Martin."

"This suits you better," she said. "Kind of reminds me of your helicopter."

He laughed at that. "Yeah, it kind of does."

The road had taken them to a small fishing village. On the shore, a group of long boats with colorful but fading paint lay motionless side by side. They looked like sea lions basking in the sun. Up ahead was a row of small buildings.

"This is it," she said. "If McCarter's still in Mexico, and he wants us to find him, he'll be here."

"How can you be sure?"

"When we came down here, we set up shop about fifty miles inland near a ruined Mayan city called Ek Balam, the Black Jaguar. But McCarter kept talking about wanting to come visit this place. I guess he and his wife spent a couple of months here," Danielle said. "Working all day and making love all night. Never slept a wink, according to him."

"Sounds nice," Hawker said. "Except for the working part . . . and the lack of sleep."

"Wow, you're such a romantic."

She pulled the jeep to the side of the road.

By an hour later they'd checked every motel in town. There were two smaller bed-and-breakfast places up the coast, but one man they'd asked had suggested the small apartment house a few blocks inland.

Danielle pulled up in front of it.

"My turn," Hawker said. He hopped out and went to see what he could find.

"Moses Negro," the front desk clerk said, after Hawker described who he was looking for. "*Este es loco.*"

Hawker remembered McCarter as calm and measured. It was hard to imagine him as "*loco*" or resembling Moses in any way.

The clerk pointed up the stairs. "*Trece, nueve,*" he said. Third floor, room nine.

Hawker climbed the rickety stairs and made his way down a short hall.

From the outside the building had looked pretty worn down, old red brick and peeling plaster, but inside it was well kept, though dated and a little cramped.

The hardwood floors beneath his feet were scratched and fading but had been swept immaculate. On a sofa table at the top of the stairs, a vinelike plant with deep green leaves and bright red flowers spilled out of its pot. Through a window he saw the courtyard; an old stone fountain bubbled in the center. Birds sat on its rim or chirped in the bougainvilleas that climbed trellises along the walls.

The place certainly had charm.

Hawker arrives outside room nine. He listened for a moment.

Nothing.

He knocked. "Professor McCarter?"

No answer. The clerk had not seen McCarter leave for the day, but that didn't mean he was in. With a key he'd bought for a hundred dollars, Hawker opened the door and stepped inside.

The room was tidy but empty. The bed was made but the blanket that covered it was slightly askew. That seemed out of place with the attention to detail that marked everything else around. Hawker guessed someone had been sitting or lying on the top of the covers. A drawer by the nightstand was not quite closed.

Something felt wrong, though Hawker wasn't sure what it was.

Movement caught his eye as the thin, gauzy drapes by the window wafted in the soft breeze. He stepped toward them and something heavy slammed into the back of his shoulders. He fell forward, stumbling to the window.

A pistol cocked behind his head.

"Who are you?!" a gruff voice shouted.

The voice was familiar. It sounded like McCarter.

Hawker began to turn around.

"Don't!" the voice shouted. "Don't you move!"

"I'm just trying to show you who I am," Hawker said as calmly as he could. "That's what you wanted, right?"

"Right," the person behind him said. "Okay, right. Just do it slowly."

And so Hawker turned as slowly as he possibly could.

His eyes locked on to McCarter, and he instantly understood why the clerk had considered him loco. The professor looked like a crazy man. Bushy beard, unkempt hair, eyes filled with more lines than a Pennsylvania road map.

"Remember me?" Hawker asked. "We had a hell of a time in Brazil together."

McCarter's face softened as if he recognized Hawker. But then he stiffened again. "Are you real?" he asked.

"Am I what?"

"Real," McCarter repeated. "Are you real?"

Hawker wasn't sure what to make of this. Perhaps there was more to the loco description than he'd thought.

"I am real," Hawker said as calmly as he could. "Though I have to point out, if I wasn't, I would probably lie to you and insist that I was real anyway."

McCarter relaxed a bit more. He lowered the gun an inch. "Good point," he admitted. "Perhaps this is not the best method of gauging reality."

Hawker extended his hand and calmly directed the gun away from him. "Whatever you decide, I'd rather you didn't shoot me to find out for sure."

McCarter uncocked the hammer and tossed the gun on the small table beside him, then looked up at Hawker again. "It's a cap gun," he admitted sadly. "All I could get my hands on."

"A cap gun." Hawker had to laugh.

"It's just . . . ," McCarter started saying. "Sometimes

I see things . . . or hear things . . . and they're not really there. And you don't seem like someone I would run into . . . I mean . . . I wasn't expecting . . ." He couldn't find the words. "What the hell are you doing here?"

Hawker looked around, rubbing the back of his neck and trying to figure out how McCarter had surprised him.

"Apparently getting suckered by the old hide-behind-the-door trick."

"Another reason I thought you weren't real," McCarter said quickly. "Who would fall for that?"

Hawker nodded. "I must be losing my touch."

McCarter smiled. In his sudden moment of happiness he looked even crazier than before. A delirious, joyful madman.

"Still it is good to see you," McCarter said. "Sorry about hitting you," he added apologetically. "I don't like hurting anyone, you know. I'm a pacifist for the most part."

Before Hawker could reply, the sound of footsteps on the wooden floors could be heard in the hall. And then Danielle popped her head in, with Yuri holding her hand.

"We didn't feel like waiting in the car," she said.

As confused as he was by Hawker's sudden appearance, McCarter seemed even more stunned by Danielle's arrival with a young child in tow.

"It's a long story," Hawker promised.

As the details of both party's stories were relayed, Danielle took a look at the wound on McCarter's leg. It was clearly still infected.

"Despite the best care of an accredited witch doctor

and my own attempts at self-medication, I've been having hallucinations and nightmares," he said. "And feeling paranoid in a way I can't quite explain."

"Fever and lack of sleep can do that to you," she said. "Not to mention the delayed reaction to being attacked and shot. You should be in a hospital."

She looked at the bottle of pills he'd been taking. "These aren't strong enough to fight what you're going through," she said. "You're probably just making the infection resistant. I'm going to get you some real antibiotics. And then I'm sending you back home."

"You're not sending me anywhere," McCarter said roughly. Then, as if he'd realized how it sounded, he added, "I mean, I'm the one who started this, remember. I'm not going home till we're done."

"This is only going to get more dangerous," she said, hoping he would change his mind.

He took a deep breath. "You're welcome to leave if you want. Or to stay and help, but I'm not finished yet."

Beside her, Hawker began to laugh. "He sounds like you."

McCarter responded, "I know you think I've been drinking the Kool-Aid but I haven't. I don't care about the NRI or the company line or any of that other stuff; I just know we have to find these stones, before someone else does."

Danielle sighed. "Just thought I'd offer. But if you're staying, I'm staying. For all the reasons we started this in the first place."

McCarter looked at Hawker. "What about you?"

Hawker laughed. "I'm pretty sure this is going to end

up in a train wreck of some kind," he said. "But as crazy as it sounds, I have nowhere better to be."

McCarter looked out the window. The ocean breeze had come wafting through the curtains once again, fresh with the salt air.

"Maybe you do," McCarter said. "Maybe we all do."

CHAPTER 27

Ivan Saravich emerged from the subway car and into the transfer mezzanine of the Park Kultury metro station in central Moscow. The opulent surroundings resembled a museum or the hall of some great palace. The floor was tiled in large squares of polished black and white like a giant chessboard; the walls were covered with marble and lined with ornate sculptures. The whole station was lit in a warm glow from rows of hanging chandeliers.

Unlike American subways, made mostly of functional concrete and steel, the .Russian metro was more than just a mode of transportation; it was a source of pride, Russian pride now, Soviet pride when they were designed and built in the 1950s and '60s. For a nation that considered itself a worker's paradise, the metro stations were to be the workers' palace, their great halls.

Saravich remembered the first time he'd walked this particular hall. A twenty-year-old recruit from the Urals, he'd come to Moscow to join the great struggle, to begin his work for the KGB. Entering this hall, he'd felt exactly what the party wanted him to feel: pride, power, and Soviet supremacy. To him it was the dawning of a new age in which the ideology of the common would overcome the oppression of the elite.

Thirty years later, the Union of Soviet Socialist Republics had dissolved and with it went any illusions about the common and the elite.

Saravich had come to the conclusion that any form of government would inevitably evolve into extensions of the elite. It was the natural progression; those who wanted power gathered it unto themselves. Those who craved equality lacked the ambition, ego, or selfishness to match up. And so the change.

With the new age in Russia, Saravich began to understand that even civilized life was every man for himself. With that in mind, he took to capitalism far more easily than he'd expected, even if he spent most of his time working freelance for the same people who once gave him a government check.

He was wealthier now, enough to retire five times over if he wanted, but he felt no desire to do so. As a widower with no children, no friends, and few outside interests, he saw little point in it. To him this was the true curse of capitalism: Work was rewarding in a way few other things could be, and so it diminished everything else in its wake.

Making his way down the concourse of Park Kultury, Saravich felt nothing of the pride it once stirred in him. He walked briskly, head down, hands shoved into his pockets. The mezzanine looked as splendid as ever, but it was just a train station now.

A gravelly voice broke his stride. "Comrade," the voice said from behind him, "you seem to be in a hurry."

Saravich slowed but kept walking. He recognized the voice and the question or at least its ilk: an old KGB habit of asking a suggestive but open-ended query, thought to startle those who might have something to hide.

The shape of a hulking man fell in beside him; the man was a hundred pounds heavier than Saravich, but not fat, just oversized, with huge arms, huge shoulders, a huge head. Saravich knew the man's name, but no one used it. They simply called him Ropa: the Mountain.

"Why are you meeting me here?" Saravich asked. "I have a report scheduled for the morning. Is that not soon enough?"

"I'm afraid not," Ropa said. "It is known already what happened in Hong Kong. The firestorm is growing. Soon someone will have to burn."

"Me?"

"Or all of us."

All of us. It was hard for Saravich to imagine that Ropa and the others who hired him would feel the heat for what had gone wrong. Most likely Saravich would find his feet being held out for the flames to lick and taste.

"What were you thinking, hiring that American?"

Saravich turned to face Ropa. "It seemed a good way to keep us out of the picture. And it has. You notice there is no backlash."

Ropa laughed and Saravich wondered if the laughter was directed at his attempt to justify the failure or some other, deeper fact. Whatever the truth, Saravich was too tired to worry about it tonight.

He turned and began to walk again, soon reaching the stairwell.

Ropa followed, just a foot or so behind him. It gave Saravich the distinct impression of being herded somewhere.

The two men exited into the frigid Moscow air. Snow was falling, illuminated by the city lights. Five inches or more already coated the streets. A light snow by Russian standards. Waiting in that snow was a black Maserati sedan. Twenty years ago it would have been a boxy Zil, the Russian equivalent of an American Lincoln or Cadillac. But with the new wealth in Russia, Mercedes and BMW were favored. Always looking to top his peers, Ropa went a step beyond.

A Maserati with oversized, studded snow tires. What would the Italians think? It was like a runway model wearing galoshes.

"You're coming with us," Ropa said.

"Where?"

"To explain yourself."

With that Saravich felt Ropa's paw of a hand fall heavily on his shoulder. It guided him to the sedan's rear door.

A moment later Saravich found himself in the back with another man, one he didn't recognize. Ropa squeezed through the front door and filled the passenger seat to capacity as the driver put the car in gear.

So this is how it ends, Saravich thought. *On a snowy night in Moscow I'll disappear. Perhaps not to be found until the spring thaw.*

The car moved through traffic and crossed the Moscow River. A minute later they were pulling to a stop at the very center of Red Square.

Would they really do it here? Maybe, if they want to send a message.

Another vehicle pulled up beside them, pointing the opposite direction and berthing so close that neither vehicle could open a door.

Ropa lowered his window. Quick words were exchanged and he snatched something being held out by the passenger of the other car.

"Let's go," he said to the driver.

As the Maserati began to move, Ropa did what he could to turn and face Saravich, handing him a padded envelope.

"You have one more chance," Ropa told him. "The orders come straight from the FSB now."

"What are they?" Saravich asked disdainfully.

"Go there, find the boy, and bring him back to the Science Directorate. If you can't capture him, then you are to kill him and everyone who has touched him."

Saravich looked inside the envelope. A new passport, cash, instructions. "I don't do that kind of work anymore," he said. "Tell them to send one of their own."

"It was your disgrace," Ropa said angrily. "Petrov was your brother."

"My half brother," Ivan insisted.

"Still," Ropa said. "It is your family that has ruined this. You must be the one to pay for it."

Saravich looked outside. He'd done much and given up much for the Soviet Union, but despite a life of work, his name was now a mark of dishonor. Then again, what did he care of honor anymore? What had it ever gotten him?

"You will be met in Mexico City," Ropa added. "The men will take orders from you, but you will not be free to leave them. Do you understand?"

Of course he understood. The men would be FSB, from the ninth directorate, assassins with orders to kill whomever he asked them to kill. And then to eliminate Saravich himself if they did not bring the boy home, or perhaps even if they did.

"You may think you have nothing to lose," Ropa told him, "but you still have nephews, nieces. These people will suffer if you do anything less than what's necessary."

Saravich stared at Ropa, but the Mountain did not blink. The threat was real. He tucked the envelope in his jacket and glanced out the window. They were approaching Moscow International. He would be boarding a plane without ever going home.

Apparently there would be no rest for the wicked.

CHAPTER 28

The thirty-foot V-hulled fishing boat sliced across the Gulf of Mexico with surprising grace; surprising because the boat itself was a battered veteran of twenty years, with dents, peeling paint, and saltwater corrosion plainly visible on every surface. Even the engines had sputtered and coughed when Danielle had started them, sounding like old tractor motors as the boat traveled at low speed.

But once she'd coaxed the throttles forward, the twin outboards had begun to sing. And now, cruising across relatively flat seas, with a long wake trailing out behind them, Danielle had begun to feel a sense of confidence and of freedom. Those feelings seemed to be mirrored on the faces of at least two of her three passengers.

Beside her, McCarter looked familiar again, smiling and shaved. Two days of proper dressings and megadoses of antibiotics seemed to have broken the back of his infection. Sleeping pills had granted him some rest and he now looked like the man she remembered instead of a lunatic who'd escaped the asylum.

Yuri seemed happier as well, much as he had on the freighter to the Philippines. She wondered about him. If he could really see or sense energy fields as the Russian captain had claimed, even a sleepy town like Puerto Azul might be something in the way of overstimulation.

It was true that autism created similar feelings of sensory overload in those who suffered from it, but for Yuri it was worse. He could be in a silent, darkened room and the waves of electromagnetic energy others could not see or feel would bombard him.

Appliances, cellphones, power lines, anything that used electricity created a small magnetic field. If one could see these things or hear them or sense them, as Yuri supposedly could, the modern world might feel like a room where everyone was shouting, blowing trumpets, and banging cymbals, all at the same time.

But out here there was little of that and it seemed that the open sea brought him peace.

And that left only Hawker to be unhappy. He stood near the bow, digging through the various boxes of equipment, looking more and more disappointed with each new find. He reached for a spot of corrosion on the metal hull, snapping off a flake of rust.

"Is this really the best we can do?" he said, tossing the flake overboard.

"It matches our jeep," she replied.

"Where are the missiles?" he asked. "The machine guns and the mini-torpedoes?"

"Couldn't afford any options," she said. "Just basic transportation. At least it's a fast boat. They normally rent these things out to chase after wahoo."

Hawker's eyebrows went up. Apparently he wasn't a fisherman. "A wahoo?" he asked. "What the hell is a wahoo?"

"A fish," she said. "An extremely fast fish. This boat is set up to catch them."

Looking out over the horizon, he grunted his approval. "I guess that's something."

She motioned toward one of the lockers he'd been through. "At least the dive gear is first-rate," she added. "That's what we're going to need."

"If we find anything," he said, looking at the control panel. "Only we would look for a sunken city with a fishfinder."

Danielle followed his gaze. The only pieces of additional equipment were a GPS receiver and a cheap sonar depth sounder. But they had checked and rechecked McCarter's calculations. If he was right, the Tip of the Spear was a spot seven miles offshore, in the relatively shallow water of the Campeche plain. The underwater data from that area was limited, but it was a sedimentary plain, relatively shallow and flat. If a ruin of some type was present, it should stick out like a sore thumb.

Danielle looked to McCarter. "I think he doubts us," she said.

"Don't worry," McCarter insisted. "We'll prove him wrong."

Hawker shook his head. "I just don't see how the Maya built something out here underwater."

"There are two possibilities for that," McCarter said. "The first is that they didn't build anything underwater. They could have built something on an island only to have it sink over time."

He waved his hand around. "The gulf is a very active zone of currents and plate tectonics. Not only that, but much of the underlying rock is sedimentary, so relatively soft. Islands can rise or fall on a human scale. A thousand years can create quite a change. As far as we can tell, the Maya and their predecessors were active in this area for two or three times that length."

"We're not talking Krakatau or anything, right?" Hawker asked.

"No," McCarter said. "More like a deflating cake or a home dropping into a sinkhole."

Danielle was glad to see McCarter acting more like himself again.

"And the other option?" Hawker asked.

"We believe the natives we found in Brazil had assistance and training from whoever brought these stones back. That's how they built the temple down there. That's why it's still standing. It's not too hard for me to imagine them building an underwater structure. Concrete hardens in a chemical reaction. Use the right forms and it can set up and cure underwater. Especially when using volcanic ash as an ingredient."

McCarter looked her way. "Our trip to the Island of the Shroud showed that these people were traveling to the volcanic regions. It was a long trek, one that I doubt they would have made without an important reason. We thought it was to create a temple to house the new stone, and in a way it might have been, but maybe we had it backward. The effort was related to housing the stone, but they weren't going there to place the stone. Instead it was to get the ingredients they needed to do the job down here."

That sounded about right to Danielle. She could imagine trains of burros loaded down with volcanic ash, trouping down the slopes of Mount Pulimundo. She checked the GPS. "I guess we're going to find out soon enough," she said. "We're almost there."

She backed off the throttles and the boat slowed to a calmer pace.

Their plan was simple: enter the area, cruise a grid pattern for an hour or two, and dive on anything that looked suspicious. Twenty minutes in, they hadn't found anything, but the depth had remained almost constant.

"That's a good sign," Danielle said.

"I've been thinking about what we're looking for," McCarter said. "The stone we found in Brazil was hidden but in a monument of some presence. And it was guarded. As if the people who put it there wanted it to be protected, but also in a known position."

"Hard to get at, but easy to find," she paraphrased.

"Not necessarily easy to find," he said. "After all, it was in the middle of the Amazon. But if 'easy to find' is the wrong description, how about 'impossible to lose.'"

That seemed apt.

Hawker nodded. "Those animals defended the temple in Brazil like a nest."

Danielle thought she understood. "Hard to lose, but well defended," she said. "You're saying this is the same kind of thing. Put a temple out here and it's even more inaccessible."

"They brought these things back here for a reason," McCarter added. "They gave the people they found a legend designed to explain what they were for, but they didn't want anyone disturbing them."

"So why are we messing with them?" Hawker asked.

McCarter and Danielle exchanged glances. At times the whole thing was too monumental to think about.

Strange, glowing stones that were actually machinery, devices of some kind sent back from a future time period. Someone had seen fit to go through whatever hell it took to send them back here, but now they were building toward something, and if the legends were correct, even tangentially, it could mean a cataclysmic change for everyone on the earth. Leaving them in place without trying to understand what they might have been for was almost too much to ask.

"We have a good reason," she said. "We need to understand what they're going to do at zero hour."

She searched Hawker's face and waited for a response. She sensed he was not quite convinced.

Before Hawker could say anything, Yuri stood abruptly, looking off to the port side of the boat. He stepped to the rail, staring at a spot ahead and to the left. He followed the spot with his eyes as they moved past it.

Danielle slowed the boat further and began to turn back toward the area. The depth sounder began to beep and Yuri became more agitated. He leaned out over the edge of the boat, moving his head back and forth as if he were trying to see through the water.

Suddenly he raced from the port side of the boat to starboard, grabbing that rail and repeating his agitated actions.

"Siren!" he shouted. "Siren, siren, siren!"

He seemed unable to control himself, shouting aggressively, rocking back and forth. He went from one side of the boat to the other and began to climb overboard. Hawker grabbed him.

"Calm down!" Hawker urged.

"Siren, siren, siren!"

The depth gauge was beeping louder; they'd moved over a shallow spot.

Yuri wriggled in Hawker's arms trying to break his grip. He lunged at Hawker's hand to bite it. "Siren!" he screamed. "Siren!"

"Get us out of here!" Hawker shouted.

She gunned the throttles and the boat leaped forward, racing away from the offending spot.

Yuri looked toward the wake behind them. "Siren," he said, softly and wistfully. "Siren."

And then he was calm.

Danielle slowed the boat once again and when Hawker released his grip, Yuri ran to Danielle and clung to her leg.

"What the hell did they do to this kid?" Hawker asked.

"I don't know," she said, stroking Yuri's hair. She crouched down beside him.

"What's 'siren' mean, sweetheart? Can you tell me?"

He just stared at her. It was no use; he didn't understand.

"It's okay," she said, looking into his eyes and touching his face. "It's okay. You're okay."

He locked his eyes on hers and it seemed as if he was troubled, but then he broke free and found his sunglasses again and began clicking them beside his ear.

"You think he's okay?" McCarter asked.

Sadly, she looked up at him. "I don't know. But I think we've found the Tip of the Spear."

CHAPTER 29

Danielle punched the keys on the dive computer to calculate their time available underwater. Air use, type of mixture, and decompression stops would all be factored in. While she worked on the details, Hawker took off his shirt and began hauling the gear from the equipment locker.

She glanced over at him. His shoulders and back muscles formed a broad V that tapered down to his waist. His muscles went taut as he stacked the heavy tanks by the boat's stern rail.

His tanned skin was marred with sets of scars: an old knife wound that traveled down from one shoulder blade, road rash or shrapnel scars on his right side, and two small, circular scars that she guessed were bullet wounds. As terrible as it might sound, she thought, they suited him, the way the beat-up old helicopter and the rusting jeep suited him.

"Don't get too distracted," McCarter said, catching her.

"Right," she replied, somewhat embarrassed.

"Don't worry," McCarter added. "I caught him staring at you earlier. He almost fell off the boat."

"Good," she said, smiling to herself. "I'd hate to think I was losing my touch."

She turned back to the computer. If the depth finder was correct, the sea floor was a sandy plain eighty feet below. But at the spot where Yuri had begun screaming, the depth finder had registered successive pings ranging from fifty-five to seventy feet. Something was down there rising out of the sediment: a reef, the remnants of some island or some type of construction.

She stepped to the front of the boat for some privacy and changed into her dive skins, a thin, formfitting suit of Lycra, similar to a neoprene wet suit but designed for warmer water. Dive skins were good against abrasion and didn't affect buoyancy, like neoprene suits could.

With the suit fitting like a glove, Danielle sheathed a four-inch titanium knife around her calf and then walked to the back of the boat. Hawker stood there, wearing dive shorts and a rash-guard of a shirt. He was examining their masks.

The full-face diving masks had radio communications built into them and a miniature head-up display that projected depth, time, and compass direction on the top right corner of the mask, like a modern fighter pilot's helmet.

They had cost a thousand dollars apiece and when added to the two diver propulsion vehicles, or DPVs, the twin aluminum tanks, the setup came to twenty grand or more.

"I see where our budget went," Hawker said.

"I had these flown in yesterday," she said. "The boat . . . well, I had to make do with what was already available."

Hawker lifted the tanks onto her back.

"We're using nitrox," he said referencing a special mixture of oxygen and nitrogen that allowed divers to go deeper, and stay down longer.

"Forty percent mixture."

For a dive into eighty feet of water they didn't really need nitrox but she hadn't known what the depth of the site would be, and if they found something in deeper waters she didn't want to go back for new tanks.

"With the nitrox we can do an hour and ten minutes without decompression," she explained. "Max time on the bottom is two hours, saving thirty-two minutes for decompression on our way up."

Hawker set his watch and heaved his set of tanks up onto his shoulders.

She turned to McCarter. "I programmed a waypoint into the GPS. Don't delete it. You're going to drift a little, even with the anchor down. You'll need to be able to home in on that spot if we need a pickup."

"I thought you had radios in the masks," he said.

"We do but the transmitters are not as powerful as the one you have on board." She motioned to the surface unit.

"We'll be able to hear each other and you, but once we go deeper than thirty feet you won't be able to hear us."

McCarter nodded and Danielle pulled on her mask and went over the side, splashing into the warm Caribbean water.

Hawker followed and a moment later they were both in the water, testing out the DPVs: torpedo-shaped machines with stubby wings and handlebars that resembled a motorcycle's.

Cruising through the gin-clear water of the gulf, Danielle activated the head-up display. A series of brilliant green lines formatted on the glass of her mask like some kind of high-definition video game.

Depth: 4, Bearing: NNW (323), Temp: 88, Time Elapsed: 1:17.

"Which way?" Hawker asked.

"We need to head back under the boat and follow the one-oh-seven bearing."

And with that she peeled off to the left like a dolphin turning away from the pod. Hawker followed and the two of them tracked back underneath the boat, heading for the hidden rise in the sand half a mile away.

As she flew through the water, Danielle heard Hawker's voice over the radio, doing a bad job of impersonating Jacques Cousteau. "And zey dove into zee murky depths, in search of zee giant octopus. Although it was not so murky as zey expected and zey weren't really diving zat deep."

She smiled to herself. Seawater absorbs and scatters light fairly rapidly but as they passed through forty feet it was bright and clear and pristine blue. With the light-colored, sandy bottom, it would only be slightly darker at eighty feet.

From the corner of her eye she saw Hawker pull up and turn.

She backed off the throttle and the two of them hung there, floating in zero g.

"What's wrong?" she asked.

He pointed into the distance.

"Sharks."

CHAPTER 30

Danielle watched as a large shape materialized in the distance,

"Hammerhead," she whispered.

"As long as it's not the one that jumps out of the water with people in its mouth," Hawker said.

In the time she'd known Hawker, she'd found he liked to make light of situations, using humor to prop up people's spirits or to defuse a situation. She didn't detect that he was actually worried, but a twenty-foot, thousand-pound shark was not something to take lightly.

"Hammerheads usually ignore people," she said, looking around in the other directions. "But the problem is . . ."

Even as she spoke two more of the oddly shaped fish came gliding in from out of the darkness, and then a third, fourth, and fifth.

"The problem is they tend to swim in packs," she said.

The sharks were cruising near the surface, moving methodically, almost lazily out toward the limit of her vision. She nudged the throttle and began to ease forward.

"What are you doing?" Hawker asked.

"I just want to see where they're going," she said.

"How about we just let them go there," he suggested.

That would have been fine by her. But the problem was she didn't think they were going anywhere. She had a sneaking suspicion that they might be moving out beyond visual range and turning back toward the two human swimmers.

She continued the slow pursuit until she could see them more clearly. The sharks *had* changed course, but not back toward her and Hawker; they'd banked left, turning due south. She wanted to follow farther, but even though the sharks were swimming at a leisurely pace, there was no way to keep up with them short of gunning the throttles on the DPVs, and that didn't seem wise, since she knew that sharks are acutely aware of vibrations.

"Danielle," Hawker said, "you might want to turn around."

She released the throttle and turned in Hawker's direction. More sharks were headed their way. Not one or two or five, this time, but twenty or thirty or fifty, strung out in a long line two and three wide, like rush hour drivers on some underwater highway.

Like her, Hawker was sinking noiselessly toward the bottom. It seemed like a prudent idea. They touched down in the sand. From there Danielle had a better view. Looking upward, with the sharks backlit by the sunlight, she followed their progress. She could see what they were doing now, swimming in a half-mile-wide circle. Slowly meandering along, turning and swimming and turning and swimming, the way fish in circular aquariums do.

"Not that I wouldn't rather be watching this from a submarine," Hawker said, "but this is pretty cool."

"I've heard they can gather in groups of hundreds," she said, "but I've never seen anything like this."

"How many do you think there are?"

It was impossible to count, but as she watched them circle, she guessed there were more than a hundred of them, maybe close to two hundred. The larger ones swam out on their own, in the outside lane so to speak. The smaller ones, seven- and eight-footers, stuck closer together in tight groupings on the inside of the circular track.

As she tried to take in the whole scene, she gazed across the seafloor toward what would have been the center of the shark circle. There a ridge of coral and what looked like an outcropping of stone rose from the silt.

And suddenly it made sense to her. Sharks, hammerheads in particular, had sensitive organs in their snouts that detected electromagnetic pulses. The small organs were called the ampullae of Lorenzini, and were basically bundles of nerve fibers that reacted to changes in electromagnetic waves.

If they were right about the possibility of another stone being present in this area, then perhaps the sharks sensed that energy and it was drawing them in, similar to what had happened with Yuri on the boat moments before.

Only, for the sharks, there were no restrictions to hold them back and their desire to be here resulted in this endless circling pattern. The same way moths flicker in circles around candlelight, thinking it's the moon. They can never quite reach it, but they can't leave it, either.

As she stared at the sharks, slowly turning above them, she found the scene almost hypnotic. Slightly dizzy, she looked away, toward the coral-covered outcropping across from them.

A few deep breaths cleared her head and she spoke.

"I think we should go over to that coral rise. It's in the right place. If one of the stones is down here, then I'm guessing that's where we'll find it."

Moving slowly and keeping an eye on the sharks above, they swam up to the outcropping of rock. Peeking out from beneath a coral blanket were great stones cut and laid in precise diagonal blocks, interlocking and supporting one another.

Danielle swam around the side, finding an exposed corner and the line of an edge.

"It looks pretty much intact," she said.

Hawker was examining the fit of the stones. "If the exterior is secure, the interior might be as well."

"Just like McCarter said: hard to find, but impossible to lose," she said.

"And well defended," he noted, nodding to the sharks. "Just like the temple in Brazil."

Danielle examined the edges of the structure. She could see designs in the stonework. They weren't hieroglyphic but they were similar to other Mayan designs McCarter had shown her. Warrior figures and the outline of the Witz Monster, a Mayan representation connected to the rain god. In this case the mouth had a pair of serpents suspended within it.

The discovery sent a wave of adrenaline through her body. In fact she felt positively rapturous. "Let's see if there is a way to get inside."

They glided across the top of the structure, with one eye on the sharks, then they dropped down on the other side.

Danielle arrived at the bottom, beside a hollow-looking area in the web of coral. She aimed her flashlight inside.

"A tunnel."

It was narrow and cramped with jagged outcroppings of coral growing along the walls, but she felt it was worth a try.

Hawker grabbed her arm. "You'll fit but your tanks won't."

In her excitement she'd almost forgotten. The double tanks on her back were bulky and their cross section was actually wider than her hips. She slipped them off.

"Don't," Hawker said.

"I'm just taking a look."

She disconnected her regulator, dropped her tanks, and kicked her way forward. After easing into the tunnel for fifteen feet or so it began to narrow around her. She moved back outside and connected to the regulator for a moment.

Hawker was staring at her as if she were crazy.

"Relax," she said, confidently. "I'm skinny and you're worrying for nothing."

She took a series of deep breaths, trying to hyperoxygenate her body as free divers do. With a little luck she'd have three or four minutes of air. It was a risk, but she felt certain that what they were looking for was right around the corner. McCarter's translation and calculations, Yuri's reaction, the sharks—it all made sense. The second stone was inside. It had to be there. And she had the power to go get it.

She disconnected the regulator for a second time and swam back into the tunnel. Kicking her legs smoothly, she followed the tunnel down to the spot where it narrowed. Bits of coral stuck out on one side but she squirmed past.

"Be careful," Hawker warned.

She couldn't reply, because it would use up her air, but she wondered when he'd become such a nag.

And then the coral snagged her in the ribs. She tried to pull away from it but there was no room in the tunnel and she began to be concerned. Time to back out.

Using her hands she pushed, but the wedges of coral that had let her slip forward now jammed into her back. She couldn't turn around and she couldn't back up. She twisted and pushed harder. She felt her heart pounding, heard the coral snapping off as she writhed against it.

"Hold on," Hawker said.

She glanced back, hearing a sudden rush of bubbles as he disconnected his tanks and came in after her. She felt a hand on her leg, pulling her, but the coral was gouging her now; she could feel it cutting her skin.

"Wait!" she grunted.

Her head was spinning. She wanted him to pull her free but the coral would surely cut her and blood in the water would be the end of them both.

She twisted over, looking upward now. Her chest felt

as if it were being crushed from the outside and exploding from inside all at the same time.

Hawker had her leg again, his hands gripping her calf.

She exhaled a small amount to let some of the pressure off and the bubbles raced upward . . . and then popped.

Hawker pulled and she slid backward a few feet.

"Let go," she said, barely getting the words out.

"No!"

"Please, let go." The words squeaked from her throat. She had no more air, she was close to blacking out, but she had realized something: Safety lay ahead and not behind.

She kicked him and kicked again, felt her foot slamming into his chest. She pulled free of his grasp, and then pushed upward to where she'd seen the bubbles burst. But before she could reach the spot, her eyes rolled and all she found was blackness.

Hawker fell backward through the water, one of Danielle's fins in his hand. He tossed it aside and tried to move forward, but his weight belt snagged on something. He broke it free but he could go no farther; his own lungs were screaming. He stretched his arms forward into the darkness, grabbing blindly for her.

Finding nothing, he pushed back out of the cave, grabbed Danielle's tanks, and snapped the regulator into place on his mask. He took deep, fast breaths and then swam back into the cave, pushing the tanks ahead of him. They jammed on something and he pulled them back and slammed them forward angrily, using them like a battering ram, breaking off large chunks of coral on both sides.

"Danielle!" he shouted into the radio. "Can you hear me?"

He took a deep breath, pulled the knife from its sheath on his leg, and cut the air hose. An explosion of bubbles burst forth and Hawker pushed the tanks forward, past the downslope and through to the far side. They settled to the bottom of the tunnel, bubbles flowing up toward the roof of the tunnel, where Danielle had disappeared.

He had no doubts as to Danielle's consciousness, but without her tanks, her vest gave her positive buoyancy. She would float upward, rolling over to be faceup like a person in a life vest and banging against the ceiling of the cave, however high above her it was.

Hawker couldn't hope to get to her quickly, and unconscious she couldn't attach her regulator, but if she was lucky, the air pouring from the ruptured hose would fill the highest point of the cave. It would create an air pocket that she could breathe in, granting her life until he could smash his way through the tunnel and reach her.

He found himself getting light-headed, backed out, and grabbed his own tanks again. Then he swam back and attacked the coral with his knife.

Large chunks broke away beneath his assault and soon he could fit through to the bottom of the tunnel where it bent upward again.

He swam down and found Danielle's tanks still venting gas from the ruptured hose.

He passed through them and swam upward, feeling around for Danielle in the darkness. He broke into the air pocket he'd created and frantically reached in all directions. His hands found the ceiling and the walls on every side.

It was impossible. Danielle wasn't there.

CHAPTER 31

The dockside agent for Gulf Boat Rental had his feet up, radio on, and the brim of his baseball hat tilted just enough to keep the sun out of his eyes. He heard the sound of people walking toward him on the wooden dock and looked up.

To his surprise he saw several Chinese men in slacks and dark shirts. They didn't look dressed for a fishing trip.

"*Hola,*" he said.

The largest of the three men pushed his way into the small booth. The rest of the group stood out in a defensive formation.

"You rented a boat earlier," the Chinese man said to him. "To some Americans."

"We rent out to many Americans," the agent replied.

"You'd remember these ones," he was told. "Two men, one white and one black. Plus a beautiful woman and a young boy who doesn't look like he belongs to them."

"Right." The agent nodded.

The questioner seemed surprised but pleased. He produced a wad of bills, handing a couple of twenties to the agent.

"Do you know if they had any weapons with them?"

"Maybe a speargun or two," the agent said.

"Where did they go?"

"Fishing for wahoo," he told them, repeating what the woman had said to him. "But they did have diving equipment with them."

This time a hundred came his way. He began to see how it worked.

"Do you have any way to track them?"

The agent shook his head. "I have only the deposit, in case they don't bring the boat back. But they only have enough fuel for about fifty miles. Where could they go? We would just call the other docks."

"Which direction?" The Chinese man said, clarifing his interest.

"Due north, once they left the harbor."

The Chinese man handed over one more note. "Give me what you have of theirs. And rent us two of your best boats to go find them."

The agent nodded and reached for the keys to the larger boats. They had pilothouses and inboard motors, designed to go for swordfish, and they were as fast as the boat the Americans had gone out in. Maybe faster.

CHAPTER 32

Hawker had surfaced in a dark void filled with the air from Danielle's tanks. He flipped up his mask and shouted.

"Danielle!"

Grabbing the wall, he steadied himself.

"Danielle!"

There was noise and reverberation from the venting tanks, like being in a hot tub gone out of control. But no sign of Danielle.

He found his LED flashlight and switched it on. The space was no more than five feet across and roughly circular. The ceiling above him was curved like the inside of a dome. He moved along the wall and found an opening.

It was like the rim of a pool. As he sloshed around, water spilled over the side and went sliding down a ramp of some type.

The inner chamber of the temple was dry.

In the dim light he saw a figure lying at the bottom. He clambered over the wall and slid down. Danielle lay on her side, coughing out water and finding her way back to consciousness.

She opened her eyes and looked at him. She was exhausted.

"What the hell is wrong with you?!" he shouted. The sound echoed around them. "Are you out of your mind?"

With great effort, she sat up. "Actually, I think I might be," she said finally.

"What are you talking about?"

"Nitrogen narcosis," she said. "Or more likely oxygen narcosis, since we're using a high-oxygen blend. I had it once before, but on a longer, deeper dive."

"You're the diver, the former marine biology student," he said.

"One of many degrees I started and then abandoned," she said. "But anyway I'm sorry. I didn't even realize what I was doing. I just felt like I could get in here. It was right in front of us."

She put a hand over her eyes, rubbing at her temples. "The problem with that type of narcosis is you don't feel it coming on. You just feel great. It's like the fourth stage of tequila, without all the drinking."

As angry as he was, Hawker had to laugh. "Bulletproof?"

"Invincible," she replied.

She had seemed to be acting a little crazy ever since they'd spotted the sharks. He looked up the ramp. "Do you even remember what happened?"

"I remember thinking I didn't want to get cut, and that I was afraid you'd get trapped, too," she said. "And then, when I was pulling away from you I exhaled and I saw the bubbles pop. It reminded me of a cave dive I was on a couple of years ago. I remembered the exhaust from my regulator getting trapped against the ceiling, creating a thousand little bubbles, perfectly round spheres like silver pearls. But when these bubbles popped, I realized they had to be reaching air. That's why I kicked you. I couldn't go back; I had to go forward."

She looked up the ramp.

"I grabbed this wall as I was blacking out. I guess I hauled myself over."

He sat down next to her and brushed the wet hair back from her face. "I know what oxygen narcosis is, but why would you get it?"

"It happens."

"On a dive this short, this shallow?"

He sensed there was something more, perhaps something she didn't want to tell him. He waited.

"I haven't been sleeping well," she said. "And they drugged me a lot in China. I don't know what it was—truth serum, narcotics, barbiturates maybe. They kept me sedated a lot. You said I was there ten days. I remember forty-eight hours."

"So the drugs are still in your system," he said.

"Some of it might be," she admitted. "I didn't think about it. Didn't want to, I guess. But I should have. Things like that can affect you when you dive, especially with nitrox."

"I'm glad you're okay," he said, aiming his flashlight around. "But where the hell did it get us to, anyway? Back down the rabbit hole somewhere?"

They were in the center of a temple of some kind, one that was sealed against the water. The tunnel, which angled down and then up, acted like an air lock. As long as the roof didn't leak, the water could never overcome the pressure of the air. It could never push inside.

Above them the ceiling of the room was curved and smooth like the dome of some rotunda. Seams between the blocks of stone were precise and almost invisible. No water dripped or leaked. It was an incredible work of construction.

The beam of Hawker's flashlight played across the smooth stone walls and stopped on what looked like a stairway covered with hieroglyphics. "McCarter would love this place."

"If he could get over the sharks," she said.

"I almost didn't get over the sharks." Hawker told her. His light followed the flight of the stairs. Lying prone on an altar at the top was a familiar shape. It looked like a sarcophagus of some kind.

"Can you stand?" Hawker asked

She reached out a hand and he pulled her up. Together they crossed the open floor and began climbing the stairs.

Up on the surface, McCarter sat in the fishing boat. Strangely, his feelings of paranoia had returned at almost the instant Danielle and Hawker had descended beneath the waves.

He found himself checking the GPS every thirty seconds to make sure the wind and the current hadn't moved him and then scanning the horizon with a pair of binoculars, fearful that there might be some miscreants coming toward their position. He hadn't seen anything so far but that didn't mean it wasn't happening.

In addition he had to watch Yuri, and he found his nerves jumping anytime the boy moved away from the very center of the boat. As a precaution he'd tightened all the straps on Yuri's life jacket and secured a second flotation device to his back.

"Think they'd be mad if they came back up and I had you tied to something?"

Yuri ignored him and McCarter had to laugh at himself.

"I used to be the normal one," he told Yuri. "Now look at me. I'm seeing things. Hearing things." He glanced over to Yuri, who was ignoring him and playing with the sunglasses again. "Talking to a child who finds plastic sunglasses more interesting than my learned conversation."

He raised the binoculars to his eyes once again and looked out over the calm gulf waters. It was midafternoon and the sun was blazing from a cobalt blue sky. To the east, some large cumulous clouds had begun to grow. They were a long distance out, but seemed to be moving his way. The last thing he wanted was to be on the water in some kind of storm.

"Come on," he whispered to his absent comrades. "Let's not take all day."

A slight breeze blew up, wafting audibly past his ears.

Why aren't you paying attention today?

He spun around, looking for the source of those words. No one there, of course.

Why aren't you paying attention today?

They were his wife's words. Said kindly, on the days when he was distracted by some problem and not listening to her.

He looked at Yuri. The boy was staring back at him as if he'd heard something, too.

"I'm not even going to ask," McCarter said.

Another sound caught his ear, a distant rumble of thunder to the east. The storm clouds were still many miles out but they stretched off to the south. He followed the line with the binoculars, wondering if they would cause a problem getting back to shore. And then he caught sight of something new: Two fast-looking boats were cutting across the sea toward them. They were probably five or six miles off, but hauling ass directly at his position.

"Shit," McCarter said, pulling the binoculars down.

He glanced at Yuri. "Let's not make those your first English words."

The boy did not react, and McCarter turned his attention back to the boats, hoping to see a pyramid of water skiers behind them.

He didn't. And though the boats could have been anything, he had a terrible suspicion as to what they were and who they were interested in.

He grabbed Yuri, strapped him into the passenger chair, and then started the engines.

Hawker and Danielle reached the top of the stairs. The body lay there in a sarcophagus of some type, wrapped in simple gauze. The setup was nothing elaborate, just simple wood, with carved notches on the sides, like handles for pallbearers.

Danielle peeled the strips of fabric back. The skull was human, barely. Its smooth bone was covered in tiny pores. A filament of wire ran from the empty eye sockets back into the brain cavity. The deformed ribs, the overlarge eyes, all the same defects they had seen on the body in Brazil. Another descendant of man, who'd died several thousand years before he or she would be born.

She looked at Hawker. There was only silence. Respect.

He aimed his light past the body. In the alcove beyond loomed a statue of a Mayan king in full ceremonial dress. It reminded Danielle of the monument taken from the Island of the Shroud, but its arrangement was different. Here the king was holding out his hands the way one might cup falling water. In those hands and protruding into his chest lay a smooth, glasslike object. The stone looked to be the same construction as the one they'd found in Brazil, but it was a different shape and smaller. About the equivalent of a large grapefruit.

Danielle reached over and switched off Hawker's flashlight. As their eyes adjusted they could see a ghostly white glow coming from the stone.

Hawker walked toward it and reached for it.

"Don't," she snapped.

He pulled his hand back, staring at her.

"Just give me a second," she said, looking around as if there might be a booby trap or two waiting to be sprung on them.

Trying to ignore the concern in his eyes, she stepped toward the stone and pulled it free. It was heavy in her hands, incredibly smooth and warm to the touch. It brought a tingling sensation in her fingers, a wave of energy coursing through her body. She felt a type of elation holding it.

"You all right?" Hawker asked.

His voice brought her back to the present.

"Yeah," she said. "I just can't believe we actually found it."

Carefully she secured it in a pouch, which she zipped shut and clipped to her belt. Following that, she pulled out what looked like an old film camera and began taking pictures.

"Is this part of our retro look?" Hawker said, noting the old-fashioned snap-and-click camera. "To go with the jeep and the boat?"

"Remember how all our electronic equipment went down in Brazil?"

He nodded.

"I figured we'd better have something that wouldn't be affected."

She advanced the film with her thumb, asked Hawker to direct his light onto the surface she was shooting, then clicked off the next shot. She took pictures of the statue, the stairwell, and the hieroglyphics there. She took pictures of the ceiling and the walls and the fading murals they contained. She aimed her camera at the body on the altar and then lowered it without snapping the shutter.

Hawker seemed to agree. "Let the poor fellow be," he suggested.

She finished up and put the camera away. When she was done she thought of destroying the carvings as she and McCarter had done at the Island of the Shroud, but there were no loose stones around and they carried no hammers or other heavy tools. Even the knives, which had been useful against the brittle coral, would be ineffective against the heavy stone of the temple.

She let it go. They didn't have much time anyway. They still had to get back out and up to the surface within twenty minutes or they'd need a decompression stop, something she didn't want to do in a shark-infested area.

While she put the camera away, Hawker dove back into the tunnel and retrieved both sets of air tanks. As he swam back in, he perched on the top of the ramp, as if he were sitting on the side of the pool. She climbed up beside him, her eyes settling on the air tank with the split hose.

"Those are yours," Hawker said.

"You really are hard on equipment," she said.

"I was trying to save you at the time," he said.

There wasn't much she could say to counter that. She crouched down and checked the pressure gauge. The tank's reserve air feature had activated. Designed to keep all the air from being expended in the event of an accident, it closed an inner valve and reserved a small portion of the mixture to be used only if the diver manually switched to reserve. She disconnected the hose that Hawker had cut and turned the valve so the reserve air would only feed to the spare hose.

"I should have about fifteen minutes on this," she said. "That ought to be plenty."

"If not, we can buddy-breathe on this tank," he replied. "But let's not waste any more time down here."

She agreed and slipped over the rim and back into the tunnel.

Just as Hawker had done on the way in, she pushed

the tanks ahead of her. In a few seconds she'd made it through and back out in the open sea, thrilled beyond belief to be bathed in the clear blue light once again.

The brief second of euphoria died as her earpiece cackled. Her transceiver had picked up a call from McCarter, one that had been blocked during their time in the temple.

". . . coming toward us from the southwest. Do you hear me? Two boats headed right for us at high speed."

CHAPTER 33

Danielle had her tanks secured by the time Hawker exited the cave. By the haste of his actions, he'd heard the call, too, and was rapidly strapping his own harness back into place. He pulled it onto his shoulders and they dove for the DPVs they'd left at the entrance to the tunnel.

She grabbed hers by the handle and twisted it to full throttle. The propeller spun and Danielle kicked with her feet to assist the acceleration. In seconds she was cruising as fast as she could possibly move, with Hawker only a few yards behind her.

Together they raced away from the sunken temple, climbing gradually as they did. Fortunately, they hadn't been down deep enough or long enough to require a true decompression stop, but rocketing to the surface was never a good idea.

They would ascend at a constant angle, giving their bodies time to reabsorb any dissolved nitrogen, and when they spotted McCarter in a minute or two they would drop the scooters and surface.

Suddenly Hawker yelled, "Look out!"

At Hawker's shout she turned her head. A shadow flashed over, one of the hammerheads buzzing them. A second one followed, brushing her and twisting violently to the right as it passed. It raced into the distance and disappeared, but others were streaming their way, rocketing toward them like underwater missiles.

On the surface, McCarter couldn't take his eyes off the boats flying toward them.

He grabbed the transmitter. "If you guys can hear me, you need to hurry. They're only two miles away at most."

If he wanted to be safe he would have to go to full throttle soon and start heading west. That was the plan, go west, call the Mexican coast guard, and hope a few helicopters were enough to scare off whoever was attacking them.

It seemed the prudent thing to do, but McCarter couldn't stand the thought of leaving his friends behind. He bumped the throttle down, wheeled the boat around until it pointed back toward the dive zone, and then grabbed the transmitter once more.

"I'm a half mile north of where we dropped you," he said. "I'll wait as long as I can."

Suddenly Yuri dropped the sunglasses, stood up, and began staring trancelike at the water ahead of them.

Danielle turned to the left, angling down to get away from the oncoming sharks, but even with the propulsion of the DPV and her own legs kicking, the sharks were moving at three or four times her speed.

A few of the smaller ones zipped past her; another dive-bombed her from above, slamming her shoulder. She looked for Hawker. He was coming her way, his own DPV running full throttle, but the sharks were basically ignoring him. For a moment it actually pissed her off, until she realized why.

The hammerheads, the circling honor guard of the sunken temple, were homing in on the object that had drawn them there in the first place: the power-emitting stone now secured in Danielle's pack.

None of them had tried to bite her, at least not yet. In fact they seemed almost oblivious to her presence, as stunned and surprised by the sudden impacts as she was. But they were unable to resist the sensory overload in the magnetic detectors in their brains and they continued to come on in waves.

She twisted to escape another hit but there were too many sharks to avoid. It soon became a blur, like being caught in a stampeding crowd. Her world spun: the gray tops of the sharks, the white of their underbellies, bubbles from her regulator exploding around her.

A glancing blow on one leg was followed by a thud on her right arm and then a shot to the ribs that bent her body and whiplashed her neck.

"Hang on!" Hawker shouted.

"They're after the stone," she managed to say.

In the next moment a large group of the juveniles hit, spinning her around and leaving her disoriented.

She saw a larger one rocketing in. She dodged the hit, but the shark crashed into the DPV, ripping it from her hands and sending the yellow device spiraling toward the bottom.

She righted herself, saw a flash of the surface above, and kicked toward it but something grabbed her. She turned to see Hawker; with an arm around her waist he pulled her close. She reached for a handhold on the DPV just as the acceleration from the propulsion unit kicked in.

Another group of sharks came racing their way. She hardened her body against the impact, but two more followed, and a third on its own.

They broke the surface and Danielle spun around. McCarter was racing toward them in the boat. Thank God he was close. He slowed and turned beside them.

She grabbed the ladder, pulling herself up as Hawker pushed her from behind.

Tumbling into the boat, she whipped around, stretching a hand toward Hawker.

He clutched at it, just as a gray-green shape split the surface, rammed him like a torpedo, and dragged him away.

She felt his hand ripped from hers.

"Follow him!" she shouted to McCarter.

McCarter punched the throttles and spun the wheel and Danielle grabbed for the speargun.

Flying through the water, pushed by the big shark, Hawker felt as if he'd been hit by a train. His mask was torn off and the DPV wrenched out of his hands as he was pulled by forces he could not overcome or even influence.

He twisted and wrenched his body to try to free himself but the animal's flat, angular head had wedged itself between his tanks and his back.

And then suddenly he flipped over and slowed. The shark had torn itself free after dragging him two hundred feet or so.

Kicking upward, Hawker burst through the surface, gulping the air and looking around for the boat. He spotted it circling toward him.

He guessed, and hoped, that the sharks would leave him alone now, as they had before he'd teamed up with Danielle. But as he caught his breath and began to tread water, he saw a line of color dripping down the edge of his nose. He touched his forehead and his hand came away red with blood.

Instant panic hit him. He shed his tanks and began kicking hard for the oncoming boat, trying desperately to keep his face above the water.

On the boat, Danielle saw him. She saw the blood and a pair of dorsal fins slicing through the surface right at him.

She threw out the cargo net. "Hurry!" she yelled to McCarter.

They sped toward him. Hawker grabbed the net. Danielle pulled with all her might, leaning back and throwing her weight into it.

Hawker rolled and tumbled into the boat as one of the hammerheads launched itself, arching its back, half its body out of the water.

It landed on the cutaway, tipping the small craft, almost swamping it.

The front third of the shark was inside the vessel. The head whipped around, jaws snapping for anything it could grab. Yuri screamed, Hawker kicked it, and Danielle grabbed for the speargun again.

And then it flipped back into the water and disappeared in a tremendous splash.

"Go!" she shouted.

McCarter punched the throttles and the V-hulled fishing boat leaped forward like a stallion launching itself from the gate.

Danielle locked the cutaway back into place as other sharks whipped by. They followed briefly before falling behind the speeding boat. All she could think of was Petrov's story of being followed by sharks and killer whales. She thanked God that she'd rented the fastest boat available.

Suddenly she felt Yuri at her side. "This siren," he said, grabbing for the stone. "This siren."

She tried to calm him and then opened the equipment locker and pulled out a lead-lined box they'd had specially made. She placed the stone into the box, sealed it shut, then slipped the box into her backpack. Beside her, Yuri stared.

"Siren," he said quietly. "Siren." As Danielle placed her pack inside the locker and latched it shut, he sat next to it and stared as if it were a television.

Danielle stroked his hair and looked out in front of them. A mile off, the boats McCarter had seen were splitting up, one continuing toward them, the other heading directly west to cut them off.

Perhaps the hard part was not over.

CHAPTER 34

The convoy of vehicles rumbled down a weathered strip of road in the high desert of western Nevada. A camouflaged eighteen-wheeler held the center position, flanked by an escort of machine-gun-toting Humvees and a pair of missile-armed Black Hawk helicopters two hundred feet above.

Fifty miles more and they'd arrive at Yucca Mountain and the erstwhile nuclear depository that had been in limbo for the better part of three decades.

The place had originally been designed to store nuclear waste, with the plan that it would accept the growing stockpiles of spent radioactive fuel from all across the nation. But the environmentalists had attacked and overwhelmed the process almost from day one. Years of litigation, impact studies, and changing political winds had left Yucca Mountain empty. As a result the vast majority of the country's radioactive materials remained right where they were: at 107 different reactor sites, most of which were only lightly guarded and just miles from the nation's largest population centers. Apparently, to those who fought against the project, that was a safer alternative.

Such efforts had left Yucca Mountain sitting empty and thus usable for the NRI. And so Moore's team had removed the Brazil stone from its vault beneath the Virginia Industrial Complex and loaded it onto a military C-17. After a four-hour flight they touched down in Nevada and then continued overland toward Yucca Mountain.

The journey had been planned with meticulous precision, designed to bring the stone out of hiding during the lowest phase of its power surge, when it was all but dormant, and get it back into hiding before the wave began to grow once again. So far, the transit had gone off without a hitch. As things looked, they would be deep in the mountain bunker at least seven hours before the next burst.

Riding in the cab of the semitruck, Arnold Moore listened as one of the Black Hawks thundered overhead, moving forward to take point in the formation. He found himself amused at the overkill of their protection force.

The convoy was firmly in the heart of military controlled property, traveling an unnamed road that cut through the center of the Nellis Bombing Range. To attack them, someone would have to cross a hundred miles of open desert and then breach the most heavily guarded military base in the continental United States. Missile-armed helicopters and F-22 Raptors patrolled the skies. Cameras and infrared sensors monitored every square inch of the perimeter and, even before Moore and his cargo had arrived, the military guards had standing authority to shoot any intruders on sight. The reason was simple: This section of desert was also home to Groom Lake, a top-secret test flight center where the Stealth bomber and other exotic aircraft had been developed. And if that wasn't enough, the land surrounding them was the infamous Area 51.

Moore glanced through the window. He saw a barren landscape, pockmarked with bomb craters, test sites, and ugly mountains of piled-up dirt. A thousand different types of explosive had been tested here, from cluster bombs to "daisy cutters." Even nuclear warheads had been exploded here.

The scars remained on the dry desert surface without even a hint of life to soften them. Not a blade of grass, nor a cactus, nor the smallest desert scrub could be seen. It looked like the moon or another planet. Perhaps that was why the UFO junkies were so certain that aliens had been brought here; they just might have felt at home.

The door to the trailer opened and one of the research scientists poked his head through.

"We have a problem, sir."

Moore's heart froze. "What's wrong?"

"We've got an unexpected rise in the energy wave," the scientist told him. "And it's growing rapidly."

Out on the Gulf of Mexico, Danielle studied the two boats charging toward them.

"They're trying to corral us," McCarter said.

"I told you we should have brought some missiles," Hawker said.

"Next time I will," she promised, only half joking.

Danielle watched as the gap between the two pursuing

vessels widened and she thought she saw an opportunity. She nudged McCarter from the driver's seat and reduced the throttles slightly and a moment later reduced them further. The other vessels rapidly closed the range.

A moment later, she chopped the throttles once again, whipped the boat through a quick ninety-degree turn, and then gunned the engines.

With the throttle to the firewall they charged for the gap.

As they raced across the water, Danielle held the boat's throttles to full, ducking down as the air and spray whipped across the deck. She was gunning for the space between the two boats that had come out after them, something the drivers of those boats must have realized as they now raced to pinch it shut.

Her eyes flicked back and forth between the two boats. It would be close.

Behind her Hawker spoke to McCarter. "Might want to get down," he said, as he gently forced Yuri to the deck. McCarter followed suit and Danielle hunkered down as far as she could while still being able to see and drive.

The boats were racing toward one another at a combined speed of seventy to eighty knots.

Seconds apart, Danielle dropped down, still holding the wheel.

She cut between them. As the pursuing boats crossed behind her, a spread of bullets whistled overhead, not aimed at her but at the squared-off shape of the outboard engines.

It was an impossible shot, taken from a pitching deck with only an instant to aim. A thousand to one, Danielle thought. She listened to the sound of the engines, felt the vibration, and glanced back at them. The odds had held. They'd come through unharmed.

She glanced behind them. One boat had been forced out to the north and the other craft had altered course and was now turning to follow.

From here it would be a race to the shore, one she wasn't entirely sure they could win.

Out in the desert wastes of Nevada, Arnold Moore stared into the panic-filled eyes of the scientist. "What the hell are you talking about?" he asked.

"A major energy spike," his man said.

Moore tried to stand and found himself held back by the seat belt.

"That's not possible," he said, releasing the belt and realizing that he had no idea what was or was not possible in regard to the stone.

He pushed into the back of the truck. There, in a makeshift version of the Virginia lab, two of his staffers were monitoring the glowing stone. Moore looked at the readout on the computer screen. The energy output had clearly spiked, quadruple its normal passive state and growing.

"When did this start?"

"Five minutes ago," the scientist told him. "First we noticed a change in the energy distribution pattern: more high-energy and less background readings. And then the countdown signal changed, becoming rapidly more complex and increasingly random."

"Meaning what?" Moore asked, sensing that the man was hiding some conclusion he'd already reached.

"I don't know," his staffer said. "Something has changed and the signal is in a jumbled state now. As if it's gone haywire and is trying to restore its order."

Moore ran a hand through his gray hair. He glanced at the power curve. It was spiking up in an accelerating fashion, the way it normally did just prior to a discharge, but the benchmark levels were almost off the chart.

The computer attached to it began flashing a warning and chirping loudly as threshold levels continued to grow. The screen itself began to blur and bend as if it were being degaussed. The radios around them and in the truck's cab began to squeal with feedback and static.

Moore shouted to the driver. "Are there any bunkers around here?"

The air force sergeant driving the truck seemed confused. "Mr. Moore?"

"Anywhere to hide this thing?"

"No," the driver said. "It's all open road."

Hawker held Yuri tight, covering him and lying almost flat on the deck. Danielle continued to pilot the flying craft, whipping the boat to the right and then curving back to the left, doing all she could to present a hard target to the people chasing them.

As far as Hawker could tell, the boats were evenly matched in terms of speed, but every twist and turn cut into the distance between them. The pursuing boats were only fifty yards behind now, fanning out and taking potshots at them.

They'd done well so far. And in five minutes they'd reach the harbor. Hawker hoped the area would be public enough to keep their pursuers at bay. But he wasn't sure they'd even get there. One hit on either outboard and they'd be finished.

A rifle shot hit the deck a few feet behind him and he heard another zip overhead.

Danielle ducked. "Now would be a good time to do something!" she shouted.

Even as she spoke, Yuri began to mumble something unintelligible and squirm out of Hawker's grasp. The kid stretched out a hand toward the locker, his eyes wide as if he'd just discovered something new.

"Two," he said suddenly, then looked at Hawker. "Two."

Hawker beckoned McCarter, who crawled toward him.

"Is he all right?"

"I don't know," Hawker said. "Hold on to him."

As McCarter grabbed Yuri, Hawker scrambled to the rear of the boat. He dug into the space beneath the seats and pulled out the anchor. They were coming up fast on the shoreline, but if they were going to make it they would need help.

"Hold us steady!" he shouted, sawing through the rope with his knife.

The boat leveled and ran straight and true for a moment. As it did, Hawker swung the thirty-pound anchor like a bolo and flung it into the air.

The anchor and a short section of attached rope

trailed out toward their pursuers, but splashed down well short of the target.

"You're going to have to throw harder than that," Danielle shouted.

"Thanks," he said. "I kind of realized that."

Next he flung out one of the oars, which landed in front of the lead boat, only to be cut in half by the flying keel.

The men on the boats answered with another spread of bullets, and Danielle cut sharply to the right as tracers ripped into the sea all around them. Hawker ducked and spotted a flare gun.

That gave Hawker another idea. He strapped a buoy to one of the spare diving tanks. "One more time!" he shouted.

The turn eased and the wake stretched out behind them in a streaming line. Hawker opened the valves and pushed the tanks overboard. They splashed down and submerged, but the bubbles and the buoy were enough for him to see it by.

He waited.

He fired off a flare.

The crimson charge raced toward the bubbles of venting gas and a wave of flame exploded out of it as the 40 percent oxygen mix ignited.

The lead boat swerved too late and the explosion sent it airborne for just a foot or so. It landed slightly out of alignment, hitting the water and tumbling like a stock car that had blown a tire at Daytona. Debris flew off it in all directions and it came to rest right side up but swamped and still.

"Great shot!" McCarter shouted.

Hawker hoped the men in the second boat would stop to help their comrades. But they swerved around the ruined craft and continued the chase.

And this time when they'd closed in sufficiently, the men on the foredeck opened fire without holding back. Bullets and tracers began ripping into their boat.

Hawker dove to the deck as Danielle guided the speeding boat around the breakwater into the harbor, swerving around anchored sailboats and other craft. Behind him Yuri began to scream. He twisted free of McCarter's grasp and lunged for the locker that held the stone. "Two!" he yelled, banging his hands on the locker. "Two! Two! Two!"

Arnold Moore shouted to be heard over the radios as they emitted a high-pitched shriek that he could hardly take.

"Get the helicopters down!"

"Why?"

"Get them on the ground now!"

The master sergeant grabbed the radio and tried to relay Moore's order, yelling to be heard over the feedback and the static. The computers in the back of the truck began to overload. Sparks blasted from the vents of one and an oscilloscope attached to the setup exploded.

"Close it up!" Moore yelled to his men, reaching for the heavy lead hatch on the box containing the stone. "Close it up!"

The radios in the cab wailed and then blew out one after another. The remaining computer shorted. Moore and his scientist raised the heavy lid and began to slam it down but a flash of blinding light came from the stone and a shock wave blasted through the truck and out across the open desert.

"Two, two, two!" Yuri was shouting, and then his eyes went wide. "One."

A blast ripped through the boat.

Hawker was almost flung overboard and Danielle was knocked forward, tumbling over the driver's panel and hitting the deck. The engines behind them exploded. Sparks shot from the depth finder and radio transmitter.

Hawker had no idea what had happened. It was like he'd been hit by a pane of glass. His breath was gone, his head ringing. He saw McCarter bent over Yuri, trying to help him. Up ahead Danielle was crawling back to the wheel.

He looked behind. Their own outboards were belching black smoke and the boat that had been chasing them was going off course, flames licking out of its engine compartment. Several of the vessels in the harbor were having similar problems.

Danielle grabbed the wheel and guided them up onto the beach with the momentum they maintained. The boat skidded to a stop.

"What the hell was that?" she asked.

"I don't know," Hawker said.

He turned to McCarter, who was holding Yuri as one might hold a sleeping child, cradling his neck and head. He pulled his right hand away; it was soaked with blood, pouring from Yuri's ear.

"Oh my God," Danielle said.

"Let's get the hell out of here," Hawker said. "I'll carry him."

Hawker took Yuri from McCarter as Danielle pulled the equipment bag with the new stone out of the locker and then hopped over the side of the boat.

She helped McCarter hobble up the beach. As Hawker carried Yuri, a thought flashed through his mind: *They'd found the second stone and recovered it, but at what cost?*

CHAPTER 35

Danielle burst through the doors to the emergency room. Hawker came behind her carrying Yuri in his arms.

"We need a doctor!" Hawker shouted.

"Necesitamos un médico," Danielle repeated in Spanish.

She looked around. The room was dark, lit only by the sunlight coming through tinted windows and by a pair of emergency lights in each corner.

"No power," she said.

The drive to the hospital had been panicked madness. The traffic lights were out, cars stalled in various places. To get them here Danielle had driven on the median and down the sidewalk at one point. But the power loss had preceded them. As had a large number of prospective patients.

Like most ERs in America, this one was overcrowded and understaffed. There were already more patients in the waiting room than the unit could accommodate quickly.

Priority went to those most in need: heart attack victims, those with life-threatening wounds or conditions.

For patients who were fortunate enough to have minor traumas and lesser conditions, the wait could be hours.

Danielle was certain that Yuri did not have that kind of time.

A nurse glanced at them from across the room, focused on Yuri's limp form. A second later she was rushing over, stethoscope in hand.

"Do you speak English?" Danielle asked.

The nurse nodded. "What's happened to this child," she asked, putting the stethoscope to his chest.

"He had a seizure," Danielle replied.

The nurse checked the blood oozing from Yuri's ear, then lifted one of his eyelids and flashed a light into it. The concern on her face deepened.

"He's nonresponsive, barely breathing," she said. "This way."

She led them down a darkened hall to a curtained-off room lit by the emergency power. It was clean but the equipment was older. Danielle wondered if they would have what Yuri needed.

"We should have taken him to the States," she said aloud.

"I assure you we have good doctors here," the nurse said.

Danielle nodded. She hadn't meant to disparage the health care they were likely to get at this place. She hadn't even meant the statement to refer to now; she'd meant after Hong Kong, instead of coming to Mexico.

"It'll be all right," Hawker said, laying Yuri down on the examination table.

"How?"

"I don't know. But it will."

The nurse ducked out and a few seconds later a doctor came in. "I'm Dr. Vasquez," she said, going right to the examination table without looking at either Danielle or Hawker.

"This child had a seizure?" she asked.

"That's right," Danielle replied.

Dr. Vasquez moved to the other side of the table, checking Yuri's pulse and blood pressure.

"When?"

"Twenty minutes ago."

The doctor looked up. "When the blackout hit?" she asked. "What was he doing at the time?"

Danielle paused, her mind searching.

"Was he watching TV? Or in a room without natural light?"

The question made sense to her now. Seizures could be caused by many different stimuli; one common cause was flickering light, like that of a television or computer screen cycling or on the fritz.

"No," Danielle said. "We were outside, on the water."

Dr. Vasquez stared at her and then looked over at Hawker. "Near Puerto Azul?"

Danielle didn't reply. She guessed that news of the strange incident there had reached the hospital despite the blackout. Boats racing into a sleepy harbor, explosions that caused blackouts, and a group of people beaching their craft and racing on foot while carrying an injured child were not likely to go unnoticed.

Danielle stared into the doctor's eyes. "Look, I have two years of medical training, and I saw this child have a seizure. Now he's unconscious, bleeding from his ear, with possible bleeding inside his skull. He needs an MRI or a CT scan or whatever you have available to make sure his brain is not swelling."

Dr. Vasquez began to look uncomfortable.

"You're not his parents," she said.

At that moment, a tall, broad-shouldered orderly stepped through the curtain, closing it behind him. He seemed to notice the tension and looked at Dr. Vasquez.

"Ricardo—" she began to say as she reached for an alarm button.

Danielle was on her, a hand going over her mouth and slamming her into the wall. Ricardo lunged for Danielle, but Hawker was quicker. He slammed the orderly against the opposite wall, producing a black handgun and holding it to the man's head.

The doctor looked at her, eyes filled with utter fright.

Danielle hated what she saw.

"Listen to me," she said, quietly but with great intensity, her eyes boring into the doctor, willing her to understand. "I promise you," she said. "*I promise you.* We are not here to hurt you, or your staff, or this child."

She took a deep breath. Dr. Vasquez took a breath. Hawker pulled the gun away but held it at the ready.

The doctor turned her eyes back toward Danielle.

"I'm not his mother, nor am I some deranged person who's kidnapped him and thinks he's my son. He's not. But he's been through hell and there are people looking for him who'd like to drag him back there. And I am not going to let that happen."

Danielle noticed a softening in the doctor's eyes and

saw her steal a glance toward Yuri. She relaxed the pressure on the doctor's mouth so she could speak, but held her hand close should Dr. Vasquez try to scream.

"Who are you people?" the doctor asked.

"We're members of an American security service," Danielle said.

"You have no authority here," Dr. Vasquez said bluntly.

"No, we don't. But our superiors are in touch with important members of your government." Danielle had no choice but to lie. "People who both know of and have approved of our presence. I don't have the time or the ability to contact them now. So please, just help us. Then we'll go."

Dr. Vasquez seemed torn. She looked at Yuri again. How could she not help? "We can do an MRI," she said. "And after that you leave."

Danielle nodded, thinking she would promise anything to get Yuri the examination he needed.

Professor McCarter sat in a public plaza, hiding among a crowd of people and the chaos of a traffic jam caused by the midafternoon blackout.

He tried to concentrate on the surroundings, looking for any sign of trouble, struggling against the flight reflex building within him.

In his backpack he carried the newly found stone, an object that had just discharged a massive burst of electromagnetic energy, an object that at least two groups of armed men were looking for and willing to kill over. As uneasy as he felt carrying it around undefended, both he and Danielle realized it would be unconscionable to bring it into the hospital, where it could interfere with countless tests and devices, not the least of which were the items needed to examine Yuri.

Across from him a fountain rose in concrete and stucco. Hundreds of people milled around, many of them out on the street and in the park because of the blackout. In an open area a group of teenagers was playing soccer. Near the borders of their makeshift field stood a group of uniformed *federales*. They walked through the mass of people looking like predators among a herd of prey.

Logic told him they were there for crowd control, to make sure an afternoon blackout didn't turn into something worse. But despite his well-founded logic, he couldn't shake the thought that they were specifically looking for him. Coming to find him and to take the stone.

Danielle stood with Dr. Vasquez in the control room studying the MRI. It showed a cross section of Yuri's brain, highlighted in red, orange, and pink. One section was blue and it was blurred.

"What is that?" she asked.

The doctor adjusted the controls and had the machine run another scan. The beltlike apparatus that Yuri laid on moved him back into the tube of the massive machine and a series of loud clunking noises were heard as the machine took another picture of Yuri's brain.

This one was slightly better, but still blurred around the blue section.

"Could something be wrong with the imager?" Danielle asked.

Dr. Vasquez shook her head. "I don't think so," she said. "I changed the angle of the scan slightly, just to be sure." She pointed to the blurred area. "If it were the machine, the blurred area would have appeared to move. It didn't. It's in a different place on the image, the same spot in the child's brain."

"What is it?" Danielle asked.

"You said someone was doing experiments on him?"

"To the best of my knowledge that's true."

Dr. Vasquez nodded sadly. "In that case I would guess that we're looking at the remnants of one of those experiments," she said. "That is an object, a powered object, inserted into his cerebral cortex."

"A powered object?"

"It's emitting its own electromagnetic wave," Dr. Vasquez said. "Minor, to be sure, but that's the blue distortion."

Danielle felt sick to her stomach. And then she heard a sound that made it worse. Yuri had woken up and had begun to scream.

McCarter moved toward the outskirts of the park. He had stopped at the table of a street vendor and pretended to examine some of his offerings. He glanced back toward the group of policemen.

They're coming for the stone.

Were they his thoughts or a voice?

Run. It was an urging, not a physical sound. *Run!*

McCarter couldn't help it. He dropped the trinket from his hand and ran for the street.

Yuri had awoken screaming but had calmed down as soon as the MRI machine was shut down. He clung to Danielle as Dr. Vasquez did a number of other tests.

"There's no sign of swelling to his brain," she said. "His neurological responses are good."

Thank God, Danielle thought.

"What about the blood from his ear?"

"It looks as if he had a cyst inside his ear canal that ruptured during the seizure," she said. "But he can hear okay. So, no damage."

The doctor smiled. "He's a lucky child," she said, then seemed to realize better. "In some ways."

Danielle stood, holding Yuri protectively.

"What will you do with him now?" Dr. Vasquez asked.

"Try to get him to somewhere safe, where he can receive help," she said.

"You could leave him with us," she said. "I'll make sure he's cared for."

Danielle hesitated. There was an undeniable attraction to the idea. Let Yuri disappear, no Kang, no Russia. No more problems for him. But she couldn't be sure it would turn out that way.

She shook her head. "There are people looking for him, people you won't be able to protect him from. If they found you, they would kill you and anyone who stood in their way."

"Why?"

"It's a long story," Danielle said. "When we leave, you should call the police. In case these men come here."

The doctor nodded, looking nervous. She glanced at Hawker still holding the gun. "I'll give you five minutes before I call. Don't come back."

Danielle turned and left the room carrying Yuri. Hawker followed a second later.

"Should I call security?" Ricardo asked.

"No," Dr. Vasquez replied.

"You're going to let them go?"

She nodded. "I think it's best," she said. "If they are who they say they are, then there is no need getting mixed up in the situation."

"And if they're not?"

"Better they be far from here when the police find them," she said.

Ricardo nodded reluctantly and then looked past her to a small device beside the door. A bright green LED was flashing rapidly.

"Was the intrusion in the child's head radioactive?" he asked.

"I don't think so," Dr.Vasquez said. "Why?"

He pointed to the LED. "The waste alarm. One of them has been exposed to radioactive materials."

McCarter tried to run in a controlled fashion, but he knew it must have looked bad. His leg was hurting and his mind was spinning, and he reckoned his pace was that of a man in a three-legged race, even if he was tied to no one but himself.

He continued across the street, thinking he had to get

away, away from the police, away from whoever was chasing him, away from Hawker and Danielle.

The last thought hit him hard. Why had he thought that? They were his friends; they were protecting him. Was his subconscious mind trying to tell him something?

He saw a bus stop in front of the hospital and a city bus coming down the crowded street. He ran over and got in line. The bus slowed, releasing a great blast of air from its brakes.

"Professor?"

He turned to see Danielle and Hawker coming out of the hospital. Yuri was walking with them. He was thankful for that.

"What are you doing?" Danielle asked suspiciously.

His mind raced. "Ahh, I'm hiding," he said. "Trying to look inconspicuous."

He gestured at the police, both in the park and on the street corner.

"The police aren't after us," Danielle noted.

"Can't be too sure," he said defensively.

Danielle looked at Hawker, then nodded toward the bus. "What do you think?"

"Time to let the old jeep go," he said, agreeing.

"We're getting on?" McCarter asked, surprised.

"Yeah," Danielle said. "Let's go."

CHAPTER 36

Arnold Moore sat in the permanent darkness of the Yucca Mountain tunnel holding a cold compress to his temple while technicians buzzed around him, connecting cables and moving equipment, turning a double-wide trailer into their new laboratory.

He watched them work, fighting the urge to throw up as he had every ten to fifteen minutes since the incident and listening to Byron Stecker bitch so extensively that he'd actually begun looking forward to the next episode of vomiting.

With the first of the lab's flat-screen monitors now operating, a review of the energy discharge event had been arranged, but there wasn't much to see.

Moore stared at the screen. The playback, which was now frozen, had been paused with a line of distortion running through the left side of the frame.

It showed the pockmarked desert floor, the smoking eighteen-wheeler, and the Humvees scattered about randomly. It also took in the two Black Hawk helicopters that had crash-landed on separate sections of the route. One seemed to have come down almost normally, but the other was smoking and crumbled over on one side, its rotor blades in dark pieces all around, shattered like old LP records.

In the freeze-frame image, the shape of a man could be seen jumping from the burning hulk.

Byron Stecker, who had been waiting at Yucca for Moore to arrive, spoke. "We have no video depicting the actual event. Nothing prior to this. Despite the fact that there are cameras all over the base—including cameras designed to catch nuclear blasts—all the data feeds are blank from a moment four minutes and nineteen seconds prior to the blast until this point approximately one minute and thirty seconds after.

"But we have one eyewitness describing it as a shock wave rolling across the desert floor, a nuclear blast with everything but the mushroom cloud."

Moore stared at the display. He'd been unconscious until several minutes later.

"At least fifteen commercial airliners were affected," Stecker said, "including nine that lost complete electrical power and had to make emergency landings. Nellis radar and communications went down and we have extensive grid failures all along the West Coast. Vegas, Henderson, and Tahoe are completely blacked out."

Moore tried to ignore it.

"And worst of all," Stecker added, "both the Russians and Chinese are accusing us of breaking the test ban treaty or of creating some new superweapon. The UN is even convening a Security Council meeting on it the day after tomorrow. And it's the damned weekend."

Moore rubbed his head. The interest of the foreign powers certainly complicated things.

"What's your point?" he asked, too exhausted to wait for the DCI to get around to it.

"I've been telling you," Stecker said, annoyed. "This thing is dangerous."

"Anything that has power can be dangerous," Moore said. "A car, a gun, a bomb. Even you. The question is how you use these things and negate the dangers."

"That's just the point, Arnold. We don't know how to use this thing. We don't even know what it does. All we know is that after two years of studying it you got caught with your pants down."

No doubt Stecker had already commissioned similar findings and sent them to the president. Moore would have to get off a response quickly and hope that the president could remain rational in the face of such a strong attack.

In the meantime, the scientific effort would kick into high gear. New equipment would be flown out to replace what had been lost in the blast and the new power-sharing arrangement would be tested.

The door to the trailer opened. An air force major came in leading three civilians. The men were scientists: Moore's own chief analyst, who had fortunately or unfortunately not been on the truck; the CIA's chosen expert, a stern-faced true believer of about forty-five who had apparently worked on some advanced projects for the military; and an older Native American man in his late fifties. He had tanned, wrinkled skin, thin white hair, and a billy goat's tuft of scraggly whiskers on his chin. He wore a bolo tie, a plaid cowboy shirt with rhinestone buttons, and an oversized pocket protector stuffed full of pens. Moore recognized him as Nathanial Ahiga, a theoretical physicist who'd once been with the Sandia Labs in New Mexico and now worked for the National Academy of Sciences.

The name Ahiga was Navajo for "the one who fights" and Nathanial's family had a pedigree in combat. His grandfather had been one of the famed Navajo Code Talkers during World War II, his father had earned medals in Korea, and his older brother had been one of the first Native Americans to join the Green Berets, earning a chest full of commendations during three tours in Vietnam.

Nathanial himself had gone to college instead of joining the military, but his contribution to the armed forces eclipsed them all, since he'd helped design the nuclear triggers used in the warheads on the Trident missile and had spent years after working with the missile-defense effort. If World War III ever did come, Ahiga's work would be instrumental in both annihilating the enemy and saving what could be protected in the United States.

It was clear from Stecker's speeches that the CIA wanted the stone destroyed, and Moore and his people already believed that such an action would be a mistake, unless there was truly no other choice.

That dynamic effectively turned Ahiga into the decision maker. When all was said and done, his opinion would be the only one that counted.

Moore shook his hand, then watched as Ahiga strolled around the makeshift lab and over to the viewing station. Leaning in and squinting slightly, he got his first look at the assignment and pursed his lips tightly. It could have been a sign of curiosity, or a simple mannerism the man often used, but to Moore it looked an awful lot like a display of disgust.

CHAPTER 37

Hawker sat on the balcony of their new hotel, a five-star resort fifty miles south of where they had been staying. Like almost everywhere else along the gulf coast of Mexico, this hotel was without electrical power. That had served them well, since the front desk manager had been unable to electronically record their arrival.

A cash bribe had convinced him not to do so even when the lights came back on. An additional payment had put them in this suite and rented the one next door as well. A thousand dollars had been promised for each of the next five days if their presence could be kept secret. That would take them up to the day of reckoning. One way or another, Hawker doubted they'd be around after that.

With no lights on and no moon to speak of, the coast looked as dark as the sea, but out over the blackness of the gulf, a pair of heavy thunderstorms was building, splitting the night with bolts of purple lightning. At times there were long delays between the flashes, but at the moment the show was intense, with flashes illuminating the clouds from inside and handfuls of forked lines spidering across their billowing faces.

Though the storm was tracking inland, the air on the balcony was utterly still. Not the slightest hint of a breeze could be felt and even the flame on the candle beside him burned without a flicker.

To Hawker there was some great truth in the scene, some lesson about life and trouble and how paying attention only to what was immediately around you did not grant a true sense of what was really going on. It was the type of folly that allowed danger to creep in. And he wondered if he was committing such an error himself.

At this moment in time he felt better than he had in years. Not physically, perhaps—the bruising events of the last several hours had left him choosing between ibuprofen and a few stiff drinks—but his mind had grown quiet for the first time in months, if not years. The gnawing sense of guilt, even the dreams of misdeeds in Africa had faded away for now.

He credited the change to being around Danielle and McCarter once again. He wasn't sure of any greater purpose behind this stone and the prophecy that was linked to it; it all seemed like guesswork to him, but two people he truly cared about were mixed up in it and they needed his help. Whatever the outcome might be, protecting his friends brought with it a sense of purpose and peace.

And yet he guessed there were clouds on the horizon somewhere. He couldn't see them, or feel their effect at this point, but like the storm out over the gulf, he knew they were coming.

In an effort to stave off the thought, he took another drink from the tumbler beside him. As he put the glass down, the door behind him opened and Danielle came out onto the balcony.

"How are the patients?" he asked.

"McCarter's infection is getting better and he's working on what we found down there. And believe it or not, Yuri is actually asleep now."

Hawker's eyebrows went up.

"I gave him a sedative. He seems to be doing fine."

"That's good," Hawker said, stretching his leg.

Danielle sat down, then reached out and took the glass from him. After a large sip she placed it down on the table between them.

"Any guess as to how they found us?" Hawker asked, giving words to one of the thoughts that had been bothering him.

"They talked to the boat guy," she said, sounding convinced.

"Okay, and how did they know to talk to the boat guy? How'd they know we would be out on the water?"

"They have the statue from the Island of the Shroud," she said. "Those were the inscriptions that led McCarter to his discovery."

"I thought you guys trashed it." he said.

"We did what we could, but . . ."

He looked away. It seemed reasonable.

"You concerned?" she asked.

"Always," he said.

She smiled. "Listen, my suspicious friend, it's all right. We got the stone, they didn't catch us, and Yuri's okay. We're all okay."

"Are we?" he said, staring at her.

Hawker had noticed an odd pattern in Danielle, a

type of behavior that had not been present in Brazil. When things went to hell, she grew concerned and introspective. And once the danger had passed, the same overly confident attitude returned. It was in her nature to be bold and aggressive, but this seemed like something else, closer to recklessness, as if she was unbalanced in some way.

She slumped back into her seat, exhaling. "Look, I'm sorry about what happened down there. I should have been more careful with the mix. Forty percent was too high, considering my situation. It was just a mistake."

A huge bolt of lightning sliced across the sky. It lit up the horizon and the sea beneath it. Seconds later the faintest sound of thunder reached them. It made him think about the stone.

"What do you think that shock wave was?" he asked.

"The stones create energy," she said. "Some kind of discharge."

"Maybe because we moved it," he said, half joking.

"Maybe," she said. "The weird thing is, if it didn't happen when it happened, we'd be dead. We'd have hit the beach and those guys would have shot us in the back before we reached the street."

Hawker took the glass back. "I call that an extremely fortunate coincidence."

He took another drink and then refilled the tumbler with two more of the little rum bottles from the minibar.

Danielle seemed to relax a bit. She gazed out toward the storm.

"Why'd you come for me?" she asked quietly.

"Moore paid me to," he said. "How do you think we can afford this luxurious lifestyle?"

She took the glass from him, had another taste, and held it. "I'm serious. The last time I saw you was two years ago. I promised I'd try to help clear your name, but I couldn't get anyone to move. And then instead of sending someone to bring you back into the fold, CIA sent some guys to haul you back in chains."

"That wasn't your fault," he said. "I knew how that would play out. It means a lot that you tried."

She sighed, took another sip of the rum, and put the glass down. "I didn't lure McCarter into this," she said, defensively. "I didn't want him to be out there alone. I thought I could protect him."

"I know that, too," he said. "It sucks to know you can't protect everyone, no matter how hard you try."

She nodded as if the words held some deeper meaning. But she didn't offer it up.

That was too bad, Hawker thought, because here for the first time since they'd known each other she'd begun to show an openness that he found endearing.

"So that's why you came to get me," she said, smiling. "To protect someone you care about."

"When I met you," he said, "you were this immaculate, type-A corporate woman. You walked around with a kind of energy that I honestly can't ever remember having. And all I could think was, here's a gorgeous woman who can help me get what I want."

She laughed. "I don't know whether to be flattered or offended."

He guessed that his statement could have been taken a number of ways.

"But then, when we were out in that jungle, you made a lot of hard choices. You did the right things, and by the time we left that place you seemed different. I thought, maybe here was someone who could help me find what I *need,* a way to believe in something, a way to find some kind of hope again."

She looked over at him as if he'd said something strange. "I don't know you as a person lacking hope. You don't give up. You don't give in."

"I don't like to lose," he said. "And if I have to go down, I'm going down swinging. But that's a long way from believing there's anything out there to win."

"Defiance," she offered.

"I guess. But it's not the same as belief."

She stared at him quietly for a moment, her brown eyes locked on his, the candlelight bathing her face and her lips glistening from the rum. They were close now, looking into each other's eyes.

He reached for her, but a shrill chirping interrupted them. It was the satellite phone.

"It's Moore," she said, standing up.

She went for the phone.

Hawker slumped back into the lounge chair, propping one foot up dejectedly and grabbing the rum-filled glass once again. "Great. Half the Western Hemisphere is blacked out and I get a girl with a solar-powered phone."

Danielle took a last glance at Hawker and the storm brewing on the horizon, then picked up the phone. Moving to the next room, she typed in her code, confirming the lock to receive the transmission.

"Sorry it took me so long to reestablish contact,"

Moore said. "I know you tried to initiate several hours ago. Things have been a little busy up here."

He went on to explain how badly the move had gone and how the CIA had seized on the incident as a moment to attack.

"You were out in the open?" she said, surprised.

"Unfortunately," he said.

"Were you delayed or something?"

"No," he said, sounding aggravated by the question. "We were on time; there was no reason to expect a spike for hours. It came off early, and a lot stronger than it should have been."

Her mind raced, going over what had occurred on the boat. It sounded identical. Both stones had discharged unexpectedly. And seemingly random events now made sense to her.

"I think I know what happened."

"Let's hear it."

"We've found another stone," she told him. "We pulled it out of a sunken temple eight miles offshore."

"That's damn good news," he said.

"Thanks," she replied. "But the thing is, this stone spiked also. I don't know if you have access to the news up there but half the Yucatan is blacked out—just like Vegas from the sound of things."

"I thought we caused that," he said.

"Nope," she said. "That one's on us. And it sounds to me like the timing was identical."

"What are you saying?"

She gathered her thoughts. "The stones sent out a constant signal, right? A carrier wave that cycles like a beacon or a searchlight, rotating over and over again.

What we've never known is what happens when that wave bounces off something," she said.

"You think the stones found each other," he said.

"One stone queried and the other answered. Like our computer networks."

"Sounds like a possibility," he said. "How come they haven't found each other before?"

"You had that one buried underneath Building Five," she said. "We found this one eighty feet beneath the gulf, shielded by a thousand tons of rock and coral. But we happened to bring it up to the surface at the same time you were transporting that one."

She expected Moore to be skeptical but he was with her.

"That makes a lot more sense than you know," he said. "We've been studying the buildup of the energy wave, what we were able to record anyway. And the main signal showed a sudden divergence from its prior, constant pattern. A change in the carrier wave that we could only account for in two ways. Either the stone was having some type of internal malfunction, or the divergence was the result of the two separate waves merging."

"It has to be," she said.

"It would help explain some other things, too," he added, sounding relieved. "To begin with, the burst we had up here was more powerful than normal by a factor of ten. That's easier to understand if something new was amplifying the signal."

"These stones were meant to do something in concert with one another," she suggested confidently. "They might even be connected now, like some kind of network."

He hesitated. "Maybe they were for a moment, but not now. Once we got the Brazil stone into the tunnel, the carrier wave reverted to normal."

She considered that. Apparently Yucca Mountain would work as a containment site after all.

"I'll have a workup done on your theory," Moore said, "but I think you're on the right track."

"So what's the next move?" she asked. "I hope you have some plan for getting this stone back there. Because I doubt I can get it through security in my carry-on. Not that I'd bring it on a plane."

"Don't even try," he said. "Just keep it with you. At least for now. Find some way to shield it or you'll be causing blackouts every seventeen hours and thirty-seven minutes."

"I can do that," she said. "But I need you to arrange travel for Yuri."

"Why?"

"He was injured by the pulse. He seems to be okay now but I want to get him out of here. Whatever the Russians did to him, it seems to have made him vulnerable to harm from this thing."

"What exactly are you talking about?"

"He has some type of implant embedded in his brain," she said. "He had a seizure during the event and was unconscious for thirty minutes or so afterward. I got him to a hospital and they did an MRI."

She took a breath. "Bottom line is this: He needs more care than I can give him, and we're endangering him by keeping him with us. We've already been attacked once and even though we've moved, we're not safe by any means."

Moore remained awfully quiet.

"Can you arrange something discreet?" she asked.

"I told you before, you risk the Agency getting their hands on him," Moore said. "My guess is that they'd take custody of Yuri if they got the chance and I don't know if that would be any better than turning him over to Saravich."

Danielle felt a wave of anger surge through her. "We can't endanger him like this," she said urgently. "He's just a child, a special-needs child at that."

"I understand what you're saying, but things are going out of control up here," Moore replied.

"They're not exactly going well down here, either," she said.

"Yuri will be safer with you," Moore said.

Moore really had only two expressions: smug satisfaction and thinly veiled disgust. Nervousness was not his way, but she could hear a type of tension and concern in his voice that was out of place.

"What's going on?"

"The Russians and the Chinese are going out of their minds over this event. They're accusing us of building and testing some new weapon that we can't control. It's giving Stecker a lot of ammunition and the president, who I thought was smarter than that, is playing right into it."

"Bottom line," she asked.

"Suddenly showing up with a Russian child who'd been kidnapped by the Chinese, before being stolen by

American agents and dragged off to Mexico, might not be the smartest thing to do right now."

"Then find me a safe house," she demanded.

"In Mexico?" he said. "Do you really think we have one?"

Danielle cursed under her breath and looked at Yuri again. She'd begun to feel as if she were risking Yuri's life for someone else's gain. Being forced to make that type of compromise was the main reason she'd quit the NRI in the first place.

"Are you telling me the safest place for him is here with us?"

"No," Moore said. "I'm telling you that if things get any worse there might not be anywhere safe for anyone."

Moore's voice was cold and unyielding. It left her wishing she'd never answered the phone. She felt a soft breeze drift in from the balcony. The storm was growing closer.

"You've got ninety-two hours," Moore said. "Make them count."

She had no choice but to trust his take on the situation. "Find out what you can about Yuri," she asked. "I'll let you know before we make our next move."

Moore signed off and Danielle put the phone down. She turned out toward the balcony. The wind had grown stronger and cooler and drops of precipitation had begun to spatter against the wall. As the lightning flashed in staggered waves, she could see the rain blowing sideways across the beach.

Hawker had moved from his chair and was now leaning against the wall in the sheltered part of the veranda, just outside the doorway. He was just standing there quietly, watching the storm.

She wondered if he was thinking of the last storm they'd been in together, a moment in time two years ago that was so fresh in her mind it could have been yesterday. She wanted to walk over to him, put her hand on his shoulder, and wait for him to turn to her, but she knew things could not be that simple.

She thought about Marcus and felt a new wave of guilt. She imagined him back there waiting, forced to trust what Moore told him about her well-being, probably worried sick over her fate. Now she wished that she'd spoken with him when offered the chance.

She took a deep breath. She didn't like this. Didn't like confusion.

Her mind flashed to Moore's statement. *There might not be anywhere safe for anyone.* She needed to focus. To stop thinking about Hawker, to stop thinking about Marcus. To stop thinking about anything but the job in front of her.

She watched Hawker a moment longer. And then she turned from temptation, walked to her bedroom, and closed the door.

CHAPTER 38

The massive warehouse on the outskirts of Campeche belonged to a subsidiary of Kang Industrial. But the normal business that was conducted there had been moved, giving way to Kang's pursuit of the stones.

From his chair Kang surveyed the effort. Through the windows near the back of the structure, he saw the Sky-crane helicopter his men had used to hoist the statue from Isla Cubierta. It sat dormant on a helipad, waiting with two others of its kind for a new mission to fulfill. Inside the building, stacks of equipment lined the walls: there were armored vehicles squatting on massive tires, containers holding inflatable rafts, a small two-manned submarine, and a flight of drone reconnaissance aircraft similar to the U.S. Army's Predators.

As Kang looked around, his heart swelled with pride and fresh confidence. His collection of high-tech equipment had been growing for years, part of a newfound reality he had embraced.

His deteriorating health had given him an unusual vantage point from which to study his empire. As he'd been forced to delegate and rely on others, he'd seen the growth of his empire stall and the number of failures and missed opportunities rise to a level he could not abide. It had taught him a lesson that he considered a revelation: Human limitation and fallibility were the greatest of enemies.

Just as his own body betrayed and failed him, the people around him betrayed and failed him. Physically Kang was forced to rely more and more on the machines. They strengthened him, healed him, and gave him mobility and independence.

To save his empire he had forced a similar paradigm into place. Ultramodern surveillance systems blanketed every square inch of his domain; predictive artificial intelligence software allowed him to move quickly in business and other fields without a large cast of human analysts to slow him down. Computer programs tracked the productivity and reliability of every employee he had. They decided who to hire and who to fire. There were no meetings, emotions, or friendships involved. Just facts, data, and algorithms. With the human element removed, his businesses had begun to thrive again.

And now he intended to bring similar changes to his quest for the stones. Despite the efforts of Choi and his men, Kang knew it would be machinery that allowed him to find and recover what he was looking for. Human power was only necessary to operate or initiate the equipment, and if the humans failed or lagged they were easily replaceable.

In Kang's eyes, Choi and his men were nothing more than spare parts, one just as good as another, but the machines . . . the machines were the key.

One of the doctors called to Kang. They were ready to begin the latest and most advanced incarnation of his treatment. At this Kang turned his chair and crossed the floor. Choi followed dutifully at his side.

They arrived at a metallic worktable. Spread out in sections were various types of familiar equipment: the electrical stimulators, the monitors, the power packs.

"Are you ready, sir?" the doctor asked.

"Is the testing complete?" Kang asked.

The doctor nodded. "All diagnostics have been run and the feedback from the earlier sessions downloaded."

This was the moment of truth.

"Then you may proceed," Kang said, extending his right arm awkwardly.

The doctor assisted him, straightening and stretching Kang's arm and sliding a gauntlet of sorts onto it. Next he connected a brace to Kang's elbow and a shoulder harness of sorts. Once Kang was strapped in, the doctors began connecting wires to various points of the harness.

"I will leave you," Choi said.

"You will stay," Kang ordered.

Choi sat down uneasily.

As the doctors worked, a yellow forklift carrying several large crates traveled methodically toward them. The forklift deposited its load and then scurried away as men rushed into position and opened the crates. Inside rested the mechanical equivalent of pack mules: four-legged machines, powered by an internal engine and controlled by an advanced computer brain that kept them agile and balanced on almost any terrain while carrying hundreds of pounds of equipment.

Kang's techs immediately began assembling them.

From the look on his face, Choi seemed to take this negatively.

"Something troubles you," Kang said.

Choi hesitated.

"You disapprove of these efforts?" Kang felt anger growing within him.

"So much equipment will slow us down," Choi said.

"No," Kang said. "This is the only way."

The doctor finished connecting the wires and then taped them flat against Kang's arm and plugged them into a power pack in the harness. Kang admired the work. With titanium braces, hydraulic actuators, and an articulated elbow and shoulder joint, his new sleeve looked like some type of futuristic body armor, but it was more than that.

The technicians tested the fit, adjusted it, and then tightened the straps again. After that they went to work connecting smaller mechanical appendages to each of Kang's fingers.

"I wish to speak of our quarry," Kang said to Choi. "They continue to elude you."

"For the present," Choi explained. "We will find them soon enough."

"But you were close the other day," Kang said. "And yet they escaped your grasp."

One of the technicians squeezed between Choi and the table, twisting and connecting tiny wires to the actuators on Kang's fingers.

"They escaped," Choi replied, sounding aggravated, "but only because of the electromagnetic burst. But prior to that, they led us directly to the offshore site. Our men are diving on it at this moment. They've found a submerged temple filled with hieroglyphic writing that we'll soon be able to translate. This information will lead us to the next destination."

That news did not seem enough for Kang. "And if you had been quicker," he said, "you would have been able to obtain what they found down there. The second stone would have been in our possession now."

"Yes, of course," Choi replied. "But we know their theory. There are four stones to be found. That means there are still two others out there."

"No," Kang said with certainty, "there is only one stone remaining."

Choi looked puzzled.

Kang's voice turned softer, a tone reserved for a foolish but loyal dog.

"Of course, I cannot expect you to know these things," Kang said. "They are beyond your ability to perceive or to truly understand. You are a simple instrument, best reserved for simple tasks."

He nodded toward the technicians, who were using tweezers to connect the thin wires to different nerve junctions on his arms. Each time they did so his arm twitched slightly.

"If a hammer is used where a fine blade is needed," Kang continued, "the workman cannot fault the hammer for its failure. And if *you* are put to a test you cannot pass, whose blame is it but mine for putting you there?"

"With the information we have, we will beat them to the next site," Choi said. "By the time they arrive we will be in possession of all that matters. And we can set a trap from which there will be no escape."

"We're ready to power up," the technician said.

Choi looked exasperated.

"Begin," Kang said to his technician. As the power came on, Kang's arm moved and twisted, then settled.

"I'm concerned," Choi said, appearing aggravated at having to conduct the conversation in front of the technicians.

"About what?" Kang asked, his eyes locked on the device that was enabling his arm to move.

Choi began carefully. "I understand why you want the stones, but the power they possess—"

"The Russian stone was used to heal the boy," Kang said sharply, not happy to be questioned.

"Yes. But you saw what they did, you saw what happened down here. Perhaps it is not safe for us to possess them."

Kang's eyes widened. "I will have what I'm after," he said sternly.

"And I will retrieve it for you," Choi said. "But I feel we must be careful."

Choi's statement was couched in all the deference a man could muster, but Kang saw something else. He saw avarice behind the concern; he saw disloyalty. Now he understood Choi's failures, the near misses. His ire flared.

"You do not want me to have it," Kang growled, seething with anger.

"No," Choi said. "That's not true."

Of course this was happening, Kang thought. If he died, Choi would take over. He was a traitor like all the others.

"You would keep it from me," Kang bellowed. "You would have me die!"

"No. You misunderstand. I want you to have it. I'm just—"

Choi didn't finish. His eyes had flashed to Kang's arm and the strange device strapped to it. The arm was moving back and forth in an extending and contracting motion, like a man stretching after a long sleep. The finger actuators that had balled Kang's hand into a fist were now stretching and flattening his palm once again.

Behind them one of the technicians pried the front off a huge coffinlike crate. It fell with a bang. Inside were similar contraptions to the one attached to Kang's arm: two legs, another arm, and a torso unit, all with hydraulic actuators, bundled wires, and racks of G4 lithium batteries.

Kang's face flushed with pleasure. Choi's flashed confusion and then fear.

"For many years I have relied on you," Kang said to Choi. "I have tolerated your failures and your thefts and your scorn. But I need not do so anymore."

Kang's hand was hovering above a large screwdriver. In the blink of an eye, the hydraulics on his fingers snapped shut. Kang's hand grasped the tool and pulled it back. And then the arm extended, firing forward with a speed and force that stunned Choi.

The screwdriver drove into him, and Choi fell backward. The chair he sat on clattered to the floor and Choi landed flat on the concrete behind it. He put a hand to his chest, clutching at the impaling weapon but unable to pull it out.

His breathing came in spurts. He looked up toward Kang, eyes searching his master. "I am loyal," he managed to say. "I would punish them . . . for . . . you."

"When I find them," Kang said to his dying lieutenant, "I will punish them myself."

CHAPTER 39

It was daytime. Yuri liked the day. There was less sharpness in the day, more in the dark. In the day most of the things were asleep, though not all of them.

From where he sat on the floor, he watched one that was awake; the light around it seemed to shimmer, floating like a ghost amid the moving blades of the ceiling fan. The wind came down from the fan but the light stayed near the hub, twirling around it. The pattern changed, shifting and bending, bulging slightly at times. But Yuri found that he liked it. It was soft and quiet, the colors pale and smooth.

Across the room the darker man sat at the table, working. This man was important; he knew things, things the other two didn't know. And he saw things and heard things. Yuri didn't see them or hear them, but the important man did. Sometimes he wondered and sometimes he seemed to be sure. Sometimes he even spoke to them.

Yuri liked him. The important man was kind. When he spoke, his voice was heavy. He liked paper and pencil, not the machine that he was working with, pressing keys and swearing at.

He could see that the machine was hot. Maybe it was burning him. Certainly it burned Yuri's eyes when he looked at it. Yuri decided that he didn't like it any more than the important man did. He wished it would go. That would be best. It should just go away, to somewhere else.

The door to the room opened and he saw the woman come in. He heard them talking but he didn't understand them. Their words were not like his.

"Any luck?" she said.

"Not so far," the man replied. "But I'll keep at it."

The woman came over to check on Yuri. Her face was warm; she brought warmth to them. He wasn't sure how; she just did. When the woman touched him, Yuri was not afraid. Others who touched him made him hurt, made him afraid, but this woman helped make others feel better.

She and the important man were trying to find something, looking for something that was lost. She was nervous, afraid that they might not find it. He was not; he was certain; he expected to find it. So much difference. Yuri thought maybe they were not looking for the same thing.

Out through the glass door, in the sunlight, stood the other man. He was different than the other two. He didn't want to find what they were looking for, but he helped anyway and he watched for things. The man outside was always looking; his eyes were always moving. He didn't see the lights or the colors like Yuri did, and he didn't hear the words like the important man, but he looked and looked as if he knew something was coming.

That was it, Yuri thought. The other two were looking for something and this man was helping them, but he was looking in a different way. They were expecting to find things and this man was watching for something that might find them.

The woman spoke again. She was trying to help the important man.

"What if we contact the embassy, have them reach out to some of your colleagues?"

"I don't think it would help," he said. "And what if it gives us away?"

"All right," she said, opening a plastic bag she'd brought with her.

She pulled out several bottles. Yuri knew those kind of bottles; they had medicines in them. Sometimes the others had given him medicines. Not this woman, but the ones who spoke like he did. Some of the medicines made the lights darker, until he couldn't see them dancing.

He didn't know why, but sometimes he liked that, and sometimes they were too bright. But other times he didn't like the medicines at all. They made him feel sick to his stomach and hurt his head. And besides, he didn't want the lights to go away.

She took two tablets out of each bottle. "Take these," she said.

"What are they?"

"New antibiotics."

"Your fever is almost gone and this should knock out the infection for good. We might almost get you back to normal."

He held out his hand and she dropped the pills into it.

"Thanks," he said.

She nodded to him, then turned and walked away.

The important man reached for a glass of water and then stopped. He looked at the medicines and then he slipped his hand into his pocket and brought it out without the tablets. The woman didn't see. She didn't know. And then he took a drink of water anyway, and turned back to the hot machine.

The medicines made things go away, Yuri knew that, and the important man wanted the things he'd seen to come back.

CHAPTER 40

After a brief trip to the infirmary at the Groom Lake base, Arnold Moore returned to Yucca Mountain, riding shotgun in an air force Humvee as it rumbled toward the gaping entrance of the massive tunnel.

Off to the right lay the giant tunnel boring machine. It looked like a Saturn V booster lying on its side. The hundred-ton machine had single-handedly carved, gouged, and concreted the tunnels that penetrated Yucca Mountain. And then, too big to move without taking it apart, the machine had been parked and shrink-wrapped by the entrance in case it was needed to do further work.

The Humvee rolled past it and through the huge blast doors that fronted the tunnel. The environment went from blazing Nevada daylight to utter darkness, only partially illuminated by the lights in the walls and the Humvee's high beams.

"You ever get used to this?" Moore asked, looking around.

"After a while," the driver said. "We check the mountain three times a day. And we're always here when science guys like you drop in. Not usually with this much firepower, though."

Moore guessed he was referring to the machine-gun-toting Humvees that had been stationed near the entrance, the squads of armed men, and the hourly Black Hawk reconnaissance sorties.

Moore turned his attention to the tunnel ahead of him. The entrance section was a triple bore, meaning it was three times as wide as the individual tunnels. It ran that way for about two hundred yards before the main tunnel narrowed into what was essentially a two-lane road, walled by rock and concrete. Moore once again found himself growing claustrophobic in the long, narrow cavern.

"What happens if the walls cave in?"

He hadn't meant the question seriously, but the driver answered anyway.

"There are a series of escape vents that go up to the surface. You have to climb a couple hundred feet of ladder but they pop you out topside."

"Huh," Moore grunted, not knowing which was worse: getting quickly crushed in a cave-in or climbing a hundred feet of ladder. "No elevator?"

The driver shook his head, and the Humvee continued on for just over a mile until the double-wide lab began to loom in the headlights.

The main shaft continued for another four miles. Concerns about whether they were deep enough in had already been raised. The truth was they were now in the central part of the "test" tunnel, which had been home to numerous experiments over the years, most of which were designed to tell if there was any chance of instability, seismic activity, or groundwater issues that might make the site unsuitable as a depository.

Because of that history, cables for power and data were already hardwired into place ready for the NRI/CIA teams to hook into. Going deeper meant extending the infrastructure, something they didn't really have time for.

As a contingency, a rocket sled of sorts was being set up. The motor powering it had been liberated from a Sidewinder missile. In the event the stone appeared to be going supercritical, it would be attached as a payload and fired into the deepest heart of the mountain. A three-second journey into oblivion.

Moore jumped out of his taxi, climbed up the two steps of the trailer, and entered the makeshift lab. He was ready to launch into battle, but a more immediate problem had grabbed everyone's attention.

The UN meeting was going badly, and the men inside the trailer were watching it all in high definition via satellite. Nation after nation stood up and took the dais to denounce the United States. Unlike the old days, when only a few enemy nations could be counted on for such outbursts, many friendly nations were demanding to know what had happened in the desert, statements that further emboldened the leaders of the lynch mob.

Unlike British parliament, where a statement was made and a rebuttal allowed, the current system in the UN permitted representatives to grab the floor and make uninterrupted speeches one after another. The U.S. ambassador could only sit there, lamely making notes and holding a hand to the translation headphones on his ear.

In general, Moore believed in the UN process, but this was turning out to be a circus.

To make matters worse, the president was also

watching, albeit from the Oval Office in Washington. In a teleconference type of situation Moore could see him on one screen while watching the UN debate on the other. Mercifully, Stecker had temporarily gone back to Langley and, at least for the day, was nowhere to be found.

"How bad is it?" Moore asked.

Nathanial Ahiga had taken a break from the reams of data to watch.

"If I was a man who liked to gamble," Ahiga said, "I wouldn't double down."

Moore listened to the feed. The Chinese delegate was claiming that some new American superweapon had destroyed one of their "communications" satellites, an act they considered dangerous and illegal, in other words a precursor to war. No explanation as to why a Chinese "communications" satellite would be orbiting over U.S. territory was offered, and everyone involved knew it was a spy satellite, of course, but that made its destruction no less dangerous.

"Is this true?" Moore asked

The president spoke. "Intel confirms the Chinese air force trying desperately to reestablish contact with one of their information-gathering satellites this morning."

"Damn," Moore said.

"It gets worse," the president said. "The Russians say they've lost a satellite, too."

Moore cursed under his breath, wondering what the hell kind of luck had spy satellites from the world's other superpowers in the wrong place at the wrong time. Then again, Nellis Air Force Base, the airfield at Groom

Lake, and Area 51 were among the most heavily scrutinized sections of U.S. real estate. Maybe he should have been surprised that they only had two.

"Any military activity?"

"Selective but heavy mobilizations and unit dispersions," the president told him. "Accompanied by stepped-up activity at all military ports."

Of course, Moore thought. Taking out spy satellites was something that all military doctrine considered a necessary precursor to war. In response the Russians and Chinese were acting both paranoid and yet with perfect logic, mobilizing their units and dispersing them to remote locations as a precaution. If it had been the other way around, the United States would have done the same thing.

He rubbed his temples, the stress level bringing on a migraine. He wondered if he should have checked himself back into the infirmary.

"What have we done in response?"

"I had no choice but to raise our own alert status," the president said. "We've gone to Defense Condition Four and the Joint Chiefs are likely to suggest DefCon Three if the Russians and Chinese continue with their activities."

Moore exhaled, exasperated. "Well, that ought to confirm their worst fears," he grumbled.

"Excuse me?" the president said.

"We should be talking to them, Mr. President, not moving tanks and aircraft into launch positions. Escalation leads to more escalation; it's the predictable result of itself."

The president grew instantly angry. "You are out of

line, Arnold. And you're missing the damn point as well. This mess is half of your making. So far I've backed you up, but you're not getting anywhere and my patience has limits. Limits which are going to run out in about three days."

"Mr. President—"

President Henderson cut him off. "You insist these things are supposed to save us from something. So far all they've done is endanger us. We need a strategy for dealing with them, and you'd better goddamned well get me one or you'll leave me no choice."

Moore heard the threat in the president's words, a warning that he had pushed the boundaries of their friendship too far. This wasn't a simple argument between policy wonks; it was the president and the commander in chief he was talking to. Moore reminded himself of this and of the fact that at a word the president could order the Brazil stone destroyed.

"I apologize, Mr. President," Moore said, adding, "I'm very tired. What story are we going with?"

The president turned to him and shrugged. "Give me one," he said. "What can we tell them?"

Moore paused. He couldn't think; it was as if his mind didn't work anymore. He couldn't fathom any type of explanation that would make much sense. He looked down. The floor of the trailer was uncarpeted, to prevent static buildup that could affect delicate instruments. Fatigued to the point of exhaustion, the cool, metal floor looked inviting and Moore wondered what the president would think if he stepped off his chair and lay down to take a nap. Probably, it would just confirm that he'd lost it.

He looked toward the science section of the laboratory. He'd had a sense, since first viewing the stone, that it was important somehow, vitally important. Had his conviction brought him too far? There were reasons, he had to keep reminding himself, to question his own judgment.

Despite two years of study, the thing was still beyond their understanding. It presented itself as an object of great power, and had at least temporarily linked itself to the second stone, boosting that power tenfold. Did that mean three stones would have a hundred times the power and four stones a thousand? If that was the case they were now talking about the equivalent energy release of several hundred nuclear warheads simultaneously.

As far as they could tell there was no radiation, no explosive component, nothing beyond the massive electromagnetic wave, but how could they be sure? The stone had surprised them once already. Maybe he was the one that had it wrong; maybe the stone should be destroyed before things got out of hand.

"Tell them the truth," he suggested.

The president just looked at him.

"Share the data with the whole world, instead of keeping it secret. With a lack of information, they're being forced to make their own conclusions, usually based mostly on fear."

Onscreen the president looked surprised and then glanced off to the side, exchanging words with someone outside the frame. Moore guessed it was his chief of staff.

"I'll take that under advisement," he said finally.

"Maybe they'll understand," Moore added, feeling suddenly proud of himself. "Hell, they might even have a few ideas as to what we should do about it."

An aide came up to the president. A folder was placed in front of him. A few words whispered in his ear. The feed was muted but the look on his face became increasingly strained. He turned back to the screen, to Moore.

"We have another problem," he said. "The Russians have just shot down a pair of Chinese spy planes."

Moore turned his attention back to the UN screen, cringing at this latest development. The Chinese ambassador had apparently gotten the word and was already railing at the Russian delegation, and worse yet, he was threatening retaliation.

Things were beginning to spiral out of control.

CHAPTER 41

McCarter had spent most of the night and all morning focused on the photographs that Danielle had taken in the submerged temple. Some of them were strikingly clear and others less so. They were low-resolution shots, taken in poor light, but with what he already knew, they gave him enough to piece together a larger part of the legend.

He began explaining it to Danielle, but she held him up. "I think Hawker needs to hear this," she said solemnly.

They exchanged a look and McCarter offered a resigned nod. Danielle had a good point, though it was something he didn't want to think about. There were reasons Hawker might be more important in the decision-making process than either of them.

So far, however, Hawker had asked for little in the way of information about what they were studying. He understood the basics and he'd pressed them on details related to Kang and the threats they might face, but as for details of legends they were mining, he seemed less than interested. McCarter guessed that would have to change.

Danielle called him over. "We're making progress," she said to him. "But you should be part of it."

A suspicious look flashed over Hawker's face and it left McCarter feeling like he was back in the classroom or on the lecture circuit.

"Do you remember our time in Brazil?" he asked Hawker.

"Of course," Hawker said. "Angry natives, mutated animals, people trying to kill us. Great fun. We should do it again sometime."

The joke put McCarter at ease. "Right," he said. "Well, if you remember, we went down there looking for Tulan Zuyua. A place we compared to the Mayan Garden of Eden, because in their legends it was the first place that humans gathered and it was also where the different Mayan tribes were given their gods."

"I remember something like that," Hawker said.

"The thing is," McCarter said, "in the story, the Mayan tribes are given their own patron gods. And some of them, including the Quiche people, left Tulan Zuyua carrying the essence and power of these gods in special, glowing stones."

Hawker clearly understood the significance. "Like the one we just found."

"And the one we found in Brazil," Danielle added.

"When Moore and I first spoke, a year and a half ago, we talked about the Mayan culture, the Mayan religion, and the Mayan prophecies. He wanted me to explain the 2012 prophecy and what it meant to the Mayan people and culture as a whole.

"I had to remind him—and myself—that there is no

'one' Mayan culture, religion, or specific set of prophecies. Just like there is no 'one' Christianity, Islam, or any other religion. There are schisms and divisions and differences of opinions. Just like you have Catholic, Protestant, Eastern Orthodox, just like you have Shiite and Sunni, there were many different sects of Mayan life, often divided along the lines of the different city-states."

"And each state has its own interpretation of things," Danielle added.

"Exactly," he said. "They worshipped the same gods in general, but each nation had its own take on things. Different philosophies, different rituals."

He needed to make the point clear because it would color everything he was about to tell them. "Unification of any religion is difficult if not impossible. In Christian faith, we have the church getting together in the fourth century to decide which books would be part of the official canon. The rest become apocryphal. But despite their official ex parte status they still exist and some believers still put faith in them. Other documents that are part of the official body are less accepted than the rest. Martin Luther considered the books of James to be heresy because they required acts—not just faith—as an instrument of salvation. The Eastern Orthodox Church rejects the Book of Revelation for different reasons. So you can see the difficulty in creating uniform religion even when you try. But in the Mayan world, you have no canonical gathering to unify the code. And the cultural and religious differences are widespread."

"Each to his own," Hawker said, grasping the concept easily. "Why does that matter to us?"

"Because this concept of 2012 being the end of time,

the end of civilization or existence, did not *ever* gain widespread acceptance anywhere in the Mayan world."

Hawker looked surprised. "It seems to have gained widespread acceptance now," he said.

McCarter had to laugh. Indeed it had, mostly because it was interesting, exciting, and mystical in a safe way. Few of the people talking about it believed in the slightest that anything might occur.

"To us it's a ghost story," he said. "Good conversation around the campfire. But to them, the Maya of that time, it was not a popular idea. Nor, I might add, one that leads to productively motivating the troops. If all is for naught, then who wants to work? Who wants to build temples or carve idols or glyphs?"

Hawker nodded.

"So it was marginalized," Danielle said.

"Almost to the point of extinction," McCarter added.

"But not quite," Hawker guessed.

"Precisely," McCarter said. "And that's where it becomes interesting. What we've found is a broken trail of evidence, linking the stones and the prophecy. It seems like this trail was created on purpose, most likely by a group of true believers who were savvy enough to keep themselves from being discovered and stable enough to pass the knowledge on without destroying themselves in an effort to prove their point."

"Destroying themselves?"

"Doomsday cults rarely last more than a few years," McCarter said. "Both because it's hard to attract followers to such an idea—sane followers anyway—and because even when you do attract them, it's awfully hard to keep them around and interested for any length of time without performing the act of self-destruction."

"Makes sense," Hawker said. "I'm guessing you guys haven't found that anywhere."

"No," McCarter said. "But what we have found is this." He pointed to places on the map that was spread out before him. "On a stone at the monument of Tohil, the oldest structure in the city of Caracol, we find reference to the 2012 prophecy and a group referred to as the Brotherhood Behind the Smoke, this means the hidden brotherhood. From there we tracked them to Ek Balam, city of the Jaguar, where they took the name Brotherhood of the Jaguar. Here we found glyphs that talk of them building temples and structures to protect and house the Sacrifices, which I think is a reference to the stones. That led us up into the mountains to the Island of the Shroud, where they quarried their volcanic ash to use in building the underwater temple."

"Okay," he said. "I'm with you."

McCarter nodded his approval. "Now, the ultimate end of this trail is a site referred to as the Mirror. We originally guessed this was another reference to the god of fire, Tohil, since he was often depicted with a mirror in his forehead. The problem is, since the first structure we've found nothing of Tohil, as if that particular iconography had been left behind, in exchange for something new."

"Which was?" Hawker asked.

"Well," McCarter said, "before we were attacked, we found a monument that seemed to reference the Brotherhood and perhaps their leader. Ahau Balam—the Jaguar King—and the glyphs we found on this king's monument directed us to the temple beneath the waves. And from the decidedly low-tech photos that Danielle brilliantly took," McCarter said, "I've found the following."

He looked at his notes.

"'It is here that the Brotherhood gather, unknown and unseen. Only a few of us now remain. To go on we must find others who will understand. Others must be tested, and once deemed worthy, must let the blood of their hands and lips. And remain until the blood will not flow.'"

He looked up. "From the reliefs carved above the stones it looks like they would paddle out to that temple, which only they knew how to find, and then they would dive down upon it with a new recruit who had passed enough tests to be worthy. This journey into the water would be the ultimate test, to risk swimming to such depths, to swim into the cave and cut their hands and lips as a blood sacrifice."

"Not to mention the sharks," Hawker said.

McCarter had to agree; in fact, he thought that was an important factor. "Yes, now imagine them inside the temple, with open wounds, perhaps little food or water. They were trapped there until the wounds had healed; otherwise the sharks would devour them. So while they remained in the temple, they grew weak, entered a trancelike state, and went on a vision quest of sorts. And then they were allowed to place their hands on the stone, the Sacrifice of the Soul."

"Some kind of initiation," Hawker said. "I get it. After going through all that trouble, the person feels a part of something. You think that's how they remained so resolute through the ages?"

"I think that's part of it," McCarter said. "But there's more." He exchanged glances with Danielle. And she took over the story.

"When we were down there, I was acting oddly," she said. "Part of it was the oxygen narcosis but there was something else. I snapped at you to stop you from touching the stone."

"Yeah," Hawker said. "I was waiting for you to call it 'the precious.'"

"That's not too far from the truth," she said. "One of the things we know from studying the Brazil stone is that a portion of its signal resonates in the frequency of human brain waves. The brain is nothing more than an extremely complex electrochemical processor. Thinking and emoting and deciding are the result of synapses discharging electrical pulses. When I was a med student I watched a brain surgery where minor electrical currents were applied to the patient's brain. The subject, wide awake, could then not remember certain things, such as his name, or, when shown pictures of a dog, what that animal was called. Stimulation to other sections of the brain caused a rise in emotions: fear in one place, anger in another."

Hawker's look went from interest to concern. "What are you telling me?"

"We believe that this final initiation, where the candidates were allowed to hold the stone, was done to program the brains of those deemed worthy."

McCarter could see Hawker's mind whirling, making the connection. It took only an instant. The lead effort on this quest had been taken by McCarter, despite all reason to the contrary, despite the fact that he'd almost been killed by the NRI's treachery, despite the fact that he was not cut out for dealing with men like Kang and Saravich. Even after being shot and losing Danielle he had still refused to give it up.

"You touched the stone in Brazil," he said.

McCarter nodded.

"Both he and I did," Danielle said. "But you didn't. And I didn't want you to touch this one, either."

"It affected you?"

"When I was back in New York, I could never sleep through the night," McCarter said. "I thought it was some type of delayed stress reaction to all that had happened, but as the months wore on the insomnia got worse. I started taking sleeping pills and they worked for a while, until one night in the summer a massive thunderstorm woke me up. I thought I was back in the Amazon for a second. And from that moment on, I could not stop thinking about the stone. When Moore and I finally spoke he mentioned that he, Danielle, and another technician who had handled the stone were all suffering from the same symptoms. Little sleep, obsessive thoughts, a need to do something in regard to the stone."

"You're saying this thing programmed you."

"It's not as far-fetched as it sounds," Danielle said. "Lots of things program the human mind in subtle ways. Studies have shown that the sound of a baby crying will affect women's thought patterns, particularly if it is the voice of their own child. Addictions do a similar thing: drugs and alcohol actually affect brain chemistry and thought patterns to where the brain of the addict has been reprogrammed to be biased toward the drug over all else. Including food, water, and sex."

McCarter pointed to the map. "The Brotherhood's continued devotion to the stones and their apocalyptic message, without them creating their own false apocalypse, is pretty much unheard of. We think the stones were designed to instill that type of devotion."

"Okay, but why?"

Danielle replied. "If you were sending some very important items to people who might not have a clue what they were, wouldn't you want to wrap them in a package that would get them accepted?"

Hawker's eyes narrowed. "The stones generate this brain-wave-matching pulse, which creates endorphins or something within the mind of the person touching it. Is that what we're talking about here?"

McCarter nodded.

"So they love the rock and they're willing to die for it," Hawker said.

As McCarter watched Hawker's face, he noticed a subtle change in his demeanor. A new level of guardedness, a slight clenching in his jaw. To McCarter he seemed more disgusted than pleased by their honesty.

"In Africa," Hawker told them, "you'll find whole villages of children, most now in their teens, missing hands or arms or legs. It's because for a decade or so it was fashionable to use what they called butterfly mines, explosives made to look like toys that would be scattered near the enemy's towns and villages. The theory being, it's easier to convince someone to blow themselves up if they think what they're finding is a prize."

McCarter looked at Danielle. A similar thought had occurred to them in a discussion months before. It was a possibility.

"And that's why I wouldn't let you touch it," Danielle said. "As strongly as I believe they're meant to do good, I don't know how much of it is my own conviction and how much of it has been planted there. I figured one of us should remain uncompromised."

Hawker seemed to appreciate that. He relaxed a little and then looked over at McCarter. "Have you figured out what all that devotion was designed for? I mean isn't that the end goal here, to decide what these things are going to do in a few days?"

"Draw your own conclusions," McCarter said. "The books of Chilam Balam tell of the unfolding darkness. The information on Tortugero Monument Six tells us the god of change will descend from a place we are guessing is referred to as the Black Sun, and he will do something catastrophic. And now this, from the Temple of the Initiation."

He looked at his notes.

"It is written: 'At the end of the Katun, the eyes of the sky were made blind and the kings of the land waged war, and kings of the sea did likewise and all the malice of time is released, and the children shall be punished for their sins of their fathers.'

"We think the eyes of the sky are satellites," McCarter said. "Like the ones that got wiped out in this burst a few days ago."

"There's only one real reason to take out a nation's satellites," Danielle said. "That's to blind them. And in such a case, military doctrine leans heavily toward using your WMDs or losing them."

"So darkness falls and everyone pulls the trigger," Hawker said.

"*If* darkness falls," McCarter said. "Perhaps the stones can prevent it."

"Prevent it?" Hawker said. "In case you forget, the stones are what caused the satellites to fail in the first place."

McCarter took a deep breath. Hawker's logic made sense, but he felt it only made sense given their limited data. Like the man who runs into an elephant's leg and thinks he's found a tree.

"I dread to see what would happen if all the world's satellites were swept from the sky at one time," McCarter said. "But I can't imagine that being the purpose here."

By the look on his face, Hawker was imagining precisely that.

"Whatever the case is, we need more information," Danielle said. "So what do you have for us?"

McCarter went back to his notes. "Glyphs in your underwater temple give us instructions for how to find the next stone, the master stone if I'm reading them right."

"Where?"

"At a place called the Temple of the Jaguar, somewhere in the mountains."

They looked on as he smoothed out the map of southern Mexico. Using a straightedge and beginning at the location of the underwater temple, he drew a line calculated from another series of numbers. It stretched across Mexico and into the highlands of Guatemala.

"We take this angle," he said, pointing to his line. "It leads to the next stone, the Sacrifice of the Body."

"Where exactly do we stop?" Danielle asked, examining the line.

McCarter looked down at the map. His course cut across low jungle filled with mangrove swamps and up onto the foothills, traveling across the ridges of the Sierra Madre Occidental before continuing out to the Pacific.

To follow that line they'd have to hike through the jungle and then up and down a series of five- and six-thousand-foot peaks. It would take months.

McCarter scratched his head. "I'm not exactly sure," he admitted. "The glyphs were written in Mayan form, but they read like someone was telling the artisan a story. It says: 'The Brotherhood shall follow the path of those who were as gods, but moved like men. Frail and mortal, mere fragments of the gods, attempts at the human kind like the Wooden People of old. There was built the Mirror and the Temple of the Jaguar at the end of the shining path, in the footsteps of the gods.'"

"I'm not trying to be unromantic here," Danielle said, "but that doesn't exactly help us."

"Sorry," McCarter said.

"So what's the shining path?" Danielle asked herself aloud. "Could it be the Milky Way? What with the Maya and all their astronomy."

"I thought about that," McCarter said. "But the glyphs don't include a time component, or even a season. And like all stars, those in the Milky Way align lower on the horizon in some seasons and higher in others. You couldn't use that as a reference unless you specified a month or day or at least the general time of year."

"What then?" she asked.

He shook his head, but from the corner of his eye he saw Hawker grinning.

"I think I know what it is," Hawker said. "Or at least I know how we can find it. All we need is—"

The house phone rang, interrupting Hawker. He grabbed it.

McCarter heard the front desk clerk shouting vigorously over the line.

"Get out, señor! Get out now! They are coming for you!"

CHAPTER 42

Hawker slammed the phone down.

"Get the kid and the stone," he shouted as he threw open a closet and pulled out a shotgun.

McCarter grabbed Yuri, while Danielle pulled a backpack from a cabinet in the suite's kitchen.

Hawker stepped to the door and opened it a crack. There were men coming down the hall, dressed like tourists but definitely not on vacation. Caucasians with grim, pale faces, not even sunburned. They certainly hadn't been out enjoying the sights. Two stood near the far stairs while three others had stopped just one door down, at the suite Hawker had originally rented.

God bless that kid at the front desk, Hawker thought. He wanted his bonus. If they survived this somehow, the kid would have damned well earned it.

The first of the two men pushed into the neighboring room. And then the third one looked down the hall. Right at Hawker.

Hawker slammed the door.

"Get down!" he shouted, diving away from the door as a flight of lethal bullets ripped it to shreds.

Hawker came up firing, blowing a hole in the wall to

the left of the door and then turning to the dividing wall between the two rooms. The concussions from the shotgun echoed as he blasted four gaping holes in the thin plaster. A howl of anguish followed one blast and the sound of something heavy crashing to the floor. He guessed he'd hit at least one of the thugs.

Crouching behind the counter, Danielle shouted to him. "Which way?!"

A shoulder slamming into the door and busting it open gave them the answer. Hawker fired at the shape in the doorway as Danielle led McCarter and Yuri to the balcony. That was their only hope: a twenty-foot drop to the sand below.

Before he could move to a new position a hail of bullets came tearing through the same wall through which he had fired, shattering the plates and glasses and the sliding glass door to the balcony. Hawker fired back blindly and scrambled to a new position. In the moment of calm he turned to see Danielle hurdle the railing, carrying Yuri with her. But several steps behind her McCarter froze.

Hawker could see him looking around for another way.

"Jump!" he shouted, just as heavy automatic fire began shredding the room again. Plaster and bits of wood flew through the air like confetti and Hawker dropped to the ground and crawled on his belly toward the balcony.

"Jump!" he shouted again.

McCarter looked back at him, one leg over the railing, frozen like a deer in the headlights. If one of the gunmen made it to the adjoining balcony from the suite next door, McCarter would be dead.

Distracted by McCarter, Hawker missed as one of the attackers kicked the remains of the wall in and fired.

Bullets hit around him, one scraping his forearm, as he spun and fired back.

His own shot was wild but the burly, dark-haired man who'd come through the wall dove to avoid it. With the shotgun empty, Hawker swung it like a club, knocking the assault rifle out of the man's hand. As it clattered across the floor, Hawker lunged for it. But the assassin grabbed him and pinned him to the ground.

Hawker rolled and tried to throw the man off but was unable to free himself. The man was reaching for a shoulder-holstered pistol.

Hawker threw his hand out, desperately grabbing for an object to use as a weapon. His hand landed on a long shard of glass from the door. He gripped it, swung it forward, and plunged it into the man's neck.

The man fell backward, clutching at his throat. Hawker scrambled away and ran for the balcony, launching himself through the air and tackling the wavering professor right off the edge of the railing.

They crashed into the sand, with Hawker on top of McCarter.

"Are you all right?" Hawker said.

"I will be," McCarter grunted. "If you get the hell off me."

"Look out!" Danielle shouted.

Hawker rolled defensively as she fired a handgun at a figure above them, hitting him just before he was able to fire down on them.

Hawker helped McCarter up and noticed McCarter's clothes covered in blood.

"Your hand," McCarter said.

Hawker looked at his hand as the four of them raced along the beach. Blood was flowing from a straight line cut by the shard of glass. He made a fist and tried to hold it against his side as they moved.

Fifty yards down they found a breezeway that cut underneath the structure, from the beach side of the hotel out to the street side. It was a maintenance access route. They ducked into it and raced through, breaking into a storage room while they were there.

By the time they came out the front, Hawker had wrapped his hand in a towel and the three of them were in worker's overalls. They walked along the front of the grounds, Yuri holding on to Danielle.

Police sirens wailed as guests began pouring out of their rooms.

Sneaking past the valet, Hawker grabbed a set of keys and in a minute the four of them were driving off in a stolen rental car.

"Everyone okay?" Hawker asked.

"Except for you," McCarter said.

"How's Yuri?"

In the mirror, Hawker saw Danielle run a soothing hand over the boy's shoulder. She looked up. "He seems fine."

He did seem fine. The look in his eyes was flat, as if the madness had not even happened.

"Those guys weren't Kang's," Danielle said.

"Russians," Hawker said. "I figured we'd have to

deal with them sooner or later. But I was definitely hoping for later."

"How the hell did they find us?" she asked.

It was the same question he'd asked about Kang's men on the water. He had no answer. They were an odd grouping, a white man and woman with an injured black man and a Russian child. That kind of diversity made them easy to spot but it wasn't like they'd stayed in one place.

Hawker looked over at McCarter in the passenger seat. "When the hell did you get afraid of heights?"

"Two years ago, in that rattletrap helicopter of yours," he said. "I pinpoint my phobia to that exact moment."

Hawker laughed. He hoped McCarter was joking, because their next move would take them back into the air.

Ivan Saravich walked through the decimated hotel suite, heading toward the balcony through which his quarry had just escaped. Glass crunched under his feet and he could hear the sound of police sirens wailing in the distance.

To the left, one of his men lay dead, a long wedge of glass sticking out of his neck; two others were badly injured and a trickle of blood ran down his own side where several pellets of buckshot had caught him.

As his two remaining men helped their wounded comrades, Saravich stepped out onto the balcony.

"Get them to the van," he said without looking back.

"What about Gregor?" one man asked.

Saravich shook his head. "Leave him," he said. "He cannot be traced to us."

The men shuffled out and Ivan looked around. A glass of rum lay undisturbed on the balcony table. He picked it up, sniffed the aroma, and then raised it to his missing adversary.

That's twice the luck was with you. The third time it will be mine.

He downed it in one gulp and stepped back inside. As he was heading for the door, something caught his eye. Lying on the floor beside the overturned table was a large, unfolded map. He crouched down to grab it. To his surprise, he saw several places circled and a black line drawn across it.

Saravich smiled. Perhaps the luck was with him already.

CHAPTER 43

Thirty minutes from the hotel, now in possession of a different, legally obtained vehicle, Danielle, Hawker, McCarter, and Yuri were traveling north, back toward the more crowded sections of the coast near Cancun, headed for the airport.

Danielle sat in the back trying to communicate with Yuri in Russian. He had grown frantic and with the stone now so close to him again, he could not settle down.

"Yuri, we're going to a new place," she said. "It will be all right."

He looked at her and then at the backpack containing the stone. "Brighter," he said in Russian. "Brighter." He covered his eyes.

They'd assumed this stone's power wave matched the one from Brazil, but what if it didn't? She wondered if it was near to peaking now.

"What do you see?" she asked in Russian.

He held his hand out, demonstrating curved lines. "Yellow," he said.

"Is it hurting you?" she asked.

He did not respond.

"Does it hurt your eyes?" she asked. "Does the brightness hurt your head?" She touched the side of her temple.

He shook his head. "Yellow is good," he said. "Blue, no good, darker then it hurts."

Danielle was thankful for what he said. She noticed he'd gotten more used to having the stone around since the night before, but she guessed that would change if it began to power up again.

Their current guesstimate had the next scheduled peak coming in about five hours, an event she suspected would be a "normal" burst, nothing like the energy wave released on the boat. It could still be problematic. They would have to time their actions accordingly.

She stroked Yuri's hair and he pressed into the seat, leaning against her. One thing for sure, the kid was a trouper.

Ahead of her, Professor McCarter sat in the front passenger seat. He seemed to be focused on pain in his leg. He touched the skin around the dressing, gingerly probing the bruised muscle.

"You all right?" Danielle asked.

"Either I hurt myself in the fall or the infection is coming back."

"I'll give you another dose of the antibiotics," she said.

"Not right now," he said. "I feel a little queasy. Let's get settled somewhere first."

She relented and looked over at Hawker. They were picking their way toward the local airport in heavy traffic along a narrow, two-lane road. They had been moving steadily earlier but it had become stop-and-go now.

"How the hell can a little town like this have so much traffic?" Hawker grumbled.

"Didn't you see all those hotels along the beach?" Danielle said.

Hawker didn't reply; he just switched on the radio. After scanning through a group of Spanish language channels he found one that was broadcasting in English. The announcer was British.

Danielle guessed it might have been the BBC Worldwide.

. . . they've come here by the thousands to celebrate this Mayan milestone. Serious scholars, curious travelers, and New Wave crystal worshippers searching for something called the vortex. Above all, tens of thousands of vacationers, mostly Americans and Europeans expecting a party that should be a cross between Mardi Gras and New Year's Eve, with much nicer weather.

Until recently, that's exactly what they'd gotten. All enjoying themselves and eagerly awaiting that ultimate moment when the Mayan calendar hits its end and rolls over to begin again. Most just smile and laugh when any talk of a cataclysm is raised. At least that was the case, until midday yesterday when an unexplained shock wave plunged half the country into darkness.

Hawker turned the broadcast up just a bit.

Officials insist the blackout was caused by an overload from the U.S. grid, after a mishap in the top-secret Groom Lake air base. But many insist a shock wave was felt here and was particularly strong along the coast. This, combined with what might have been a terrorist attack at one of the hotels earlier today and the sudden uptick in tensions worldwide, has the vast majority of these travelers trying desperately to get home.

End of the world or not, most of the travelers I talked to aren't in the mood to stick around and find out.

Hawker shut off the radio and Danielle stared through the traffic up ahead of them. They were a mile or so from the entrance to the airport. She could see units of the Mexican army and riot police around the gates. Every car that passed was being checked and rechecked.

"They may have our description," she said. "Not sure I want to chance making it through security."

"I wasn't planning on buying a ticket," Hawker said. "I was planning on borrowing a helicopter."

"You mean stealing one," she replied.

"It's not stealing if you bring it back."

She laughed. Perfect Hawker logic.

"This is too hot, though," he said. "Too many people. Too much security."

McCarter seemed pleased. "I can't say I'm completely disappointed."

"Me neither," Danielle said.

He smiled at them. "Might want to hold off on that," he said. "You haven't seen plan B yet."

With that, he turned into a gas station, waited for a few moments, and then accelerated calmly back out onto the street, moving opposite of the traffic and away from the airport.

CHAPTER 44

Kang's warehouse in Campeche had become a command center to rival Mission Control at NASA. On one side were scholars he'd hired to translate the glyphs from the submerged temple; on the other were banks of computers, dozens of screens, and groups of trained men working the equipment like air traffic controllers.

It was a face-to-face search with a twenty-first-century twist. Kang had teams scouring the various towns, villages, and archeological sites that he suspected the NRI team might visit, including the Museum of Anthropology in Mexico City. All in all two hundred men were running about, carrying cameras and other remote sensing equipment. They simply wandered around, scanning faces, moving from section to section, through plazas, airports, restaurants, and hotels, wandering up and down streets and avenues. His men did not have to find the NRI team; in fact most of them had no idea what they were looking for. They just had to execute the simple orders they were given. Kang's computers would do the rest.

Behind him, racks of high-powered servers hummed

as they absorbed and processed the data. Facial recognition software running at blazing speeds examined every image. A man moved down one street, and five hundred faces were scanned and ruled out. Another man wandered the airport from gate to gate, and in thirty minutes Kang could be certain that the NRI personnel were not there.

In this way his two hundred men could scour the countryside like a veritable army of spotters.

Kang checked the readout. His artificial intelligence system had initially predicted a 31 percent chance that the NRI team would access one of these points for additional information.

But that prediction was updated constantly based on the rate of progress. As Kang checked the readout, he saw a diminishing likelihood of finding the Americans at any of the known Mayan sights. And with all the additional faces that had been scanned and rejected at the university, that probability was falling as well.

The current analysis graded the possibilities in the following manner:

Probability that

- NRI party has been captured or incapacitated: 3.27%
- NRI party no longer in Mexico and heading for the United States: 9.41%
- NRI party will use McCarter's remote access to New York University mainframe: 11.74%
- NRI party has sufficient information to locate precise point of next site: 14.69%

- NRI party will access a local university or museum for data: 28.91%
- NRI party has sufficient data to begin generalized search for next site: 31.08%
- Possible other outcomes: < 1%

Kang considered the data. The most likely category, that the NRI party now had sufficient information to begin a *generalized* search, had been the second *least likely* category twenty-four hours before. He had watched with both concern and hope as it rose steadily in the rankings.

If the NRI party was truly out in the jungle somewhere, they were much closer to finding the next stone than he'd hoped. On the other hand, that was what he needed them to do eventually. And by leaving the metropolitan areas and entering the jungle they played into his hands. Out there Kang had ways of finding and tracking them that were not feasible in the crowded streets of urban civilization. And when he found them, he would deal with them away from the harsh light of any witnesses.

He turned to the project leader. "Prepare to launch the drones."

CHAPTER 45

The plane was a Lake Renegade LA-250, an amphibious, single-engine aircraft that floated on a boatlike hull instead of pontoons with struts. They'd found it at a tourist trap called Sea & Air Tours, where for a hundred and fifty dollars vacationers could go up on a forty-minute ride and see the coastline. A few more dollars arranged for a two-hour trip and a landing at a secluded bay, where the passengers could have a romantic picnic on an uninhabited beach. The NRI team had no time for such luxuries.

After casing the dockside and the small building that acted as Sea & Air's offices, Hawker had decided this was the plane they needed.

And then they'd waited until almost midnight, partly because they needed the dockside to be deserted but more importantly because they needed the stone to finish its energy wave and reenter the lull phase before they took off in a small aircraft.

This time Danielle had taken it in the car out into the hills. Again she had found a spot in the middle of nowhere, dug a deep hole, and placed the case containing the stone into it. It was not exactly glamorous duty, and as she dug, she waited for a *federale* to arrive and ask what the hell she was doing. It never happened.

Forty minutes later, she'd dug the stone out and driven back to where Hawker, McCarter, and Yuri waited.

"Anything happen?" McCarter asked.

"Nothing," Danielle said. "Even the radio still works."

It concerned her, actually. Perhaps the stone had blown a fuse when it had flashed the day before.

"What do you see?" she asked Yuri.

The child grinned sheepishly. "It is asleep," he said.

From there they had ventured to the coast again, where Hawker had broken into the shedlike building and come out with a set of keys. A minute later he was in the aircraft, waving to Danielle to come aboard. She'd led McCarter and Yuri along the dock and they'd climbed inside, strapping themselves in and lowering the clamshell doors into place.

After starting the engine and taxiing the waddling craft away from the dock, Hawker had pushed the throttle to the wall. In thirty seconds they were airborne.

That had been two and a half hours ago. Since then they had flown along the dark line that McCarter had drawn, with Hawker insisting that he knew where he was going.

Danielle looked around. A large windscreen and big panoramic windows that curved up into the roof of the plane—designed to give the tourists the best views possible—gave the plane a spacious feel, especially with the wide-open sky and the stars twinkling in the distance.

As they droned along in the dark, Danielle began to

relax. At least for the moment they had nothing to worry about. It seemed unlikely that there would be trouble up here. She didn't consider it impossible, but at least it was highly doubtful.

And so she allowed her mind to rest, to stop worrying and planning and compensating, and mostly she just stared out the window at the stars.

She turned her attention from the beautiful night to the other passengers in the aircraft. It seemed there was some correlation between the insomnia and the times when the cycle peaked during the night. With the stone "sleeping" both McCarter and Yuri were finally sleeping themselves. She could even hear McCarter snoring over the intercom.

"Any way to turn that off?" she said into her microphone.

Hawker flicked a switch, restricting the intercom system to the two of them.

"Better?"

"Much." She gazed out the window again. "I can see why you like flying so much." She had always considered it just a mode of transportation, usually working on her laptop as the hours flew by.

"It's quiet up here," he said. "Especially at night."

The Renegade had a 250-horsepower engine that was mounted above the cabin on a pylon. It was horrendously noisy, even through the protective headsets.

"You call this quiet?"

He nodded. "Up here there's no one yapping at you to do this or explain that. No traffic, no horns, no jagged, random noises."

He smiled to himself, apparently pleased with his reasoning. "Yeah," he said. "To me this is quiet. And straightforward. Go from point A to point B and back again. Try not to get shot down while you're doing it."

She had to laugh. She guessed that qualified as quiet. "I'm sorry about the other night," she said. Since their night on the balcony she had avoided looking him in the eye. That wasn't her way.

"You mean ditching me to talk to Arnold Moore on the phone?"

"Yeah," she said. "That and . . ." The words were hard to come by. She decided to be direct. That *was* her way.

"I wanted to kiss you," she said. "I haven't felt that close to anyone in a long time and I wanted to kiss you. It's just that there's someone in my life already. Someone back home, waiting for me. I think."

For a second Hawker didn't react. Perhaps the whole conversation seemed too absurd to him. People were trying to kill them even as a cataclysm of some kind loomed up ahead. And she was talking about her almost-fiancé, who maybe even wasn't her friend anymore. This was why she hated relationships; somehow they always made her feel foolish.

And then she wondered if maybe he didn't care. Maybe their almost-kiss had just been a way to pass some time. Like watching the storm and drinking the rum. His world was so different from hers. Was it foolish to even talk like this to someone who didn't know where he would be next week, next month, next year? She was worried about home. He didn't have one.

"Basically I'm supposed to be engaged right now,"

she said in explanation. "I'm supposed to be home planning a wedding and wishing my dad was there to give me away."

"Maybe you should be," he said, finally. There was some pain in the statement, but sincerity, too.

"Maybe," she said.

"Does he know what you do?"

"He was my first partner," she said.

Hawker raised an eyebrow.

"My second year in the NRI I got a field posting. Marcus was the guy they teamed me up with. He was a few years older, a lot less naïve, and just as ambitious."

"Sounds like instant attraction," he said.

"We kept it professional for about eight months," she said, somewhat defensively.

He smiled. "You don't have to do this," he said. "This isn't twenty questions."

She wanted to. She thought it might clear the air, at least for her. "They always tell you it's dangerous to mix business and pleasure, that it dulls your edge or makes you sloppy. But that wasn't the case. There was a high from it, the work, the relationship, the partnership. If anything it made us sharper, made me feel invincible."

"Fourth stage of tequila again?"

"Better," she said.

"What happened?"

"I pushed like I always do," she said. "And because he was the same as me, there was no voice of reason to hold us back. An operation we were on went bad. He took a bullet in one kidney and a second bullet in the leg. He rehabbed for almost a year and then when he was healthy enough to come back he decided not to."

"What about you?"

"Not a scratch on me."

"Lucky as always."

"I guess," she said. "I took time off to help him get better. But back then, seeing me made him angry. A sort of reverse version of survivor's guilt. Eventually he asked me to leave. To just go away and let him be. So I did."

Hawker was silent, listening and scanning the instruments. "So when you quit the NRI, the two of you found each other again?"

She nodded. "Becoming a civilian was sort of disorienting: too much routine, not enough to worry about. It felt good to have someone to talk about it with. Things progressed from there."

"So why wouldn't he be waiting for you? I mean has he gone insane or something?"

She laughed. "I think I wrecked it by coming back. We started arguing, things got out of hand, and I decided to make the arguments as harsh as I could. He didn't deserve that."

She understood Marcus's objections on an intellectual level. She was making a leap that he could not. But she still wanted his support and when it hadn't been there, she had lashed out.

"I felt guilty about leaving," she said. "But I'm painfully aware that I have avoided every opportunity to go back. I could have gone back after you rescued me. I could have gone after we found McCarter, slapped him in cuffs, and dragged his ass home."

"But you didn't want to."

"Remember how you said I wouldn't like 'normal life'?"

"I was just talking. It didn't mean anything."

"I think in some ways you were right."

"Look," he said, "I don't believe in trying to convince anyone to do anything. But assuming the world doesn't blow up, this mission is going to end in a few days, and when it does, I'd get out of this madhouse if I were you."

"You're on his side?" she said, surprised.

Hawker shook his head. "I'm not talking about him, I'm talking about you. If you have a chance at something good in this life, something worth going home to most of the time—whether it's him or someone else or just being home and safe and surrounded by friends—you should grab it and never let go."

She stared at him in shock.

"I'm not saying go bake cookies," he explained. "Run for Congress, like you said. Kick some ass up on Capitol Hill. God knows they could use someone like you."

"It sounds like you're saying 'pretty good' should be enough for me?" The words came out as if she were challenging him, but she hadn't meant them to sound that way.

"I'm saying I'd settle for half decent and no one trying to kill me."

"And what if I don't want to settle at all?"

"Then maybe it's not leaving that made you feel guilty," he said. "Maybe it was wanting to leave in the first place."

His words hit close to the mark, closer than she'd been able to get on her own. Prior to Moore's call for help there'd been no reason for her to go anywhere, but in a way she'd already begun to feel trapped. Had she just run to the NRI to escape that? Based on some glamorous selective memory of how good life had been there? Maybe Hawker was right: Maybe she was throwing away a chance at happiness, whether it was with Marcus or someone else. She wasn't sure, but suddenly she didn't want to talk about it anymore.

"And what about you?" she asked, changing the subject. "Is there some gun-toting mercenary girl waiting for you out there?"

"Lots of them," he said, as if it were an admission. "One in every port."

She laughed, half hoping it was true. It sounded like a simpler arrangement "Good for you," she said, as sincerely as he had earlier. "Now, how about telling me where we're going?"

"Take a look out the window."

Danielle turned and gazed through the curved glass. Beneath the plane she saw nothing but darkness; endless miles of unlit jungle and impassable terrain.

And then she caught sight of a flash. A fleeting glimpse of silver, as if someone had flipped over a giant mirror and then hidden it away.

She couldn't say what it was. In fact she'd never seen anything like it before. It seemed to have come up through the trees.

She continued to stare into the darkness as the plane droned on, looking, searching. And finally she saw it again. This time it moved, traveling through the darkness like a snake in the grass. It slithered, disappeared, and then reappeared, traveling with a calm precision that exactly matched the movements of the plane.

It took another sighting for her to realize what it was. She looked up. The full moon had risen to a spot almost directly above them. Its light was being reflected off a narrow river below.

"You've seen this before," she said.

"Not here," he said. "But on one of those long, quiet flights we were talking about."

"You get shot down on that one?"

"No. Not that time."

"Maybe that's a good sign."

Hawker laughed. "Better wake up Sleeping Beauty back there. He wouldn't want to miss this."

Danielle woke up McCarter and showed him what Hawker had found. They followed the river, which coincided nicely with the line McCarter had drawn. It snaked across the jungle to a series of small lakes arranged in a kind of offset pattern. One lake was on their left with the next one on the right, and the next one back on the left again.

She saw at least a dozen of them. From the air, with the moonlight reflecting off their surfaces, they really did look like a set of divine footprints.

"Incredible," McCarter said.

"Not too shabby," Hawker admitted. "Now, if we can just find one big enough to land on, we won't have to crash in the jungle."

CHAPTER 46

Hawker's statement provoked little alarm from either Danielle or McCarter, but as he stared down at the small lakes passing beneath them, Hawker began to sense a miscalculation on his part.

He'd guessed correctly that a small river winding through the jungle and a series of lakes or ponds would mark the silver path and the footsteps of the gods. He'd seen the same type of thing before in night flights over outlying terrain. If the moon was in the right place, its reflection would travel along the water as the aircraft moved, a silver marker leading the plane as if it were urging him to follow.

A brief look at McCarter's map and the line he'd drawn showed it heading into the highlands where small streams joined together and meandered along. There were no major lakes depicted on the map, but Hawker knew that the terrain and its climate would mean intermittent lakes that came and went. With the rainy season having passed only a month before, Hawker guessed that some of the lakes would still be present, and when they'd been blocked from acquiring a helicopter, he'd figured that a float plane like the Renegade would do just fine.

This guess had turned out to be correct, but as Hawker studied the lakes in the moonlight he'd begun to worry that they were all too small.

He searched for forty minutes, flying in a zigzag pattern, looking for a larger body of water, but found none. As their fuel began to dwindle he knew they'd have to make do with the lakes they'd already seen.

He dropped the nose and swooped in over the two largest lakes. The first had a roughly circular shape, while the second was elongated and narrower. It offered more room to land but forced a crosswind landing and as Hawker flew its length with the landing lights on, he saw the remnants of drowned trees sticking out in places.

He pulled up and buzzed the first lake once again. They would have about a thousand feet to stop in, which wasn't really enough, but at least he could make an approach into the wind.

"All right," he said over the intercom. "Make sure your tray tables and seat backs are in the upright and locked position."

Beside him Danielle checked her belt and put away the flashlight and the sectional map she'd been holding. McCarter woke Yuri and made sure he was strapped in while Hawker climbed five hundred feet, reduced power, and put the flaps down to full.

The Renegade slowed noticeably and Hawker had to use a lot of pressure to keep the nose up.

"How's our fuel?" Danielle asked.

"Just about gone," he said.

"We have enough for a go-around at least, right?"

He looked at the gauges. He didn't think so, but he didn't say anything.

"What if get down there and there are more trees?" she asked.

That was a concern, but trying to climb out and do it again would be more dangerous. At this point they were committed to landing, regardless of what they saw at the last second.

"There's an old pilots' saying," he told her. "If you're making an emergency landing at night, you wait till you're a hundred feet above the ground and then you turn your landing light on. If you don't like what you see, you turn it back off again."

"There better not be trees down there," she said.

"Don't worry, there won't be," he said, hoping it was true.

Hawker brought the Renegade in slowly, keeping the nose up and using a bit of power in a technique devised for a short-field landing. He could barely see over the nose and was yawing the craft to the right so he could look ahead through the side window.

At a hundred feet he began to see the tops of the trees. They were reaching up toward him and the plane was sinking faster than he'd planned.

He nudged the throttle forward and the engine noise increased but the aircraft was still descending. He was too low now. The treetops were blocking his view. He saw nothing but branches and fronds catching the light.

Where the hell is the lake?

They needed to be a little higher. He bumped the throttle forward and pulled back on the column. The nose came up a bit and then the engine sputtered.

It didn't die, but it was running rough.

"Hawker," Danielle said.

He pushed the mixture to full rich and pumped the throttle, hoping to dump a little more gas into the cylinders. The stall horn began to whine, an annoying whistle. The engine sputtered loudly, shaking the plane.

He dipped the nose.

"Hawker!"

They caught the treetops, snapping a branch here and there and then crashing through a thicker strand.

Suddenly they were out over the water, dropping and hitting hard. The deceleration was sudden, whiplashing the passengers forward against their seat belts.

They came up off the water for a second and touched down again. The Renegade settled this time, cutting a white swath across the glassy surface of the lake.

"Hold on," Hawker said.

"Why? We're down," Danielle said.

He looked over at her. How to explain it? "We don't have any brakes."

She looked up.

He did the same. The lake's embankment was coming at them fast, at twenty or maybe thirty miles per hour. They were slowing marginally but they were not going to be able to stop.

Hawker braced himself and the Renegade slammed into the bank and skidded up onto it.

It stopped abruptly.

Leaning forward over her seat belt, Danielle looked over at him. Her thick brown hair had covered her face. With a puff of air she blew some of it back and then used her hands to pull the rest of it behind her ear.

"No brakes," she said, looking anything but amused. "You got us a plane with no brakes."

"It's a float plane," he said. "None of them have brakes. I guess maybe they have anchors or something. I don't know. I never flew one before."

"You took us up in a type of plane you never flew before, to a place you weren't sure we would be able to land safely in?"

For some reason he found her anger amusing, endearing. "To be fair," he said, "I actually *was sure* we'd be able to land safely, I just also happened to be wrong."

She unbuckled her seat belt and popped the latch on her door, pushing it upward.

"Get me out of this contraption." she said, grabbing the flashlight and climbing out onto the sloping embankment.

The seat popped forward and Yuri climbed through.

McCarter followed behind him. He clapped Hawker on the shoulder. "I hate to tell you, but this hasn't done anything to assuage my fear of flying. Especially with you. But since I thought we were about to die, and we're somehow still alive, I say 'good landing.'"

Hawker stayed in his seat for a few minutes to shut the plane down. They weren't going to be flying out of there, but the battery still had juice and the plane still had radios. Hawker guessed there was a chance they might need them.

He climbed out and shut the door.

The stars and moon were brilliant. They cast a fair amount of light around the edge of the lake. It was smaller than he thought, maybe seven hundred feet across, with fifty-foot trees around its edges. It had been like trying to land on a runway with walls at each end.

It was a hell of a landing, all but impossible to pull off safely, yet they'd done it. He didn't know whether to pat himself on the back or be surprised by their good luck.

Then his eyes turned to the tree line up ahead of them. He saw a flicker of light, white light first, from the beams of flashlights and then several glimpses of orange flames. A group of people were marching through the trees toward them, carrying flashlights and torches and who knew what else. And all Hawker could think of was the angry villagers coming out to seize Frankenstein.

CHAPTER 47

Danielle noticed the smell of smoke even before she saw the torchlight flickering in the forest ahead of them.

A moment of apprehension gripped her, but she didn't share Hawker's overriding suspiciousness of everything and she thought there could be a chance that meeting other people out here would be helpful. Certainly the men and women of Oco's village had been fundamental to their initial success.

Still, she shielded Yuri by stepping in front of him as she waited for the oncoming party to reach them.

"I'm telling you," Hawker said, "we should get out of here."

"It'll be all right," she replied. "I'm almost *sure* of it."

McCarter stood by expectantly. He turned on a flashlight and waved.

The train of torches changed direction, heading straight for them.

"There must be a town around here," McCarter said. "If we're looking for another Mayan ruin, the locals might know about it. There are hundreds of structures hidden in the jungle, most never seen by outsiders. This could be a stroke of good luck."

The torches grew closer, winding down a slight hill, until several men came through the brush and trained a series of powerful flashlights on the NRI group. The glare blinded Danielle and she put a hand up.

"*Nos puede ayudar usted, por favor?*" she said. Can you help us, please?

The lights continued to shine in her eyes.

"*Necesitamos ayuda,*" she said. We need help.

A rough voice answered her. "*Ponga los manos,*" the man said. Put up your hands.

And then she heard a sound that needed no translation: the pumping of a shotgun and the racking of the slides on several other guns.

Danielle raised her hands, trying hard not to look in Hawker's direction.

In a minute they were surrounded by a group of eight men, several of whom had weapons. They were led by an older, shorter man with a full beard and mustache who carried a flashlight and a pistol.

While one of the men searched the plane, another took her backpack and McCarter's. A third man patted them down and confiscated a black handgun from Hawker.

The man with the beard walked around them, making a wide, slow circle. He seemed to be studying them, at the moment focusing on Yuri. Finally he put his pistol away.

"What are you doing here, señorita?"

That, Danielle thought, she could not explain without sounding crazy.

"We crashed here," she said. "My husband was trying to fly us over to Puerto Vallarta. But he forgot to check winds or to fill the tanks before we took off."

The man came closer, looking into her face and then at her hands. "If he is your husband, then where is your ring?"

Before she could answer, he added. "And if you had not circled overhead for an hour, you could have easily made it to the coast. So I think maybe you have a different story to tell. No?"

Danielle felt a sense of fury at getting caught in the lie. It was a stupid lie, easy to see through. She wondered why she'd even thought it would work.

Hawker leaned over to her. "I told you we should have run."

"Now is really not the time," she said.

"I'm just pointing it out."

"Point it out later," she shot back.

The bearded man turned to the others. "Hmm . . . maybe they are married after all."

The men laughed. And the leader stepped over to McCarter. He shone the light in McCarter's face, studying him for a long time.

"Could you please lower the light?" McCarter said. "It's hurting my eyes."

The man turned the beam away, aiming it at Hawker's face in a similar manner. Hawker squinted into the light as if it were some kind of challenge. He said nothing.

The man who'd gone to search the plane popped out of the cabin. "*Nada aquí,*" he said. Nothing here.

Another man had been going through their backpacks. He handed the satellite phone and the spherical, glasslike stone to the bearded man.

As it passed in front of them, Yuri tried to pull free from Danielle; he wanted to touch it. She held him back, but the bearded man had seen his reaction.

"Is this your child?" he asked.

"He's adopted," she said. "And he has special needs, so if you don't mind . . ."

The bearded man handed the stone back to the underling who'd found it. Yuri tracked it as it went, relaxing only when it had been placed in the sand-filled, lead-lined container.

"So many lies," their captor said. "I think you might need to see a priest."

He turned and began marching back toward the forest.

"Bring them," he said.

CHAPTER 48

Led by the armed group and their bearded leader, Hawker, Danielle, McCarter, and Yuri hiked through the tropical foliage. The trees and ferns and brush had a junglelike feel to it, but more sparse and reduced in scale because of the altitude. As they neared the end of the two-mile hike the terrain became flatter and the foliage was replaced by tilled land, fields, and pastures.

Beyond the fields lay a small town made up of white-washed stucco buildings. Children played in the unpaved streets while livestock, mostly chickens and goats, moved about in various gated yards.

It was not what Danielle had expected. Certainly it didn't look like a hideout of some criminal gang. But they remained under armed guard, and as their captors walked them blatantly down the main street, activity in the town around them came to an abrupt halt. Onlookers gawked in their direction.

The man with the beard walked ahead of them and waved to a handsome woman of about thirty, dressed in plain, simple clothes. She came to greet him and, after a brief conversation, looked at Danielle and then Yuri, who walked beside her.

Danielle guessed what was about to occur and held Yuri's hand tightly.

"Do not worry," the bearded man said. "Maria will take care of him while we talk."

The woman led Yuri to a small adobe house.

Danielle turned her gaze forward, ready to argue with the man, but he had stepped through a gate in front of a mission-style church. Writing beside the doorway dedicated the church to San Ignacio, the founder of the Jesuit order and the patron saint of Catholic soldiers.

They were forced inside and the doors closed behind them. Once the bearded man had genuflected and crossed himself with holy water, he pulled off his poncho, hung it on a peg, and turned to face them.

He wore a black cassock and the white collar of a Catholic priest. "Welcome to San Ignacio," he said. "I'm Father Domingo."

"You're a priest," Danielle said.

"*Sí,*" he said. "I'm sensing you feel differently about the lies you told now."

He seemed amused with himself, but Danielle didn't share the feeling. "Has the church taken on a new role that I'm unaware of? Beginning with kidnapping people at gunpoint?"

Beside her McCarter stumbled. Hawker moved to support him and then led him to a bench that sat against the church wall. Father Domingo watched Hawker sharply.

"Don't worry," Hawker said. "I've got enough going against me already."

Father Domingo turned back to Danielle. "My actions are necessary to protect the citizens of this town."

Danielle could feel her anger beginning to burn. Of all people to deny them help, a member of the clergy seemed to be the least appropriate. "I asked you to help us. Did that seem like a threat to you?"

"We did not exactly act the Good Samaritan," he said. "But there are reasons for this."

"And what might those be?"

"Drug smugglers."

"Which we are not," she explained.

"Yes," he said. "It seems to be the case, but we needed to be sure. Several years ago, some men came here with money, trying to buy our silence, while they cut down trees for a dirt runway and took over good lands to grow their drugs.

"As soon as they were entrenched, the kind talk and the money ceased and they became tyrants. But the spirit of the people here is strong. We decided to run them off but it was not easy. Threats were made; some people were harmed," he said, catching the look in her eye. "Blood was spilled on both sides. We vowed to never let them come back; it is always easier to keep the predator out than to deal with it once you've let it through the gate."

He nodded toward a window, through which blue sky could be seen. "Your plane circling for an hour in the middle of the night and then landing on the lake was very suspicious to us. We had to be sure. Even Saint Ignacio was a soldier before he became a priest. Sometimes that is what we must be as well."

Danielle relented. Now she felt the fool for judging too quickly. With a history like that, she could guess how their actions might have appeared.

"I understand what you're saying," she said.

"And knowing how things looked from your side," he replied, "I can understand why you lied. But that doesn't tell me what you're really doing here. Would you like to explain?"

Danielle uncrossed her arms and sat down. "You probably wouldn't believe it."

"Try me," he said. "Belief is my business."

"We're looking for an ancient Mayan ruin called the Temple of the Jaguar. We believe it might be located nearby. And our suspicious"—she glanced at Hawker—"and somewhat foolhardy flight out here was part of that search process."

"Why didn't you go back?"

"By the time we'd figured out where we needed to be," she said, "we were too low on fuel to get back, so we landed on the biggest lake we could find."

"I see," Father Domingo said. "And why would you feel it necessary to keep such a thing secret?"

She hesitated, not wanting to lie to the priest again, but not wanting to tell him, either.

It was Father Domingo who spoke first. "Perhaps," he said, "because you've brought something with you that you don't understand, and you fear both using it and failing to use it. But your greatest fear is what other forces might do if they found it first."

CHAPTER 49

The Situation Room of the White House was more crowded than the president had ever seen. The Joint Chiefs of Staff, the director of the CIA, the secretaries of state and defense and their aides had filled the sitting areas. Other cabinet members stood in the space around the main table.

The world situation had deteriorated harshly in the past twenty-four hours. In response to the downing of their fighter plane, the Chinese had captured a pair of Russian spy boats in disputed waters and now troops were building up on the border between the two countries.

Because an American vessel had been approached in the same area but had managed to leave the vicinity and escape capture, the Russians were claiming U.S. duplicity. They were lashing out at both nations through every available channel.

The Chinese, on the other hand, wanted to know why U.S. and Russian spy boats were in its waters and operating together, as a second round of finger-pointing and paranoia got into full swing.

The president sat in his chair quietly. He glanced

through a situation report while the head of the Joint Chiefs explained the particulars using a flat screen monitor.

"... and in addition to that the Chinese have deployed forty divisions on the Russian border; strategic aircraft have been dispersed or launched and parked in racetrack patterns a hundred miles from the borders."

He clicked the screen and a new satellite photo appeared: a Russian ICBM silo. What looked like steam could be seen escaping from hoses attached to a large, odd-looking tanker truck. "The Russians are making serious preparations, but their activities are balanced, half in Asia, half on the European side."

A new photo showed mobile SS-20 launchers being dispersed into the countryside. The following one showed the Russian port at Murmansk. The docks were empty, and the channel, normally frozen solid at this time of year, had been cleared by a flotilla of massive icebreakers.

"From our point of view this is the bigger problem," the chief said. "In twenty-four hours, in some of the worst conditions of the season, their entire ballistic missile fleet has put to sea. Not only did we believe this could not be done so quickly, it hasn't been done since the Cuban Missile Crisis."

He turned to look at Henderson. "This is a grave sign, Mr. President. The Russians are very serious about things. And I think we should be, too."

These latest actions were highly unwelcome. And they left the president with a growing dilemma. He believed the Brazil stone was secure and no longer an immediate threat as long as it remained in the Yucca

Mountain depository. Sensors placed on and around the mountain had detected no emissions of electromagnetic energy escaping the complex. But neither the NRI staff, the CIA's newly involved experts, nor Nathanial Ahiga could say for sure what would happen if another superspike occurred.

Another event like that, in the current state of heightened readiness, might be more than they could afford.

In that sense the incident had been terrible luck. It had led directly to the current predicament—spy satellites destroyed, tensions flaring. One more hour and the stone would have been safely ensconced in the depths of Yucca Mountain and nothing would have occurred.

But in a different sense, he felt it might have been good luck. Had the stone sent forth this burst while still housed at the NRI headquarters in Virginia, or, worse yet, at the beginning of the journey, on the road to Andrews Air Force Base, all of D.C. and most of the eastern seaboard would have gone dark—including the Pentagon, the White House, and Congress, not to mention CIA headquarters in Langley and Andrews itself.

The pulse had fried almost every circuit and backup system at Groom Lake, and even the backup systems at Nellis Air Force Base, eighty miles away, had been inoperable for almost five hours.

The president had served in the military and he believed in their professionalism and training. But he feared what the reaction would have been if Washington and most of the East Coast had gone suddenly, utterly dark. It would not have been like the blackout in 2003, where the grid went down but phones still operated, with places with backup power remaining functional and military communications online. It would have been complete darkness, complete silence.

To the western command, five hours without communication would have been incomprehensible. All public television, radio, and Internet feeds gone, nothing but static on the box, no response to calls, no word from either military or civilian personnel, no flights arriving from eastern airports. To any rational person, and especially those charged with the task of protecting America, the sudden loss of contact with anything and everything from New York to Washington—all without any warning—could have only seemed like a nuclear strike of some kind.

He wondered privately if that scenario would have caused the western command to launch some type of counterattack, firing back against anyone anywhere who might have been responsible.

The president was thankful that burst had happened so far from civilization. But it had caused a shift in his position. He'd begun coming around to what the director of central intelligence had been pushing all along: that these stones, these devices of unimaginable power, were incredibly dangerous instrumentalities. If the men who studied them did not understand them, or even know what they were capable of, how could anyone accurately predict their intended or even unintended consequences?

For the past month, he'd been swayed by the opinion of his longtime friend, Arnold Moore. But for all his well-known gifts of discernment, Moore didn't seem to feel the danger.

"Mr. President," the head of the Joint Chiefs said, "in

the interests of national security I must formally request we move the military readiness status to Defense Condition Two."

"Two?" the president asked, stunned.

"Yes, Mr. President. I feel in light of the Russian and Chinese actions it's necessary."

Escalation, the predictable result of itself. Certainly Moore had been right about that. Even if he was blind to his own part in the cause.

The president looked down at the photo in the briefing folder. *Russian ICBMs fueling up.* For the first time in decades. He felt a thin sheen of sweat on his palms. Things were beginning to come unglued. Prior to this moment he'd felt a conviction that he could do what was needed and keep everything and everyone reined in. Now he knew that was beyond his grasp. And he also knew with certainty that he could no longer protect both his old friend and the American people at large.

"Mr. President . . . I'm afraid we need an answer."

Henderson closed the folder and looked up.

"No," he said. "DefCon Three only. Take all defensive measures, but I don't want any ships going to sea early, bombers on airborne alert, or ICBM activity. Do one damned thing to make them more afraid and I'll fire your asses on the spot. You understand me?"

So forceful was the president's voice, so unexpected, that the entire room shrank back. Henderson considered that a good sign. He knew there would still be visible signs of the upgrade but they would be minimal and perhaps it would be the start of a de-escalation.

"Yes, Mr. President," the head of the JCS said.

As President Henderson stood, the room came to attention.

"I want updates in two hours," he said, then glanced over at Byron Stecker. "Come with me."

Henderson strode from the Situation Room and down the hallway. The glare on his face was dark enough that staff members who'd been waiting hours to speak with him pulled back into the shadows and let him pass.

Stecker caught up with the president halfway to the White House elevator.

"What's your take on Moore?" the president barked.

Stecker fumbled for a moment, and then spoke. "He wants his way," Stecker said, struggling to keep up. "Wants to win his argument."

That wasn't Moore's style, the president thought. Moore could be obstinate but not for the sheer sake of it. If the facts were plain he would surrender his case. There was something else.

Turning the corner, he launched his next question. "Could he be withholding information?"

Stecker looked away, as if considering the possibility.

"I've had issues with the NRI since day one," Stecker said. "And especially since Moore took over. I wouldn't put it past him if he thought it was the right thing to do, but . . ."

"But?"

"But in this case it would take a hell of an effort. We have access to the stone; we have everything in their database. My people have been all over it for the past couple of weeks. Everything is linked to everything else. Every report they ran built on a prior one. If there were holes in the data we'd have found them. So if he is holding something back, it's something he never disclosed in the first place."

The president doubted that. Moore had been upfront that the stone had been brought here from the future, that it was creating ever larger waves of energy, and that it was ticking down to something cataclysmic. *If you weren't going to hide those facts, what the hell could be worth hiding?*

And yet Moore's actions in this particular instance seemed out of character: his initial reluctance to explain what his people were doing in Mexico, his private hiring of a mercenary to rescue his friend—a loss that the man Henderson used to know would have borne stoically out of duty's sake, even with all its pain and anguish.

The president stopped thirty feet from the elevator and the Secret Service guard who stood beside it.

"Do Moore's actions seem rational to you?" he asked.

If Stecker ever wanted to fire a broadside at Moore, the president had just given him the green light. But Stecker was subtle.

"If you have to ask, Mr. President . . ."

He did have to ask. And now he found himself furious with Moore for putting him in this position to begin with.

"I want you to go back out to Yucca," he said. "I want you to keep an eye on Moore, personally."

"Mr. President—"

"He's too wrapped up in this thing to pull him off it now. He knows the stone and the research better than anyone else. But I'm strongly leaning toward destroying that damn thing, and on the chance that Moore finds that option unacceptable, you are to prevent him from interfering."

The president paused and then added, "By any means necessary."

CHAPTER 50

Ivan Saravich sat at the end of the poorly lit bar. A tepid shot of bad vodka sat in front of him.

He looked at the man beside him, the head of the FSB unit he now commanded.

Commanded. The word was a figment of someone's imagination. Not his.

These men of his were as much his guards as his subordinates. They answered to him, yes, but only in regard to the quest. Their real masters resided in Moscow, with Ropa and the FSB.

"Let me get you a glass," Ivan said.

"I don't drink," the man said.

Ivan shrugged. "Perhaps you should. You look upset."

"We should not have left Gregor," he said.

"It could not be helped," Ivan said.

"We should have continued the pursuit," the man said insistently.

Ivan downed his shot and poured another one.

"Along the crowded beach, with your weapons held high?" he scoffed. "How long do you think before the Mexican police arrived? How long before a helicopter and waves of cars made it impossible to escape? What would happen to our quest then?"

The man backed off a bit, but he still seemed angry and there was a sense of arrogance that would not fade. Finally he spoke. "I wonder if you really want to find the boy."

Ivan smiled to himself, disgusted.

The man stood up. "We leave in the morning. You should know, I will not let you act that way next time."

The man walked away. He was half Ivan's age, thirty pounds heavier, and strong. Ivan guessed there was little beyond disdain in his heart for the old warrior.

How things change. He had once been a hero of the Soviet Union, and since its disintegration he had become a successful capitalist. He marveled at the differences. For him communism had meant honor without wealth, and capitalism wealth without honor. And now he was a disgrace, his only hope for redemption to assassinate a child.

Not a satisfactory end to either part of his life. The capitalist in him saw no profit in it and the communist saw no honor.

He downed another shot of vodka to quell that thought. The vodka was beginning to grow on him.

The truth was, if he didn't succeed or do as ordered, these men would kill him. And if he did succeed . . . they would probably kill him anyway.

CHAPTER 51

Professor McCarter held the church pew with his right hand for balance. He suddenly felt light-headed, as if he was swaying—or the ground was.

"Could you say that again?" he asked the priest.

Father Domingo stepped toward McCarter. He put a hand on McCarter's shoulder. "The prophecy of Kukulcan," he said. "The writings of Chilam Balam: December 21, 2012, the day in which darkness will pour from the sky. There are tourists everywhere in Central America because of it. But I sense you are different."

"How can you tell?" Hawker said sarcastically.

"For one thing, you carry weapons. For another, none of you have cameras."

He turned to Danielle. "And then there's the object you brought with you. Something we have been waiting to see. You wish to deliver it to the Temple of the Jaguar, but you're afraid of what will happen if you do."

McCarter did not know how this man knew what he knew. But in McCarter's weakened state it seemed ominous to him. "Or if we don't," he replied.

Father Domingo nodded in response to his statement. "Fear is the domain of the evil one," he said. "Jesus told the mourners who believed their daughter had died to *fear not and believe only.* And she was healed. If you act out of fear, you will always make the wrong decision. You must act out of faith, whichever way you decide to go."

"Easy for you to say," Danielle replied. McCarter would have seconded that.

Father Domingo nodded. "Perhaps it is. And perhaps I can show you something that might make it easier for you. Come."

He led them past the altar to a small door. Using a key on the modern padlock he released the cast-iron latch. The door creaked open. A long, wooden stairway beckoned.

With Hawker and Danielle's help, McCarter followed Father Domingo down stairs made of old, lacquered pine. They arrived at a large wine cellar. Brick walls faced them on two sides and five huge oak barrels sat recessed within the earthen wall.

"San Ignacio was originally a fort and then a mission," Father Domingo explained. "And after the conquest of Mexico it was turned into a monastery. The soldiers began to grow grapes here and when the monks took over they improved the vineyards and had these casks built. We still make wine and much of it will be served tonight as part of the novena, our celebration of the nine days before Christmas."

Father Domingo walked slowly as he spoke, stopping finally at the last of the heavy casks. He slid a flathead screwdriver between two planks on the face of the barrel. Using a small hammer, he tapped it in farther. Taking great care not to bruise or split the wood, he levered the plank outward.

"Nice hiding place," Hawker said.

"It even works," he said grinning. "This one is the best wine of the bunch."

He reached inside and pulled out a thin, flat box, like those used for long-stemmed roses.

McCarter hobbled forward as Father Domingo placed the box on the wine presser's table. An inscription on the lid read: EN EL AÑO DE DIOS MDCXCVIII.

"In the year of our Lord," McCarter read aloud. "Sixteen ninety-eight."

"Must be a rare vintage," Danielle said.

Father Domingo looked up. "Very rare," he said. "There is no other like it that I know of."

Father Domingo opened the box. Inside, wrapped in a towel and then a layer of fireproof Nomex fabric was a sealed plastic bag. Within that was a cracking folded parchment wrapped partially in silk.

Father Domingo laid the parchment down, unfolding it with the greatest of care. On the top half of the yellowing paper they saw Spanish writing in faded blue ink. The bottom half was covered with symbols: Mayan hieroglyphs.

"What is this?" McCarter asked.

Father Domingo smiled. "The history of the church is not one of honor at times. Certainly not in this part of the world. When the conquistadors came, the church followed, and what wasn't stolen by the men of Cortez was burned and broken by the church. Soon almost everything that had once been here was swept away. Lives taken, traditions banned, books and parchments thrown into the bonfire by the thousands, until there was little left but a pile of useless ash. If they could have, they would have swept the stone monuments into the sea."

McCarter nodded sadly and turned to Hawker and Danielle. "Only four parchment books of Mayan writing are known to still exist. We call them codices—the Madrid codex, the Paris codex, the Dresden codex, after the cities they're stored in. There is a fourth called the Grolier fragment. Four out of thousands. A few short pages of astrological studies are all that remain from hundreds of generations of Mayan civilization."

"And the church was the chief destroyer," Father Domingo said sadly. "A sin we shall bear until the day of judgment."

"But this book," McCarter noted, seeing there were several folded pages. "How did it survive?"

"Much of what God has done, he does through the fallen and the weak," Father Domingo said. "In this case, in the darkest parts of the church's shame there were those who spoke out. A missionary named DeVaca was one. One of the men whom his testimony reached was among the first to come here to San Ignacio. His name was Philippe Don Pedro. He had come from the Basque region of Spain, where he had owned a vineyard, only to see it burn once, and then after he rebuilt it, to see a pestilence destroy his vines.

"He came to the New World a broken man, a peasant priest. But when he arrived here he saw hills that would bring good wine and flat lands that could be irrigated and turned into productive fields. But he also saw that the people who lived here were happy and peaceful even if they were not yet Christian. And so he lied. His reports to the diocese described a place no one would want to set foot in, teeming with mosquitoes and fever and swampland. Surrounded by the most unproductive soil."

"And Philippe Don Pedro found this parchment?" McCarter asked.

"No," Father Domingo said. "When the oldest man of the village lay dying, he called for Don Pedro. He said he had lived in other villages before fleeing to the mountains and that Don Pedro was the only honorable man he had seen among the new regime. He promised he would convert to the religion of the cross, if only Don Pedro would protect for all time the last words of the old man's dying world. Words no longer written, barely spoken."

"The hieroglyphics," McCarter said.

Father Domingo nodded. "As the story goes, Don Pedro asked the old man if he knew what converting meant. His reply was that his people, the Maya, had always known that only sacrifice and blood could atone for sins. If Don Pedro would tell him that Christ had done this for all, then he would believe."

McCarter nodded. For many Central American religions, the story of Christ sacrificing himself on the cross, his life and blood offered for salvation, made perfect sense. Their kings and priests gave blood sacrifices of their own, cutting themselves and passing barbed ropes and other serrated objects through earlobes, lips, and tongues.

And while most in the church saw no similarity whatsoever in these actions, it made many of the indigenous people of the region easy to convert. At least partially.

It seemed they could be inclusive and worship both Christ and their own gods in a side-by-side sense. Only when they were forced to give up all other trappings of their former religion did the resistance began to stiffen.

"So the old man converted and gave Don Pedro the parchment," Danielle said.

"And Don Pedro promised to protect it," Hawker guessed.

Father Domingo nodded. "He wrote on it in Spanish the words that the old man told him. It reads, *En los últimos días antes del Sol Negro, ellos vendrán. Tres blancos y uno negro, tres hombres y una mujer, y tres viejos, uno joven, tres sin ira, uno sin paz. Ellos decidirán el destino del mundo.*

As McCarter listened to these words, he translated them roughly in his head.

He looked at Danielle, and then Hawker. Danielle spoke very good Spanish and by the look of shock on her face she'd clearly translated the words. Hawker looked suspicious but wasn't as fluent.

"What does it mean?" he asked.

"In the last days before the Black Sun, they will come," Father Domingo said, his voice resonating off the stone walls. "Three white, one black; three male, one female; three old, one young, three without anger, one without peace."

As he heard the words, Hawker's eyes narrowed and his square jaw clenched as if he were grinding his teeth to dust. He seemed more angered than awed by what they'd found and as McCarter studied his friend, he guessed that the final sentence would only make it worse.

He looked at Danielle; she knew. He returned his gaze to Father Domingo, who finished the translation, tracing his hand along the flowing lines of the Spanish script.

"*Ellos decidirán el destino del mundo,*" he said, once again. "And they shall determine the end of the world."

CHAPTER 52

Hawker stared at the priest as he uttered the words. It was plainly evident that their little group matched the exact description on the parchment, but what did that tell them. Could it really have been meant to be them? Him, Danielle, Yuri, and McCarter?

He could see the gears in Danielle's mind whirring. McCarter looked as if he'd just found some place of enlightenment himself, and Hawker could think of nothing more dangerous.

"Don't get any ideas," he warned. "It's just a coincidence."

"These are the last days, before the day of the Black Sun," Father Domingo said. "When I saw the four of you, I must admit, my heart shook. With time growing short I have considered this parchment greatly and I wondered if anyone would appear. These words were written four hundred and ninety years ago."

Hawker watched as Danielle moved to McCarter's side and the two of them studied the parchment paper. There were several pages of Mayan hieroglyphics spread across its leaves and McCarter was instantly engrossed.

Danielle seemed to have caught her breath quickly.

Her eyes were bright in the dimly lit wine cellar, and there was a sense of accomplishment about her, a sudden aura of success, as if the burden she carried had been lifted. He understood it: Their search had not been in vain. The pain, the suffering, the carnage all around them—most likely she felt as if there was some reason to it now. Some destiny beyond it. And that was what scared him.

Hawker didn't believe in the concept of destiny. Certainly it had its value. There were occasions where it gave people the will to push on, to succeed against monumental odds. But more often than not, Hawker had seen the concept as a destructive one.

Those who thought they were on a mission from God—any god—were capable of horrendous things. All actions and atrocities could be rationalized if they were the will of some supreme being.

For the arrogant and power hungry there was no better rallying cry. It was a lie that made even the good people of society capable of carrying out acts of an evil nature.

And for oppressed peoples it became the mantle of fate; their lot in life to suffer; defeat preordained and thus accepted and unchallenged.

As he thought of these things, he wanted to point them out to both Danielle and McCarter, but he could already see the fever burning in their eyes.

CHAPTER 53

Deep within Yucca Mountain, the scientific arguments continued. Despite all the technical data regarding the stone, neither Moore, nor Stecker, nor any of the scientists could say exactly how it worked. Nor what it was meant for.

As a result, the teleconference had turned into a grilling, with questions fired at Moore from all angles. It could mean only one thing: The burden lay on him. Either he would sufficiently justify the stone's existence or the defense would fail and the stone would be destroyed.

"Where is the energy coming from?" President Henderson asked point-blank. "How is this stone creating the type of power you've described? Is it nuclear? Is it through some type of fusion process?"

"It's not, Mr. President. The stone is not radioactive. It's not a process of cold fusion, as we once thought. It's certainly not hot fusion. In fact, there is no process we know of through which this stone can be creating energy in the magnitude we have seen. Which leads us to believe that the stone is not *creating* energy but is actually drawing it from somewhere. Acting as a conduit."

"Explain this to me," the president demanded.

"Think of a wire in your house," Moore said. "You stick your finger in the socket, you get shocked, but neither the socket nor the wire create the energy; they're merely conduits. The electricity is created in another place, at a power station, probably many miles from your house. We now think this stone is receiving energy from somewhere and disbursing it."

"Where?"

"The place it originated in," Moore said, wondering if the president would grasp what he was saying, without elaboration.

"The future?" the president asked.

Moore nodded. "It's not as far-fetched as it seems," he said. "Even in the original example I gave you, the energy was created in a different time, albeit milliseconds before it reached your house. The difference is only one of magnitude and direction. In this case, the time displacement is farther away."

The president seemed to understand what Moore was telling him but he clearly remained suspicious. "How good is the science on this?"

Moore didn't hedge; no time for that now. "Most physicists are certain that the universe is made up of more than three dimensions. String theory and quantum mechanics currently suggest eleven dimensions, but at the very least we know of four: the three spatial dimensions—height, width, depth—and the fourth, time.

"In general, we consider time as unidirectional, moving forward and not backward, but we know for certain that it can be distorted by relativity, and if we're correct about where and when this stone came from, then we can be fairly certain that that unidirectional concept of time is wrong. If that's the case, then the transfer of simple electromagnetic energy through time would likely be far easier to accomplish than the safe travel of a human person through it."

"Why don't we see any other manifestations of this?" the president asked.

It was a difficult concept to explain. "Maybe a demonstration would work better," he said.

He grabbed a foot-long piece of metal that had broken off of some cabinet. He placed it on the ground, its curving, silver shape looking like a flatter version of the St. Louis arch.

"Can you see this?" he asked.

"Yes."

"Okay, now imagine a two-dimensional world," he said. "Flat, like this floor. If there are two-dimensional beings living there, they would only be able to see what exists within their two dimensions: things that exist on either the north-south or the east-west axis. But nothing up or down. Anything going vertically above or below this flat plane is literally beyond their ability to perceive."

Moore pointed to the arch/handle. "So if we place this three-dimensional arch in their two-dimensional world they see only the points that intersect their world."

Moore touched the base of the curved metal handle. "Here and here," he said. "They would identify each point as an independent two-dimensional object. What they would not be able to recognize is that the two objects were connected and were in fact one."

He ran his hand along the arch.

"Now, if this were an electrical circuit and there were a power source attached to it, they would be able to sense the output at both ends, and they might even be able to determine that the two things were acting in concert, fluctuating at identical moments, but they would have no way of knowing where the power was coming from or why, because their entire plane of existence is contained in the flat two dimensions of the floor."

President Henderson seemed to grasp this. "What you're saying is that these stones are the same as those intersecting points on the floor, only in four dimensions."

Moore felt he was getting somewhere. "Exactly. We can see and sense only the parts connected with our three-dimensional world, but if we're right, there is some invisible conduit going through time that leads back to a power source, one that is pumping energy into the stones in massive quantities."

Okay," the president said. "For the first time some of this is starting to make sense."

Across from Moore, Stecker rose to his feet.

"Mr. President, there's another possibility to consider here," he said. "One that relies on more than a wild theory, and in fact actually comes with direct evidence linking it to these stones."

"Which is?" Moore asked, aggravated by Stecker's untimely interruption.

Stecker didn't respond directly to Moore. Instead he spoke into the camera lens, focusing on Henderson. "Mr. President, have you ever heard of the term *geomagnetic reversal*?"

"North Pole shifting?"

Stecker nodded and motioned for his scientist to make their case. "Talk to the president, Ernest."

The man in the lab coat got up and cleared his throat. He seemed a little nervous in such company, clearing his throat twice before speaking.

"Over the last hundred million years the north and south magnetic poles have switched places dozens of times. The most recent shift occurred seven hundred and eighty thousand years ago, in an event we call Brunhes-Matuyama reversal. But in the billion years before that, the poles reversed on an almost random time frame, sometimes as quickly as forty or fifty thousand years, in other cases remaining stable for fifty million years or longer. Periods we call superchrons. The truth is that no one understands the timing or mechanism of these reversals."

Moore studied the man, considering what he was saying and wondering where this was going.

"Now," the man continued, adjusting his glasses and beginning to sweat, "for the past several years, research specialists from NOAA and other organizations have been actively studying the magnetic field in an effort to better understand this phenomenon."

The president interrupted. "All very interesting," he said with undisguised frustration. "What the hell does it have to do with the stones?"

The CIA's scientist gulped at a lump in his throat. "I'll show you," he said meekly and then went back to the computer and began tapping at the keys. A graph appeared on one of the flat screens in the lab; a remote screen in the White House displayed it as well. Across the bottom axis was a timeline, beginning in 1870 and ending in 2012.

Even before the CIA's man explained the graph, Moore began to feel sick. What the hell were they getting at?

"There are fairly accurate measurements for both the field strength and the position of the north magnetic pole since the late eighteen hundreds," the scientist explained. "This graph displays the magnitude of the pole's movement by year."

He pointed to the thick red line, cutting across the chart. "What we see here is the beginning of a more rapid phase of movement. The movement, already in effect in 1870, accelerated sharply in 1908 for reasons unknown."

He traced the line with a pointer. "And from there we see a continuing slow deterioration, with the north magnetic pole moving southward, approximately seven or eight miles per year over most years of the past century. A pace that quickened to over twenty miles per year in the last few years."

A few more clicks on the computer and a second graph appeared, this one representing field strength, with the timeline now stretching back some three thousand years.

"As you can see, the field strength has decreased almost continuously from a high point achieved roughly two thousand years ago. As of last year, the earth's magnetic field had weakened thirty-five percent from its peak, with almost half of that drop coming since the falloff in 1908."

The year 1908 was reverberating through Moore's mind, but he couldn't say why.

A third chart with a more volatile line popped up on the screen. The time frame on this chart extended back only through 2009.

"This is the field strength over the last three years."

Moore stared. There were two more dramatic drops and two minor spikes, but if the time index was right, he now knew what the CIA was getting at.

The field strength had dropped an additional 5 percent in the winter of 2010, the exact time when Danielle and what was left of her team had recovered the Brazil stone and brought it to Washington.

A small spike could be discerned, near the end of November of the current year, perfectly coinciding with the burst over the Arctic. And an additional large drop occurred at the far right edge of the chart. Moore guessed that would be tied into the event that had occurred a few days earlier, the same moment that Danielle had pulled the second stone from beneath the Gulf of Mexico.

After that latest drop, the earth's magnetic field was down almost 50 percent in relative terms, and sitting at an all-time low for the last fifty thousand years.

Unless the data had been faked, even Moore could see that the stones were intimately connected with the weakening of the magnetic field. Their current estimation of the stones' arrival even coincided with the beginning of the drawdown, around 1000 B.C.

Just in case the president hadn't seen it yet, the scientist lowered the boom.

"As you can see, Mr. President, these dramatic reductions in field strength coincide exactly with two events:

the NRI recovery of the stone from the Amazon and the event that took place here forty-eight hours ago. And just as incredibly, the survey data tells us that magnetic north has traveled south by over a hundred and forty miles in the past five months, ninety miles of that since November twenty-first."

With Moore struck silent, Stecker took the spotlight.

"In one sense," he said smoothly, "we think the NRI is actually right. The stones are drawing energy through some conduit beyond our understanding, beyond our ability to see, but I assure you, Mr. President, it ain't coming from the future. It's coming from right here, right now, in our current time frame. These stones are draining our magnetic field. It's virtually collapsing before our eyes. Every time Moore's people recover one of these stones and bring it out into the open, the situation grows a hell of a lot worse."

"Damn," the president said, clearly disturbed.

Stecker wasn't done. "What really scares me is this, Mr. President. These stones are drawing all that energy to themselves, storing it perhaps, and when they release it . . . I don't know about the end of the world, but it could be the end of the modern, electronic world as we know it."

Moore felt like a lawyer who'd just been blindsided, wanting to know why this information hadn't been disclosed. But this was no courtroom and no one cared if he was surprised. In some ways it made things worse. For the CIA to come up with something he and his team had not found made him look incompetent.

"Fine," the president said. "Now, in practical terms

what does a failing magnetic field do to us? It's obviously happened before. Do we see any die-offs, any great extinctions like the dinosaurs?" He paused. "Arnold?"

Moore looked up, still reeling. "No, Mr. President," he mumbled. "But our world is different than theirs. Our world depends on electrical power for absolutely everything that matters. And with no magnetic field, we are exposed to the solar wind."

"Meaning?"

"An unending torrent of charged particles that will, over time, affect human tissue. But at a far quicker pace it will destroy the electrical grids, computers, processors, and any other device with modern circuitry. While it will not melt the earth, as some in Hollywood have suggested, a large solar flare or an event known as a coronal mass ejection could set us back to the stone ages. Or at least the late eighteen hundreds."

The president went silent. He seemed to be mulling this over. And then he offered the drowning man an unexpected branch.

"I'm guessing you think these stones were sent back here to prevent that?"

Moore perked up. "Yes, Mr. President. Seeing this data, I would come to that conclusion."

Stecker scowled. "Oh, Arnold, you are naïve. After all this, you think these things are a blessing?"

He pulled out a printed sheet of paper. "From your own man's translation: 'The children won't learn so they must be punished. War of man and man, food no more shall grow, blood shall endless flow, disease shall take the most. The day of the Black Sun has brought the doom of man. Five Katuns, a hundred years, of endless killing, Fifty Katuns, a thousand years of disease and dying. To stop it there must be sacrifice for all.'"

Stecker dropped the paper. "Millions killed in war, billions from disease and starvation. These things are weapons, Arnold, bombs sent to destroy us quick and clean before we do it in a way that will ruin the world for them."

Moore fumed. "It's patently illogical to think you can go to the past, destroy a huge section of society, and not have it affect you down the line. Your argument makes no sense, Stecker, and if you were actually smart enough to understand what you are saying, you'd see that."

Stecker bristled but he didn't back down. "If these things are supposed to help us, then why'd they hide them?" Stecker asked. "You ever hide a first-aid kit? A fire extinguisher? Of course not, but you hide mines and booby traps and bombs. Hell, if this thing were meant to help us they would've dropped it in our laps, not buried it in some ancient temple three thousand years ago."

With that statement all hell broke loose. In a minute Moore was shouting at Stecker, the two scientists were arguing, and the president was repeatedly demanding calm, like a judge in a courtroom gone wild.

"This is goddamned ridiculous!" Moore shouted. "The most incredible journey in the history of mankind, quite possibly the single greatest achievement of all time, and you think they did it to destroy their ancestors?"

"Stop deceiving yourself," Stecker retorted. "Man's greatest achievements are the efforts put forth in war. Countries, continents, and religions mobilize everything they have, every ounce of physical, mental, and spiritual energy in the struggle for survival."

Moore felt himself on the defensive, wanting to shout back but having nothing intelligent to say. In the absence of any defense, Stecker pressed the case.

"And yet you have these people of yours from the future, sending something back to our time, something that seems to be affecting us negatively, and you believe they come in peace? If they wanted to help us why not just send the stones to our time? I'll tell you why: because these things needed time to load themselves up. They sent them to a time before ours so that they can gather energy unto themselves, store it in this four-dimensional loop you keep talking about, and then unleash it on us all at once. To teach us the error of our ways."

Moore burned with the temper of his youth, but restrained himself from physically striking out at Stecker.

He turned to the screen. "Mr. President, we're not talking Arnold Schwarzenegger, H. G. Wells, or *Star Trek* here. We're talking about an act of supreme effort, one that taxed and debilitated and mutated the men and women who undertook it. One that eventually left them here to die on what is essentially a foreign shore."

"Suicide mission," Stecker interjected blithely. "You ever hear of the kamikazes?"

"This isn't a damn joke," Moore said.

"No, and it's not a puzzle, either," Stecker said. "That thing is a danger. It's a ticking bomb that we don't know how to defuse. And your messing around with it is going to get us all killed."

A quick study of the president's gaze told Moore that

he was losing the argument. And yet he couldn't throttle back. He found himself railing further at the director of the CIA despite the president's urging, despite his own realization that he must have looked like a lunatic by now.

He turned to his own scientist and then the screen with the president's image and then across the room to where Nathanial Ahiga sat quietly, watching the whole thing like a spectator, drinking a grape soda through a straw.

"You!" Moore shouted. "Say something, damn you. The president sent you here to share your opinion, to decide who's right. Well, it'd be nice if you opened up your goddamned mouth once in a while."

As Moore lashed out at anyone in reach, he realized that he was now attacking the referee. He didn't care anymore; he was beyond exhaustion, and in his current state it was all he could do to recognize his self-implosion. He was powerless to stop it.

Ahiga looked at him curiously and the whole room went quiet. Even the White House feed only buzzed with static. Perhaps realizing that the spotlight was on him, the old Gallup, New Mexico, resident took another sip from his grape soda.

"You want me to speak," he asked, rhetorically. His voice was soft and gravelly, like smooth-sided stones rumbling together. "Of course. I can do that, as long as all the yelling and shouting is done."

He cleared his throat, and put the soda bottle down. "In my opinion," he said, shrugging his shoulders and looking straight at Moore, "you're wrong."

It seemed as if he'd just decided randomly, a flip of a

mental coin. Or perhaps it was because Moore had yelled at him. Could the man take his job any less seriously?

"That's it?" Moore said. "That's all you have?"

"No," Ahiga said, nodding toward Stecker. "He's wrong, too. You're both running around in circles. Shouting and yelling and making all this racket. Hard to think with so much noise. I'd like to say it's white man's noise, but my father made it, too: the sound of people who want to be right, not people who want to know the truth."

As Moore stared at Ahiga, he shrugged again. "Do I know what the answer is? No," he said. "I don't know. But I know enough to see where you've gone wrong."

"And where's that?"

"Both of you are trying to decide what to do based on what these men of the future have done. Based on their actions and what they've sent you and whatever record they left of it. And by doing that, you're missing the whole point."

Moore struggled to follow the logic.

"You're mixing up cause and effect," Ahiga elaborated. "When they made their decision a thousand years from now, all of this—the finding of the stones, this argument, whatever results from it, if anything—it was already done and gone. Ancient history, so to speak. And that means they made their decision based on what we did. They didn't send these stones here to make us *do* one thing or another. They sent them here because in some way, we asked them to."

In his polite way, Ahiga looked around at them.

"We're the cause, and their actions are the effect. Our

choice is their destiny, not the other way around. If they live in misery because our warlike nature finally got the best of us, then it's our choices that caused it, regardless of these stones. And if they live in paradise, then we should get the credit for that, too."

"So you're saying we don't have a choice?" the president asked.

"No, I'm not saying that at all," Ahiga said. "Of course we have a choice, but whatever we eventually choose, it *will* lead them to send these stones our way, be it for destruction or for salvation."

Moore sat down and exhaled. Even Stecker had been stunned into silence.

"Well, that kind of circular logic doesn't help us much," Moore mumbled.

"I know," Ahiga said, sitting back down and grabbing the soda bottle for another sip. "That's why I was keeping it to myself."

CHAPTER 54

Even through the slightly distorted, electronically encrypted satellite transmission, Danielle could tell from the sound of Moore's voice that things had gotten worse. But it was not just the geopolitical news or Beltway power grabs that had him upset.

"I have some information on Yuri," he said. "Some from a source of my own, some from Stecker, of all people, courtesy of a highly placed source in the Russian Science Directorate. I believe it's accurate."

"What's wrong?" she asked, fearing the worst.

"I'll download the details for you, and you can use the data screen on the phone to view them, but here's the gist of it: Yuri was born just outside the hot zone near Chernobyl. His parents, whoever they were, could not take care of him, as he came into this world with the degenerative nerve disease you see in him now. The actual diagnosis remains a mystery but what is known is that it attacks the nerve fibers relentlessly. At first the afflicted person notices tics and shudders but soon they turn into full-on tremors and even seizures. By stage three the person has lost all motor control and by stage four involuntary muscles like the heart cease to operate, resulting in death."

Danielle reeled as Moore spoke the words. "What's the progression?"

"Under normal circumstances, five years to get to stage three, ten years maximum before the terminal condition."

She thought about what he was saying. "Are you sure? Because I don't see many symptoms at all, and unless there's something wrong with your math, Yuri would be dead already."

"Nothing wrong with my math," Moore said. "Yuri is still alive because the Russians have been treating him in an unusual manner. In rare cases, high levels of direct electrostimulation of the nerve fibers, spinal column, or cerebral cortex have been shown to slow the progression of the disease."

"He has an object buried in his cortex," she said, relaying what they'd discovered at the emergency room. "Some kind of implant."

"Yes," Moore said. "It was an experiment. And in addition to retarding or reversing the disease, it's that implant that seems to have given him the abilities you've noticed, the power to see or sense electromagnetic disturbances."

She had felt nothing but a sense of revulsion when she'd learned that Yuri had been the subject of experiments, but now her perspective changed. "The trial seems to have worked," she said. "At least physically."

"It's not all roses," Moore said.

"Why?"

"After looking at the data and the rather strange etymology of the device, we've come up with a guess as to what they implanted in Yuri's brain. It isn't a piece of medical equipment, it's a shard of the Russian stone, which the Russian Science Directorate has been in possession of since the fifties."

"What?" She could not believe what she was hearing.

"It seems the Russians found their stone long ago, or at least they found what was left of it," Moore said.

"What are you saying?"

"Yesterday I got blindsided by Stecker. He and his team tied these stones into the continued reduction in the earth's magnetic field. Quite a competent job," he added, sounding disgusted. "They appear to be correct in some ways, including a link between the stones and a weakening magnetic field."

"Are you kidding me?" she asked.

"No," Moore said. "Each time we've pulled a stone out of the ground, there has been a corresponding reduction in the field strength and a shift in location of the north magnetic pole."

Danielle listened and thought. She was suddenly back in Kang's brig, listening to Petrov tell of how his vessel had lost its way, sailing north instead of south, relying only on the magnetic compass. The pole had moved, but he didn't know it. She thought of the GPS going out, the sharks following them, and now she knew why: Yuri and the shard embedded in his brain. The small pulse on November 21 in the Bering Sea had to have come from him, with the sharks tracking them, just as the sharks in the gulf had homed in on her when she carried the stone.

"There was a similar weakening in 1908," Moore added. "It took me awhile to understand why."

"The Russians pulled the stone that far back?" she asked.

"Not exactly," Moore said. "We think the stone detonated or self-destructed in central Russia in June of that year."

June 1908. The date was familiar. "The Tunguska blast," she said.

"You know the story?"

"Of course," she said. "Summer 1908, a massive explosion shook the Russian tundra. Fireballs were seen in the sky from three hundred miles away, trees knocked over like dominoes for twenty miles in every direction. Most people think it was caused by the airburst of a meteor or perhaps even a small asteroid. Expeditions have gone looking for the remnants but as far as I know, nothing was ever found. Last figure I saw equated the burst with a thirty-megaton bomb."

"Try fifty," Moore said. "According to the Russians anyway. Two thousand times the power of the Hiroshima bomb."

"And you're telling me it was one of the stones?"

"It's the only thing that makes sense," he said. "The drop in the magnetic field coincides exactly with the event. The blast itself has remained unexplainable even with the theory of an airburst. No crater, no radiation. And then there is the one thing the Russians did find."

"The remnants of the stone," she guessed.

"As it turns out," he said. "In 1957, amid the chill of the cold war, the Russians mounted an expedition that they have never admitted to. And using the latest technology of the time they were able to find what they considered a ground zero of the event.

"Highly distorted magnetic readings led them to believe they had zeroed in on the nickel-iron core of a fallen meteor, at the bottom of Lake Cheko. A year of underwater work recovered nothing, until suddenly the magnetic readings shifted and all electronic systems failed in the main dredging boat. During the repairs a magnetometer led them to a single shard that had been hauled aboard just prior to the meltdown."

"And the Russians had it all this time," she said.

"One of the prize possessions of the Science Directorate."

"And they used it on Yuri," she said. "I can see why they want him back."

"They want the shard back," Moore said, "and they don't want the world knowing what they've been using it for. As I said, it was an experiment."

"And at the end of the experiment?" she asked.

"It was to be removed," he said. "A procedure that would likely kill him."

Danielle shuddered. She couldn't believe what she was hearing. "How did he end up with Kang?"

"It appears that some members of the directorate thought that removing the shard from Yuri was an inhuman decision. They kidnapped him with the help of some contacts. They sold him to Kang under promises of his good treatment. We think they're all dead now."

"And why did Kang want him?"

"Because Kang, who hasn't been seen in public for years, suffers from the same disease that Yuri has. Based on the timing of his disappearance, it's believed he came down with it five years ago. If the rumors are true, he'll be dead in a year or so."

Now it made sense, at least some of it. "He had

Yuri," she pointed out. "He could have operated on him right then."

"It seems Kang doesn't want just a shard," Moore said. "He believed Yuri could lead him to the stones that remained. And with those stones he could do more than gain remission; he could be healed completely."

"So there is no fourth stone," she said, wondering what that meant for the prophecy, either good or bad.

If the stones were designed to help, she wondered if they would have enough power to complete their task. And if they were designed to cause some havoc, would Russia now be spared while North and Central America bore the brunt of it?

"At least not anything more than a splinter," Moore said.

Danielle took a moment to absorb what she'd just heard and then asked the obvious. "And what's going to happen when these stones fulfill their mission?" All along she'd felt they were pursuing the right road, but now . . . she suddenly felt her conviction shifting.

"I don't know," Moore admitted. "I should think you and McCarter would have a better grasp on that than I do."

"What's going to happen to Yuri?" she asked pointedly.

Moore hesitated, and then spoke remorsefully. "We believe the next pulse will be far more powerful than the last. Maybe a hundred times more powerful. Maybe a thousand. And if Yuri is affected proportionally . . . "

"He'll die," she said, finishing his sentence.

Moore didn't reply. He didn't need to.

It seemed impossible to her, unfair beyond comprehension that Yuri could have gone through all he'd been through just to die now. She could not accept that this would be his end. There had to be a way to save him. There had to be.

She heard Moore talking, but her mind had gone numb.

"There's more at stake here than just Yuri," he said. "You have to stay clear on this, remain unemotional."

Once upon a time that had been her forte.

"If you even tell me to look at the bigger picture I'll—"

"You do need to look at the bigger picture," he said. "If the legend is true, if it's history and not speculation, then billions will die if we do the wrong thing. Hundreds of millions of them will be children just like Yuri."

She took a breath and tried to harden herself as she'd once been able to. Finally she spoke. "What do you want me to do?"

"I've been instructed to give you the following order: Set your watches to count down independently. If you do not hear from us prior to the reading triple zero on the clock, you are to destroy the stone and bury the remnants in the deepest hole you can find."

"They gave you a contingency order," she said, realizing it had come from someone other than Moore. "Fine, it's noted. But what do *you* want us to do?"

"I don't know yet," he said. "I feel they're misreading this thing badly, but I can't ask you to violate the order. Not without absolute proof."

She knew what he wanted to say, but she understood why he held back.

"Figure out your own thoughts on this," he added. "Find some peace with whatever you decide, and then tell me if you can do what I ask or not."

She looked around the small guest room. Out the window at the gathering dusk she saw the people of San Ignacio. There were children getting ready for their posada play. She wanted to go see Yuri.

"I will," she said.

"Good."

She signed off, put the phone down, and fought hard against the tears that were trying to break through.

CHAPTER 55

Hawker sat on the steps of the guesthouse watching the procession in the street. A group of the youngest children from the village were reenacting the journey of Mary and Joseph to Bethlehem. A young boy was wearing a long, blue cloth as if it were a robe; beside him a young girl wore white with yellow trim as she rode atop a small burro. The rest of the town's children followed them. Hawker even saw Yuri mixed in with the group.

The boy playing Joseph dutifully led the burro and its passenger from door to door, knocking politely and asking if there were any *"habitaciones en la posada."* Any room at the inn.

At each door the children of the group inhaled with expectation, but one by one they were told no. Finally, at a house several doors up from the church, a face looked out on the young Mary and Joseph and smiled.

"Sí," the woman said.

And the children went wild.

Minutes later the party was in full swing, with music playing, a piñata being smashed, fresh food and drink for everyone. Scenes like this were taking place all over Mexico on the nights leading up to Christmas.

In the Mayan towns like the one McCarter had temporarily resided in, a different festival was being celebrated, one that focused on the winter solstice and combined it with the looming end date on the Mayan calendar.

Scenes of joy and happiness everywhere. Hawker wondered what they would think if they knew what he knew.

Watching the party from a distance, Yuri saw him and smiled. Hawker waved and Yuri swirled away with the other kids, running and playing like a normal child.

A town like this would probably be paradise for the kid. It had electricity, but not all that much ran on it: small bulbs strung across the street to give a little public light, a few radios and televisions and phones, but nothing like the cities.

Maybe when it was all over they could just leave Yuri here, let the family that was caring for him adopt him, and allow the little guy to actually live for once. To some extent Hawker wouldn't have minded staying here himself.

He put the thought out of his mind, picked himself up, and made his way across the street. He entered the church intending to check on McCarter and was surprised to find Danielle lighting a candle by the altar.

She wore a cotton, flower print dress of red and black. It fit like it was made for her. Her chestnut brown hair spilled over her shoulders in long, straight locks. He almost didn't recognize her.

"Danielle?"

She turned.

"Look at you."

She actually blushed slightly, then glanced toward the door as firecrackers went off outside at the party.

"You like it?"

It was so different. "I've never seen you like this." He couldn't stop smiling.

"I borrowed it from the woman who is taking care of Yuri," she said.

"I just saw him," Hawker said. "He's enjoying himself."

Her smile faded. "At least for now."

"What's wrong?"

"Moore thinks Yuri will die when the stones release their energy tomorrow."

"What?" Hawker said, shocked. "Why?"

"Because the object buried in his cerebral cortex isn't a medical device; it's a shard from the Russian stone."

She went on to explain what Moore had told her, what it meant. Hawker looked away. It was like they just couldn't win.

Danielle turned back toward the altar. She took the candle she was holding, whispered a prayer, and placed it beside the others.

If ever there was a time for it.

"Maybe he doesn't have to die," Hawker said.

She looked over her shoulder at him.

"The wine cellar downstairs," Hawker told her. "The one our mad scientist professor won't leave until he's found the secret formula. It's twenty feet belowground. It might shield him, the way the temples in the Amazon and under the gulf shielded those stones. The same way the tunnel at Yucca Mountain is keeping that one from linking up with ours."

She looked up at him.

"As someone reminded me awhile ago, this *is* a sanctuary," he said. "So why not let it be one?"

Her eyes were locked on his, and he felt as if she were reaching out to him.

"I don't know how you can say you have no hope," she said. "Because you bring me hope whenever you're around."

The statement caught him off guard. The look in her eyes and the tone of her voice touched him deeper than he would normally allow. He thought instantly of the way his life had progressed, of lost friends, lost battles, some of which had been caused by his reckless, arrogant choices. He thought of the day Moore had come to meet him, when he'd been sitting in Devera's church in Africa, unable to sleep or speak or think.

"The last time I was in a church, I was literally covered with blood," he said. "I kind of felt like Pilate, you know? At some point it doesn't come off."

"Might be the only trait we share. I feel guilty for everything. For McCarter, for Yuri, for Marcus . . . for you."

"Me?"

Her eyes tracked him. "I don't know what it is that haunts you so deeply," she said. "But that's the past. And today I've come to realize that we can't change that. No matter how hard we try. No matter what we have in our possession. Including these stones."

There was something in her voice, a partial resolution of her own issues, he guessed.

"All we can do is fight for a better future," she added.

"With the stones," he said.

"With everything we have," she replied. "For everyone we love."

She continued to gaze at him and he again had a sense of her searching him, as if he were hiding something and she was unwilling to let him continue.

"What would you decide," she said, finally, "if it was up to you?"

He held her gaze in the quiet of the church. He'd long since lost faith in most things: governments, churches, himself. The thought of having this decision rest on his shoulders had not weighed easy on him before. Since arriving in San Ignacio that feeling had grown worse.

"You're the only one who hasn't been affected," she said.

"Let's see what McCarter finds," he said.

"I just spoke with him," she said. "It's not going well. And he didn't look particularly good, either, so I don't know how much we are going to get out of him."

Hawker didn't like the sound of that. Without McCarter's translation they would be left with little more than guesswork.

"So if you have to decide," she said, pressing him.

He felt more than a sense of ambivalence toward the stones; he felt anger. They were like some kind of blank piece of paper to him, letting everyone see what they wanted to see.

"Most of what I've seen from humanity is brutality, selfishness, and greed. You want me to trust in mankind?" He looked toward the crucifix, the image of Christ battered and bleeding. "This is what we do."

He stared into her eyes. "Better hope McCarter figures something out, because if using those stones means harm to you, or him or Yuri . . ." He shook his head. "Then the hell with them. I'll smash that stone into a thousand pieces. And if the world burns around us, so be it."

Her eyes were locked on his. She didn't blink or move or speak. She just stared at him in the silence. And he didn't know if that was a good thing or a bad thing.

He looked around the church, feeling out of place, much as he had in the simple wooden building in Africa. "I should go," he said.

"I'll go with you," she replied.

She looked back to the altar, crossing herself, and then turned and walked with Hawker to the church door. Together they stepped out into the cool night air.

For the briefest second, as they stepped outside, Hawker thought he heard the sound of a small plane. But he tilted his head and couldn't pick it up. A moment later the musicians in the street began to play and Danielle led him off to where the town folk were dancing.

Three hundred miles away, at Kang's command center in the warehouse, Kang's men processed the incoming data. The foot patrol units with their networked cameras had scanned nearly two hundred thousand faces with no sign of the NRI team, while the aerial drones surveyed the terrain along the line that led into the mountains. They probed the jungle with a combination of infrared cameras, magnetometers, and a specialized receptor designed to pick up the faint signature of medical-grade radioactive material.

So far they'd found several parties of hikers, a crashed military trainer that had rusted to pieces in the trees, and three possible sites of undiscovered ruins. But there had been no sign of his quarry, at least until now.

One of the drone operators received an alarm. He sat facing a pair of large computer screens displaying what looked a great deal like a modern military cockpit. And indeed it was similar. The readouts on his screens were created by remote telemetry from the sensors and instruments in the drone. Three hundred miles away, sitting on the ground in Campeche, the "pilot" controlled the drone and he had taken this one to the very end of its range, before picking up a signal.

The strength of the signal faded rapidly and he decided to risk one more pass before turning the million-dollar machine for home. This time the signal came in stronger.

He pressed the intercom switch, which buzzed Kang's office. "I report contact from drone number five. I repeat we have contact. I'm locking the location in now." He typed the coordinates into the computer and hit ENTER.

The computer ran the sensor analysis and confirmed the signal.

"San Ignacio," he said, looking at the map. "They're hiding in San Ignacio."

CHAPTER 56

Arnold Moore remained at Yucca Mountain deep into the night, running simulations on a program his technicians had put together. The simulation had confirmed Stecker's theory. The stones and their energy waves were intrinsically linked to the weakening magnetic field, but no matter how Moore tinkered with the variables, the numbers did not match up. Close, but slightly off.

Using assumptions the NRI had come up with, he changed the inputs several times. The numbers skewed slightly high.

He changed them again.

The numbers were off to the low side.

Frustrated, Moore ordered the simulation to do a reverse analysis, to take the actual data and back out to what the numbers should be.

He waited. The screen flashed.

Operational parameter invalid.

Something in the equation was preventing the operation, like dividing by zero.

Moore typed. *Suggested parameter adjustment?*

The computer ran through a series of calculations and then offered its best guess.

Parameter with highest likelihood of successful adjustment: Number of Magnetic Fields.

Moore stared at the blinking cursor. *Number of Magnetic Fields. What the hell could that mean?*

Sliding a pair of reading glasses back onto his nose, he clicked over to the input page and scrolled through all of the preset parameters. Among them he found a box to input number of magnetic fields. It currently was set at 1.

Moore looked around, feeling foolish. Could there be more than one magnetic field? The program came from the North Pole survey group; it was designed to calculate the speed and magnitude of future changes. Moore's people had modified it to assess the impact of the stones.

The stones.

Could they be considered their own magnetic field? Moore looked over his glasses and changed the number to 2. He then designated the output for field number two to match the believed power level of the stones. Hitting ENTER, he ran the reverse query again.

The screen blinked. *Operational parameter invalid.*

"Damn," he cursed.

He went back and changed the number to 3. The computer asked for the strength of the third field and Moore had no answer. He typed "X" and hit ENTER.

The computer began to think. It was connected to a group of mainframes and networked through an advanced system of processing that one of the NRI's former member companies had developed. Working together, the mainframes had the power of a supercomputer. But by entering "X," Moore had created a massive need for calculating power. And as he stared at the nonresponsive screen, Moore wondered if he'd crashed the system.

After several minutes, Moore sighed. He was about to give up when the screen flashed. A series of numbers came up relating to field strength, where the pole was, and where it should be. Moore studied the numbers. They matched exactly.

If the computer was right, they were dealing with not one earthbound magnetic field but three.

CHAPTER 57

Professor McCarter found himself struggling once again. Beneath the exposed bulbs in the church's wine cellar, he found he could not focus.

He sat back and looked at the notes he'd written so far, from glyphs he'd already translated. *These were the words of the Fallen Jaguar, the last of the Brotherhood. I write them in the language that is no more.*

He guessed that this was the author of the scroll, and that the language he referred to was the hieroglyphics of the Maya.

McCarter glanced at his next line of notes. He could see his own handwriting deteriorating. He noticed his hand shaking visibly now, but it must have been doing so even then.

In their wisdom the gods gave the four stones to the first people, the Wooden People. After the great storm, the falling of the Black Rain, only the Brotherhood remained to carry the secret.

McCarter was certain that this referred to the Mayan creation story, in which the gods of the Maya tried to bring forth the human work. After several failed tries they used wood as the catalyst in the effort and succeeded, creating beings that looked somewhat like humans but were more like stick people, with deformed bodies and dry cracking faces.

Some scholars said these people were actually monkeys who ended up living in the trees, but McCarter had always rejected that notion, as the Wooden People were never described to have fur, or tails, or any type of grace or athleticism. Instead they were said to be ungainly and weak. Much more like the body they had found in the cave below the Amazon temple. The body of a human from the future.

And if he was right, after the Wooden People were killed in the storm and the flood, the regular people, whom they seemed to have exercised control over, left, fleeing the Amazon and heading north. Most of these people, and indeed the legend itself, gloried in the destruction of the Wooden People. But the Brotherhood, perhaps a group of priests or acolytes, knew better. They had taken the stones that were accessible and brought them on a journey, several journeys to be exact, and placed them as they'd been told.

The Sacrifice of the Heart remains at Zuyua.

This was the Brazil stone, which he and Danielle had found two years earlier.

The Sacrifice of the Mind has followed the sun, over the great sea.

McCarter guessed this was the Russian stone. The one they had yet to look for.

To the Temple of the Initiation was taken the Sacrifice of the Soul, and the last went to the mountains. Here I have placed it: The master stone, The Sacrifice of the

Body lies beneath the Mirror, in the Temple of the Jaguar.

The Brotherhood, the regular humans from the current time period, stretched all the way back to the original shrine in Brazil. It made sense. The travelers from earth's future appeared weak and deformed; they needed help, assistance. They could not be expected to do the task alone. They must have recruited certain members in secret, and thus the Brotherhood was formed.

McCarter gazed at his notes, pleased that the past made sense now, but he realized that nothing he'd found would tell him what they really needed to know: what they should do now.

Feeling dizzy, he went back to translating.

He leaned over the hieroglyphic book and a drop of sweat fell from his face and hit the parchment. He dabbed the parchment with a towel, wiped his face, and studied the next group of symbols.

One for the earth, the land. One that represented healing, and another that he'd come to realize indicated the stones.

Would the stones heal the earth? And from what?

He leaned forward again, studying a glyph that represented men or mankind or the human kind. Another glyph represented nature, the earth in a sense, and a third glyph represented darkness. He had seen glyphs before that signified that nature would destroy man, as when a volcano erupted or an earthquake flattened a village, but here the order was reversed. Could it mean what he thought it meant? So much of the prophecy, especially as it was treated today, seemed to indicate nature destroying man, but this was different: The parchment in front of him suggested that man destroys nature. Was the catastrophe not natural in origin but in fact man-made? Or was it his liberal prejudices coming out? He remembered a debate with a conservative friend who told him he put trees ahead of people. He could not be sure, but the words were there.

His eyes blurred suddenly, watering and burning. His body ached. He wrote his notes and looked to the next set of glyphs. They seemed familiar to him, in fact he was certain he knew them, but he could not divine a meaning. It was an odd sensation, like not being able to recall the name of someone you knew well. He traced the outline of the first one with his finger, hoping it would jog his memory, but nothing came to him. He drew it with his shaky hand but still his mind was blank.

A jolt of anger and frustration hit him. It was almost impossible to do what he was trying to do without a database, or at least his old notebooks or an anthology of known glyphs. But he had nothing to work with, nothing but his failing memory.

He sat back again. Despite the warmth of the wine cellar he now had the chills. He was running a fever and as often happened to the patient whose temperature rises rapidly, he'd begun to feel as if he were freezing.

He held the towel to his face. He felt as if he might throw up.

He put a hand to his leg and touched the outlines of his wound. It was hot, burning with infection once again, swollen and painful to the touch.

What had he done?

In a vain, desperate effort to hear his wife's voice again, he'd stopped taking the medications Danielle had been giving him. The sickness had brought his wife to him once, or so he'd thought: the sickness and the stone, the conduit through time. But as he'd become well, her face had vanished; her voice no longer touched his mind. It was like waking from a dream and wishing only to go back to sleep and find it somehow. And McCarter could not bring himself to let that happen.

In response he'd shunned the antibiotics in hopes of seeing her again. But the only result was a growing fever and a cloudy mind just when they all needed it to be sharp.

CHAPTER 58

At the celebration, Father Domingo made a great fuss over Hawker and Danielle. The women of the town found it hard to believe Danielle could be happy in her thirties without having a husband. They insisted she dance with a few of the men, and then, realizing she had come with Hawker, they made it a point to get them dancing and drinking as much as possible.

By midnight the celebration had begun to wind down and Hawker and Danielle found themselves alone in an alleyway outside the guesthouse.

They leaned against the building and looked at each other.

Hawker found himself both captivated by her and concerned. The events of recent days flashed through his head and, strangely, Arnold Moore's arrival in Africa settled in his mind.

"A peso for your thoughts," Danielle asked.

He hesitated. "Just thinking about something Moore said to me in Africa," he told her.

"And what might that be?"

"By the pricking in my thumbs," he said, "something wicked this way comes."

"Bradbury?"

He shook his head. "It's from *Macbeth,* actually."

"Shakespeare?" She smiled. "You surprise me."

"I know a thing or two."

"So it would seem," she said. "You feel like Macbeth?"

"The witches said those words to him, after he became a traitor and murdered the king," Hawker said.

"You're not a traitor or a murderer," she said, "and Arnold Moore certainly doesn't think so."

He guessed that she was right. Certainly Moore had hired him to save the thing he valued most in this world, Danielle. "There are those who would disagree," he said to her, "but even that's not what I'm getting at. Macbeth was a loyal soldier, a general who crushes the king's enemies until the witches stir up his ambition and ego by telling him that he would soon become king himself. The question is, would he have done anything had they just kept their damned mouths shut?"

She guessed his line of thought. "You're thinking about the stones and us, and the parchment Father Domingo had. Afraid we're doing the witch's bidding?"

"I don't believe in destiny," he said. "But people can be manipulated into doing things they otherwise wouldn't."

She took a deep breath and looked into his eyes. "Fate and destiny don't have to be an evil thing. Where would I be, if you hadn't come into my life?"

He studied her. So much in his world was darkness, but somehow she was like the light. The flickering glow from the fire bathed her face, laying shadows and mystery across her skin. A strand of dark hair had fallen across her eyes.

Hawker reached out to put it back behind her ear. He didn't pull his hand away, and she didn't ask him to. Instead he ran the tips of his fingers down the side of her face, softly brushing her cheek. She turned toward it, then looked back up at him as he leaned in and kissed her.

She kissed him back, pressing her lips into his. He could taste the wine on her tongue, feel the warmth of her breath in his mouth.

They kissed hard, then parted, looking into each other's eyes for a second. He laced his fingers through her hair, placing his hand behind her neck, and cradled the back of her head. She closed her eyes and moved toward him again.

In a moment they were sitting on a stone bench with no backrest, facing each other, their legs straddling the bench. They were hidden in an alcove in a quiet alleyway. She kissed him again and rubbed her face against his, the soft skin of her cheek moving across his, the smell of her hair and the perfume of the night around them adding to the intoxication.

Holding her mesmerized him. It wasn't as if he'd been waiting for her; there'd been plenty of women in various places. They had been comfort on hard nights, a chance to forget the hell that life sometimes was. But this was different. It felt like breathing again after drowning, a chance to rediscover what made life worth living.

He pulled her close, his fingers tracing the smooth curve of her neck, sliding down to the top of her back, to the top button on her dress. He opened it.

She traced a finger across his chest, leaning in and kissing him again. His hand slid down the side of her neck, across her shoulder, and down the smooth skin of her back. And then he stopped.

He pulled back.

"What's wrong?" she asked, looking at him. Her hair was a mess, her eyes half open.

He moved his hand to her back, just above her bra strap. But the movement was different, clinical, searching.

She seemed amused. "Having some trouble back there, sailor?"

"Have you had surgery recently?" he asked.

"No," she said, slightly aggravated. "Why?"

"Because you have a fresh scar, between your shoulder blade and your spine. And there's something solid underneath the skin."

A minute later they were back in the guest room. Danielle slid the top half of the cotton dress past her shoulders and leaned forward in front of the light. Suddenly she remembered the pain in her back after regaining consciousness in Hong Kong. She remembered the bright room that she'd thought had been an interrogation room.

Could it have been an operating room? Could they have implanted something in her?

"What is it?" she asked.

"I'm guessing it's some kind of tracking device," he said. "Probably short range, but able to be picked up by remote sensors, like LoJack."

Now it made sense. Of course they had given her boots back; of course they'd allowed her to escape. They knew what she was looking for and they realized she would find it more quickly than they would. Kang wanted her loose. He probably wanted Yuri with her, because of what he could do.

"This is how they found us on the water," she said.

"Probably," he said.

"And you thought you heard a plane earlier," she said.

"It could have been anything."

"But you know it's not," she said.

She stood up holding the dress against her chest to prevent it from falling.

She turned, trying to see the scar in the mirror, but it was in a place that was almost impossible to reach or even to see clearly. That had been done on purpose, so she'd never know it was there.

"How deep is it?" she asked, thinking she would have felt a lot more discomfort if they had cut into the underlying muscle.

She felt his fingers pressing for the edges. "It's just under the skin."

"Subcutaneous," she said. That made things easier.

"What do you want me to do?"

She looked dead at him. "I want you to get a knife and cut the damn thing out of me."

"Are you insane?" he asked. "Does this seem like a sterile environment to you?"

"We can account for that," she said, knowing they had strong antibiotics on hand.

"Okay, fine," he said, "but I'm not a surgeon and I've been drinking for three hours."

She fixed her gaze on him. "I'm not asking you to

take my gall bladder out. It's nothing more than a big splinter. You just have to cut the skin and pull it out."

Hawker did not look pleased by the thought but he seemed to realize there was no other choice. "Fine," he said. "Lie down."

She took off the borrowed dress and laid a towel on the bed, wrapping another one around her waist. A second later Hawker was back with a bottle of rubbing alcohol and Danielle's first-aid kit.

He pulled out the Zithromax she'd been giving McCarter and handed her two pills, which she gulped down with a large glass of water.

"This is going to hurt," he said.

She almost laughed. "Not as bad as I'm going to hurt you, if you don't hurry up and get it over with."

She watched as he pulled the scalpel from the kit. Using the rubbing alcohol, he sterilized it repeatedly and then put it down without letting the tip of the blade touch anything.

She folded her arms up around the pillow and closed her eyes, trying to focus on anything but the cut that was about to come. She could feel Hawker's hands against her bare skin. They were warm and strong, and they felt heavy against her back. His leg pressed tight against her thigh and the feeling of his body over the top of her was distracting in an intimate way.

A sudden touch of cold brushed her back; an ice cube to numb the skin. She drew in a sharp breath and held it. Several droplets of water ran across her shoulder blade. One trickled to the side, curving over her body and down toward her hips, clinging to her skin until it trailed across her stomach.

The chill brought on goose bumps and she found herself holding her breath. She wanted to tell him to wait. To turn over and pull him close to her and to make love to him before all this would be done. But they'd run out of time to enjoy life.

"I'm ready," she said.

She felt his hand pressing heavy on her shoulder, holding it still, and then the edge of the scalpel cutting a shallow line in her skin. She tensed, fighting the instinct to cry out in pain.

CHAPTER 59

Back in her own clothes, with her shoulder bandaged but still bleeding, Danielle hiked to the church with Hawker by her side. She carried the pack with the stone in it. Hawker carried the first-aid kit, with McCarter's antibiotics.

As they walked, she tried to bottle up the waves of emotion running through her, pushing aside the feeling of having Hawker hold her and kiss her. She needed her wits about her now; she needed to be a professional again.

The tiny object buried under her skin turned out to be a radioactive pellet, an isotope that with the right equipment could be sensed from a distance. The fact that it wasn't a transmitter made sense. If Kang knew about the stones, he knew that a small microtransmitter would not operate long in their presence. But the pellet was a simple solution. Danielle guessed and hoped it was a low-grade isotope, with a short half-life and capable of little damage, but she didn't know.

She wrapped the pellet in a cloth and slid it into the lead-lined case that contained the stone. Then she and

Hawker hustled to find McCarter. The plan was to go now, to lure Kang's forces away from the town and ditch the pellet along the way, hopefully distracting him further.

They entered the church and immediately made their way to the wine cellar.

As they descended the stairs, she called out to McCarter. "Professor?"

She heard a crash and raced down the remaining stairs. She spotted McCarter in the far corner, the table overturned next to him. They ran to him.

"Professor," she said, helping him up.

He was drenched with sweat.

"He's burning up," she told Hawker.

"Are you all right?" she asked him.

"I couldn't . . . ," he mumbled. "I can't . . ."

She pressed her hand against his forehead. His temperature had to be over a hundred. McCarter reached into his pocket and produced five days' worth of antibiotics, which he had been pretending to take.

"I'm sorry," he said. "I wanted to see her again. I thought that the stone could bring her to me. Make it real."

"I've got to get you upstairs," Danielle said, as she and Hawker helped him up.

With Hawker under one arm and Danielle under the other, they began to move. "I tried to figure it out, but I don't know," McCarter said. "I can't think."

"What did you find out?" Hawker asked.

"The stones, they heal the earth," he said.

"The earth?"

"The ground," he said meekly. "The land."

"What about the Black Sun?" she asked. "What does the sun do?"

"Not the sun," he said. "The land."

"What are you talking about?"

"The land blackens the sun," he said.

She looked over at Hawker. He shrugged.

"It comes . . . ," McCarter sagged, almost unconscious. "From down here," he said.

They were holding him up now, a two-hundred-pound rag doll. He seemed on the verge of delirium.

They'd made it to the top stair and out into the church.

"I'm sorry," he said. "I wanted to see her again."

"You will."

The words came from Hawker, surprising to her as so many things about him were. She didn't know if he was just trying to put McCarter at ease or if he believed them, but the way they'd been spoken, filled with conviction, seemed to indicate that he did.

"Outside," she said. "The cool air might help his temperature a bit."

They dragged and carried him outside, laying him down on the church step. He looked horrible.

"Can you do anything for him?" Hawker asked.

"I can force-feed him some antibiotics, I can jury-rig an IV with fluids, and I can clean out that damn wound again," she said, then looked up at Hawker. "What I can't do is leave him here alone."

"What about the stone, the destiny?"

"I came back for a friend," she said. "I realized that

last night. Whatever other reasons there were, whatever the stone programmed me to do, I came back for Mc-Carter. I'm not leaving him now."

Both of them knew what that meant. Hawker would go for the Temple of the Jaguar alone.

CHAPTER 60

As Danielle worked on McCarter, Hawker went to find Father Domingo. Sneaking into his room, he switched on a flashlight.

"Forgive me, Father, for I have sinned," he said.

Father Domingo blinked in the bright light. He blocked the beam of light with his hand. "What have you done, my son?"

"I woke a priest up in the middle of the night after he threw a heck of party."

Hawker lowered the light.

"Is that all?" Father Domingo asked.

"No," Hawker said. "But that's all we have time for."

Father Domingo sat up. It was a heavy, ponderous movement, like a bear coming out of hibernation. "You're leaving," he said, looking at Hawker's manner of dress.

Hawker nodded. "Tell me where I have to go."

"What makes you think I know?"

"You asked us if we planned to do anything with the stone, not what we might do or where," Hawker said. "I figure that's because you already know."

"Are you sure you want to go there?"

Hawker nodded.

"You want to, or you believe you must?" Father Domingo asked.

"Other people believe," Hawker said. "Right now, that's good enough for me."

"Then you must hike back to the lake where we found you," Father Domingo said.

"Go past it and past the long, narrow lake beyond. There you will come to a series of hills. Between the third and fourth ridge you will find a sinkhole, much like the cenotes of the lowlands. At this time of year it is filled with water, with a small island in the center no larger than this room."

"That's the temple?" Hawker asked.

"The island is the temple; the cenote is the Mirror."

"Why do you call it the Mirror?"

Father Domingo nodded. "The water is like glass. Like any mirror it shows us who we are."

Hawker tried to take it all in. "Where's the stone? The others were hidden."

"Get onto the island. The Temple of the Jaguar is a simple place. Up close you will see what looks like a common drinking well. But it is different. Instead of dropping a bucket and working to pull it out, a system of counterweights was developed. All you must do is release the lever. The weights will drop, the shield of rock will move apart, and the stone will be brought up to you."

"You've been there." He guessed.

Father Domingo nodded. "I have seen it. I have touched it."

"Last of the Brotherhood," Hawker said, admiringly.

A gleam appeared in Father Domingo's eye. "I should hope not," he said, staring at Hawker.

Hawker didn't know what to think. All he knew was that he had to get away from San Ignacio as fast as possible, to lure their pursuers in one direction and make his way in the other. "Thank you for trusting us."

The priest stood and took a sip from a glass of water. "The Mayan people that I know would tell you this day is not doomsday but a day of transformation. Perhaps like many transformations it will be painful, even destructive. But they believe it will lead to a new dawn."

"What do you think?" Hawker asked.

Father Domingo looked to the Bible at his bedside. "When he was on the earth, the Lord told us that *he would make all things new again.* He did this through his death and resurrection, and by granting us the faith to believe we could do the same. Painful, destructive, but leading to a new dawn. So who am I to say this isn't another way of his making?"

Hawker stood to go. "I just wonder why they didn't design these things to do what they're supposed to do automatically."

"You've said they are machines, sent here to save us?" Father Domingo replied, echoing an earlier conversation.

"Some people think so," Hawker admitted.

Father Domingo smiled. "My son, even God requires an affirmative act of faith. Machines cannot save us alone. We must have a part to play. It seems that part is yours."

Hawker did not know if he had the faith everyone

was placing in him, but he had no time left to worry about it. "I have to go," he said.

"I will pray for your safety," Father Domingo said. "*Vaya con Dios.*"

A moment later, Hawker was leaving the village, sneaking out of town two hours before dawn, the stone and the pellet secured in his pack.

In a small house near the edge of the village, Yuri awoke in the darkness. He had heard something, as if someone had shouted. But there was no sound around him, no light or noise. The other children slept, some of them breathing loudly, but there was no movement.

And yet he could feel movement.

He sat up and looked around. He was certain now; he could hear it again. He could feel it.

Carefully, he picked his way across the room and looked out the window. There was no light, but there were colors to be seen. He could see it off in the hills just past the edge of town: The siren was moving.

He found his clothes, put on his shoes, and snuck out the door.

CHAPTER 61

At the helipad in Campeche, armed men piled into the bay of the Skycrane, taking seats and stowing their weapons. There were twenty men in all, followed by their leader, who strode calmly up the ramp, most of his body wrapped in what looked like Kevlar armor.

Kang stepped aboard the Skycrane and looked into the hearts of his men. They had no fear of what was ahead, but they regarded him with a sense of foreboding. He was a man encased in a machine now and they were not sure what to make of it.

He turned toward the cockpit, finally getting used to the speed at which the hydraulic actuators responded to the electrical input from his own nerves. At first it had felt too quick, as if he were being shoved around by some will other than his own. But now that he was used to it, Kang had begun to revel in it.

In the suit, he had the strength of a bear and the quickness of a cat. He had already decided that once he was healed he would continue to develop this suit and use it as he saw fit. He had been right all along. The machines would save him.

"We will find the boy and the other stones," he said

to his men. "And we will take them without pity. And when we return, there will be fortunes waiting for you all."

A cheer went up from the men, instinctive, unplanned for, like soldiers from the dynasties of old. They had just needed their leader back and now that they had him, Kang knew they would follow him to the end.

He motioned to the pilot and the engines began to roar.

CHAPTER 62

All through the night, Danielle had worked to stabilize McCarter, rigging IVs that she hung from a lampstand, cleaning and dressing his wound, and dosing him with antibiotics. Shortly after Hawker left, Father Domingo had come down to help and sometime around dawn, the fever had broken. McCarter wasn't out of the woods yet, but she believed he would survive and recover.

Relieved by his progress, she'd rested, until being awoken by the church bells ringing across the street. Was it Sunday? She had no idea.

She checked her patient. He was doing well, lying on the floor of the small guesthouse, conscious now.

"You're awake," she said.

He strained to get the words out. "Who can sleep with all those bells?"

He had a point. The church bells were ringing rather insistently.

Insistently.

Danielle sprang to her feet, suddenly realizing that the bells could be a warning. She grabbed her gun and ran outside.

A pair of armed men waited there, aiming weapons at her. Two others held a couple of the town folk as hostages, and an older man, who seemed like their leader, stood off to one side.

"Put it down," the scruffy-faced leader said.

She dropped the pistol as he walked toward her. "I'm Ivan Saravich," he said. "And you have something that belongs to me."

Twenty miles away, Hawker was picking his way toward the fourth ridge. He had hiked through the night, one hour on, ten minutes off. Upon crossing a small canyon, he'd taken a slight detour and flung the radioactive pellet down into it. If he was lucky Kang's men would track the pellet to the canyon and begin a search there. With all the nooks and caves he'd seen, it might be awhile before they knew they'd been had.

Since then he'd come five miles, though exhaustion was slowing his pace considerably. He stumbled on, scratched and cut from the briars and thornbushes, drenched in grime and sweat. He was exhausted, trudging forward, not thinking anymore, not looking at anything but the ground right in front of him.

In that semi-oblivious state, he failed to hear the sound of danger until it became too loud to ignore. A buzzing noise in the air, not a plane or a helicopter, it sounded more like a flying lawn mower.

He turned and ducked down, then glanced around, scanning sections of the sky. A mile or so behind, he spotted a small object cruising directly toward him. He knew what it was: a remotely operated drone. It meant Kang had found him.

He ran from the sound of the drone. He didn't bother ducking or hiding in the scrub; the drone had seen him. His only hope was to get to some real cover. The ridge-line up ahead looked like a possibility.

As he scrambled through the brush, the drone made a pass, buzzing by so closely that it almost clipped him.

He glanced at the stubby wings and gave thanks for the fact that it seemed unarmed. Then he heard a second drone coming in behind him, followed by the shrill whistle of an unguided rocket.

He dove to the ground. The missile whipped past him and exploded a hundred feet ahead. He felt the shock of the concussion and a wave of heat, but it was far enough away to be safe.

As the second drone passed him and broke into a turn, Hawker sprinted to the ridge and clambered up and into the rocks. He took cover, near the top, surrounded by a crown of boulders.

Safe for the moment, he looked around for the drones. They had pulled up higher, cruising in a lazy circle above him like mechanized buzzards. That could mean only one thing: They were there to keep their quarry treed. The real hunters were still on their way.

At gunpoint, Danielle was forced back inside the guesthouse. The man who identified himself as Saravich followed. Father Domingo and several of the townspeople were brought in. Danielle recognized Maria, the woman who had cared for Yuri and had given her the dress. They were ordered to their knees.

"Don't do this," Danielle pleaded. "They have nothing to do with me."

Ivan raised a vodka bottle to his lips. "You deceive yourself, young lady. They are here *only* because of you. They're hiding the boy," he said, "just as you did."

Danielle looked at Ivan's men. They were young, with hard faces, the same type of men who'd come to the hotel. Undoubtedly they would want revenge for their friends. She could see it in their faces.

And Ivan . . . Ivan had a look in his eyes that suggested he'd done this work before, done it for a long time.

For the first time in many years Danielle felt a type of fear she could not control.

She was ordered to sit next to Father Domingo.

"Where is the boy?" Ivan asked.

She did not want to give up Yuri, but she was certain that the Russian would kill everyone if she didn't.

"I don't know," she said.

"You lie!" he shouted, flying into a rage and smacking her in the side of the head with his Makarov pistol.

She fell and he aimed and fired. The crack of the powder charge shook the room. Everyone jumped and dust drifted upward from a hole in the floor just inches from Danielle's face.

Cautiously she returned to her kneeling position, her hands raised up beside her. Saravich stepped back and took another long swig from the bottle, like a man preparing for something he didn't want to do but could not avoid.

"We have already searched the church and the house of this woman and each of the houses on this street. And still the boy is not found," he said.

"He's missing," Maria said. "We don't know where. He must have run off."

Saravich wandered behind her to where McCarter lay. With a finger he flicked the IV line.

"I'm not afraid of you," McCarter said.

"You don't look so good," Ivan said. "Maybe I should put you out of your misery."

Danielle held her breath, realizing any response might be enough to set him off. She relaxed only slightly as the sound of Ivan's footsteps circled away from McCarter.

He walked out in front of the prisoners, eyeing them, waving a finger at them.

"You have all spoken the same," he said, sounding as if he approved. "But a well-concocted lie is not equal to the truth."

Danielle's mind whirled, desperately searching for a method of escape. It seemed impossible. The four younger Russians stood near the exit, weapons aimed at the floor, but ready and eyeing her and the other prisoners. Ivan continued to pace. She could sense his patience growing shorter.

He pounded the floorboards, slow and ponderous.

He crouched in front of her. "You know how this is going to end," he said. "I will kill everyone and kill you last. Spare them. Tell me where the boy is."

She looked down toward the floor, avoiding eye contact with him and hoping to disguise the fact that her emotions had gotten the best of her. But the position caused the tears to stream across her face. She watched the drops fall and splatter on the simple wooden floor.

She closed her eyes, tight. And when she opened them, there were no more tears left to come. The fight had returned to her.

She met his gaze.

"I know who you are, Ivan Saravich," she said. "And so do the people I work for. We take care of our own. A man from your era should know what that means."

"'A man from my era,'" he laughed. "Yes, once we were professionals. Now we are just roaches scavenging for what we can get."

"If you harm me," she said, "or any of these men and women, my people will hunt you down. You know that. So shoot me if you want, but dig your own grave while you're at it."

Danielle thought she saw a flicker of concern cross Ivan's weather-beaten face, but then a sickening laugh bubbled up from deep in his being. He took another drink, then offered her the bottle, but she refused it.

"Mine was dug long ago," he whispered.

For just an instant he looked sad, remorseful. And in that moment she recognized him: the round face, the flat bridge of his nose, and the sharp eyes that seemed to miss nothing.

"I know you," she said.

He stood and raised the Makarov slowly, as if it were heavy in his drunken hand.

"You knew my brother," he corrected. "The man who kidnapped Yuri."

"He was trying to save him," she said.

"Yes," Saravich said, as if it were some hated admission. "And he failed."

Turning, Saravich centered the gun on the back of Father Domingo's head.

"No," Danielle pleaded.

"I'm afraid it's time," he said.

"May God forgive you," Father Domingo said.

"We can only hope," Ivan replied. He flicked the gun to the right and fired two quick shots. Two of the Russians fell. A quick turn to the left and three more shells crashed.

Bang, bang, bang.

The other Russian men went down in heaps, one squirming and writhing until Saravich finished him with a shot to the head.

Father Domingo and the other prisoners dove in opposite directions. Maria scrambled out the door. Danielle pushed back to the wall and froze beside McCarter as Saravich aimed the gun her way.

"I don't understand," she said.

"It is simple," he said. "I do not wish to die today."

"Neither do I," she replied.

"You won't," he said lowering the gun. "Not by my hand, at least. But these men would have buried us all."

Before she could ask anything else, Ivan turned to Father Domingo. "Do you have Yuri?"

"I swear, we don't know where he is," Father Domingo said.

"I hope for his sake you're lying," Ivan replied. "I hope you have hidden him well and just find it impossible to trust me. But do not worry. I have no intention of taking him back to Russia."

Father Domingo shook his head. "I don't know where he is."

"Hmm . . . ," Ivan grumbled. "You must look for him, then. If you find him, or if he comes back once we've left, please keep him safe. I will tell the men who sent me that he died."

Danielle studied Ivan's face. It seemed etched with regret.

"I still don't understand," she said.

"All this time," he told her, "I have been thinking that my brother disgraced me. That it was he who had ruined our names. But it was I who disgraced him and what he tried to do."

"And now?" Danielle asked.

"Now?" he repeated. "Now an army of men and machines are speeding toward your valiant friend, the one called Hawker. And though he seems to be very resourceful, he will soon be involved in a battle he cannot hope to win."

Ivan offered a hand. "Unless we help him."

"He's a long way from here," she said.

"I know," he replied, "and Comrade Kang has helicopters with him. But I promise you, they're nothing like the one I've brought."

Danielle found herself dizzy from the sudden reversal, but the thought of Kang killing Hawker was something she could not allow her mind to grasp. She reached out and grabbed Ivan's hand, pulling herself up.

"Then let's go help him."

CHAPTER 63

In the darkness of the Yucca Mountain tunnel, Arnold Moore jumped out of the Humvee before the driver had even stopped. He raced toward the trailer laboratory and burst in.

Nathanial Ahiga, Byron Stecker, and the rest of the two science teams looked up. With only half an hour to go, they had been discussing the procedure for destroying the stone.

"Where the hell have you been, Arnold?" It was President Henderson's voice over the speaker on the flat-screen monitor.

"I'm sorry, I've been working on a new theory," he said.

"Oh, please," the director of the CIA grumbled.

"Shut up, Stecker!" Moore shouted, then turned back to the president.

"It's a little late for this, Arnold," Henderson said.

"Just hear me out," Moore answered. "Then do whatever you want. Shoot me if you want. Just listen for two minutes."

Without taking a breath or giving the president the

chance to say no, Moore continued. "Stecker's information was correct, but the numbers weren't the perfect match he told you they were. They massaged the data to fit it into the graph, but for reasons that would take too long to explain, if you extrapolated the numbers in either direction, their graph diverges from reality."

"Stecker?"

"It's called rounding, Mr. President. Other than that I don't know what he's talking about."

The president looked open to suggestion but he glanced at the clock nervously. "Be quick, Arnold."

Moore took a breath. Light-headed and sweating, he looked around. Stecker rolled his eyes, Moore's staff members looked at the ground, and Ahiga shook his head sadly and looked away. Not a friend in the room. He didn't care.

"Mr. President, standard geology holds that earth's core is a huge, spinning ball of liquid metal, mostly nickel and iron. Because those elements are conductive, the spinning motion creates the magnetic field that protects us."

It was the quickest primer Moore had ever given.

"The problem is, no one knows this for sure; no one's dug down that far to find out. And no one has been able to match this theory up with an explanation of why the earth's field reverses at seemingly random intervals, a million years between one changeover, fifty thousand between the next." Moore ran a hand through his hair, tamping down his wiry mane, trying to look like something less than a lunatic.

"The reason is," he said, "it's not a single magnetic

field—I mean in the aggregate it is—but it's being generated by three separate layers interacting with each other."

"Oh, come on," Stecker mumbled.

Moore ignored him. "A similar thing happens in the sun. Even though the sun is a million times more massive than the earth, and it creates a magnetic field millions of times more powerful, its magnetic field reverses every eleven years. And it doesn't go easily. The sun's equator rotates faster than the sections near the poles. As a result the magnetic lines of force get dragged across the face of the sun, much like spreading a sheet out over your bed and then pulling it only from the middle. The center moves, the edges stay. Instead of nice parallel lines everything gets skewed.

"In the sun, the lines get so tangled that they can snap like a rubber band stretched too tight. This is what causes solar flares and other events like the coronal mass ejections. Both events release incredible amounts of energy in a single instant."

"How much energy are we talking about?" the president asked.

"Enough to fling a hundred billion tons of material into space at a single moment," Moore said.

The president looked drawn. "How does this apply to us?"

"We keep acting as if the earth's core is a single, uniformly rotating thing, and for the most part it is, but the inner layer is solid and the outer layer is liquid. In the simulation I've run we can line up the graphs of field strength and reversal timing, allowing that this outer layer is spinning at a different rate near its equator than it is at the poles. That's the second field."

"You said there were three."

"Yes," Moore said. "The third is created by the stones. It's only been present for the last three thousand years. Sent here in an effort to stabilize that second field to stop it from doing what it's about to do."

"Which is?"

"Snap exactly like the loops on the sun."

The president cleared his throat. "And what happens when this, um, rubber band snaps?"

Moore took a breath. "There won't be any mushroom clouds, if that's what you mean, but there may be some physical effects, possibly minor earthquakes or tremors, but mostly just a massive electromagnetic burst. I don't have all the numbers, but you can expect something close to ten thousand times the energy of the burst we felt here."

"Ten thousand times?" The president's voice trailed off as if the concept were inconceivable to him.

"A tsunami wave of electromagnetic energy rampaging from the current pole across North America and downward, wiping out every electrical circuit in the Western Hemisphere. It will blind every satellite in near-earth orbit at the same moment, while a weaker shadow wave crosses Asia and central Russia and the northeastern corner of Europe. Unfortunately for us, the wave crossing Russia and China will be lighter, meaning they will be stung hard and blinded, but some of their hardened military equipment will survive, especially missiles in hardened silos. They will likely retain the capability to wage war, both on each other or on us, at a time in which we will be utterly defenseless against any foreign attack."

"And the stones' part in this?"

"Designed to counter it while they were hidden, to hold the wave back so the rubber band never stretches in the first place," Moore said. "But something went wrong. When the Russian stone exploded that plan began to falter. But I think they have a fail-safe mode, and if we bring them up to a place where their signal is not blocked, they can find each other and they can vent this wave safely into space, channeling it like a lightning rod. But to have any chance we must surface all of them: the ones in Mexico and the one we have here."

The president was quiet. The room was quiet. Finally, even Moore was quiet.

He did not know whether he had convinced the commander in chief, but he'd exhausted himself in the attempt.

"Clear the room," the president said finally. "I will speak with the director of the NRI alone."

Sitting next to Moore, Nathanial Ahiga grabbed his soda bottle. "You put on a good show," he said somberly, sounding like he was talking to a valiant but defeated warrior.

As Ahiga stepped back into the lab section of the trailer and shut the door behind him, the other scientists picked up their notes and exited into the tunnel. Stecker followed them, a smirk on his face as he stepped out into the darkness.

CHAPTER 64

Pinned down by the circling drones, Hawker had cowered in the crown of boulders as three lumbering helicopters approached. In a flat area between the ridges, two of them touched down, disgorging a small army.

He saw twenty men fan out from the lead craft, while the second helicopter released what looked like a group of pack mules, moving in a precise and ominous fashion.

Through his binoculars he could see that these "pack mules" were some kind of mechanical walking machine, like four-legged donkeys with machine-gun turrets where their heads belonged.

"You've got to be kidding me," he mumbled.

The men hung back, allowing the strange walking machines to take the lead. He watched their hydraulic legs propel them forward, their turreted heads swiveling from side to side. He counted six of them, and all he could be certain of was that he didn't want to see them up close.

Wedging the assault rifle into a gap between the rocks, he sighted the lead machine and opened fire. Shells from the rifle ripped into the lead beast. Sparks flew and it stumbled. But somehow it regained its balance and continued on its course, climbing the slope toward him. He fired at another with the same result and then let the rifle whale away on full automatic.

One machine crashed to the ground, its front legs damaged, the rear legs still trying to push forward. The others turned toward him and opened fire.

The rock wall in front of Hawker exploded from a convergence of shells. He dove to the ground, crawled fifteen feet, and tried to steal a glance out the other side. But the machines seemed to be waiting for it. The instant he poked his head out, another burst tore into the boulders around him. Whatever type of sensors the machines were using to find him—heat sensors, motion detectors, shape recognition software, whatever it was—they'd locked on to him now.

As the barrage continued, Hawker took cover. He pressed himself into the largest of the boulders, listening to the strange sound of the machines marching closer.

Danielle sat in the gunner's seat of a massive Russian helicopter as it thundered across the countryside. The craft was a Hind-D, a huge military gunship armed with a 30mm cannon and racks of air-to-ground missiles, and powered by a tremendous turbine engine that pushed the craft through the air at up to two hundred and fifty knots. The sense of speed, the vibration, and the visceral feeling of power that coursed from the airframe was undeniably intoxicating. For once in her career she felt as if she were charging into battle on a stallion of superior power.

As Ivan piloted the craft, Danielle familiarized herself

with the weapons systems. And as they approached the target zone, she was looking forward to wreaking havoc.

"How the hell did you get this thing in country?" she asked over the intercom.

"Officially it is part of a movie production," Ivan said. "Not a bad cover, don't you think?"

"Not bad at all," she replied. "As long as it doesn't fire blanks."

Ivan laughed, a genuine belly laugh with a sense of warmth that could be felt even through the intercom. "I promise you, I didn't come all this way to fire blanks."

With that they rocketed over the third ridge and the helicopters on the radar scope came into visual.

One of the Skycranes was hanging back. Ivan was already angling toward it.

"Three seconds to range," Ivan said.

The amber light on her targeting display lit up and an instant later it switched to green. Danielle pressed the fire switch and a heavy buzzing shook the craft as the rotary cannon unleashed the fury of a hundred shells.

The tracers laced into the hovering Skycrane, ten explosive shells in between each glowing marker. The hovering craft lit up with smoke and then exploded and fell toward the ground.

Euphoric, Danielle searched for the next target.

With the burrolike machines blasting at his stronghold, Hawker lay flat on the ground, slithering toward the back edge of the space. He was considering making a break for it when the sound of a thunderous explosion echoed across the landscape.

From the corner of his eye he saw a fireball in the east. It was one of the Skycranes. How or why, he didn't know. But when he saw the drones spiraling out of control and crashing into a canyon wall, he didn't waste time trying to find out.

He took off running. He had ten minutes.

As Stecker and the scientists left the trailer, Moore caught sight of the rocket sled, the vessel of destruction designed to send the stone into the deepest part of the mountain. It was ready and waiting.

The president shouted at him. "What the hell have you gotten us into, Arnold?!"

"What are you talking about?"

"You were late to a briefing about Armageddon, looking like you've been out drinking somewhere all night, and you offer some cockamamie theory about the earth's core."

Moore was acutely aware of his appearance. He was unshaven, looking haggard, in the same clothes he'd worn the day before.

"I've been working on this all night with no sleep—"

The president cut him off. "That's one of the problems, from what I hear: You haven't been getting much sleep."

Moore was stunned.

"When you didn't show on time, I asked your staff about your behavior," Henderson said. "They answered honestly. The way you should have months ago. Instead of endangering the country like you have."

"I would never purposefully—"

"You brought this damned thing here, you sent your people after the other stones, you even mounted an illegal operation to rescue Danielle, despite the fact that I told you not to. And I covered your ass for it. Yet you couldn't be honest with me?"

"I tried—"

"Stop lying to yourself, Arnold! You've put us at risk, and maybe the whole world along with us! I want to know why."

"Mr. President—"

"Why?!" he shouted. "What are you holding back? Some hidden part of this prophecy you haven't shared, something else you found down there in Brazil, or some bit of data you don't want to give up? What is it that makes you believe in this thing beyond all reason?"

Moore looked away. His old friend knew him, knew he wasn't being completely truthful. He caught sight of the blue countdown clock: seven minutes to zero.

"Now, Arnold!" the president shouted.

"I touched it," Moore said finally, the admission feeling like a fool's last act and a weight off his shoulders all at the same time.

"I held the damned thing when Danielle brought it back from the Amazon. And since that moment, since that very moment, I've had an unshakable sense that this thing, this stone, was sent here to help us. Not to harm us or hurt us, but to save us from something. Maybe from ourselves. The stone affects everyone who touches it that way."

For a moment Moore wished he'd let the president touch it. They wouldn't even be having this conversation. But at the time it had seemed unwise.

"There are patterns in the signal that mirror brainwave activity," Moore added. "We think it was done that way on purpose, to give us a message, to condition us and teach us."

As Moore spoke, the anger on the president's face resolved into despair and a look of utter disgust. It became so obvious, so deep-seated and evident, that Moore could not stand to gaze at his old friend. The president offered no challenge, no angry rebuke. He was just done with Moore.

"You're relieved," he said. "Get Stecker in here."

CHAPTER 65

Danielle watched as the cannon fire she'd triggered tore into the second of Kang's Skycranes, shredding the thin aluminum fuselage and blasting off the tail rotor. The flaming craft came apart and careened into the ground, where it exploded.

"The third one is running," Ivan said, turning toward it.

"Let it go," Danielle said. "There are men on the ground."

"Can you see your friend?" Ivan asked.

The Hind-D had a camera system with a telescopic lens, designed to sight targets visually and help prevent friendly-fire incidents. She scanned the terrain and saw only Kang's people and the strange mechanical mules.

"No!" she shouted.

"You're sure he's not with them?"

Kang's people were still pursuing something, still making their way toward the top of the mesa. "I don't think so," she said. "Why?"

"Because once we pass, there will be nothing left down there."

"So be it," she said. "For your brother."

And with that, Ivan banked the helicopter fifty degrees,

finishing the turn and lining up the figures on the ground. He bore down on them relentlessly and Danielle flipped the toggle to arm the cannon.

As they thundered in, the men started turning and firing. Danielle pressed the trigger for the cannon and fired a batch of air-to-ground missiles at the same time. The rotary gun blazed away, loosing three hundred shells in five seconds, missiles streaking out from the left and the right. Explosions rocked the terrain, and parallel balls of fire merged into a rising inferno where the men had once been.

The Hind raced past, pulling up to clear the smoke and flame. Only then did Danielle notice a second group of men.

"On the left," she said. "Ten o'clock. Look out!"

The second group opened fire as they passed. But the Hind was built for low-level combat. Its armor shook off the rifle bullets as if they were BBs. Not so with the rocket-propelled grenade that exploded above their heads.

The windshield was instantly streaked with oil and fire. Smoke poured in and the helicopter shook like a speeding car that had lost a couple of wheels.

Ivan tried to control it, but the rotors were damaged. "Hang on!" he shouted.

Shuddering wildly, the helicopter lurched to the side, spinning and dropping from the air.

Aboard his personal Skycrane, Kang saw the Russian craft go down. His men had done well. "Turn us around," he ordered.

"To the men?"

"No, up on the ridge."

He could see a figure near the far side of the mesa, sprinting across it.

"That's the one," he said. "Run him down."

The pilot turned the helicopter toward the target and accelerated. "We have no weapons," he warned.

Kang shouted above the noise. "Just get me close. I'll kill him myself."

In the darkness of Yucca Mountain, Byron Stecker watched Arnold Moore step out of the trailer carrying his suit jacket awkwardly over his shoulder. His gait was slow, as a beaten man's should be.

"What's the word?" Stecker asked, keenly aware that there were less than five minutes to go before the zero state.

"You win," Moore said. He nodded toward the rocket sled. "Might want to get that thing ready."

Moore shuffled away, moving toward the big wrecker tow truck that had been used to drag the trailer in.

Stecker grinned and took a moment to soak up the glory of victory. He turned to his staffer. "We have four minutes. Get the sled primed. We'll need to do this quick."

He stepped inside the trailer.

The screen inside was still glowing with the president's image. "About damn time, Stecker."

"Moore just informed me," he said. "We'll destroy the stone immediately."

"Good. Contact me when it's done."

The president cut the line and Stecker switched the

screen off. He walked to the lab section and opened the door. The room was dark except for the glow of computer screens.

He stepped toward the viewing platform and nearly slipped.

"What the hell?"

Looking down, he saw a puddle of grape soda. Nathanial Ahiga lay sprawled on the floor, semiconscious, with a large welt across his forehead.

"What the hell happened?" Stecker asked.

Moaning, Ahiga opened his eyes, but before he could even say a word Stecker realized the truth. He rushed to the observation stand and looked into the vault. The stone was gone.

Without stopping to help Ahiga, he ran out of the lab and burst through the trailer door, into the tunnel.

The box truck was rumbling away with Moore inside it.

"Stop the truck!" he shouted. "Moore has the stone!"

CHAPTER 66

Whatever madness was going on behind him, Hawker could only guess at, but as he reached the edge of the cenote, he saw a different problem. The opening was a huge depression, a circular well carved from the granite, two hundred feet across and a hundred feet deep. From the precipice it looked like an open-pit mine flooded with unmoving water.

"What am I, a cliff diver?" he said aloud.

At the center he saw the tiny island that Father Domingo had told him about. It looked like the top of a spire, a pillar of stone twenty feet in diameter, with its foundation disappearing into the water, like a bridge stanchion. A set of stairs, carved into the side of the pillar, descended into the water, but no bridge or cable ran to it.

Apparently it would be a swim and then a climb.

He noticed a narrow pathway that wound down and around, but he didn't have time for such a long route. He dropped in over the side, skidding down the slope until he reached a narrow ledge. As he stopped, a sound like thunder roared in above him.

Looking up, he saw Kang's Skycrane fan out in a

braking action. He expected a sniper to be targeting him from the open door, but instead he saw a man in body armor.

To his absolute astonishment, the man leaped from thirty feet above, falling toward Hawker and clotheslining him across the chest. The impact sent both of them tumbling down the slope.

Despite Ivan's efforts, the Russian Hind-D was finished. It crashed and skidded forward on the mesa, sliding to a stop.

The impact threw Danielle about, but her seat belt held and she was uninjured. She pulled out of her harness, helped Ivan to extricate himself from the wreckage, and then dragged him away as the helicopter began to burn.

"Are you okay?" she asked

Ivan shook his head. "My feet," he said. A quick look told her that both of his ankles were broken. She glanced toward the valley, where Kang's men had been.

"Give me your gun!" she demanded.

Ivan held out the Makarov.

She grabbed it and crawled toward the edge of the ridge. The last of Kang's men were headed the other way. Done with the battle. *Thank God for that.*

Now to find Hawker.

She made her way back to Ivan. "You should be safe here," she said. "Which direction was the line?"

"West."

She looked that way. A thousand yards off, the last of the three Skycranes hung in the air, circling something at a snail's pace. She saw no sign of Hawker. And yet halfway between her and the hovering copter, she saw something else: a small figure, no more than three feet tall, running across the top of the mesa.

It was Yuri.

Hawker's bruising ride stopped on a midlevel outcropping, fifty feet above the water.

He sprang to his feet and threw a punch toward his attacker's head, but the man blocked it with his armored wrist and fired a punch into Hawker's chest that knocked the wind out of him and sent him tumbling backward.

Landing hard, Hawker coughed uncontrollably and tried to shake off the blow. He'd been in plenty of fights in his life, a lot of them losing ones, but short of being hit with a two-by-four, he'd never felt a shot like that.

Still hacking, he tried to scramble away, but a hand grabbed the back of his shirt and yanked him up. Before he could react, he took a blow to the side of the head and went spiraling down again.

Hawker looked up at his opponent. The man himself was average and frail looking, but built up around him were hydraulic actuators, padding, and armor that made him into a hulking brute.

"You are inferior," the man said.

The statement rang out like a discovered truth. Not a boast or a threat, but a simple statement of the facts. Hawker couldn't argue it.

"You should give me what I want," the machine-assisted man told him. "I will make your death easier."

Breathing hard, Hawker answered. "Why is it . . . you guys always think . . . that's such a good deal?"

Kang stepped toward him and Hawker spun to one side, delivering a solid kick to the man's knee. It should have shattered the joint, should have bent the knee sideways, tearing the ligaments to shreds, but the armor and the bracing prevented it from doing any damage at all.

In response, Kang thrust a knee into Hawker's ribs. He went flying backward, slid off the ridge, and tumbled down to the lowest of the ledges.

Kang slid down after him, planting his feet firmly and standing ominously over Hawker.

Groggy from the last blow and tenuously holding on to consciousness, Hawker crawled a few feet, grabbing a rock from the rubble of the slope.

Kang reached for him. The hand was like a vise crushing his arm. It yanked him upward. And even as Hawker swung the rock, Kang's other arm slammed down on his shoulder.

Hawker fell to his knees.

"Give me the stone," Kang said.

Too dizzy to speak, too physically exhausted to argue, Hawker looked over the edge, to the water. He saw his own reflection, battered and bleeding; the vanquished man. He saw Kang standing over him, the hulking, victorious machine. He remembered what Father Domingo had said: *The Mirror shows us who we are.*

He pulled the backpack off one shoulder.

"Hurry," Kang demanded.

Hawker pulled the other strap off, shook his arm loose, and then wound up and threw it past Kang. It sailed over his head onto the farthest part of the ledge. Kang's eyes followed it.

In that instant, Hawker launched himself at Kang. He grabbed the air vents in Kang's suit of armor, locking on to them like handles, and leaning back with all the strength that remained in his body.

The two men fell toward the water, shattering the calm surface of the Mirror with a tremendous splash.

Suddenly more alert, Hawker righted himself. Despite his hope, Kang remained operational. His suit must have been insulated against water. Hawker pushed off him but one of Kang's mechanically assisted hands locked on to his ankle. With his arms and his free leg, Hawker kicked and stroked for the surface. Kang might even have been doing the same, but the hundred pounds of his armor, hydraulics, and battery packs pulled both of them toward the depths of the well.

CHAPTER 67

Byron Stecker rode in a Humvee, chasing Arnold Moore.

"Shoot him!" he shouted to an air force SP in the back. "Do you hear me? Shoot the son of a bitch!"

The man leaned out the side of the Humvee, firing with a rifle. But items of equipment, including the heavy vault that the stone had traveled in, were piled up behind the flatbed's cab. Shells struck the vault repeatedly, but they would never penetrate.

A second Humvee tried to race up the driver's side looking for a better angle to fire from, but Moore swung the big truck sharply, and the tail end slammed the smaller vehicle against the wall of the narrow tunnel.

A shower of sparks lit up the darkness. As Moore pulled away, the Humvee tumbled out of control, rolling over and almost wiping out Stecker's vehicle in the process.

His driver swerved around it and a third Humvee joined the chase. But Moore had now built himself some space and was still accelerating.

"Shoot out the tires," Stecker ordered. "Stop him or we're all dead."

As if on cue, alarms, hooked up throughout the complex, began to sound. "One minute to EM Burst Event," a computerized female voice announced. "Shut down all electrical systems. Repeat, shut down all electrical systems."

Stecker glanced at the digital readout that had been hastily installed in the cab of the Humvee. It was ticking unnervingly fast. The voice rang out through the tunnel. "*Fifty-five . . . fifty-four . . . fifty-three.*"

Up ahead, Stecker saw the proverbial light at the end of the tunnel. A place he did not want Moore to reach.

"Seal the doors!" he shouted into the radio. "Seal the damned doors!"

Sinking fast, Hawker could feel the pressure growing in his ears. His hands scraped the walls, searching for something to grab, but the granite was smooth and the weight of Kang and his mechanical armor continued to drag him down.

He slammed his heel into Kang's chest, trying to break free, and Kang tried to grab his other leg. Neither succeeded and they crashed into the bottom. The impact jarred Kang's hand loose, and Hawker pushed off, pumping his arms and legs, desperate to reach the surface.

Below him he saw Kang trying to swim or climb, but the weight was too much and he fell back, landing at the bottom of the well, like some kind of offering to the gods. A spot beside him waited for Hawker if he didn't keep going.

On the verge of blacking out, Hawker pushed harder, kicking and clawing for the surface.

He burst through, exhaling a cloud of carbon dioxide and sucking in a breath of clean air. The closest land to him was the island at the center of the cenote. He swam for the stairs.

By now he could feel the waves of energy whipping, a staticlike feeling that ran through his frame. The water around him began to churn and vibrate with a sound so deep that it shook his body from the inside.

Reaching the stairs, he dragged himself out of the water. He crawled up toward the well that Father Domingo had spoken of.

The Sacrifice of the Body.

Hawker stared at the altar. The vibration inside him had sharpened into pain; the sound in his head became a scream. With each piercing wave, ropes of water whipped up into the air around him, like some beast trying to break its chains.

To the left, on the shore, he saw movement. He turned to see a figure scampering down the slope. Yuri.

How was it possible? How had he come here?

Yuri made it down the side of the embankment to where Hawker's backpack had come to rest.

"No!" Hawker shouted.

Yuri opened the pack and pulled the lead case out.

"Yuri, don't!"

Yuri did not hear him. He opened the case and stared at the stone as if the gates of heaven rested inside.

The ground trembled from the next surge of energy, but Hawker remained locked on Yuri.

This can't be happening.

He heard shouting. Over the noise in his head, and

the chaos around him, he somehow heard shouting. He looked up. Danielle was sliding down, racing to Yuri.

Another wave of energy whipped through. The pillar he stood on shook to its foundations, knocking him down. More ropes of water whipped off the surface, lashing the walls and flying around like deranged spirits.

With the world coming apart around him, and the ground shaking so hard he could no longer stand, Hawker crawled forward. He saw the counterweights and the ropes. He spotted the lever that Father Domingo had said he would find.

Moore kept the pedal floored, but up ahead the light was dimming. The monstrous doors to Yucca Mountain were closing.

"Twenty-nine . . . twenty-eight . . . twenty-seven."

He crossed into the triple-bore area near the entrance; the tunnel widened. Almost immediately the second Humvee pulled up on his left. Moore swerved toward it.

Shots were fired, blasting into the cab. Moore flinched as the mirror shattered. His arm took a hit and flew off the steering wheel.

Moore's truck swerved, a front tire exploded, and the big rig went over on its side. It crashed down hard and skidded toward the exit, grinding to a stop twenty feet from the threshold.

"Twenty-three . . . twenty-two . . . twenty-one."

Moore looked out through the shattered windshield. Blood ran down his face; one eye was swelling shut. But there was still a chance.

He grabbed his coat, extricated himself from the wreckage, and crawled toward the narrowing band of light.

He heard the klaxons sounding, heard the voice warning.

"*Nineteen . . . eighteen . . .*"

Suddenly he was unable to move. He looked back, straining to see through his swollen eye.

Stecker was standing on the tail of his coat, looking down at him like an owner who had caught the leash of a disobedient hound.

"You're too late," Stecker said. He yanked the coat from Moore's grasp as the doors ahead of him slammed shut with a monstrous metallic clang.

Stecker opened Moore's coat but found nothing inside.

"*Fifteen . . . fourteen . . .*"

"Nothing in here!" one of the guards yelled from the cab of the overturned truck.

"Where is it?" Stecker shouted.

Moore stared up at him, battered and shaking. "I don't have it," he said simply.

Stecker's face betrayed utter confusion, but suddenly he seemed to understand. He looked back down the tunnel.

"Ahiga."

In a distant part of the Yucca Mountain, at the top of a ventilation shaft that served as an escape route should something go wrong, Nathanial Ahiga heard the alarm go critical. He pushed upward, slamming against the hatch.

"Three . . ."

His mind reeled from the darkness and the fear of falling that gripped him. He pushed again, barely moving the heavy door.

"Two . . ."

Shouting a Navajo curse, he forced the hatch open. The blazing Nevada sunset burned his eyes and he tumbled out onto the mountainside holding the stone aloft.

"One . . ."

Hawker lunged for the handle.

"I believe," he whispered as his hand slammed onto the lever.

The counterweights released. Heavy stones dropped into tunnels on either side of the well and the ropes spooled out over metal pulleys at tremendous speed. Something came racing up the tunnel toward him. The blocks slammed home and the fourth stone was jammed into position.

Hawker saw it for an instant. Then the world went still. His hearing shrank to nothing. And everything vanished in a blinding flash of white.

CHAPTER 68

Hawker became aware of being conscious, and by extension alive, when the pounding in his head became too much to bear. He woke with his back to the stony ground and some type of wet cloth over his eyes.

The quiet around him seemed complete—the exact opposite of all he remembered.

He tried to move but found it too painful.

"Hawker?" a voice called to him. "Can you hear me?" The voice was kind but worried. He recognized it as Danielle's.

He managed to move his hand, trying to bring it up toward the cloth, but he lacked the strength even to do that.

Danielle pulled the cloth from his eyes.

At first he saw only shadows, blurs of light, and the outline of her face. But slowly his eyes focused and the details appeared. She was a mess, but God she was beautiful.

"What happened?" The words croaked from his throat, dry as dust.

"You put the stone into place," she said. "The blast knocked you a hundred feet, and you landed in the water."

He looked at her. Her clothes were damp, and muddy in places instead of dusty. "You end up in the water, too?"

"I didn't want you to drown."

He was thankful for that. He tried to prop himself up. She helped him.

"How long have I been out?"

"Two hours," she said. "I thought I'd lost you."

They were up on the mesa. It was completely dark. "Aside from getting my ass kicked, did anything happen?"

She smiled for the first time, but there was still a sense of sadness in her eyes. "See for yourself."

She helped him turn around.

Out over the cenote, against the backdrop of the night, he could see ghostly filaments of light rising upward. They poured from the island at its center, a twisting, almost invisible column of light.

He followed the strands upward, into the dark of the sky, where they spread into a shimmering curtain of white and blue. The display moved in a curious fashion, flowing and bending back in upon itself. At times it seemed to flicker and fade, as if it might be a mirage, but then the brightness would grow once again and the color would become more intense than it had been before.

"What is it?" Hawker asked.

"Charged particles in the atmosphere, channeling along the magnetic lines and funneling themselves harmlessly into space," she said.

"How do you know that?"

"It's an aurora," she said. "I've seen one before, although normally the charged particles are coming down into the planet."

"Shield of the Jaguar," Hawker said.

She nodded, but the sad look returned.

Suddenly he remembered about Yuri.

He looked around. Back toward the cenote he saw a man whose features he couldn't make out sitting and staring at the curtain of light in the sky. Beside them a smaller figure lay draped beneath a jacket.

"Please tell me . . . ," he began.

She shook her head. "It was too much for him," she said.

Hawker closed his eyes, choking back a wave of emotion.

"He fell limp the instant it happened," she said. "The soul stone flew out of his hands toward the well at the same moment you were being flung away from it."

Danielle paused, trying to control her own sadness. "There was a trickle of blood near the base of his skull. A tiny hole like he'd been hit by a dart. I think the sliver was pulled from his body in the same way."

A wave of numbness flowed through Hawker's body. He'd known, even before he released the counterweights. He'd known what was going to happen to Yuri, but in that moment he realized that something far worse was going to happen if he didn't. The only comfort he could find was that Yuri had given his life for many, perhaps for billions around the globe.

Sacrifice of the Body.

It was a Mayan belief, a Christian belief, a Jewish and Muslim belief as well. Innocent blood, shed for the rest of us. To make the rains come, to make the crops grow. To save the world.

Four days before Christmas, on the turning point of the Mayan calendar, a day known as 4 Ahau, 3 Kankin, the story found truth once again.

CHAPTER 69

Bethesda Naval Hospital, Bethesda, Maryland

Forty-eight hours later, Hawker, Danielle, and McCarter arrived back in the United States aboard an air force transport. For Hawker it was the first time he'd set foot on American soil in over a decade, though so far none of them had seen much of it. Lingering problems with Hawker's eyes, official secrecy, and a tight security cordon meant waiting in ambulances at Edwards Air Force Base and several days in the confines of the Bethesda Naval Hospital.

During that time, Hawker's eyesight returned to normal, Danielle was treated for low-level radiation poisoning, and McCarter's leg was operated on and his infection finally, adequately addressed.

With those efforts winding down, Danielle found herself growing frustrated. Aside from the treatment and long debriefing sessions, she and the others had been confined to their individual rooms. She wanted to talk with Moore, to check on McCarter, and mostly she wanted to speak with Hawker. But so far she'd been unable to either sneak past the guard at her door or convince him to look the other way.

Arnold Moore arrived on her fourth day in "captivity." He looked like he'd been fifteen rounds with a prize fighter.

"What the hell happened to you?" she asked.

"Took a wrong turn at Albuquerque," he said, before explaining the truth, his theory of twisted magnetic lines and how close they had come to Armageddon. "The wave still affected the world," he said. "The three stones and whatever energy was created from the shard Yuri carried had acted to dampen it and channel the excess, but there were blackouts all over the country and across the Pacific, from Kamchatka to Mumbai. It would have been far, far worse had we not succeeded."

"Were we really that close to war?"

"The fact that most satellites were spared kept it from happening," Moore told her. "The president used the hotline; he was able to convince them that wave was a natural occurrence, but I don't think it would have worked if they could not look down on us and be sure we weren't launching missiles."

"The children will not learn," she said. "Maybe we'll learn now."

"Let's hope so."

"What happens next?"

Moore brightened. "Well, for one thing, your intrepid chief might get an award of some kind, maybe even a Nobel Prize for his revolutionary new theory on the workings of earth's magnetic field. What do you think sounds better: 'Moore's theorem'? or the 'Arnold axiom'?"

"Go with the first one," she said smiling.

"Noted."

"I want to get out of here," she told him.

"Of course you do," he said. "Someone's coming to see you first. And I figured you'd want something proper to wear when you meet the president of the United States." He offered her a tote bag filled with clothes from her home.

She took the bag eagerly and started pawing through it. She couldn't have been more excited if it were filled with gold.

He turned.

"Where are you going?"

"To find McCarter and relieve him of his temporary status and then to see Hawker. It's a long story but I still have a rather large check to write him."

She shook her head. "He'll never take it," she said.

"He earned it."

"I'll go half with you. It was my butt getting rescued."

Moore nodded.

"Something good better be happening for him," she said sternly.

"It's in the works" was all he would say. He ducked out the door.

Danielle turned her attention to the tote bag and examined the selection of clothing. Moore had chosen surprisingly well.

After four days in the hospital, Hawker was getting used to it. He liked pressing the button and asking for new pillows or more ice water or another serving of whatever it was they'd been feeding him. He didn't know why so many people complained about hospital food. So far he liked it. And besides, it was great to have things brought by.

On her fifteenth trip to his room, the nurse scowled at him.

"What else do you have to do?" he said.

"Plenty," she said, shoving a bottle of water at him.

"Here," she added, offering him papers and a clipboard. "You're being discharged. You're to meet Mr. Moore in the conference room."

Five minutes later, Hawker walked past a group of guards that looked like Secret Service agents. He stepped into the room to find McCarter and Danielle. They embraced, reunited at last.

"What's going on?" Hawker asked.

"President's coming," Danielle told him.

"Do we like him?" Hawker asked.

"What do you mean?" McCarter said.

"I've been gone for a while. I haven't voted for anyone since Perot in 2000," he said.

"Perot didn't run in 2000," Danielle said.

"I wrote him in," Hawker said. "Bush, Gore?" He shook his head and shivered as if the chills had just come over him.

A moment later the door of the conference room opened and a pair of Secret Service agents entered. The president followed, accompanied by Arnold Moore and Byron Stecker.

The three patients stood at this unexpected arrival.

"Sit down," the president said, as he himself took a seat.

Hawker noticed that Moore's face seemed to bear

some healing abrasions and other wounds and his gait included a pronounced limp. Despite that he seemed a hell of a lot happier than Stecker.

President Henderson offered his thanks, and the thanks of the nation. He explained the story that was being released in bits and pieces.

"We're telling the world that a joint effort between the United States, Mexico, Russia, and China has averted this catastrophe. Of course, the ranks of the conspiracy theorists are running wild with the occurrence and its perfect coincidence with the Mayan prophecy, but we are reporting that this system was designed eleven years ago, during a solar flare event that had similar, if less pronounced effects, and that it was only a fluke that the event occurred on December twenty-first."

"I'm guessing that very few are buying that," McCarter offered.

The president shrugged. "Conspiracy theories are a growth industry. I'm just glad they don't need a bailout."

McCarter laughed. "It would be appropriate if we could find a way to credit the Mayan people, their religion. They kept this legend alive for thousands of years. In the face of all they've been through since the Europeans reached the Americas, they maintained their beliefs and that was the key."

The president seemed to make a mental note of this. "No doubt you're correct," he said, with great sobriety. "I'll make sure we discuss it with our counterparts in Mexico."

Danielle asked the next question. "And what about Saravich? Where is he?"

"He's been treated and released," the president said.

"Released to where?" she pressed.

"He's boarding a British Airways flight to London," the president said. "From there it's direct to Moscow."

"And then what?"

Hawker could hear the concern in her voice, perhaps more plainly than she'd like. But she'd told Hawker the story. Saravich had saved her, and together they had saved him. His brother had saved Yuri from the Russian Science Directorate and then from freezing to death on the Arctic ice. By extension those acts had helped save them all. In both cases the men had violated the directives they'd been charged with. Hawker's kind of people.

"Don't worry about him," the president replied. "Ivan Saravich is a hero of the Russian people. Like the three of you, he is a hero to the world at large. The leaked story will indicate that his guards were killed in the battle with Kang and his army, but that his actions were instrumental in destroying that army, which they were. And if I know anything, I'd guess that Ivan Saravich will become a Russian celebrity of some sort and enjoy a long and honored life."

Danielle sat back, seeming satisfied and hopeful.

"And what about us?" McCarter asked.

This time Stecker answered. "In your case," he began, "it's simple. First, you'll be sworn to secrecy under the Anti-Espionage Act of 1949. Under the terms of that act—"

"Oh, spare me," McCarter said, holding up a hand.

"I've been down this road before. I get it. I promise you, I have no intention of returning from sabbatical to announce that I've been working as a spy, escaping from hired killers, and carrying around a magic stone that saved the world."

He paused, then added, "Although maybe I should. They'd probably send me on another sabbatical, this time for mental health reasons."

Hawker almost laughed. The feeling bubbled up within him and he just barely held it back. Without seeing the truth, it was too absurd to believe.

Across the table, even the president smiled. He turned to Stecker. "I'm thinking we can cross that one off the list."

"And what about Hawker?" Danielle asked, attacking like a good lawyer.

Moore reacted first. And Hawker guessed there were additional considerations, no doubt involving the CIA.

Fine with him. If ever there was a time to fight it out, this was it.

"A deal has been crafted," Moore said.

Before Hawker could reply, Danielle jumped to his defense. "There's no need for a deal here. I mean, my God, what could he possibly still owe you?"

"Nothing," Moore admitted. "In fact, it's my understanding that he's come into a large sum of money. Enough to make certain that he'll never owe anyone anything."

Moore looked at him. "If I were you," he said, "I'd take that money and disappear, and never work another day in my life."

Hawker leaned forward. "And on the odd chance I don't want to do that?"

Moore raised an eyebrow. "Then you can have a full pardon," he said. "Or a grant of immunity at all levels, or whatever you want to call it, accompanied by the CIA's express, written apology for the situation they put you in years ago."

As Moore spoke, Stecker squirmed, but he made no move to refute what was being said.

"In return for what?"

"Your agreement to continue working as an agent of the United States for the next five years."

"Undercover," Hawker said to clarify. "For the CIA?"

"No," Moore said. "For the NRI."

Hawker sat back, surprised.

"You don't have to do this," Danielle interjected. "You can still go find that beach."

Yes, he could still go. And where would it lead him? Out on his own again. Certainly she didn't mention coming with him.

"There is a catch," Moore said.

Only one? Hawker thought. *Must be a hell of a deal.*

Moore cleared his throat again, and it seemed to Hawker as if he were looking for the words.

"Among other things," Moore said, "it is your particular status in the world, as a known pariah of sorts, that makes you uniquely valuable. As has been discussed among the three of us behind closed doors, you are a unique asset in all the world. You can go to places we could never get an agent; you can find your way into organizations that would be impossible for us to infiltrate or even get close to without ten years to set up a cover. For you to be most effective, you'll need to maintain that status."

Moore cleared his throat again. "In other words," he said, "it must appear as if you are still on the run. Which means you will have to leave the United States within twenty-four hours."

The words were like a dagger to the heart. He looked over at Danielle.

"Give me a few hours to think about it," he said.

"I think we can do that," the president said.

And with that the meeting adjourned. Stecker left immediately, muttering to himself. The president shook hands with all three heroes and then left with the Secret Service. Moore lingered, speaking to Danielle, before departing.

And then Hawker, McCarter, and Danielle were left looking at one another.

"What are you going to do?" Hawker asked McCarter. "Maybe you should join up full-time. I mean look, they want to hire me; they must be desperate."

McCarter laughed. "No thanks," he said. "I have a son and a daughter who both have their mother's eyes. I'm going to go see them, and stay until I'm driving them crazy. Might even reprise my Moses Negro look."

He laughed. "At the very least I have a couple of great stories to tell my grandkids, while they're still young enough to believe them."

Danielle hugged him.

"Stay in touch," she said.

"I will," he promised.

McCarter shook Hawker's hand and then they hugged.

"Stay out of trouble," Hawker said.

"Godspeed," McCarter told him. "Whatever you decide."

McCarter left to collect his things and Hawker found himself looking at Danielle, fixed on her eyes. Lost for a moment.

"So what are you going to do?" she asked.

"I don't know. Want to help me figure it out?"

"Yeah," she said.

"I got to go get my stuff before the nurse burns it," he said.

"You have stuff?"

"A few things."

She smiled. "All right. Meet me downstairs. I'll wait for you."

Danielle went back to her room, thrilled to be leaving, excited for a chance to be out in the free world again.

As she was packing up her stuff, the door opened. From the corner of her eye, she saw a huge bouquet of flowers. Somewhere behind it stood a man.

"You can give those to another patient," she said happily. "I'm getting out of here."

"Okay," the man said in a surprised tone.

She recognized his voice.

"Marcus?" she said, spinning around. "What are you . . . what are you doing here?"

He looked good, looked fit. Serious as always.

"I blackmailed Arnold," he said. "I wanted to make sure I came to see you."

"Why?" she said. "I mean not why. It's just I'm . . . I'm getting out. I would have come to see you tomorrow."

She felt her equilibrium tumble. She had planned to go see him as soon as she got out of the hospital, but she hadn't expected him here. She was unsure of how to react. She wasn't ready. "You got your hair cut" was all she could come up with.

"A couple of times," he said. "It's been eight months."

He moved toward her and they embraced and still she didn't know what to say.

Hawker thanked the nurse for not throwing his watch and his pen away. That was the extent of his things.

"It doesn't work," she said, pointing to the watch.

He knew that. In fact the dial was cracked, the hands frozen at the exact time of the blast. For reasons he found hard to explain he didn't want to let it go. It was proof of what had happened. Proof that man had done some good to his fellow man, despite what must have been a horrendous cost.

"It works for me," he said.

She gave him a look that said he was even crazier than she thought and he stepped out of the room and headed down the hall.

Danielle sat on the bed. Marcus sat beside her, holding her hand. It felt so familiar and yet strange at the same time.

"So much has happened," she said. "I don't know where to begin."

"Who was it that took you?" he asked.

She was about to answer but caught the words in her throat. He wasn't part of the institute anymore; he wasn't cleared to know.

"Right," he said. "This again."

She gazed at him, her eyes asking for some slack.

He seemed to get the message. "I have something for you," he said. "I know I handled things badly when you left but now that you're back . . ."

He pulled out a small case. She knew it held a ring.

She did not reach for it.

"I know we fought about the job," he said, "and about you going back. But now that—whatever you were doing is over—we won't have anything to cause those arguments anymore."

Her mind whirled. He was right about all that, but she didn't want to do this now. She needed a minute.

"I said a lot of things that were cruel," she began. "I was angry at you for not supporting me."

"I didn't want you to go, because I was worried about you and I didn't like being left behind. So I'm sure I was just as much in the wrong as you."

Maybe time did change things. They were finally saying the right words instead of just trying to win the argument.

"You know this can be good," he added. "You know it was, before our egos got in the way."

He opened the case. Of course, the diamond was perfect.

On his way to the elevator Hawker passed the nurse's station. All smiles for him. "Having a good day?" he asked.

"You're leaving," one of them said. "We're ready to party."

He had to laugh.

He stepped into the elevator and rode it down to the first floor. From there he walked to Danielle's room. Hearing her talking to someone, he glanced inside. They were sitting on the bed holding hands.

He pulled back quickly, surprised, stunned. He was certain that they hadn't seen him, but feeling like an intruder, he backed away. Right into Arnold Moore.

Moore stepped past him and peeked into the room, then came back to where Hawker stood.

"Bad timing," Hawker said.

"There's some history there," Moore advised. "I'd tread lightly if I were you."

Hawker clenched his jaw as the reality of the situation crashed in on him. Things happened when people were under pressure and far from home, but the normal world was something different. He wanted to talk with Danielle, tell her how he felt, most of which she already knew or guessed at. But what would that lead to? She was getting out and lining up on final approach for a normal life, one without blood and death and destruction around every corner. Just as he'd suggested she should. How the hell could he ask her not to?

"Might be better if I don't tread at all," he said.

Moore nodded, noncommittal. He shoved his hands in his pockets and looked down the hall. "You make a decision?"

"Yeah, I'm in," Hawker said, making it that moment. "Send me on my way."

Moore pulled a passport wallet from his coat. "Instructions are in there, along with new ID and papers," he said. "We have a car waiting outside, and a ticket for you to Miami. Transport will be standing by."

Hawker studied Moore. He had a new sense of the man. He guessed they'd argue plenty over the next five years. But at least he knew he could trust him.

"I'll give you your money back," he said. "When the five years are up."

"Interest?" Moore asked.

"Probably not."

Moore shrugged. "It was worth a shot."

Hawker took the papers. "Don't you drag her back in," he warned.

"Once was too often," Moore assured him.

Hawker nodded and then reluctantly started for the far door. "Tell her I said goodbye."

"I will," Moore promised.

Danielle pulled the ring from the case. The facets caught the light and it sparkled almost like the Brazil stone. It was awfully pretty. But pretty things did not move her anymore. Never really had. She pushed it away.

"I don't want you to be angry," she said.

He looked as if he was. But it didn't matter. She'd decided something in San Ignacio, even before she'd kissed Hawker. It had to do with living for the future.

"I went back to the NRI because I had to," she said, stating her original position. "But also because I wanted to."

"Why?" he asked.

"You like your life," she said. "You like teaching, and your friends, and the university. You like the consulting work and the lobbying firm. But for me those things were just okay."

"You'll get used to them," he said.

"I don't want to get used to anything," she said.

He inhaled a deep breath and looked away, as if trying to hold back.

"I don't feel pity for you," she said. "You have almost everything you want in life. You got shot and almost died and instead of crawling into a hole you're in the world building an empire. The only thing about your life that brings you pain is me."

"That's not always the case," he said with conviction.

"No, not always," she said. "But it shouldn't ever be. If I stay and live your life, I will resent you forever, because this isn't where I belong. And if I continue with the NRI, you will always worry about me and always be reminded of what happened to you. I don't want either of those things."

"What do you want?" he asked.

"I don't know," she said. "But until I find it I'm not willing to give up the search."

He looked as if he was about to launch into the full-court press, the all-out effort to change her mind, but he didn't. Reluctantly, he put the ring away, closed the box, and stood up. A long moment of silence followed. "You win," he said finally.

"No one wins," she said. He leaned toward her. They hugged and he walked out.

She watched him go, knowing she'd hurt him again, but feeling like she had finally done the right thing for everyone including herself. She gathered up the rest of her belongings, walked out and down the hall. Moore waited there for her.

"You okay?" he asked.

"Yeah," she said, certain of it for the first time in a while. "I am."

"I saw Marcus leave," he said. "You not going home?"

"The NRI is my home," she said. "And I'm grabbing on with both hands."

He smiled. "You'll end up old and lonely like me."

"I can think of worse things," she said. "Where's Hawker?"

"He's gone," Moore said.

Her heart dropped. This could not be happening. If Hawker vanished into the haze she might never find him again.

"You've got to be kidding me. Did he say where he was going?"

"No," Moore replied. "But he'll check in when he gets there."

"What are you talking about?"

"He took the deal," Moore said.

She was very surprised. "You're serious?"

"Uh-huh," Moore said. "Now, I just need to find

someone to be his contact. Someone who might be able to keep him under control and out of trouble. I was thinking Carson or Palomino or . . ."

She glared at him. "You give that job to anyone but me and I will kill you right here and now."

"Well," he said, false shock covering his face, "since I can't even afford a funeral these days . . . I guess the job is yours."

CHAPTER 70

Hawker was riding shotgun in a Bell JetRanger as it crossed the Everglades of South Florida and descended toward the tarmac in an isolated corner of Miami International.

Someone in the NRI or CIA had telegraphed his whereabouts to the State Department, part of the cover he would now maintain. As a result, U.S. marshals and members of the FBI were undoubtedly searching for him, possibly even in Miami. To keep the cover clean he would have to stay on the run. He was used to that.

As the JetRanger descended, Hawker gazed across the flat expanse of Florida. The air was warm and humid, an incredible difference from frigid Washington. To the west the sun was setting, a giant orange ball once again, falling through the hazy sky.

The latest estimates had the poles returning to normal after thirty-seven days, and a similar event as not likely to occur for another five thousand years.

In the meantime, the aurora that had sprouted over central Mexico was being watched closely, guarded by an impressive phalanx of military hardware but left alone. All involved agreed that ignorant interference in the device would only risk its failure.

Yuri had been carried back to San Ignacio and buried on holy ground, a martyr unknown to most of the world. Perhaps as it should be.

The JetRanger touched down at the center of the helipad. The pilot pointed across the ramp, to an old, unadorned cargo jet.

Hawker shook the pilot's hand and grabbed his pack. He jumped out of the helicopter and made his way across the apron to a forty-year-old DC-8, retrofitted with new engines.

The plane carried no markings. But the men who stood outside it were most definitely retired military. Thirty-year vets by the look of things: weathered, confident faces, gray buzz cuts and steely eyes.

Hawker walked up to them.

"There's trouble," the captain said. "You must be our passenger?"

Hawker nodded.

"My name's Samuels," he told Hawker, shaking his hand. He pointed to the man across from him. "This is Halle, my copilot. And for God sakes don't tell us your name. We'd have to go through six months of brainwashing to get it out."

Hawker smiled; there was something undeniably positive about these men. And he had a sense that they'd been told he was one of the good guys.

"What's the plan?" Hawker asked, assuming something had been set up.

"We take you anywhere you want to go," Samuels said. "I have ten thousand miles of gas and a tanker standing by in every direction in case for some reason that ain't enough for you."

The captain looked across the airport to the setting sun. "What I don't have is time. We have to be wheels up by sunset, with or without you. So, whoever the hell you are, you're cutting it damned close."

Hawker glanced over his shoulder. The sun was just touching the horizon. If he was right, the FBI was on its way, chasing a hot tip as to his whereabouts, someone's bright idea to make sure he didn't change his mind. It was okay; he had no intention of changing it now.

"Let's go," Hawker said.

"Where to?"

"I'll tell you when I decide."

The captain nodded and ushered Hawker aboard.

Taking a seat in the passenger compartment of this particular aircraft was not much different than being part of the cargo, so Hawker chose the jump seat behind the pilots instead.

He strapped himself in as they ran through the checklist and received expedited taxi clearance.

Several minutes later the roar of the engines announced the beginning of the takeoff roll and the big DC-8 rumbled down the two-mile strip of concrete.

Three-quarters of the runway behind them, the plane rotated and finally broke free from the earth.

The old bird climbed at a steady pace, engines roaring, the cabin shaking and rattling around him. He felt a sense of kinetic energy, of freedom and gathering momentum. His world had changed. It had been painful and destructive, but he'd come out the other side. He wasn't sure what the future held, but he would rush forward to meet it, much as he was rushing forward now, surrounded and enveloped by something greater than himself. He was part of life once again, instead of death. And for the first time in years the darkness had left his soul.

EPILOGUE

High desert of Nevada, three months later

Arnold Moore stepped out of a gray four-wheel-drive Humvee with the USAF logo stamped on the door. He stared at the open expanse that stretched out before him. It was the same type of barren terrain he'd seen on the journey between Groom Lake air base and Yucca Mountain, with one minor difference. This was the desert in its natural state—unscarred by bomb craters, piles of rubble, or endless rounds of weapons testing.

In the distance, whitish salt flats shimmered in the morning sun. Beyond them lay rugged mountains the color of chocolate, as if the endless waves of heat had blackened them over time.

To his surprise, Moore found it beautiful, majestic, awe inspiring.

As he admired the scenery, a second man exited the Humvee behind him. Moore turned to Nathanial Ahiga. "Ready for a hike?"

"I really think I've had enough of climbing," Ahiga said.

"No ladders this time," Moore said. "I promise you."

With Ahiga following, Moore took to a winding trail that snaked up the side of a weathered hill, about a hundred and fifty feet high.

"I thought you might want to see this," Moore said. "In a way it was your idea."

"My idea?" Ahiga said.

Moore nodded. "I was trying to figure out what we should do, based on what they sent back to us. You told me it was the other way around. That our descendants weren't asking us to do anything, but were responding to what we asked of them. That being the case, I thought we'd better send them a message. Just to be sure."

They crested the hill. Ahead of them, a deep circular section had been hollowed out. In the center, a hundred feet below, stood a tall, thin obelisk, gleaming like polished silver.

"You're leaving them a marker," Ahiga said.

"The Maya called them Stelle," Moore said. "According to McCarter they carved stones like this around most of their major monuments. Ours is made of hardened titanium, covered with a layer of clear Kevlar, but the principle's the same."

He pointed to the side facing them. Markings could be seen in the surface.

"The larger details of what occurred have been engraved on its sides, laser cut and protected, in four different languages. English, Russian, Chinese, and—out of respect for those who kept the legend alive—Mayan hieroglyphics."

"The Brotherhood of the Jaguar," Ahiga said.

Moore nodded. The small sect had kept the truth

alive as they journeyed from South America to the jungles of the Yucatan and the surrounding countries. Protecting the secret of the stones, passing it on in the best way they could, energized by the feeling given to them by the stones themselves.

In some ways Moore, Danielle, and McCarter had themselves become members of the Brotherhood. Certainly, as he looked back on it now, Moore found many of his own decisions irrational, even if they were ultimately, desperately needed.

In some strange way, he'd felt a sense of fulfillment and release only as he watched the laser cutting the glyphs into the sides of the marker. He knew then he was doing his best to pass the message on.

Was it the influence of the stones and the effect they had on his brain chemistry, or was it his own sense of duty?

He couldn't be sure. Ultimately he'd decided that it didn't matter. Certainly others had made the decision to help without such influence, Hawker and Ahiga chief among them.

Remembering that, Moore turned back to the scientist.

"Thank you," he said, "for what you did."

The old Navajo shook his head. "For giving me a chance to help the world? I should be thanking you."

Moore didn't feel that way, but he understood what the man was saying.

At the edge of the hollowed-out section a large crane swung a bucket of fill dirt into position and released it, allowing it to cascade down the side of the crater.

"Why are you burying it?" Ahiga asked.

"For the same reason we're keeping it all a secret," Moore said. "We're not sure that the world at large is ready to comprehend it yet. But this way, the people who need this information should find it about a hundred years before they decide to do something about it."

Ahiga cocked his head.

"The erosion in this valley is ninety-five percent wind driven," Moore explained. "It progresses at an extremely consistent rate. About a thousand years from now, the bulk of this hill will be scoured away and the obelisk will begin to appear."

Ahiga looked out over the barren plain. "What if no one's here to see it?"

"Three others are being set up," Moore explained. "One each in Russia, China, and Mexico. In addition, each marker contains a small nuclear core, an atomic clock—like those on the Voyager spacecraft—and a transmitter. If no one has found these things by the time they're needed, the markers will begin broadcasting a signal to draw someone to them. Inside, stored in multiple formats, is everything we know about the stones."

Ahiga put his hands in his pockets and looked out over the expanse once again. He seemed pleased.

"Symmetry," he said. "They sent us four stones that were transmitting signals. We send them four that are doing the same. I like it."

Moore liked it too.

"Any worries?"

"Tons of them," Moore said. "I worry about everything I ever do. But this . . ." He waved a hand over the hollowed-out mountain, and the obelisk slowly being buried within it.

"Nathanial, this is the first message I've ever sent that I'm certain will be received."

AUTHOR'S NOTE

Thank you for joining me on this latest adventure. For those interested in the creative process and the blend of fact and fiction in this novel, I offer the following, beginning with my own thoughts on 2012.

At this point in time, it would be almost impossible not to have heard of the Mayan prophecy. Knowing that other authors and filmmakers had already explored the same subject, I felt it was important to take a different path. That path centered on three questions:

1. What did the Mayan people really think about 2012?
2. What type of event could possibly change the world or destroy a good portion of it?
3. If the prophecy were to come true, how could the Mayan people have possibly known?

In answering the first question, I found that the concept of a 2012 cataclysm is far more ingrained in our society that it was in the Mayan one. The primary source of the 2012 prophecy is the writings of Chilam Balam, the Jaguar Priest. These texts were written after the

Spanish conquest, and while they do contain references to dark events occurring at the end of the thirteenth Baktun (December 21, 2012), the vast majority of the writing focuses on other, more mundane parts of Mayan life, and in some ways serves as a method of explaining the oppression of the conquistadors.

Interestingly enough, the Jaguar Priest's books were actually written at different times, in different places, and by different people, yet they are referred to as if they were the work of a single person, as if some greater force was behind the whole. In time, this thought worked its way into the novel, with the fictional concept of the Brotherhood of the Jaguar: a hidden group acting as one, carrying out their mission, throughout time and despite all odds.

Beyond the words of Chilam Balam, there is less to go on than one might imagine. But less is not nothing. The Tortugero Monument Six is indeed a reality. It lies in a place once ruled by Ahau Balam, the Jaguar Lord, in what is now the Mexican state of Tabasco. Tortugero Monument Six is one of the very few—in fact some say the only—hieroglyphic carving directly referencing the end of Baktun 13. As described in the book, it tells of Bolan Yokte, the god of change (or the god of war, according to some), descending from the Black "something" and accomplishing a great feat. Interestingly enough, Bolon Yokte is as much a mystery as the 2012 reference itself. Little is known about this god and his place in Mayan theism. As described in the book, a portion of the carving is damaged and thus a full translation/interpretation is impossible. Could it be the Black Sun, or the Black Sky? No one knows at this point, and unless something new comes to light we probably never will.

To answer the second question, I had to find a new way to destroy the world. Not as easy as you might think! This earth and the creatures that live on it have proven incredibly adaptive to change. Ice ages, droughts, plagues: Life has survived all of these. Earthquakes, volcanoes, tsunamis, no problem. Life even survived a rock the size of mount Everest hitting our planet at 70,000 miles an hour (the Chicxulub impact, which is believed to have destroyed the dinosaurs).

As I considered this, it occurred to me that we constantly hear how nature is going to rise up and throw off the burden of man, destroying us in the process. And yet, even nature's greatest efforts have little effect on mankind as a whole. So I chose to write from the opposite perspective: Even if nature could not destroy man, man almost certainly had the power to destroy nature and himself.

And that left the question of how the Mayan people could have known or predicted this. There were only two ways that I could fathom: either they could see the future in some form of clairvoyance (an answer that was not concrete enough for me), or it was told to them by someone who knew it. In the greater sense, the theme of time travel had been settled on during the writing of *Black Rain,* the novel that preceded this book, but I had chosen that theme with this end already in mind. Of course, as far as we know, no one has ever traveled back to meet us, but there are enough theoretical physicists who think it might happen someday for me to believe in the possibility.

As for other facts and fiction in *Black Sun,* please read on.

Geomagnetic Reversal

According to the geologic record, the earth's magnetic field has reversed many times throughout its history. During certain eras it has been incredibly stable, including forty million years during the Cretaceous period. At other times it has reversed quickly, with only fifty thousand or a hundred thousand years between changes.

Our current field orientation has held for 780,000 years, but it is weakening. As described in the book, this weakening has accelerated over the past hundred years or so, for reasons unknown. As the magnetic pole weakens, it also moves, but there are other, perhaps more sinister effects—cracks and fissures that have already begun to expose us to the radiation of the solar wind.

The largest of these is known as the South Atlantic Anomaly. Discovered in 1958, the SAA is a weak spot or low point in the earth's magnetic field, and it is growing larger. While the SAA isn't dangerous to humans on Earth, it is big problem for spacecraft in low earth orbit. Astronauts have reported strange vision problems when transiting the area. The International Space Station was designed with enhanced shielding because it often operates in this zone, and many satellites and even the Hubble telescope are shut down as they pass through this region, as a precaution against failure.

So is this a sign of things to come? No one can be sure. If the magnetic field continues to weaken, it is expected that other anomalies will appear; perhaps the earth will be covered with them. In essence, the premise of this book is the question of what would happen if one massive anomaly appeared instantly during a time of great political turmoil and blinded the eyes of the world.

Sharks: Ampullae of Lorenzini

All sharks contain such magnetic sensing organs called ampullae of Lorenzini. They are believed to assist the sharks in navigation as they prowl the dark seas with nothing else to guide them. The ampullae are also used in hunting prey, as all organisms give off a small electric charge.

Hammerhead sharks are known to have an acute sense of electrical charges, as their wider heads create better platforms from which the electrical sensing organs operate. Hammerheads have often been observed swimming in schools of a hundred or more (as Danielle and Hawker encountered), though they are thought to separate at night and hunt alone.

The Tunguska Blast

On June 30, 1908, a massive explosion rocked the Siberian tundra. A flash was seen in the sky and a shockwave was felt hundreds of miles away. When explorers reached the area years later, they found trees knocked over in a strange butterflylike shape that measured forty-five miles across. No crater was ever found.

Current theory centers on an air burst of a meteor or asteroid, though dozens of other theories have been proposed, including a super volcano residing underneath Lake Cheko. As far as I know, the Russians never found any items of extraordinary power during their many expeditions to the area, but then again, do you think they would tell us if they had?